SILVER Brewer

L.B. DUNBAR

Love Notes

www.lbdunbar.com

L.B. Dunbar

♡L.B. Dunbar

Books. Kissing included.

Cover Design: Shannon Passmore/Shanoff Formats
Beta Editor: Heather Monroe
Content Editor: Melissa Shank
Editor: Jenny Simms/Editing4Indies
Proofreader: Karen Fischer

Other Books by L.B. Dunbar

Silver Fox Former Rock Stars
After Care
Midlife Crisis
Restored Dreams
Second Chance
Wine&Dine

The Silver Foxes of Blue Ridge
Silver Brewer (Giant)
Silver Player (Billy) – coming 2020
Silver Mayor (Charlie) – coming 2020
Silver Biker (James) – coming 2020

Collision novellas
Collide

Rom-com for the over 40
The Sex Education of M.E.

The Sensations Collection
Sound Advice
Taste Test
Fragrance Free
Touch Screen
Sight Words

Spin-off Standalone
The History in Us

The Legendary Rock Star Series
The Legend of Arturo King
The Story of Lansing Lotte
The Quest of Perkins Vale
The Truth of Tristan Lyons
The Trials of Guinevere DeGrance

Paradise Stories
Abel
Cain

L.B. Dunbar

<u>The Island Duet</u>
Redemption Island
Return to the Island

<u>Modern Descendants – writing as elda lore</u>
Hades
Solis
Heph

<u>Penny Reid's ™ Smartypants Romance</u>
Love in Due Time
Love in Deed
Love in a Pickle

Dedication

For the love of a small town, a tight community, and a loving family.

L.B. Dunbar

1

A long and winding road

Where the hell am I?

I'm losing the GPS on my phone, and I feel as though I've passed the same copse of trees three times.

Who can tell?

Birches, maples, and cedars surround me, and those are the trees I recognize. Everything is a sea of thick bark and greenery, but soon, this forest will be ablaze with golds, reds, and oranges. The changing season is the reason for my rush. I need to secure the property before winter so the ground can be broken first thing next spring.

Working for Mullen Realty, I've climbed my way up from assistant office manager to assistant seller to commercial real estate agent. Not exactly my career choice but it's been a steady income. When I didn't have a job at twenty-four using my college degree in English, my mom made me go to work for my uncle, a real estate mogul in Chicago. I'm now forty, so I guess you could say I settled into the family business. Uncle Frank prides himself on buying and selling, and what he wants is to buy this godforsaken property in Georgia and sell it to a hotel company who wants the space for their next lodge-like resort and spa.

As the only vehicle in sight while I wind through the curving roads, I'm waiting for Jason to jump out with his creepy hockey mask and start swinging a chainsaw at me at any second. I might have mixed a few horror movies together, but that's the scene in my head as I weave along the narrow drive. I'm not even certain I'm in the correct county, let alone the right state anymore. I need Blue Ridge, Georgia, but all I've seen for miles is tree trunks and foliage, and occasionally, the inconspicuous marking for a turnoff. From the office, Marcus tries to assure me I'm in the correct place.

"There are only two tire tracks leading to nowhere," I say into the phone, struggling to drive the rented Jetta over the rough terrain.

7

L.B. Dunbar

"That's it. You're in the right place. Don't mess this up," his gruff voice barks through the speaker.

I hit a bump, and the phone jostles out of the cup holder to the floor. *Dammit.*

I can't risk reaching for it, and I'm too afraid to stop until I see the place I'm destined to find.

Harrington cabin.

I'm not certain what I expect. I've been told it's rustic, but I don't know if that means quaint or just plain rough. Either way, Mullen Real Estate wants the property.

"I think I'm almost there," I shout, as the phone lies facedown on the passenger side floor. I can't hear Marcus's reply. He's not only my assistant but one of my best friends, and he knows this acquisition is important to me. I'd prove myself as a skilled real estate buyer if I can book this deal. I'd also solidify my position in the company and earn myself a cut of the business.

Partner.

The word echoes through my head. The sound has a nice ring to it.

Olivet Pierson. Partner.

As the dirt road narrows, I see light at the end of the tunnel of trees. A clearing of sorts opens before me, and I slow even more than the five miles per hour I've been driving. As I break through the lane, a vision of masculinity stands before me. With his shirt off, the bare back of a muscular being slings an ax over his shoulder, splitting a piece of wood standing upright on another log. The thwack isn't heard inside the car, but the thunderous power in which he cracks the wood seems to vibrate under my vehicle and into my foot. I'm frozen at the appearance of his rippling back, sweaty spine, and low-slung pants that suggest he wears boxer briefs by the sliver of waistband exposed. In red. The hair on top of his head is short, trimmed close but not military style to his skull, while a bush of facial hair covers his jaw. My eyes focus on his profile as he stands and straightens, then quickly turns to see my car. Deep, dark eyes narrow, zeroing in on me in anger. He drops the ax and raises his hands, his mouth opening, but I don't hear what he says.

8

I'm blinded by the gleam of sunlight bouncing off his firm chest, a sprinkle of hair in the shape of a V between the flat plains of his pecs and above the slow hills of his abs. More hair leads south, dipping into the red band exposed above his waistline, and my mouth waters until two large hands hit the hood of my rental car, and I notice his mouth move as he shouts.

"Stop."

Oh. My. God.

My foot slams on the brake, causing me to jolt forward and narrowly missing the bridge of my nose on the steering wheel. I stare out the front windshield, taking in the appearance of the man I almost hit. He's a mountain of a man, someone I envision people wrote tales about long ago. He's lumbersexual by modern standards, and then I note his hair again. Cropped and charcoal. It isn't black but more like the smoky color before the coals are ready. A perfect blend of dusty silver covers his head and jaw. He's a silver fox, but from the size of him, he looks more like an angry grizzly.

"I'm so sorry," I mutter as I place the car in park and scramble to remove myself from the rental. My ankles twist as the heels I wear can't balance on the uneven dirt beneath my feet. I clutch the open driver's door for support, expecting to fall and knock my chin. How many stitches would I need? Is there even a doctor out here? A hospital nearby? Oh God, I might bleed to death.

Then I take note of the puzzled man before me, still leaning against my hood.

Staring at him, I'd die a happy woman.

However, the vibe coming off him is anything but pleased. His chest heaves as his eyes nearly disappear while he squints at me.

"Who are you?" He emphasizes each word as he speaks. I certainly can't use the statement "I was in the neighborhood" because I doubt you'd find another human being within miles.

Oh Lord, if I screamed, would anyone hear me? If a tree falls in the woods, does it make a sound if no one is around to hear it? My thoughts are out of control.

L.B. Dunbar

"I'm Olivet Pierson, and I'm looking for George Harrington the second. Is this the Harrington cabin?"

I'm here for the land, but the cabin catches my sight. The two-story building is of medium size, balanced with a window on either side of a single front door, standing open and inviting. A heavy metal overhang shadows the porch, which runs the full length of the cabin. The weathered gray structure with the deep black shingled roof doesn't look worn. It appears brand new. With a small yard and a forestry backdrop, the place looks quite homey.

"How did you get here?" His gruff voice returns my attention to him. His curiosity causes him to look up over the back of my car, staring down the pinched lane I traveled.

"Are you George Harrington?"

His head swings back to me, and his lips twist. Pressing off my car, he turns for a cloth on the pile of wood and wipes his face with it. Absentmindedly, he travels down his chest, or rather purposely, as he must know I'm watching his every move. I'm practically salivating as he takes his time to swipe across his broad pecs and dip to the trail leading lower. He pats himself with the cloth over the zipper region of his pants, and I flinch. My eyes flick upward, and his lips mockingly smirk.

I can't say it's a smile. His face looks far too serious for such a thing. Crinkles mark the edges of his eyes, and his cheekbones are well-defined. He might have been teasing me, but his face gives nothing away.

"So…" I repeat. "Are you George?"

"You must be looking for my father," he states, tossing what I realize is a white T-shirt back onto the pile of wood. He picks up the ax, and I try to catch my breath. I'm gripping the open door for support, peering at him as he turns his back on me and lifts the wood-chopping instrument. The sound of a splintering log resonates loudly around us, echoing in the deep quiet. I take a second to look around me, no longer lost in the woods, but noticing the beauty of various shades of green. Steeples of pines and broad sweeps of maple whisper in the breeze with a glorious blue sky as its backdrop. The landscape is breathtaking, and the silence reminds me this is the perfect location for a spa and resort. Secluded. Rustic. Peaceful.

Thwack.

Another log splits, and I shift my attention back to Mr. Lumbersexy.

"Do you know anything about the property?" I ask, interrupting him mid-swing. He doesn't miss the log, but it doesn't crack. The ax bounces back, and the log topples to its side. When he turns on me, the move is aggressive in nature, yet I find I don't fear him. His mouth opens, but I speak.

"I'm told it's owned by George Harrington II. A Miss Elaina Harrington on Mountain Spring Lane told me how to get here. Told me I'd find him here." I pause as he glares at me. I stopped at the original address given to me by the office. Mountain Spring Lane was a dirt strip with three impressive antebellum homes along the private drive. Old money covered the white paint of each house.

When he doesn't speak, I continue. "It's a beautiful piece of property." I turn my head as if I'm noticing the land, but all I can concentrate on is the weight of his eyes on me, knowing he's following the twist of my neck as I gaze around me.

"What do you want?" he snaps. The gruffness of his tone snaps my attention back to him. Maybe Grumpy is a better name for him instead of Sexy Lumberjack.

"I'm looking to discuss purchasing the land."

The ax slips from his hand while his other hand fists into a ball of knuckles. He's scary, but again, I don't fear him for some reason.

"It's not for sale."

"Everything's for sale, Mr...." He still doesn't offer his name, but I'm sensing I'm in the right place, so he must be George Harrington.

"Listen…" He pauses, and I offer my name.

"Olivet Pierson. Mullen Realty," I say, walking around my door and closing it. Reaching forward for his hand, I realize my palm already sweats with the anticipation of touching the paw of his. The closer I get to him, he appears even bigger, and we stand in contrast to one another. He's bare chested in wood shaving-covered pants and rustic work boots while I'm wobbling in my heels with a pencil skirt, blazer, and uncomfortable blouse.

L.B. Dunbar

His eyes glance down at my hand, but he doesn't reciprocate and reach for mine. Instead, he crosses his arms, puffing out his barrel chest and producing two large biceps, flexed in warning.

"Cricket," he begins, but I correct him.

"Olivet."

"This place isn't for sale, so you can just reverse out of here, hopefully without backing into an unsuspecting tree, and return to wherever you came from." All those words in his definitive tone add up to one: *Leave.* But I'm not going anywhere without the security of this property signed on a dotted line.

"Now Mr. Harrington," I say. Lowering my hand, I place both on the hood of my car. The problem is I'm still looking *up* at him, so I'm not really in a position of authority to talk him down. This always looks good in the movies, but it's clearly not working with my five-foot-seven stature compared to his six-foot-plus-too-many-extra-inches height.

"Giant," he states, and I stop.

"Excuse me?"

"Everyone calls me Giant."

"Well, Mr. Giant—"

"What do you want with the land?" he interjects, his voice still thunder deep but not so menacing.

"I work for Mullen Realty in Chicago, and we'd like to acquire this property for a resort—"

"A resort?" he huffs, his arms falling to his sides as he interrupts me. He turns his large head to the side, giving me a view of his profile. Strong facial features, a sharp nose broken at least once, and a tic to his jaw as he concentrates on something in the distance. "Do you know anything about this property, Cricket?"

"Olivet," I correct. "And yes, I do. I know it's a fine piece of land situated perfectly for a beautiful resort that will offer people peace and tranquility away from their hectic lives." I ramble off the future brochure sure to include such words to entice potential visitors. The serenity around us reminds me I'm not far off from my speculation.

12

He harrumphs, crossing his arms again. Not as fierce as the first time and more casual in nature, he shakes his head as though he's laughing at me. Only he isn't laughing. "It's not for sale."

I dismiss his words, considering what he would look like with laughter on his face. Would his cheeks glow? His mouth spread? I bet he has white teeth. A smile and a good chuckle might set him on fire. He's already larger than life in size, but with a good guffaw, he'd be bigger than thunder. A Greek god of sound and stature.

He's staring at me, and I realize I've taken too long to respond. I eye the cabin behind him. Rustic is one word for it. Cozy, graying, inviting. I rid the possibility of seeing the inside from my head. *He probably hides bodies under the porch.* I chuckle with the thought. He's fierce but not fearsome. There's just something about him. My head tilts, and my eyes pinch. I decide to change tactics. A new appeal.

"If it's a matter of money—"

"I don't need money." He scoffs, cutting me off and glaring at me again with a look of offense. "There isn't enough money in the world for me to give up this place."

My mouth pops open. "So, you are George Harrington the second?"

"I told you, I'm Giant, and I think we're done here, Cricket."

"Now, Mr. Harrington—"

He turns his back to me, that beautifully muscular back. My mouth waters, and I want to kiss up the river of his spine and along the flexing plains of his shoulder blades, which is absolutely ridiculous, considering he's a stranger. Besides, I've sworn off men. Pretty men with fancy names. *No thank you.* Although this man isn't pretty. He's weathered and worn like the cabin behind him, and for once, I'd like to be a little less straitlaced and buttoned-up. The collar of my blouse itches.

"Name your price, Mr. Harrington," I shout to his retreating back. He's abandoned the wood pile and stalks toward the low porch. Without touching the first stair, he steps up to the platform, swallowed by the shade of the overhang. My eyes are fixated on two firm globes filling out his Carhartt pants. *Oh my.* Within seconds, he's disappeared inside the cabin, closing the door on my proposal.

Well, that certainly didn't go as planned.

2

No Sale. Maybe.

[Giant]

Who the fuck was she?

I'm still pondering the answer to that question as I return to the main house on Mountain Spring Lane—nicknamed the Lane by those of us who grew up on it. I'm still fired up over that insect of a woman, chirping away, asking questions, and wanting me to sell. *Ha.*

"Who sent that woman up the mountain?" I bark. I hold back the profanity itching to explode out of my mouth, knowing my mama would still whoop my ass for such words.

"Giant, I don't know what you're talking about," Elaina Harrington says all sugar sweet and false honey. My mother is the queen of nosy, and from the look on her face, she's put her nose where it doesn't belong. I didn't need to stop at the house, but I was passing the Lane on my way back to town.

"Better question is why would you think I'd sell the cabin?" My mother believes I spend too much time up there hiding out to avoid life. Unfortunately for her, I don't care what she thinks. The cabin is mine, and I'm not avoiding anything. I like it up there. In the peace and quiet, I'm away from my mother's attempt to intervene in my life. For God's sake, I'm almost fifty.

She doesn't miss a beat as she sets the dining room table. I internally sigh. The size of the spread means my younger sister will be coming over with her new beau—or rather her former best friend, newly returned to finally profess his love for my baby sister some twenty-years later. The bloom of love my sister has found after the death of her husband has my mother playing matchmaker for me. The formality of the dinner plates hints that more than Mati and Denton will be joining us. My mother hasn't answered my question before I add, "Who's coming to dinner, the queen?"

I shouldn't ask.

"Mati's friend, Alyce Wright. She's perfect." *For you.* I don't have to hear the words to know what she isn't saying. My mother straightens from setting down the knives and looks up at me. "You know, it could happen again." Her voice softens. She's wrong, and this isn't up for discussion—*again*. Damn Mati for being happy.

"You didn't answer my question," I snap a little harsher than I intend, but my mother's matchmaking efforts piss me off. Or maybe it's the little spark inside my chest at that firecracker of a woman spewing her offer.

Name your price, Mr. Harrington.

As I told her, no sale. There isn't enough money in the world to take the land off my hands, but my irritation ignites from more than her pecking away at me with her fancy marketing jargon. It's the look she was giving me. Her bright blue eyes narrowed in on my chest, walking their way down my midsection and landing at my zipper. I had a little fun with her without intending to do it in that respect. She didn't even flinch at getting caught, just looked as if she might be hungry. *She probably eats nails for breakfast.* I snort to myself. A pretty brunette like her, all city slicked up in her dark suit and heels, isn't going to go for someone like me, even if I do have money to my name.

The money is of no consequence. I'm a fourth generation Harrington. Fourth generation George Harrington, to be specific. The second at the end of my name marks I'm the son to the junior, named after his daddy. We're beer men, making it behind barn doors until it became legal to craft beer in Georgia. Our granddad used to joke we were here before Georgia began. Giant Brewing Company is our brand, and I'm the chief executive operator under my so-called retired father.

"Mama," I say exasperated, and she sets a vase of flowers down with more force than necessary.

"Fine, I sent her up the path." My mother doesn't look at me. She knows that land means everything to me, and while she understands why, she doesn't understand how I can spend so much time up there. I don't want to have to remind her it's my life. I'm forty-nine. She can stop mother-henning me.

15

L.B. Dunbar

I spin and head for the front door. I have a house closer to town, one I avoid most days since I find solitude up at the cabin. *Who cares?* I want to scream. I'm alone anyway. Empty nester, that's the term, although I think I've been empty for longer than the absence of my daughters going off to college and moving on with their lives. It's the way it should be with my girls, yet lately, I feel as if I've missed too much.

"Giant," my mother calls after me, a warning in her voice. "You be here for dinner at six."

I won't disappoint her, but I want to. For once, I'd like to do something spontaneous and not show up to a family dinner or a matchmaking setup or a pre-scheduled anything. I'm free to do as I please with my days, yet as I approach fifty, I feel trapped. As if something's crawling under my skin wanting to be released.

My thoughts rush back to the bug of a woman leaning over her car, trying to appear all tough but instead looking adorable as her wide eyes skim down my body. Wonder what she would have thought if I placed her on her little silver hood and kissed her senseless just because I could and I wanted to?

Whoa. I slow my F-150 truck with the large Giant Brewing Co. logo on the side as I near the gravel lane heading to town. *Where did that thought come from?* My palms sweat on the steering wheel. It's been a while since I've been with a woman, but still, she's a stranger. I don't know her. *I don't even want to know her*, I admonish, but something taps at my skull.

Yes, you do, whispers through my thick head. I shake the thought.

Whoever she was, she talked too much. But then there were her eyes—bright and blue as the day—and the way she scanned my body. *Hungry*—that was the look. It was a nice look.

She also had that fierce attitude as though she wouldn't accept anything less than what she wanted.

Name your price, Mr. Harrington.

I'll give her a price: no sale.

Never mind my subtle attraction to her. I'm not going to know her because I'm not parting with my land. That property is special to me in

16

a way no piece of ass will ever be, and besides, I don't want a piece of ass. If I need to get laid, I can go down to Elton. *When was the last time I got laid?* I mentally count back as if flipping sheets on a calendar.

Cripes. It *has* been a bit.

My dick whimpers in my outdoor pants when thoughts of a chirpy brunette with big blue eyes matching the sky come into play. *Down boy*, I curse, and then decide against the reprimand. The image of her pretty little mouth begging me for my land—begging me for anything—will make my shower-time fodder all the faster this evening.

And I'm going to need a release before another matchmaking session from my mother.

L.B. Dunbar

3

Proverbial gauntlets and
other hammering instruments

[Letty]

"It didn't go well," I tell Marcus as I stand in the fluffy bathrobe provided by the Conrad Lodge. A thick towel swipes over my hair as I hear Marcus sigh through the speakerphone.

"Letty, you have to secure this place. This is your future we're talking about." If Marcus wasn't forty, like me, I'd swear he was an old man or my dad. Too bad my father is dead, and Uncle Frank is the only father figure I've ever had.

"I know." I exhale as I toss the towel aside and then throw myself on the extra-high mattress in the four-poster bed. *Who sleeps on such a thing?* Then I consider the giant of a man I saw earlier in the day. Giant. What an interesting name. It certainly suits his stature. "We didn't get off to a good start."

"What did you do?" he singsongs, assuming it's my fault. Then again, most errors in my life are. Hudson was the biggest mistake.

"I almost hit him with my car."

"What?" Marcus shrieks, releasing the mother in him. He wants to be a parent with his partner, so he understands my struggles. We aren't getting any younger as *my* mother likes to remind us.

"It would have been a little love tap. Not even marking him." Thinking of his long legs, I'm curious about their thickness within those low-slung pants. *They're the size of tree trunks*, I surmise, proportionate to the rest of his body.

"Letty, way to make a first impression."

That's just it. I botched my first impression—nearly running over a man will do that. But in general, I struggle with sales as my career. I'm not good at introductions. I go in for the kill too quickly because I want the haggle process over. I also don't make a lasting impression, which is why I've failed at life.

Sigh.

"You need to go back to him with blazing saddles and double barrels and those big breasts of yours."

I laugh. "Marcus, there isn't one drop of hope that man is interested in my breasts."

"Oh, and do you want him to be?" The tweak to his tone and the higher octave bring visions of an eyebrow raised in question. Did I want Mr. Lumbersexy-and-steamy to be interested in my breasts? No, of course not. Absolutely not. That would be unprofessional, inappropriate, and not plausible.

"No." I chuckle. "But I do want his land."

"And how hung is his land?"

I laugh outright at the poor euphemism. I couldn't even guess at the expanse of *his land* as it's been almost a year since I've experienced the private property of another person. Damn Hudson. The thought sobers me.

"I need to obtain his land."

"Now, you're talking, honey."

"No, I mean the actual property. The Harrington cabin and surrounding woods need to become mine."

Marcus remains quiet for a moment. "And what are you willing to risk to possess his wood?" He's still speaking in innuendos, but I'm not playing.

"Anything," I say breathlessly. *Anything.*

The declaration is reinforced when the next call I receive is from my uncle Frank.

"Olivet," he snaps sharp on the third syllable of my name. "How did it go today?" From his tone, it's clear he's concerned I can't get the job done, and he isn't off in his assessment. I begged for this deal.

Give me a chance. I wanted to prove I could do this, but most of all, I wanted the contract. I need the commission a property this size would offer.

"I'm still working on Mr. Harrington, Mr. Mullen." Uncle Frank doesn't care for me to call him uncle in the office. He doesn't want to appear to play favorites with family members even though he clearly doesn't when it comes to me and clearly does when it comes to my older sister. But Uncle Frank has a soft spot for *his* sister, my mother. She was married to his best friend, who died too young from cancer, and Frank promised my father he'd look after us. He does value family even if he doesn't say it. It's a strange duality to his personality. But money is his first love.

"Work harder, Olivet," he demands. There is no confidence boosting. No words of encouragement. He doesn't believe I can pull off this deal, so I'm surprised he even gave me the opportunity. Perhaps he believes when I fail, my lack of sales ability and partner potential will be proven once and for all.

You pull this off, and we'll finally talk partner. Like a child, I swallowed up his promise. For some reason, I want to make him proud although I don't like him much—as a boss or an uncle. Still, I can't dismiss all he's done for our family.

I sigh with the thought.

"Yes, sir. I'm meeting with Mr. Harrington again tomorrow."

"Well, shut that deal down. We need you back in the office."

Why? I wonder. Does he need more coffee? Maybe another copy made? A contract signature that he's too lazy to get on his own?

"I'll be on it first thing."

"Anything you need to do," he warns.

Anything, I repeat as the line goes dead.

+ + +

The following day, I return to the Harrington cabin with renewed determination. I'm only supposed to be in Blue Ridge for a few days. I could stretch it a week, but the longer I'm away from home, the more I worry my backstabbing nemesis Dayna will steal prospects out from under me. Real estate can be a ruthless business, especially if you're good at wheeling and dealing like Dayna is. Plus, my sister is getting married in two weeks. Thinking of these things fuel my spirit, and after getting lost only once, I arrive at the secluded cabin with fortitude and fierceness, to be deflated when I find no sign of George—*Giant*—Harrington.

"Now what?" I mutter, looking around the small span of flat land surrounding the cabin before deep woods take over the landscape to the front and a sharp slope rises up the back. The mountain climb looks easy enough, inviting actually, but it's been a while since I've hiked anywhere other than the nearest Starbucks. Blue Ridge doesn't have a Starbucks, but thank goodness the local bakery has good coffee. I set the second cup beside me and hold mine in both my hands. It isn't cold here, but there's a chill to the air. Though I'm dressed casually in jeans and a sweater, my booties still don't cut it on the uneven ground. My toes tap on the wooden step as I allow myself a seat on the porch and take a moment to let the quiet surround me.

As a city girl, born and bred, the silence is eerie. I need a plane overhead, a train in the distance, and a car horn honking down the street, but there's something to be said for the peacefulness. Closing my eyes for a second, I feel as if I can hear the few clouds in the sky move in the slight breeze.

"What the hell are you doing?"

The gruff, masculine voice startles me, and I'm thankful for the lid on my coffee even though drops slosh out of the sipping piece. Hot splatters of coffee stain my jeans, and I'd feel the burn if it wasn't for the glacial stare and giant boulder of a man blocking out the sun.

"Well, good morning to you, too," I say, cheerfully, trying my best not to cower under his pinched glare.

Be brave. Be strong. I repeat the chant Marcus sang before ending our phone call the previous night.

As I look up at Giant, his presence says he's a million times stronger than me, and it's more than his physique. His body language screams command and control, and I briefly wonder what it would be like to have that energy focused on me. My breasts tingle as my breathing labors. My core clenches, and I force my knees together.

"I brought you a coffee," I say, realizing my fingers shake as I reach for the second cup sitting next to my hip and lift it toward him.

L.B. Dunbar

Looking off in the distance, he crosses his arms over his massive chest, displaying those bulging biceps once again. His stature says he's trying to shut me out. He's dressed in a flannel today, covering the awesome body underneath the clothing. *Too bad.* But then again, from my vantage point, I'm eye level with another area of him, and it's a struggle to keep my eyes upward. I'm suddenly thinking about *the size of his property* and *the lay of his land.* The width. The girth. The length. Damn Marcus for his innuendos.

"You'd have to do better than a cup of coffee to butter me up." For a moment, I want to believe he's teasing me. Did his voice lower? Is he holding back a laugh? What would a deep chuckle sound like from a man of his size? How much would it rock my world if he gave his laughter to me?

"Yeah, and what would a woman have to do to butter your biscuit?" I joke, fully aware I mean myself and fully aware he has no interest in me. As a woman. As a human being. In fact, when he turns his head back in my direction, I'm convinced he thinks I'm an alien, and he's ready to report me to the Department of Defense for unidentified objects.

"Do you know anything about these woods?" he asks, surprising me as his face softens and his voice dips. I know the specs of the area. The property survey reports it's a nice chunk. We're hopeful of securing the woods on either side of this place to offer a decent spread of land to our prospective investor. I'm ready to spew all the particulars, but the way he holds my gaze tells me he's asking me something else, something deeper, and I'm afraid I don't have an answer for his question.

"Why don't you tell me about them?" I pat a hand on the decking of the porch where I've made myself comfortable. It is comfortable, I note. Quiet. Pretty. The view before me isn't too bad either.

He harrumphs and gazes away from me for another second. His arms remain crossed, but his shoulders slump, and I'm almost disappointed. I like our little game, and I don't want him to give in to me too easily.

What am I thinking? I curse myself. Of course, I want him to make this as easy as possible. Just look into my eyes and give me what I want. I will the energy out into the universe and almost fall back when his eyes

22

immediately return to mine. The dark chocolaty orbs have turned midnight, and a spark flares in them.

Oh no, I think without knowing what I'm oh-no-ing about.

"Want my land so badly?" he begins, and I'm about to interject, giving away my desperation for this sliver of space, but he continues. "What do you even know about this land?"

"I—" He holds up a hand to cut me off before I can even form a thought.

"Have you ever spent a night under the stars? Or bathed in a stream? Have you seen a bear cub with its mother? Or what about hiking in the peacefulness of nature, listening to the birds sing?

"I…" This time, my voice fades, and I don't know how to respond to him. "I went to Girl Scout camp when I was ten."

He stares at me as if I've just told him I can speak Martian.

"Before you try to steal my land, perhaps you should learn a thing or two about it."

I stare up at him as his expression turns virile.

"I know this piece of property could earn you millions." I look beyond him, taking in the small bit of landscape I can see around his broad hips and crossed arms.

"I told you, I don't want the money." He scoffs. "I'm talking about dirt under your toes. Wind in your face. Stars in your eyes." His eyes nearly dance as though he has undisclosed information he's waiting to share with me, and strangely, I want to know his secret. And though dirt under my toes doesn't sound pleasant, it doesn't sound terrible either.

Still.

Tell me. Tell me all your wisdom and woes. I swallow with the intensity of his glare and rub a hand down the thigh of my jeans.

"Okay, so I'm not Pocahontas. How would I learn?" My voice cracks, sounding meek. *Teach me, Yoda.*

"From the land." He pauses. His crossed arms bulge before me and lift with the heave of his frustrated inhale. What would those arms feel like around me?

"And your land will just *teach* me?" Oh God. Did my voice just drop? Did I exaggerate *your land*, implying something other than the

23

greenery around us? Damn Marcus and his damnable innuendos, but if this man means I can hike his landscape, I volunteer as tribute. "How?"

"Camping."

"What?" I stammer. My mouth falls open.

"Camping. Three nights of roughing it and then I'll think about your proposition. You break before that and no deal."

My proposition? Did I proposition him? Can he see the images racing through my mind? I want to do all kinds of things to him, starting with the body part closest to me. My heart races, and my sweaty palms...sweat more. My breath catches.

Anything whispers through my mind along with the song "Colors of the Wind."

My eyes narrow. My heart thuds to a screeching halt.

This is crazy.

But I slowly rise, pressing up on my thigh as I stand. I come to my full height, which doesn't quite match his, but with the help of the two step difference, I'm close. My gaze meets his fiery eyes. There's one thing this man needs to learn *about me*. I like nothing more than to prove others wrong.

"Challenge accepted."

4
To camp or not to camp.

"Reporting for camping, sir."

She salutes me, and I'm reminded of how not one of my soldier friends looked like her. She looks as if an L.L. Bean magazine spit her off their pages, but judging by the newness of the clothing, I'd say she didn't happen to have these things on hand.

"Are those new?" I nod to the Timberland lookalikes on her feet that don't boast a scratch, dent, or smudge. Her jeans hug her body, and the flannel shirt open a few extra buttons exposes a tank top underneath, hinting at the swell of her breasts. Her chestnut colored hair is pulled back in a ponytail, and each time I see her, she looks different. Fresher. Younger. She can't be more than forty.

She peers down at her footwear and twists her ankle. "Do you like them? I got them at Duncan's." Duncan's Hardware is the local shop for everything as the closest Walmart is a good half hour away.

"Those are gonna hurt, Cricket," I warn her. "You can't wear new boots for a lengthy hike. You'll have blisters for days."

"I'm tough," she tells me, holding herself upright and facing off with me as best as she can despite our height difference. She props her hands on her hips, and it's almost comical how her expression turns hard. Her face doesn't allow her to be stern. It's the curve of her lips, her pert nose, and those bright blue eyes. "Besides, it's Letty."

I stare at her in confusion.

"My name. Olivet," she emphasizes. "Considering we're going to spend a few days together, you can call me Letty, my nickname."

I stare more.

"People typically wonder, how do you get Letty from Olivet? I should be Livvy, or Vette, or even Olive, but I'm not really an Olive and—"

"I'll just keep to Cricket," I interrupt her rambling.

L.B. Dunbar

Her lips twist, but she doesn't say anything more. However, she has more to say. I already know this about her—she'll have more to say.

"Spit it out," I snark, trying not to let my eyes roam to the hint of cleavage popping out of the tank top under her open flannel.

"Well, I..." She wraps her hand around her ponytail and smooths down the length. An image of my hand curling the tail to wrap around my fist and yank her head back to take her yammering mouth fills my vision. I'm blinded by the thought. She clears her throat, and I return to the quandary.

"And...?" I prompt.

"I just wondered if your wife is okay with this. Maybe she should come with us or...?"

My arms cross, and my glare stops her chirping.

"Are you worried about your safety?"

Her brows pinch for a second, but without much thought, she responds. "No. I trust you." Her words surprise us both. Her forehead furrows, and my eyes widen. "I know I don't know you, but I'm not afraid of you."

I want to warn her to be afraid, be very afraid, but then again, I don't want to frighten her away. We haven't even started this adventure, and strangely, I've been looking forward to the possibility over the past twenty-four hours. I wasn't even certain she'd show.

"Does someone know where you'll be?" I ask. Does she have a husband? A boyfriend? Someone who will worry about her.

"Marcus knows."

I nod with a scowl as if my stomach hasn't just roiled. Of course, she has a man. She's too pretty to be alone. Suddenly, she laughs.

"He's my friend. Friend-*friend*, not a boyfriend," she clarifies. "He's gay. I'm single as a Pringle," she admits, then points at me. "You should see your face." Her laughter is like a rain shower on a sunny day, unexpected and refreshing. As I stare at her, absorbing the sound, her chuckle subsides.

"Anyway, and your wife?"

"She's dead." I don't mean it as harsh as it comes out, and I hate how my voice cracks despite the years since her death.

26

"Oh, I'm so sorry," she whispers, and I hate the words on her lips even more.

"Cancer sucks," I mutter, and she looks away with a pained look on her face.

"Yes, it does." Her face drifts back for mine. We hold each other's eyes for a moment, and I wonder what it would feel like to hold *her*. It's been a long time since I've known the comfort of such things.

"So." She claps. "Should we…?" She raises her hands and tips her hitched thumbs over her shoulder to the cabin.

"And you're okay with being alone with me?" I'm suddenly second-guessing myself.

"I don't have anything to worry about, right?"

There's an unspoken question, but I don't know what she's implying. "Nope, not a worry in the world. I'm gay." I wink, and her mouth pops open. The pink circle of her lips makes my dick flinch with thoughts of what she could do with such a mouth. I point back at her. "You should see your face."

"Are you…teasing me? Is that actually a grin?" Her grin grows, and her eyes twinkle to match the day's sky. Does she think I don't smile? My lips twist, attempting to hold back the unnatural curl. "Are you laughing at me?"

"I never laugh," I say, holding back the rumble in my throat. She makes me want to laugh a little.

"I didn't think so," she mutters, a smile still on her lips, and turns for the side of my cabin. "So, camping?"

I step up next to her and point upward. Her eyes follow the line of my finger. "Up there."

The strip of land I own is narrow and long. Up an old miner's trail about three miles is the place I plan for us to share our nights. Not together, of course. Just trying to break her of her idea that she wants this land.

"But I thought…" She hesitates. I eye her outfit again as she eyes my cabin.

"Nope. Outdoors. Tent. Campfire. Stars." She's going to back down before we even start, and I have to admit the disappointment niggles at me. She blinks in the sunshine, looking up the slope of the mountain behind the cabin.

"Okay," she whispers.

Okay? My feet want to do a happy dance, and I'm not a happy dance kind of guy. My chest swells with pride that she didn't back down so quickly, and I worry I'm having a heart attack from the excitement. I can't believe she agreed to this scheme.

"Got a bag?"

"Oh. Oh yes." When she rushes back to the Jetta, a little city car, I wonder how she's made it up and down the rutted ridges of the two-tire lane leading back to my cabin. Her vehicle isn't made for such travel. I follow her to the trunk, and she pops it open. Inside is a large backpack.

"You gonna carry all that for three miles?" I whistle. I don't believe she has the strength, and I'm ready for her to argue. She tilts her head around the vehicle and looks up the mountain rise behind the cabin one more time.

"I didn't know what I'd need."

"I have all the provisions already." Her wide eyes almost make me chuckle, but I bite the inside of my cheek, reminding myself I don't want to like her. She wants my land. "It looks like you packed for a week." I have no faith she'll make it past one night, let along three, but that swollen heart thing feels like hope that she'll stick it out, and hope is dangerous.

"I didn't know what I'd need," she repeats, her voice lowering as she lugs the overstuffed hiking bag—also brand new—from her trunk. The effort almost knocks her over, and I reach for the thing.

"What's in here?" I snap. The bag probably weighs more than her.

"I didn't know—" she begins, but I hold a hand up to stop her from speaking. I tug the bag from her and unceremoniously unzip the pack. Rummaging through her clothing, I notice several with price tags and a few unmentionables that are nothing more than scraps of lace. I pull out one slim piece in black.

"You're going camping, not to a fashion show."

"Are you finished fondling my undies?" she snaps, reaching around me and pushing my hands from her bag. My dick does a dance as I consider her wearing only the lacy fabric and nothing more.

I snort and hand the flimsy strip back to her. "Suit yourself." I stand, leaving her opened pack to head for the porch where I have my own bag to carry.

"You have a tent in there?" she asks, coming up behind me.

"I've already taken everything up." I turn to face her, noticing her backpack is almost bigger than she is. She stares at me a moment, and I note again how much I like how she looks at me, even with the quizzical expressions and wrinkled nose. Then realization hits.

"You've already been up there and came back to get me. That's like a ten-mile hike in a day."

"It's six but good to see you can do math."

Her eyes narrow as I slip on my pack and tip my head toward the mountain.

One last chance to back out, lady.

But she follows me.

+ + +

To my surprise, she doesn't complain, but she jabbers on as we climb.

"You're not an ax murderer, right? Not leading me to a lair where you'll cut me up and leave me to rot. Let the bears eat me. I already told you Marcus knows where I am. I have a tracking device on my phone."

"Thanks for letting me know. Your phone will be the first thing I destroy." I continue walking, but her sudden quiet gives me pause, and I turn to find she's stopped following me.

"What?" I question. She has one hand resting on her cocked hip as she stares up at me. "You already told me you trust me."

"I know, but…I don't think that's funny." Her voice turns serious even though she had to be joking when she asked if I was an ax murderer. The thought hits me like a bullet to the chest, which I already suffered a few years back from my days in the service. In my defense, I have killed people, but I don't think now is the time to tell her that. On second

29

thought, there won't ever be a time to explain my history to her. I don't want her to know me.

"Well, you asked," I remind her. Her hand drops, and the other hand lifts for her hip. She glares at me. "Look, here's the rundown. My brother is the mayor of Blue Ridge. I don't think I'd get away with murder even if I wanted to commit it, which I don't. And even if I did, a prison term isn't on my bucket list."

"You have a brother?"

Jesus. "Do you know anything about the Harringtons? Aren't you supposed to research a prospect before you hound someone for their personal property?"

"I don't look into the personal lives of the owners, no. That would be an invasion of privacy. I only look at the property and the value for my client."

Heartless. "What about the value *to* the current owner?"

"I already told you to name your price." Incorrigible. Does she really believe everything has a dollar value? Then again, her new boots and the fresh backpack filled with clothing containing sales tags answer my question. *Gold-digging, money-driven city woman. Ha.*

I turn away from her and continue up the mountain, ignoring her suggestion.

"Tell me about your brother." She sounds farther away, but I tell myself not to look back. If she can't keep up, she'll just have to find her way.

"Why, so you can exploit him as well?"

She ignores me and begins to talk about herself. "I have a sister. For a long time, it's been just the three of us. My mother, my sister, and me. I lost my brother so long ago that I don't remember what it was like to have one."

The thought rips at my chest. I love my brothers and Mati, my sister. We're a tight-knit family, but I don't want to explain myself to her. Since she didn't bother to research the Harringtons before she approached me, that's her loss. She has no idea who she's going up against.

When I don't answer, it feels as if only a few seconds pass before she starts chirping at me again. "How about a girlfriend? Got a lady friend?"

Not that I think that's any of her business either, but I stop and turn back to her, finding she's farther behind me than I thought. I briefly think of Alyce Wright, Mati's friend, whom Mother invited to dinner. I've met her on several occasions. With curly blond hair to her chin and light eyes, she's fine, but she just doesn't do it for me. And I'm pretty certain I don't do it for her either. Despite being the assistant volleyball coach at BRHS under my sister, she's more like a cheerleader with her high-pitched voice and constant enthusiasm. She talks too much, which reminds me of a certain someone who's too busy looking up at me to notice where she's walking. Cricket trips and falls to her hands and knees.

Instantly, I race the few feet back to her.

"Are you okay?" I ask when she doesn't look up, remaining on all fours. She nods slowly, and my heart pounds because she went down hard. *Is she hurt?* "Here." I reach for her chin, intending to make her look up at me, but she tugs her face away. I'm squatting, and the rejection almost forces me to fall backward.

"Letty?" She shakes her head and slowly lifts one dirty hand. She brushes under her eye and peels the other hand from the dirt. Gingerly, she lifts her upper body and then twists to sit on her backside. Her hands cover her knees, and her forehead lowers to them.

"Let me look," I offer, but she shakes her head again, dismissing me. She removes her hands, and I note how one knee of her jeans are torn and blood seeps through the opening. "You're hurt."

"I'm clumsy," she mutters, her voice choked. "I hit a rock." I search for the offending piece of nature and find the sharp edge of a long stone sticking up from the earth.

"Hang on. I have bandages." I slip off my pack and search for some cleansing ointment and a large adhesive. "It might sting," I warn as I rip the ointment package with my teeth and then tug at the opening in her jeans, making the rip larger.

"Darn. These were my favorite." I bite the inside of my cheek, not wanting to chuckle at her expense, but it's funny that she's more worried

L.B. Dunbar

about her ripped pants than her broken skin. Her liquid-filled eyes tell me her joke hides the pain, and my chest pinches. She doesn't flinch as I swipe the gel over the cut and then open the bandage. I blow on the damaged skin before working the bandage into her jeans as best as I can. Her voice is soft near my ear as she says, "Thank you."

Slowly, my eyes lift, and I find her watching me. I swallow. Why is she looking at me like this? And why do I like it so much?

"Let me see your hands." My command comes out a little too sharply, and her soft expression turns edgy.

"I'm fine." She brushes her hands on her hips and tries to press off the ground. I don't miss the wince.

"Here," I mutter, reaching under her armpits and hoisting us both upward in one awkward movement. Her hands grip my biceps for support, and we stand. I'm hyperaware of her breasts brushing against my abs with our height difference. Her hands come to rest on my chest, and she gently presses off me.

"I'm fine," she repeats softer, but I'm quick, and I circle her wrists, twisting them to expose her palms. Both are nicked and punctured from the gravel on the ground. I turn them back over and force her open hands to rub down my shirt. It isn't the cleanest move, but she needs the bits and pieces scraped away.

"Does it feel like anything lingers? A sliver of something?"

"A sliver...of something." Her voice is hardly more than a whisper. Her eyes remain on my chest while I remove her hands and blow over the broken skin like I did her cut knee. "That...that tingles."

My gaze leap to hers, and suddenly, I tingle as well. In my heart. In my gut. And in my dick.

Dammit. I release her wrists and reach for her backpack, attempting to remove it from her shoulders.

"What are you doing?" she snaps.

"I can carry it for a while."

Her head begins to shake. "Oh no. No, you aren't going to make me feel like I can't pull my weight and lose out on this place. I'll manage."

The mention of the land may as well be a slap in the face. Of course, she isn't turned on by me like I'm suddenly worked up over her. She just wants my land.

"I was trying to be a gentleman," I bite back, taking a step away from her.

"Well, just…don't gentleman me."

Yes, right. Why am I being nice to her? I should have left her on her knees, hands digging into the gravel and leg bleeding, but it goes against my nature to leave a wounded animal unattended. On second thought, I hope she rots from gangrene in her leg. I hope it festers and falls off. Then I reconsider the wish as I've known my share of men who had such a thing happen to them. It wasn't fair, and it wasn't pretty.

"Fine," I bark, releasing her backpack strap and leaning over for my bag.

"Fine."

5

This isn't glamping

[Letty]

My eyes fill again with traitorous liquid, but I rapidly blink back the sting. I should have let him take my backpack. It's heavy, and I curse myself for overpacking. My knee really does ache, and my other knee throbs from the tender bruise hidden under my jeans. My hands burn. And I'm thirsty. I reach for my water bottle and take a hardy drink of lukewarm liquid. I don't want to waste precious water, but I pour a little over my cracked hands. The initial drops force me to hiss, but I allow the liquid to cleanse the cuts. Looking up, I find Giant has continued moving, so I follow for the remainder of our climb.

The slope is steeper than it appears from the base, and he's right, dammit. My feet are killing me. My toes feel cramped, and my heel rubs uncomfortably. I'm going to have blisters, and I want to curse Giant. It's all his fault, I swear, but the blame is really mine. If I wasn't so determined to prove myself to him, I wouldn't be in this position.

You also wouldn't be getting this land, I remind myself. I need this promotion and the financial security it will bring; not to mention, the agency is depending on me. *Anything.* Thoughts of my future drive me forward but at a much slower pace than I'd originally set. Giant's strides are naturally longer than mine as his legs are three times bigger.

Okay, maybe not three times, but I swear he's hardly broken a sweat when all I want is a shower.

Tenting, whispers through my head.

I don't suppose that thing has a clawfoot tub with fragrant bubble bath and a few scented candles. Oh, or a glass of wine. Conrad Lodge, the place I've stayed while in Blue Ridge, had all those luxuries before I began this adventure.

My eyes travel to Giant's backside, still visible despite the length of the pack on his back. Even in his rugged pants, he has a fine ass. He's the epitome of outdoor sexy. The way he blew on my knee had my girlie parts swirling in wonder at how his warm breath might feel down there. It's been a long time since anyone's given attention to my nether region. My eyes leap up to the fine curve of his firm globes, and I curse him again.

I don't want to think about him. I don't want to be attracted to him.

A sliver of something. What was it that punctured my lungs, stealing my breath when he looked at me? His deep eyes warming to liquid iron instead of cold steel.

I lose Giant in a copse of trees, and I shake my head. He's doing this on purpose. He's trying to ditch me so I'll give up my pursuit. Well, he doesn't know me, and the second I'm told no, I redouble my efforts. Only my efforts are waning as my feet pinch. When I near the thickness of the trees, I notice Giant leaning against one, his arms casually linked, and his ankles crossed. He looks like a man ready for a photoshoot for *Outdoor Life* or *Lumber Men.* I don't know if either is a magazine, but I'd subscribe if all the images inside matched him. He's watching me, his lips twisting as though he's thinking. Probably wondering how he can toss me down this mountain or hide my body.

I must have been crazy to agree to this scheme. I didn't even know if he was married, and I said yes to a camping trip. In the woods. With a stranger. I don't know anything about his history. Prison records. Background check. Unknown felonies committed. Yet here I am, traipsing up a mountain with him. Of course, a quick Google search on him last night didn't produce any illegal dealings in his past. In fact, he's a decorated military veteran from what I learned.

Still.

Hysteria wells in my chest, and I'm ready to break out in song. *The hills are alive with the sound of music...* Anxiety-riddled laughter builds in my throat. I'm going to sound like a madwoman.

What was I thinking?

Be brave. Be strong. Marcus's words come back to me, and I try to muster emotions I don't feel. I've made a mistake. I'm going to die. This man wishes I would.

I exhale heavily as I reach him, realizing I'm turning into a drama queen.

"Well, fancy meeting you here," I mock.

"Won't meet another soul." It's a warning and a reminder I'm alone with him and at his mercy. I'll need him to survive whatever awaits me for the next three nights. Then again, the thing I fear most is him.

I step into the shadow of the trees, and he swipes an arm forward, suggesting I lead the way.

"There's a path from here."

The worn-down trail, crushed by well-traveled feet, leads deeper into the trees. I keep my eyes on the flattened leaves and broken twigs before me, not wanting to take another fall.

"My great-great grandfather brewed beer up here."

I'm startled by the sound of his voice, both the deepness and the nostalgia in it.

"I thought the mountains were known for moonshine."

"He might have done that, too, but beer was his product. Even though it wasn't legal to distribute craft beer in Georgia until recently."

"That seems a little archaic. I'm from Chicago. We're fond of our liquor and have the history to prove it. It's called Prohibition."

He snorts behind me, and I concede this to be a chuckle.

"He hid his talent up here and made runs along the miner trails." Pride fills his voice with this heritage. "Today, we don't need such a thing for our beer."

I'm stumped once again as I don't know the personal side of his story. "Which is?"

"Giant Brewing Company. I'm Giant."

I stop and spin to face him. "You own a beer company. Like Budweiser?"

I found this information during my Google search but didn't realize he was the *Giant* in Giant Brewing. His slow grin is evidence of both his answer and his pride, and I'm blinded by the effect of his lips slightly curling along the heavy scruff on his face.

"We're more of a craft beer company. Our sales have jumped since my brother opened the pub, but we aren't quite at the success of a major beer distributor."

"I thought you said your brother was the mayor?"

"He is. This is a different brother." I remember what he said while we stood outside his cabin. He thinks I'll expose his family, so he isn't sharing much, but this is another tidbit about him.

"Well, I'd love to sample Giant Beer one day." Did my voice just drop? Did the statement sound suggestive? I turn away from him, heat rushing to my cheeks, and we continue walking in silence a bit before the trees open into a clearing.

"Do I hear water?" I ask as a rushing liquid sounds in the distance.

"There's a river nearby. We don't want to be too close as animals venture there as well, but we aren't far." Giant's voice sounds all business-like, and I notice a pile of camping equipment before us.

I mumble a reminder to myself. "Right, you were already up here."

As we step closer, I see a collapsed tent, two sleeping bags, an extra-large cooler, a smaller one, and a fire pit. The space has been used before as the pit is a scorched metal ring buried in the ground a few inches to contain the flames.

"It gets dark early, so we should set up." Giant pauses. "Maybe we should head to the stream to wash your hands."

"Actually, I need a bathroom." I'm wary to admit such an act of human nature, but I have to pee.

"It's right through there." He points toward another clump of trees. I'm ready to say, *You've got to be kidding*, when I realize he isn't.

"I don't suppose you have toilet paper." He tilts his head a second and then reaches into his backpack. A small cylinder travel container contains a limited number of sheets.

"I'd use them sparingly."

I shudder but realize it isn't the first time I've had to pop a squat. Mustering up my college days, I stomp my feet as I march to the trees. It feels good to remove my pack. My back aches. I'm afraid of what I'll find when I eventually remove my boots because my feet are screaming.

"And watch out for poison ivy."

Have I mentioned how I curse him? I complete my business, eyes scanning the ground as if poison ivy is a living being that can climb up my backside. When I return to camp, Giant has laid out the tent, but he directs me to help him pitch it. We work collectively under his direction.

Silently. He isn't much of a talker, and I've already learned he isn't going to willingly offer me any information. I tend to chatter to fill the quiet space, but I'm too tired to make small talk.

The tent appears rather small, but I don't give it another thought as we force the stakes into the earth. When we finish, he starts a fire in the ring as the late afternoon begins to grow dimmer.

"If you want to wash up, the stream works best. It's cold for bathing, but a little quick in and out works well enough."

Bathing in a stream? Is he crazy? I'm not getting naked near this man nor am I dipping in a stream. I don't know what I thought, but all practicalities escaped me when I said yes to this challenge. Toilets. Showers. What's going to be missing next? I turn back to the tent.

"There's only one tent." The statement echoes between us.

"And?" He pauses from laying wood in the pit. "Is there a problem?"

"Only if I need to sleep outside of it." I hadn't thought this through. His lips curve at the corner, and my fear dissipates a little at the welcome expression on his face.

"No, you can sleep inside."

"And you'll sleep out here?" I question.

"No, I'm sleeping inside, too."

My mouth pops open and then clamps shut. He's serious. "And what are the sleeping arrangements?" I sound haughty and prudish, but he's got another thing coming if he thinks I'm giving him cuddle time in order to prove myself worthy of this land.

"I brought two sleeping bags. One for you. One for me. You'll want to zip up tight. It can get cold at night."

His statement should settle me, but it doesn't. I need some separation from him.

"Maybe I need that stream after all," I mumble.

Giant points in the opposite direction of the makeshift bathroom, and I march off for fresh water. My breath hitches as I see the low water rushing over the rocks. The sun streaming through the surrounding foliage to the crystal clear water gives the scene an otherworldly feel. Taking a moment, I breathe in the crispness, allowing the air to fill my lungs. A shiver ripples up my arms as I feel strangely alone. It's peaceful, but I don't like the sense of loneliness.

I lower for some water, scrubbing my hands together and then cupping a fair amount to drink. I should have brought my water bottle to refill. A twig snaps from somewhere nearby, and I assume it's Giant. When a second snap occurs, I look up to find a deer with a giant rack standing opposite the stream looking back at me.

"I wish I had my gun. He's eight points."

I turn on Giant in my crouched position. "You wouldn't dare," I hiss. The horror in my voice raises his brows, furrowing his forehead.

"It's called survival."

"It's called there's a grocery store."

"How do you think that meat gets into those stores?" He glares back at me. His hands come to his hips with a water container in each one, making him look imposing as well as ridiculous.

"The freezer fairy." I meet his stare until his face cracks. His mouth remains closed, but his chest rumbles. Was that a chuckle? He shakes his head as he closes his eyes for a second.

"City girl," he murmurs, before opening his lids and holding out my water bottle. He squats next to me to refill his canteen, and then we silently watch the deer trek away.

"Beautiful," I whisper.

"Yeah," he says just as quietly, but he isn't looking at the buck. His eyes weigh on the side of my face.

"You scared him with your evil thoughts," I mock.

"I hope not." His voice remains low, gravelly and rough, as his eyes linger on me. Then he shakes his head again and effortlessly stands. "Let's eat."

Following him, I suddenly don't feel hungry.

+ + +

"What's this?" I ask although I know full well what he's offering me.

"It's from a grocery store," he mocks me, holding out the long twig with meat on the end.

L.B. Dunbar

"That's a hot dog." I can't remember the last time I had a hot dog, let alone one roasted over an open fire.

"Don't tell me you're some highfalutin, non-meat-eatin', I-won't-even-eat-a-vegetable-because-it-hurts-the-plant kind of person?"

His sass gets under my skin, and I want to wipe the smirk from his face with the bun he offers me.

"I'll have you know I eat meat." The tone of my voice is suggestive as I stare back at him. He sits perpendicular to me, but he's close as the fire pit is small. The temperature has dropped considerably under the cover of darkness, and with the elevated location, I expect nothing less.

"I'm sure the hot dog gods are grateful."

"*Hardy-har*," I snap. "I eat hot dogs. Once a year at the ballfield." I'm a Cubs fan, and the food is part of the experience in Wrigley—hot dogs with bright green relish, peanuts in the shell, and an ice-cold beer, which reminds me...

"Got any Giant Beer in one of those coolers?"

I'm not really a beer drinker, but I'm curious. His proud grin returns, and he reaches back for one of the coolers to remove two bottles. Cracking each open on the edge of the container, he hands me one.

"It's our October blend. We haven't distributed it yet because we save it for Oktoberfest, our annual street party."

"So I should be honored to taste an early sample?"

"Among other things," he snarks.

"What's that supposed to mean?" He can make me go from zero to sixty in a heartbeat.

"Nothing." He tugs the hot dog stick from my hand and holds it over the flames. "Burnt or lightly roasted?"

"Roasted, I guess." I sound sullen when I should be grateful. At least he hasn't tossed me off the mountain. He was even slightly sweet when I tripped. And he hasn't said no to selling this property. It's a pretty piece of land, and I imagine future resort goers sitting under a starry sky around a blazing fire pit. Of course, that pit will be in a raised fireplace made of stone with cushioned bench seating around it and a wine bar nearby.

40

Giant hands me the perfect hot dog, and I hold out the bun, using it to tug the frankfurter off the stick. Marcus would have a million innuendos for this meal.

"So why do you want this land so badly?" It's an honest question, and I wonder if I can give him an honest answer without revealing too much. I need the deal for the commission.

"Have you heard of McIntyre Farm?" His head pops up, so I'll take that as a yes. "Rumor is a corner of the farm will be used for a music festival in the future."

I might as well be speaking a foreign language with the way he stares at me.

"Does Magnolia know this is going to be done to her land?"

"Who's Magnolia?"

He huffs and shakes his head, and I realize I've made another mistake. Magnolia must own the farm property.

"Do you really think people coming to a music festival want a resort? They want the experience of a night under the stars." He glances up, tipping his head back, and I follow his gaze.

"Wow," I mutter, my throat clogging at the beauty. It's rare to see a clear sky in Chicago. It's even rarer to see one like this—filled with pinpricks of light. I want to connect all the dots.

"Yeah. Wow." Giant's voice struggles. When I lower my head, I find him watching me. My face heats, but I attribute it to the fire. It's a good flame for a small space.

"Do you need to call someone? Check in?" The questions surprise me; it's as if he read my thoughts of home. I shake my head.

"How about you?"

He replies with a simple headshake as well. The sadness in his face makes my hot dog lodge in my throat. Cancer, he said earlier. He must miss his wife, and I wonder how long ago she passed away. Instead of asking, I take a hardy drink of the fall blend. Crisp. Light. Apple-ish.

"This is good," I say with hopes of shifting our conversation, but Giant doesn't take the bait. He only responds with a chin tip, and I realize discussion time is over. It's going to be a long, quiet night.

6

A touch is too much.

[Letty]

Giant offers me privacy to change into something more comfortable for sleeping. It's difficult on my knees and then on my back to slip into my pajama pants and a crew-neck sweatshirt, but I manage. A battery-operated lamp offers minimal light in the tent. He warned me not to use my phone for light.

"Conserve the battery as there's obliviously no electricity around here." Another thing I hadn't considered—charging my phone. I really should have called Frank, checked in, and assured him things were going well. My family knows I want this commission almost as badly as I want the partnership. Although I haven't secured the property or discussed the particulars with Giant, our companionable silence tells me he won't murder me in my sleep.

I slip into one of the two sleeping bags, which seem relatively close in the narrow pop-up tent. Giant asks if I'm finished, and then he enters the tent as well. His big body fills the remaining space, and I catch a whiff of him. Manly. Musky. Soap. Did he bathe in the stream after all?

Crawling on his hands and knees, he reaches for the lamp and switches off the light. I hold my breath at the sudden darkness surrounding me, blinking several times in hopes to see something, anything. Giant rustles around in the blackness before sliding into the bag next to me. A heavy exhale from him fills the air under the canvas, and I hold my breath as I lie on my back, tugging the edge of the sleeping bag under my chin. It's weird to consider sleeping next to a stranger, and I wouldn't have to consider it if I were exhausted. I should be dead tired, but suddenly, I'm wide-awake. It's been a strange day.

Sigh.

"What?" The sound of Giant's low voice next to me startles me. He's been relatively quiet since our short meal, and we spent a long time watching the flames dance or gazing up at the stars. I wish I knew all the constellations. I bet he could have taught me, but each time I looked over at him, he appeared deep in thought as though his mind was a million miles away even though his body was present. He seems a little closed off. Is he thinking of his dead wife? Does he miss her?

I roll my head on the pillow in his direction. He isn't facing me, but I can see the rough outline of him. The visual rests in my head. Strong jaw. Edged cheeks. Firm lips. The tent is the darkest dark I've ever experienced, but I can *see* him. Large, silent, brooding type. On the other hand, the silence again is eerie. Where is an airplane? How about a train in the distance? The sound of an eighteen-wheeler on a highway?

"Relax," he suggests, his voice startling me again.

I inhale. Exhale. Breathe.

The silence continues, pressing down on me as I stare up in the direction of the ceiling.

"What?" he snaps again, his voice gruffer, and I sense his head roll near mine. *Is he looking at me?*

"I didn't say anything," I remind him, whining like a teenager.

"I can practically hear you thinking over there."

"It's nothing," I murmur.

"Speak," he snaps, his voice still low as if someone might hear us.

"I typically read before I go to sleep."

"Me too," he says, rolling his head once again and surprising me with the comment.

"Really, what do you read?"

"Thrillers."

I huff.

"What?" he asks. I hear him shift next to me, his nearness overwhelming me. Though his voice remains quiet, it's closer. "I bet you read romances."

I chuckle, caught with the truth. "And if I do?"

He snorts and flips to his back again. "Nothing."

Minutes pass again, and his breathing grows shallow. I hope he doesn't snore. Hudson snored, although he swore he didn't. Of course, the great Hudson Rockford would never make such a crude noise. He hardly made noise during sex, I recall, and then will away thoughts of him. Camping is an adventure he'd never risk.

I sigh again.

"What now?" Giant speaks, his voice a little louder, and I flinch. *Wasn't he almost asleep?*

"I just thought this would be a little more exciting. Lions and tigers and bears, oh my."

"You don't want bears close to us, sweetheart." He mocks me with the endearment. "It's why we hitched up our food." Before entering the tent, Giant had me help him secure the coolers in some kind of rope netting which he hoisted up to dangle from a tree branch. The thought of a real bear coming near our camp makes me inch a little closer to Giant despite the zippered bags separating us. He doesn't seem to notice as he doesn't question me nor does he move away.

More silence. More deep breathing.

With assumptions of him sleeping, my mind races. One of my favorite romance novels comes to mind, and I'm hopeful my memory of particular scenes will help lull me to sleep as if I'm reading the words. Unfortunately, the scene that creeps into my head is a sexy one, and now all I can think of is Giant and me in compromising positions, which isn't going to happen. He's about as interested in me as a fish wanting to be out of water. But my sex clenches, pulsing more rapid than my heartbeat, and I consider getting myself off in hopes of relieving the tension.

I'm not wearing a bra, so I slip my hand under my sweatshirt, palming my stomach as I lie on my back. Slowly, I work my way under one breast, feeling the weight of the achy swell. I curve my hand upward and tweak my nipple. It's already hard, and I tug at the nub. My thighs press together, rubbing against each other, and I cross my legs for more friction.

It isn't enough, and I listen for Giant. Will he know what I'm doing only inches from him? Will he think I'm a creepy, unstable, insatiably horny woman? Images of him in my head further ignite my desire.

His broad back splitting wood before he made our fire this evening.

His fingers brushing mine as he handed me the beer.

His eyes on me while I observed the stars.

I wonder what it would be like to have him on me. His full body over mine. His large hands palming my breasts.

My fingers release the heavy globe and travel south, slipping under the waistband of my flannel pajama bottoms. Curling into my underwear, they head to my core. My fingertips just breach the pulsing nub when Giant's voice startles me again.

"Awfully quiet over there, Cricket."

I groan, adding a little cough to make it sound like resolved boredom instead of disappointment. Caught red-handed with my fingers in the cookie jar, I quickly retract my hand, only to have a heavy palm land on my forearm, over the sleeping bag, stilling my retreat.

"Cricket?" There's a question in his voice, and my mouth goes dry. I can't tell him what I'd been planning to do. That I've been thinking about him. How I wanted to take care of myself with fantasies of him.

He sniffs and sniffs again, like a hound dog on the hunt. Oh God, can he smell me? Smell the essence of my arousal?

"Are you…touching yourself?" Mortification and a strong desire to be swallowed by a sinkhole fill me. My eyes roll back, and I close my lids as if he can see me, and I'm shutting him out.

"I couldn't sleep yet," I whisper, hoping the explanation is enough to appease him, force him to release my arm, and roll away from me. Instead, the pressure of his hand pushes at mine, suggesting I move it lower.

"Giant?" I question.

He shifts next to me, and his free hand comes to the edge of my sleeping bag. I can't breathe. He's going to know what I was doing, know my dirty daydream of him. He's going to tug me from this bag and throw me off the mountain.

I'm so worked up by this scenario that I miss the rapid unzipping at my side. He reaches inside my bag for my arm and lifts my hand to his nose. Then two of my fingers enter the warm cavern of his mouth, and his tongue twirls over them. It's so unexpected and intoxicating that my back arches and my sex screams.

He releases my fingers from his lips and guides my hand back into the sleeping bag. His palm covers the back of my hand, collectively lowering our fingers under my waistband and diving deeper. The pulse at my core sets a beat more rapid than my heart. With Giant's fingers over mine, he leads me to the place I need attention, and then he stills his hand while I brush over myself. He's so close to touching me, and the tease spurs me onward. This is the craziest thing I've ever done. We're virtual strangers, yet this man does something to me. Something I've never felt, not even with Hudson. Especially not with Hudson. I toss away thoughts of my ex and concentrate on my fingertips over the swollen hood.

As the intensity of my fingers increases, I notice movement next to me. A subtle scratching, jerking motion from Giant. Is he getting himself off while torturing me with his hand so close yet not quite close enough? I hum, and his breath hitches. It feels scandalous and delicious. Forbidden and necessary.

"Giant," I squeak. Asking. Warning. Telling. I'm on the verge of one of the biggest orgasms I've ever given myself.

"Finish, Cricket," he demands, and the command breaks me. My knees separate as much as they can within the confines of the sleeping bag, and my back arches. I give in to the pleasure rippling through my lower belly and the slick proof of my desire.

I hear Giant grunt next to me, and the sensual noise echoes straight to my clit. My knees come back together, holding Giant's and my fingers pinned between my thighs. I could go again, but I've rarely had a second orgasm. I'd need his fingers on me, yet I could never outright ask him to touch me. Suddenly, I'm so embarrassed by my behavior.

The slick sound of skin on skin next to me fills my ears, and I roll my head to the side, wishing I could watch him but settle for imagining it in my head. I need another go, but Giant slowly retracts his hand, sliding his warm palm up my wrist and over my sweatshirt-covered arm. He frees his hand from my sleeping bag and awkwardly zips up the side. Movement rustles next to me, but I can't see him, and I'm cursing the darkness. More shifting. Another huff. And then the stillness alerts me that Giant has turned onto his side, leaving his back to me.

This was the most adventurous sexual experience I've ever had, and with a stranger, no less. But Giant rolling away from me, building a wall between us, is reminiscent of Hudson and his quick, no-nonsense pace. The immediate rejection stings. My heart crushes under the weight of memory and the lack of words from Giant. *Did he think that was crazy, insane fun? Or just crazy and insane?*

I should say something—thank him or apologize— but within seconds, I hear his breathing deepen and then a soft snore. I release my hand from inside the sleeping bag and reach toward Giant as if to touch his back, but I don't. Hovering over the broad expanse, I whisper to deaf ears, "Good night."

Then I roll to my side and allow the traitorous tears to silently fall.

7

The day after.

[Giant]

I shouldn't have done it, I think as I grip myself in my large palm for the second time in less than eight hours. With one arm braced on the tree before me, I rest my forehead on my forearm while my other hand jerks and juts, squeezing harder.

I couldn't help myself. She thought she was so stealthy next to me, but I'm military trained for slight noises. The hitch of her breath. The movement of her arm. And then there was the scent. Heady. Feminine. Sex. I smelled her fingers, sucked her essence off them, and then I couldn't stop myself. My twitchy fingers rested over hers—so close yet not close enough. My dick leaped to life, and I gave in to the raw pleasure.

Like I've never done before.

Like I'm doing again next to this tree.

When I woke this morning, the pressure at my back told me Letty had curled into me. I should have said something last night. I should have apologized or thanked her. I should have held her. She was a spark of that spontaneity I'd been longing for and never in my wildest dreams could I have imagined what we'd done.

I loved my wife. Clara and I had been similar—quiet and reserved. She was my high school sweetheart, and when I joined the military, the natural progression of things suggested I marry her before I went away. But when I returned, we were strangers. I'd been gone from home for too long. My desires were different, and she was hesitant with me. Then she died.

I hear a rustle of leaves to my side, but I don't look up. *Please be a curious animal instead of her.* I pray the mountain opens and swallows me if she catches me getting off again, but I can't seem to help myself. It's been a long time since I've been with a woman, and Letty isn't like any woman I've known, especially Clara. Uninhibited. Daring.

Seductive. I woke with the hardest morning wood I've ever had, and it refused to go down no matter my thoughts.

Baseball…and traveling the bases on Letty's body.

My grandmother…and pulling Letty into a closet.

Giant Brewing Company…and then pouring beer all over her body and lapping it up.

I am a mess over this woman and making one in my hand. It was rough going with spit in my palm, but fast work as the fantasies would not cease. I bit into my forearm as relief quickly came, coating my fingers.

Fuck, it felt good, but dirty and shameful. I'm not ashamed of touching myself but using Letty as my woody wet dream seems disrespectful. We don't know each another.

But you want to get to know her, my heart beats. *You want the spontaneous spark she ignites*.

Removing a bandana from my back pocket, I wipe up the mess, then tuck myself back in my pants and zip up. It's only a few short steps to the quiet campsite, and I stoke the fire when I return. I don't even know what I'll say to her this morning or how I'll address what happened last night. I'm expecting her to demand I take her back down the mountain, and I admit the thought hurts my chest. I don't want her to go. Not yet.

I step over to the tent and discover Letty missing, but so is the towel and cloth I left behind for her. *I shouldn't do it*, I warn myself, but I rise from my haunches and trek to the stream. I'll be shocked to find her in the water. That rippling river is damn cold.

Instead, I see an unexpected sight. Her back to me, she stands naked from the waist up. She rubs a wet washcloth slowly up her side, taking her time to outline her body, and I realize I could watch her all day. Lowering for the stream, I'm mesmerized by her backside. Her snug jeans accentuate each curve and hug the hips my fingers long to touch. Rinsing the cloth, she then adds more soap. The all-natural, easily dissolvible body wash works wonders when a full shower can't be had. After she stands, she slaps the cloth over her shoulder, and her hands lower to the waistband of her jeans. My throat clogs, and I cough. The noise startles her, and she crooks her head. *She can't see me*, I tell myself, as I remain under the cover of trees.

What am I doing? *Creeper. Stalker.*

What is she doing to me?

When her jeans come undone, and she lowers them to her thighs, a perfect white ass shines at me, and the cloth disappears from her shoulder.

Goddammit, I'm turned on again. It never happens this quickly. I'm almost fifty, for heaven's sake, yet I want her. Right here on this shoreline, next to the cold stream, I want to bury myself deep inside her.

Then I remember the land.

She wants my land.

She's here because of that.

Not because of me.

I turn away from her, fighting the urge in my pants and the ache in my chest. My punishment for wanting her will be the blue balls I suffer.

I return to the fire and begin the process of making eggs and bacon over a campfire. The large cast iron skillet works wonders, and I remain crouched down, focused on the sizzle of meat and the slow curl of eggs, allowing my thoughts to wander.

Clara would camp. She liked the outdoors as much as I did, finding peace in the quiet. But we were too silent as a couple. We didn't argue with each other. We didn't yell at our children. We didn't speak about all the things missing between us, and we didn't make noise during sex. She was a good woman. The best. She made a home with my military earnings and loved our girls, the only gift I believed I'd given her. Clara wanted to be a mother, and fortunately, she was pregnant after my first tour. The girls became her focus while I was gone. When I returned home, she didn't know how to handle me. The PTSD. The brewery. We weren't those silent high school sweethearts anymore. Then she got sick.

"Good morning." Her cheerful female voice breaks into my morbid memories.

I snort in response and glance up to watch Letty's face fall. She's not the reason I'm gruff, and I curse myself for responding as such, but her singular nod and the twist of lips tells me she'll take no excuse for my rudeness. She walks over to a log and lays the towel and washcloth on the bark to dry in the sun. I want to reach for the material and rub the scent of her over my face and breathe her in again, but I don't.

Instead, I focus on cooking the bacon and eggs.

"May I?" she asks before reaching for the camp coffeepot. I nod again as if my throat's clogged.

Why am I not speaking to her? *Answer her with something, you big oaf.*

"Did you sleep well?"

She stops pouring her coffee and looks up at me. Her eyes narrow, and I raise a fist to cover a forced cough.

I'm an idiot.

"It's surprising how well I slept," she answers. "I mean, it's quiet here and dark, and I'm not used to that. Planes, trains, and automobiles zooming, and bright orange streetlights are more my scene, but a lumpy ground and a thick sleeping bag weren't too bad. I can't say I'm ready for *Naked and Afraid*, but it wasn't awful." She reflectively smiles, and her response draws a grin from me.

Maybe we don't need to talk about last night.

"So last night…" she begins, and my head heavily lowers, pulling my eyes away from her. *Or maybe not.* "You mentioned bears."

My head pops back up.

"I wonder what I'm supposed to do if I see one. I read once I should fall to the ground. Another report told me to make myself large and yell."

"You could always talk him away," I scoff. Her face falls again, and her lips purse.

I amend. *Fucking idiot* describes me best.

"My mother teases me about how I talk too much. It's a nervous habit. I feel the need to fill the silence, so the words just spew. Maybe it's that my mind can't settle. I struggle to relax, so I ramble. I don't know. It just…" She glances up at me, and the words fall away. Whatever her reason for speaking so much, it's happening again, and she realizes it.

Her expression dampens again. "Smells good," she offers with a nod to the sizzling breakfast, and then she shuts her eyes as if willing herself not to speak.

"Was there anything you'd like to do today?" I ask, not having a plan. I rarely have anything specific on the agenda when I come up here. That's the point. The brewery keeps me busy with schedules and meetings, so I use this place for a break from life.

"Ax throwing. Archery. Hunting."

"Hunting?" The thought of her holding a gun surprises me.

"Actually, no. Firm pass on killing any Bambis."

"Right. Freezer fairies are so much better."

"Exactly." She chuckles, and I like the sound. Bubbly, popping, like pebbles in a rain puddle, it fits her personality, which reminds me, I think it's going to rain later. It was in the forecast, and the haze to the sky concerns me. Not for me. I love the rain, but my city-slicker friend here might melt under a mountain downpour.

"So ax throwing? Practicing for murder or got a hot date?"

"Something like that," she huffs. I stare at her, not liking the idea of her going on a date. "Actually, it's my sister's wedding."

"Planning to kill people at the wedding?" My brows rise higher.

"If only I could," she mumbles, and I continue to stare. *Is she serious?* "Actually, ax throwing is on the itinerary of events leading up to the big day."

"Ax throwing?" I question again. City people are so strange. "Got a date for this ax-throwing wedding?" I don't know why I ask. I shouldn't care, and I don't, but I'm curious. She told me about Marcus, her boyfriend-friend, but she hasn't mentioned anyone else.

She huffs. "Nope. Single as a Pringle, remember, and going stag." My lips twist, fighting the smile and the ripple of pleasure in my belly as I make a mental note of what she says. I don't know why I make a note. I don't care that she's single. *I don't.*

"I guess I could teach you how to throw an ax."

"Really?" She sits up from the log she's been perched against. "It's all the rage lately, and there's a bar dedicated to it. I'd love to kick some ass there one night. Show them all."

Her enthusiasm grows, and I wonder who *them all* is, but I don't ask, too surprised by her first comment. "All the rage?"

"Yep. It's replacing darts as the new bar sport."

I should tell Billy. He might want to consider it for Blue Ridge Microbrew and Pub. Letty sets down her coffee, which she hasn't drunk, and lifts both arms over her head, cupping her fists together as if she's going to toss something. She lets out a hefty grunt as she throws her imaginary ax. Then she sighs in relief as if the weight of the world went with the toss.

"I think you might need help with your technique."

"There's a technique?" Her eyes open wide, and I can't help the rumble climbing up my throat. I laugh. Her eyes widen more. "Was that a laugh? Did Giant Harrington just chuckle?"

She's teasing me, and I clamp my lips as if I've given her too much.

"I like it," she says, her voice softening, and she brushes a wisp of hair behind her ear. Her soft brown tresses are piled on top of her head today, and she looks different again. Business suit to blue jeans—I like her in this attire better. My eyes flip down to her knees.

"How are the knees today?"

"Sore." She glances at the cut in her pants. "But I'll live." Her exhale hints at worse things in life, and I know all too well what she means.

"So…ax throwing after breakfast?"

"Sure thing." I sigh with relief as I've dodged the ax of discussing last night.

8

Ax throwing

[Letty]

A battle cry bellows from me along with the thrust of releasing the ax.

I miss the tree completely.

"That was…" Giant's voice drifts.

"Not good," I mutter. Giant chuckles, and the sound makes my belly flutter. I meant what I said earlier. I like his laugh—deep, rich, rumbly. We've been at this for a bit, and each time I toss, he steps away. Way away.

"At least you're nearing the tree," he states, coming up behind me.

"Hardy-har," I tease, but he isn't wrong. My throws have been wild. "I need to get this."

From behind me, he steps to my side. "Lots of axes to grind in the city?"

"My sister's wedding, remember? She's getting married in two weeks."

"Unusual for a bachelorette party," he scoffs.

"Oh, no. The bachelorette party was back in March. Mardi Gras in New Orleans." His brows pinch. "Destination bachelorette parties are *all the rage*," I mock. "As if a few shots and dancing at the local pub isn't enough." I scoff, but there's no humor to my voice. I bend for the next ax and stand, but Giant grips my wrist, a subtle warning of caution.

"She sounds like a pain in the ass."

"You have no idea," I mutter, trying to lift the instrument, but Giant holds me still, probably worried I'll miss and nick him.

"Tell me." His commanding request surprises me.

"Dayna is my older sister. She's the princess. Everything was perfect. Perfect life. Perfect wife. Until her husband left her. She calls him the practice husband, and now she's getting married again." My chest heaves as I relay my sister's history.

"So she's on marriage number two, and you haven't had marriage number one?" He questions as if he's all-knowing, but he's so wrong. Well, I haven't been married yet, but that's beside the point.

"Hardly. I'm definitely *not* jealous of her. She can have him."

Giant's dark eyes narrow. "Who?"

"Hudson."

"And Hudson is…?" Hudson Rockford. My ex-boyfriend, former fiancé, and the scumbag of the Earth.

"Not important. Not one bit unless you consider we were living together, and he slept with my sister. The one who is going to marry him."

Giant flinches. "Jesus."

"Nope, not Him. Hudson likes to think he's God's gift, but he's anything but. Small-minded, micro-penis, no-emotion Hudson. She can have him."

Giant laughs, another full-on burst of sound, and the thunderous noise ripples over me, comforting me. "Micro-penis? Poor guy."

"Wrong again. Poor me." I break free of Giant's grasp and lift my ax arm. Giant catches it above my head, and those dark eyes narrow again.

"Okay, let's not chop my head off for his faulty pipeline." His tone sobers, and he lowers my arm. "Be safe here. Smart."

He releases my arm and steps behind me. His chest brushes my back. "Drop the ax for a second but watch your toes."

I toss the blade forward, and it lands on its side. Giant covers my shoulders with thick palms and then smooths them down my arms. I'm wearing a tank top as my flannel is tied around my waist. I'd grown warm from the exercise, but I shiver under his touch. The pads of his hands are callused but comforting, and he circles my wrists. He places his scruffy cheek next to mine. His lips graze my ear.

"Concentrate," he whispers, but with his chest at my back and his breath in my ear, the only focus I have is on him and his closeness. He places my hands together and holds them collectively out in front of me. My fingers entwine as if wrapped around the shaft of the ax.

L.B. Dunbar

"Aim." Warm air brushes the skin of my exposed neck, and I try to keep still, but my body quivers. He turns his head, skimming the slope of my neck with his nose. "No matter what's going on around you, you must focus."

I force my eyes to remain on the tree trunk before me, my arms aligned with the thickness, but as his nose reverses the path up my neck, I can't think straight. I want his mouth to suck on my skin. I want his teeth to nip me. Then again, if he does, my ax-throwing lessons are over, and a new lesson will begin—the art of kissing.

His palms slip up my extended arms to my elbows. Those thick palms curl, and he simultaneously taps each elbow with a finger.

"Bend." Oh Lord, why does the word sound sexy? Heed to his will. Kneel before him. My core clenches. My legs spread apart from the slip of his knee between my thighs. I have a new target in mind, and I want to drop the figurative ax throwing to rub against the tree trunk-sized thigh between mine.

"Cricket," he quietly commands, and I bend my elbows to a ninety-degree angle. He presses on my underarms, guiding me to lift and hold the position. His chin rests in the crook between my shoulder and neck, and his mouth hovers near my ear. His beard was trim when we left, but it's quickly growing thicker. The scratchy sensation on my neck makes my mouth water.

Kiss me.

"Stay," he murmurs to my shoulder and then slides his hands down the underside of mine. I want to turn my head. I want to take his mouth, but my eyes remain forward while my body trembles under his tender touch. His fingers spread once he clears my pits, and he swipes the sides of my breasts, outlining my body. Whether intentional or not, my breasts tingle and my nipples pop. The nubs harden and strain against my bra, exposing what he's doing to me. Finally, his hands settle on my hips, and he squeezes.

"Don't lose this stance." His front taps my backside for emphasis, and I lose control. My ass presses back at him as my arms drop. I can't take the tension rippling up my inner thighs or the beating of my sex. My hands come to my knees, forcing my ass against him.

56

Take me, I scream inside my head. *Bend me over your knee.*

But instead, he instantly releases me, taking a step back.

"I think you're ready." He walks around me, ignoring how I've pressed into him. No reaction. Last night must have meant nothing to him because he hasn't mentioned it, and he doesn't appear even remotely affected by me today. I don't know what I expected, though. I don't know what I want from him.

You shouldn't want anything from him. You need his land.

My heart clenches as I watch him reach for the ax on the dirt. When he holds it shaft out, I tug it from him with more force than I intend and narrowly miss nicking the pad of his hand. My eyes lift to his, and he raises one eyebrow. He must know what he's done to me, though. I'm a hot mess.

"Take all the negative energy you hold for micro-penis and sister bitch and toss that ax."

He rushes back a step or two as I aim with extended arms and lift to the angle he suggested. I reach behind my head and then pitch forward, tossing the ax with all the strength and anger and regret.

I hit the tree, but the ax doesn't stick.

"Goddammit."

Giant retrieves the two axes we've been using and comes back to me. "Each try is one step closer to the goal. Don't give up."

Without meeting his eyes, I focus on the trunk once again.

Giving up isn't in my nature.

+ + +

My arms ache from my many attempts. I lost count somewhere after the thirty-seventh throw. Giant has the patience of a saint and the willpower of one as well. His near kisses and brisk touches are my driving force to continue throwing the ax long after the burn begins in my shoulders. He thinks Hudson and Dayna spur me onward, but I've long since let go of them. Bitterness weighed me down at first. Overhearing Hudson telling someone—*my sister*—he couldn't wait to see her soon, and then discovering they'd rented a room at a hotel to meet up was a sour pill to swallow.

I was so lonely, my sister told me. Was I supposed to sympathize with her? Was her after-divorce loneliness heavier than the weight I bore in a relationship with an unemotional man? The very man she decided would end her bout of being alone.

Four years I wasted on Hudson. Four years thinking we would get better. Moving in. Getting engaged. Making plans. Discussing marriage. I missed all the signs in my quest for happily ever after in a relationship that left me complacent and not content. Hudson is in finance, a business closely linked to real estate acquisitions and mergers. He also is a Rockford, and his family owns one of the largest privately held financial institutions in Chicago. He is Midwest royalty, and I was a blind fool.

Marrying me would have secured his family to Mullen, which would have pleased my uncle. When I broke everything off, Hudson wasted no time moving on to my sister. Or perhaps he'd already moved on to her after he broke all emotions within me? They'll be a match made in hell and definitely deserve one another. Both perfectionists. Both filled with pettiness. They are better suited than Hudson and I ever would have been. *Still*. It hurt to find him cheating on me, dissolving all his promises for a roll in the sheets with my sister.

Dayna and I had never been close. As the middle child, I was closer to my brother, Owen, even though he was years younger than me. I wipe away thoughts of him and focus my energy on Dayna. In two weeks, she'll be getting married, and I'm the maid of honor. What a fucking farce.

Put on your brave face and show them what you're made of, Marcus told me when my sister asked me. Awkwardly, the invitation came during a family dinner. Not only do I lack negotiation skills, but my ability to think on the spot struggles, and so I said yes. A whirlwind of dress shopping, engagement parties, and wedding plans followed, and my dislike of Dayna has grown deeper with each step of the process. As for Hudson, I've long since surpassed feeling hatred for him. I just want the wedding over with so I don't have to speak to either of them again.

Of course, that will be impossible as Dayna works for Mullen Realty with me, and she's probably figuring out what else she can steal out from under me while I'm here throwing axes.

I hit my mark. The ax sticks for eight out of ten consecutive throws.

"You did it," Giant says encouragingly from my side, and his voice draws me back to my surroundings.

I turn to him with a huge smile on my face.

"I did it."

I survived almost a year of in-my-face Dayna and Hudson, and it's almost over.

Giant grips my bare shoulders and rubs. "You're so tense, but it's the muscle strain. You worked hard. Just relax." His thumbs dig into the nape of my neck.

Relax.

If only he knew how *hard* I want to *relax* with him.

9

Lightning does strike twice

[Giant]

Bad weather was coming. The ache near my bullet wound told me as such, and I didn't trust how Letty would fare. After our day of ax throwing and a night of burgers, we chatted more about her upbringing in Chicago. Her eyes drooped in the heat of the fire as she sat wrapped in a camp blanket. She was so pretty sitting there under the stars with the flames casting a glow on her cheeks.

"I think I'll retire early," she says, pressing off the ground, and my breath hitches. I want her to ask me to join her, but she doesn't. I've dodged a bullet, or rather an ax, all day as we never discussed last night. In some ways, I'm bothered by this as Clara and I never talked about awkward situations in our relationship. It was one of the strains on our marriage. In an effort not to argue, we didn't confront one another.

I'm not a talker, so it isn't as though I want an emotional chat, but I would like to know what she thought of last night. *Did she enjoy herself? Did I make her happy?* Last night wasn't like anything I'd ever done before, and selfishly, I want a repeat with more experimenting.

I wait out the flames a bit by stringing up our food, and then the first raindrop plops. Before entering the tent, I dump dirt on the dying embers. Once undercover, I strip down to my boxer briefs and a T-shirt like I did last night. I run hot, and the thermal sleeping bag makes me too warm. Slipping onto my back, I stare at the tent's ceiling, taking in deep breaths to calm my memories of yesterday evening. Letty's steady breathing next to me tells me she's fast asleep. She worked hard today, tossing axes and helping me build a fire for tonight's feast, so I imagine she's exhausted.

I don't like what I've learned about her former fiancé. What an asshole. And her sister, well, there aren't enough words to string together for her. I'd kill one of my brothers if they ever went after a woman I'd been interested in. Then again, I've only ever had Clara until ten years ago, and after her, it's been rather sporadic. I don't fault Clara. I loved her, but without communication, we didn't understand what the other needed when it came to sex. And while I wanted more, Clara wasn't curious or adventurous.

With that thought, I exhale and roll to my side, my back to Letty.

A rustling occurs behind me, and I hear her shifting in her sleeping bag, its nylon covering rutting against the tent canvas. Unconsciously, Letty scoots into me. She doesn't wrap around me but burrows into my spine, and I stiffen for a second before giving in to the sensation. I don't question the movement, liking the way she feels behind me. It's comforting until the first crack of weather hits.

Letty shoots upright.

"What was that?" Her voice is filled with fear.

"Thunder," I mumble, rolling onto my back. I can't see her in the darkness, and then the lightning strikes. Her wide blue eyes meet mine for only a second, and the look on her face is pure terror before we are submerged in darkness again.

"Hey," I say, sitting up and reaching for her cheek. Her skin is soft but clammy. "It will pass."

She's nodding continuously as I guide her to lie back down. It's awkward in two sleeping bags, but I wrap an arm over her, attempting to hold her. There's nothing romantic or cuddle-worthy in the position. Letty trembles under my arm. Both her hands cover her face buried into my chest.

Thunder rumbles again. Lightning filters into the tent. And Letty shudders.

The rain hasn't started in earnest, but the wind picks up. The tent rattles, and Letty's coming unhinged, trembling under my arm.

"You're really scared, aren't you?"

She shakes her head against my chest, but it's the opposite of her body language.

"Is it the lightning?"

"It's the thunder." She pauses a beat. "If it's okay with you, I don't want to talk about it." Her voice quivers, and whatever she isn't telling me is bad, and the thunder is a trigger. I know all about triggers, and this tent isn't going to be enough to settle her.

"Get dressed."

She pulls back from me, and I hastily sit up.

"There's bad weather coming, and we need to get you out of here. We can't make it back to my cabin, but there's an old ranger station about a hundred yards from here. If we hurry, we might miss the rain."

I switch on the camp light and watch as her hands shake. She slips off her pajama bottoms under the sleeping bag and then crawls forward for something in her bag. Her smooth backside faces me as she's wearing a thong, and I try not to lose focus as I scramble for my pants. It's tight quarters in the two-person tent, but we somehow work in sync like a well-timed machine. She slips black yoga pants out of her bag and tugs them up her long legs. I notice her toes. Blisters swell on her pinkies as well as on each heel. My eyes leap to her face, but she isn't looking at me as she struggles to tug on her socks. I toss her my thin rain slicker.

"What about you?" she asks, pulling it on over her sweatshirt.

"I'll be fine." I don't consider being modest as I slip from my bag and pull on my pants. I finish dressing quickly, tugging on a flannel but not bothering to button it. Then I grab my backpack and the battery lamp. Letty reaches for her pack.

"Ready?"

She nods before she follows me out the tent. Thunder cracks again, and Letty screams. I tug her to me.

"Sorry. I'm sorry," she mumbles into my chest. Her trembling is unbearable. I don't know what she's apologizing for, but I walk us forward. I want to keep her pressed to me, but we won't move fast enough with her wrapped under my arm. She must sense this as she slips from my side. "Just go." She reaches for my hand, and I tug her along behind me, holding up the lamp to lead the way.

We haven't made it ten feet before the rain pours from the sky. Thankfully, the heavy branches keep us relatively protected from the pelting drops. We race among the trees, Letty keeping up with me until we break into a small clearing with the old station. She shivers uncontrollably next to me as I fumble for the key hidden on the upper jamb. When I press the door open, she flings herself inside, tripping, and then scrambles to the wall opposite the door. The rain falls in earnest as the thunder and lightning increase in frequency. The storm is over us.

I drop my backpack and set the camp light on the floor. I want to turn it off to conserve the battery, but the fear in Letty's eyes tells me to leave the soft glow on. I fall to my knees and crawl over to her. The old station has wood floors. Not hard wood, just uncovered boards. A single cot lines one wall while a metal desk and squeaky rolling chair stand on the other side of the room. The only other door in the place leads to a small bathroom. A kitchenette is next to the bathroom.

"There's electricity here. I can go outside and find the switch."

Her frightened eyes meet mine, wide and worried. "Please. Don't leave me."

I nod and continue to crawl closer. When I get to her, I shift to sit against the wall and slip an arm around her.

"Come here," I whisper, forcing her pack off her back. She dips her head into my chest again. It isn't enough. I need to distract her. I skim my hand down her side and then cup her hip. Repeating my command, "Come here." I hoist her over my leg so she falls between my spread thighs. The wetness of the rain slicker soaks through my shirt, and if we don't remove some of this wet clothing, the cold will be the new cause of shivers. I remove the jacket from her and shake it so some of the water releases. The inside is lined and warm, and I return the slicker over her like a blanket.

"Your shirt is soaked," she says, and I press us forward. I tug the flannel plus T-shirt over my head and toss it to the side. *My skin will warm her better anyway*, I tell myself. She falls back against me, and my arms circle her waist.

Another roar of thunder. Another flash of light. Letty whimpers. My lips come to her neck, and I kiss her under her ear.

"Let me distract you."

She nods, elongating her neck as she tips her head to the side. She has these fine hairs that curl along her nape, and they've teased me all day while she learned to throw an ax. I suck hard at her skin with my open mouth, marking her. She whimpers in response, and I lose control of my thoughts. I don't hear the thunder or see the lightning. Only her. My hand roughly moves between her thighs.

"So warm," I mouth into her skin, drawing my tongue down the side of her neck. Her knees spread, and I rub over the soft cotton covering her heat. I suck at her neck, latching on to the dip near those fine hairs. She whimpers under me, and I slip my hand under the waistband of her yoga pants, delving deeper to her center. My fingers brush over moist, lacy cotton.

"Fuck," I mutter at her ear, and she shifts her hips to lower the pants a little, allowing me better access to her. She's wearing another one of those thongs I found while rummaging in her backpack before we started this trip, so the material easily slips to the side, and my middle finger slides into her. She welcomes me by spreading her thighs wider. Her head tips back to my shoulder as she hums. She made the same noise last night.

"Always chirping." I chuckle, nipping at her neck.

She bites her lip, and I worry she'll stop making those sounds. I need the noise. I want to hear her satisfaction.

"Don't you dare stop, Cricket," I warn, adding a second finger to the first. Her head lolls forward as she moans.

"So full," she whispers, and I smile, nipping her earlobe. My fingers slip back and forth, drenched in her essence.

"You're so wet."

"You do this to me."

The comment startles me. There's no denying I'm attracted to her, and her body's response to me tells me she might feel the same. But this? This admission sounds like something more. Or am I projecting my feelings? Am I hoping for something…spontaneous?

I continue to coast in and out, adding my thumb to the nub outside her, the place I was so close to last night but didn't dare to touch. Tonight, however, I'm all in, and there's no going back. Her hips thrust forward, drawing my fingers into her. Softly, she moans, mumbles, and mutters. Her head rolls on my shoulder as she takes my fingers deeper and deeper.

"Giant," she warns, humming along with my name on her lips, and then she clenches. Her knees come together, and she rides my hand pressed between her thighs. My fingers work her until she collapses. Her legs fall open as she relaxes, but I'm too worked up. I want this woman, and touching her wasn't enough.

Quickly, I slip my fingers from her, the sound of slick suction and the scent of her fills our tight surroundings.

"Not enough, Letty," I warn as I press at her shoulder blade to move her forward. She scrambles up to her knees and then falls to her hands, similar to the position when she tripped over the rock. I follow her and hold her hips, pressing her bare ass against the front seam of my jeans. I thrust forward, and Letty collapses to her elbows. She struggles to tug her pants to her knees with one hand and then slips them to her ankles.

"Letty?" I question although my chest hammers and my dick strains.

"Please," she hisses. I've never done anything like this, taken a woman without regard, without thought, without knowing her a little better. But my only thought is how much I want in *this* woman. How spontaneous this act is. How raw, and wild, and uncontained. I'm grateful I left my belt behind when I fumble to undo my pants. Pushing the sides to my knees, I tug my briefs along with them. My dick twitches, slapping Letty on the ass. The warm skin-on-skin contact makes us both sigh.

I'm not a noisemaker during sex. I've always kept it quiet, but I have a feeling this woman is going to make me roar. I drag my tip along the seam of her ass and then lower, finding her soaked folds. As I coat the head of my dick, my legs tremble with anticipation. She's more than ready for me, and I eagerly thrust into her. Letty makes her purr-like hum as I still, seated deep within her.

"Letty," I rumble like a beast inside me has come unleashed. She moans in answer, and I exhale deeply. My God, she's so warm, so tight, so wet. One arm wraps around her waist while my hand grips her hip. Looking down at our position, I watch myself slide free but keep the tip inside her. Then I rush forward, filling her until my pelvis hits her ass.

"Ohmygod, ohmygod, ohmygod." Her breath hitches on each praise. As I pull back again, she follows me, greedy to keep me buried

L.B. Dunbar

within her, and I don't disappoint, but I tease. I draw out to the edge and then slam forward. She hums louder as her hands fist.

"Again." The word echoes through the small room, and I repeat the motion. Skin slaps, grunts grow, and Letty clenches around me. My balls tighten. My lower back pinches, and I fill this woman with every drop of my seed. The only movement for a moment is me pulsing inside her as the largest orgasm I've ever known takes me.

I collapse over her, forcing us to the ground. It all happened too fast, and my breath comes ragged and restless. Quickly, I pull out of her and flip to my back. Staring up at the ceiling, I flop an arm over my forehead as my chest heaves, and stars dance before my eyes.

What just happened?

The weight of her eyes presses on my heated cheeks, and I roll my head to face her.

Please don't let her be disappointed.

I don't know why that's my first thought, but when I find her eyes in the dimming glow of the battery light, she slowly smiles.

"So tired," she whispers as she lays flat on her stomach, her head tilted in my direction. "Thank you," she mutters before closing her eyes. She drifts off to sleep, but I don't think I'll sleep tonight. Not with this beautiful woman next to me who just breathed life back into my hollow lungs.

10
Cold night and shoulder

[Letty]

I'm drifting to sleep when Giant rolls to his side once again, giving me his back. The storm has passed, but a different one rumbles through my chest. I want to scoot into him and press against him, but I fight the urge. Actually, I'd like him to hold me, wrap his arms around me and draw me into his chest like he did before we left the tent. Still, I shouldn't fool myself into thinking anything other than sex is happening between us, but it would be nice to be held for a few minutes before he dismisses me again—before he rolls to his side and forces a wall between us instead of his arms around me.

I remind myself he took care of me during the storm. He sensed my fear and tried to comfort me, tried to distract me. Maybe sex is simply a distraction for him. I wish I could be so casual. He's the first man I've slept with since Hudson. I probably shouldn't have slept with him, yet I wanted nothing more than to feel him inside me, blocking out the thunder and my thoughts. Pulling my knees up to my chest to add another barrier between us, I brush away the dangerous desires.

I wake to heavy footsteps on the decking outside the station, and Giant instantly rolls over me, covering me like a blanket while his eyes stay trained on the door. It swiftly opens, and a man stands just behind my head, pointing a gun at us.

"Fucking hell," the man swears.

"Stand down, James," Giant yells.

The man slips his gun into the back of his jeans. From my upside-down angle, I see he's tall, leaner than Giant, and has more salt than pepper in his hair. A patch of scruff dusts his jaw, and his eyes match Giant's—dark and dangerous—but intensely blue instead of brown.

Giant peels himself off me, and I press myself up slowly, shaking as I go. I'm not a fan of guns, and the reality of a man standing over me

67

L.B. Dunbar

with one catches up to me. I twist and scoot back toward the wall where Giant and I first sat upon entering the station.

"What the fuck are you doing in here?" the man named James asks as Giant kneels and then easily unfolds to stand to his full height. His pants are righted on him. It occurs to me that neither of us removed our boots during what we did last night. I curl my arms over my middle, not wishing to think of the raw sex we had, how much I enjoyed it, and how Giant then turned away from me again.

"I'm camping."

James glances at me and back at Giant. "This isn't a campground."

"I fucking know that," Giant snaps. "We were over by the stream, but a storm rolled in. It was too much for the tent." I'm thankful he doesn't rat me out by exposing my freak-out over the thunder.

The man steps forward and offers his hand. "I didn't mean to scare you. As this oaf won't introduce us, I'm James."

"I thought you went by Ranger now," Giant bites, clearly upset that James has approached me and holds out his hand. I reach up to shake it, and I'm surprised when he tugs me, forcing me upright to stand. His eyes roam down my body and then he turns to Giant. "I'm impressed."

"You're an ass," Giant says, stepping forward and slipping an arm around my waist to drag me behind him.

"Uhm, excuse me, but the woman doesn't need to be shoved around like a rag doll."

James's brows rise, and his mouth crooks up in the corner. "Oh man." He chuckles, warm and rich, and not half as menacing as his overall appearance, which includes heavy black boots, like one would wear on a motorcycle, along with washed-out jeans and a leather jacket with a light gray crew-neck sweatshirt underneath.

"And you are?" James addresses me.

"Letty," I say from behind Giant's back at the same time Giant counters, "None of your business."

"Don't be like this," the motorcycle man speaks to Giant.

"Then come home." Giant's gruff demand startles me. Are they friends? Related possibly? The longer I look, the more I see the resemblance. The shape of their noses. The set of their mouths. James turns his head away from Giant and stares out the open door.

"You know I can't," he whispers, and something in his voice resonates with me. Heartbreak. Loss.

"What are you doing here?" Giant questions again.

"I needed a break." James meets Giant square in the face.

"You know I get that," Giant responds, his voice softening as his head slowly shakes. He looks at me over his shoulder. "We're set to go. The storm is over."

His tone is curt, and I nod without a word, leaning down to pick up Giant's jacket and his shirts. I hold the flannel out to him, and James's brow lifts again. There's a twinkle to his dangerous gaze. He's correct in his assumptions. Giant and I had sex. Raw, unadulterated, dirty sex. I loved it even if I hate him a little this morning.

Giant slips on the flannel and balls up the T-shirt before shoving it in his backpack. He lifts one strap over his shoulder while picking up mine.

"James." Giant gives the man a sharp nod and heads for the door.

"Nice meeting you," I mumble as I pass James and exit the ranger station after Giant. We barely clear the porch steps when he finally speaks to me.

"I'll take you back." Something in his tone has my Spidey-senses rising, and I glare at his broad back as he leads us into the trees.

"Back to camp?" I clarify. He'll escort me to the site by the stream and return for some unfinished business with James.

"Back down the mountain."

I stop walking and cross my arms. "You'll do no such thing."

He spins and stalks back to me. "It isn't safe if James is up here."

"Who is he?"

"He's my brother."

"He can't be the mayor," I state, surprised at my judgmental tone but questioning whether a mayor would look like a motorcycle thug. "Is he the pub owner?"

"No, this is another brother."

"How many brothers do you have?"

"Three and one sister, and none of this is relevant. Down the mountain we go," he firmly states.

"Is this because of last night?" I blurt. "We had sex, and now you're done with me."

"What?" Giant's eyes widen as his arms cross his chest. "No. No, I'm protecting you."

"Well, the only person I feel threatened by right now is you." I'm fuming without a real fuse. I don't know why I'm so upset. Maybe it's because deep down I'm not ready to leave the mountain or the man who brought me up here.

"Me?" Giant grumbles. "*Now* you're afraid of me?" He's aghast at the notion. His fists clench at his sides as he looks off into the distance a moment and then turns back to me with narrowed eyes. For the first time, he looks scary. "Forget it. I don't need this headache. We're going back." He turns back for the woods, but I stand firm.

"That's right, turn your back to me like you've done each night."

Giant pauses and twists back to face me. "Woman, what are you talking about?"

"First night, we…" I point between us. "And then you give me your back." My voice cracks, and I swallow, forcing unwanted tears to retreat. "And then last night, we…again…more…better…" I close my eyes, embarrassed to admit how much last night meant to me. "And you just dismissed me."

Giant doesn't owe me anything, but I'd have thought he'd open up a little bit. Thought we'd continue to learn more about each other, discover each other. We did have sex after all, but maybe that's why he's ready to take me down the mountain. Sex? Check.

Giant's brows pinch. "I didn't dismiss you. We went to sleep." He's serious. Something in his tone tells me that holding me wasn't even a thought. We finished, and he rolled to his side of the bed. How very Hudson of him.

"You know what? You're right. Forget it."

"Right. Down the mountain we go," he states as he waves a hand to emphasize his point.

"No can do," I say, brushing past him. "It hasn't been three nights."

"You've had enough nights."

"Nope. I get one more, then we talk. I'm not leaving without fulfilling my part of the deal."

"We talk?" he questions, pausing a reflective moment. His expressions shifts darker. "About the land." His voice falters as realization dawns. The quieter tone concerns me more than his gruffness, but I'm not backing down. I need this property. I need the commission.

"Yes, the land," I yell back at him. Should there be another reason to stay? He isn't giving me one.

He shakes his head. "You're delusional."

"And you're...you're standoffish-*ish*." It's a weak retort. I don't know why I say it. As I've mentioned, I'm not good with on-the-spot comebacks.

"I'd keep her if I were you." I twist to find James leaning against a column holding up the overhang covering the small porch and realize we have an audience.

"Mind your own damn business, James. You're good at that." My eyes flicker from James to Giant.

"Seems like he's not the only one," I mutter. Stomping around Giant, I head for the path cutting into the woods but then stop and turn back one more time. "And don't ever treat me like I'm not there again." I point at the station, reminiscent of the way he and his brother spoke to each other without including me. This is how Hudson would act, as if I wasn't present, as if I didn't have an intelligent opinion or couldn't make a decision. I spin for the path. I don't even care if I get lost. I just need *away* from Giant.

Ironically, I find my way back to camp, and it doesn't seem half as far as it did while we raced through the darkness under rain and thunder. As I see the waterlogged fire pit and the soggy ground around our site, I turn on Giant who's kept his distance behind me.

"No bathroom?" I huff. "Yet less than a hundred yards off, there is one." Not to mention a solid roof and a small kitchen, but these things are the least of my ire. My anger festers into a storm of rage. I hate how he treated me like I was invisible. Not introducing me. Acting like nothing happened between us. I also do not like how he's willing to break our agreement and take me back. *Was it only sex to him?* Did he not enjoy it like I did?

"And you'd like to traipse a hundred yards to pee?" he questions. "You didn't seem to mind the woods." His voice lowers as if the remark surprises him. No, I didn't complain because I accepted we were roughing it. He wanted to prove something to me, and I...I wanted to prove something to myself, I realize. I wanted to prove I could do this.

"Never mind." I sigh and shake my head, turning away from him. I scratch at my scalp. My hair is dirty and grimy, and I just want a hot soak and clean sheets and wine. Lots of wine. But not tonight. *One more night.* I stomp over to the fire pit and sit on an upturned log. I have one more night to survive this hell and rid myself of Giant Harrington once he signs on the line.

Only it hasn't really been hell. It's been rather wonderful, if I'm honest. The sexy time. The ax throwing. Even the hot dog roasted over a campfire was pleasant. I'm surprised how much I've enjoyed myself. Giant has catered to me in every way—organizing our menu, cooking, and cleanup. He's trying to encourage me to appreciate the natural environment around us, and I've absentmindedly soaked it up. Do I really want to leave him? *Why has he done all this?* Did he just want sex with me? I hate to think this is the truth, and a bigger question niggles at me. Will he really give up his land after a three-night camping trip?

Giant sets his pack on the ground and rummages through it before pulling out something rolled up and tucked in a small bag. I watch him walk to two trees and clip one end of the material to a hook I hadn't noticed drilled into the trunk. He crosses to a second tree and fastens the other end of the nylon cloth to a second hook. As he steps back, I notice it's a hammock.

"You said you read." The statement startles me. I stare up at him, wondering what this has to do with anything. The tension between us is thicker than the humidity lingering from last night.

"My reader's in my bag." Without permission, he rummages through my pack and pulls out my tablet.

"Why don't you read for a bit? It's too wet to sit on the ground, and I need to dry everything from last night. I'll make breakfast." Now I am curious. What is this behavior? He hands me my e-reader, and I stare after him as he lowers the food from the trap in the tree. I should offer to help, but I don't want to talk to him. I stand and walk to the hammock.

"Straddle it. Then set your butt down first. It makes it easier to lie back and get your legs in it." I do as he directs and lounge back. Within a few minutes, my anger dissipates from the sway of the hammock, the whisper of the trees, and a warm breeze. I can't concentrate on any words in my book, so I stare at them instead. Unfocused. Disappointed.

Why couldn't sex always be like it was last night? Maybe only random sex can feel so liberating. Then again, if how I'm feeling today is a side effect of random sex, I don't think my heart can take it. I haven't been with anyone in a year, and Giant's behavior is a reminder of why I've held back—I'm too emotional to have casual sex. My eyes close with memories of last night. Images of Giant touching me fill my head. His thick fingers. His mouth on my skin. His big dick. He's a large man, and his private property is proportionate. I've never been so full, so satiated, and so at a loss when it was over.

I scratch at my scalp again.

Maybe I'm destined never to understand men. Hudson was closed off, unobtainable even when physically present. Why can't I have a man who can be affectionate?

"Breakfast is ready." His voice should startle me, but I've learned to listen for his quiet movements. I'm not hungry, but I roll from the hammock, nearly turning all the way over and falling to the ground. Giant catches me, but I shrug off his touch. "I got it."

I stalk to the fire pit and sit. Fried eggs and corned beef hash—I haven't had such a breakfast since I was a kid. The combination reminds me of my dad, and I suddenly feel lonelier than ever.

"My dad died when I was a kid, so I don't remember much about him, but this was his favorite breakfast." I don't know why I tell Giant this tidbit. *You're filling the empty spaces.*

"I'm sorry. About your dad." Giant says, staring down at the meal in the skillet. He doesn't add anything more, and we fall into awkward silence, and for once, I don't feel the need to chatter and fill the quiet.

11

Silence is too quiet.

[Giant]

I can't handle her silence.

For the talker she is, she hasn't spoken since breakfast. In such a short time, her constant chatter has grown on me, and I miss the noise. The hum of life she whispers no matter what she's saying. The chirping beat she stimulates in my quiet heart. I didn't realize how empty my world felt until this vibrant woman entered the place I hold most sacred. My land.

She's only here for the land, I remind myself, but she certainly seemed upset about last night.

We had sex, she blurted, but those brilliant blue eyes were filled with hurt. The expression surprised me. Did she not want to have sex with me? Did I force her? Did I go too far? Her adventurous spirit tells me I didn't, so why did she look so offended? Was it only because I suggested we return to the cabin? Did she want something more from me? Other than my land, I can't imagine what I could offer her.

Her quiet unnerves me, and she scratches at her hair for the tenth time.

"Got an itch?" I don't think she has bugs. The insects are mild as the temperature drops this time of year. Still, a tick would love her hair. *I* love her hair.

"My hair. It's just dirty, and it feels gross. I think I'll go down to the stream."

"Not alone. I don't like James being around." What is he doing up here? I love my prodigal brother, but I don't trust his motives for anything. He claims he has his reasons to leave the family, but we all have "reasons" in our lives, and that's when we need family the most. "I'll go with you."

Letty's eyes narrow at me. "Fine." She stands and heads into the tent, returning with shampoo and a towel. She stalks past me, heading for the stream. I follow, once again keeping my distance. When we get to the edge of the water, she tugs off her shirt and then looks at me over her shoulder.

"You can turn your back." It takes me a moment to realize what she means. She wants me to turn around, but I don't think I can pry my eyes from her. The ripple of her spine. The dip at the base. The nape of her neck.

I'll be damned if I let her out of my sight with James in the vicinity, but I begrudgingly spin around. She could give me the slip if she wanted. Then I hear the slap of the washcloth hitting the water. I imagine her rubbing up her sides and over her breasts. My mouth waters as I haven't had a taste of them yet. *Hell, I haven't even kissed her.* I envision her dipping the cloth lower, swiping her sex, and I'm a mess. She's mumbling something behind me, and I slip my hands into my pants, adjusting my dick which is moving toward its new status around this woman—perpetually hard.

"Giant." My name is a strained attempt at a whisper. "It's…" Her voice stops.

"What now, woman?" I shift from foot to foot. She whispers my name again. Detecting something in her voice other than her easygoing chatter, I quickly spin and note a bear on the other side of the stream.

Fuck.

"Letty," I whisper as loud as I can, hoping not to draw any attention to her. "Don't move." Then again, she's in a precarious position. Her pants are down near her knees, underwear included, and two white globes of perfection shine at me. But I can't think about my hands on that ass or driving into her from this angle like I did last night because she needs to get away from that water.

"Now slowly, lower for your pants, Cricket." My eyes don't leave the bear who is intent on watching the rippling water. With Letty in my line of sight for the wild creature, I see her slowly bend forward and drag up her jeans. Then she takes one step back and another. When her foot steps on a twig, and the sound snaps like a shotgun, the bear looks up. We both hold our breath. I'm calculating how quickly I can reach her, hike her over my shoulder and run when the large, black creature turns away and slowly moseys in the opposite direction. I step forward and grip her bare shoulders. She claps a hand over her mouth and melts against my chest. She's trembling under my fingers.

"He's so beautiful," she mutters once she uncovers her lips, not yet fazed that a bear caught her with her pants down, literally. Or that she's standing shirtless before me, leaning back-to-chest against me.

"Beautiful and dangerous," I hum next to her ear, not certain if I'm talking about the bear or the woman before me. She relaxes another second before leaning forward, removing herself from my touch, and scratching at her hair. Her arm attempts to cover her bare chest, but it's hopeless. Both swells are hardly contained. "I have an idea. Let's head back to camp. Are you finished?"

"As good as it's going to get, I guess." Her irritation with me lingers in her tone. I should tell her I'm sorry for whatever I did and beg for forgiveness with my tongue, my fingers, and my straining erection. Her festering, fiery energy makes me want her again. I haven't been able to calm myself for the second day in a row. *What is it with this woman?*

When I woke to the sound of James, I'd been dreaming of her, her lush body underneath mine. My mouth finally meeting hers. As I pressed over her, shielding her from James, my thoughts shifted to driving her down the mountain.

My truck. She's going to hate me when the truth comes out.

I scrub a hand down my beard. It's grown bushier as the days pass.

"I'm done," she mutters, and my gaze shifts back to her. Her hair is rolled into a tight bun at the base of her neck, and she scratches at it again. Greasy hair or not, she looks beautiful.

I walk her back to camp.

"Let me fetch some water. I'll be right back."

"I thought you were afraid to leave me alone," she snarks, but the bite is no longer present in her tone. She can hold her own against the likes of someone like James, but still, his presence has me cautious. Ignoring her comment, I grab a bucket and a water jug, and then head back to the stream. When I return, she jumps up from the log she was sitting on. Her eyes wide with fear.

"What's wrong?" I set the water-filled containers near the fire.

"I-I thought you were a bear."

"Ah, I see the reality of nature is settling in with you. Lions and tigers and bears." I repeat her line from the other night.

"He was beautiful," she whispers, but fear still laces her voice. He could have been dangerous. She has her arms wrapped around her, and her hands rub up and down her flannel-covered arms.

"Here. Sit." I direct her to the fire pit. She folds down onto the log for a seat and stares at the dying flames. I kneel to stoke the fire and pull the water-filled bucket closer to the heat source. With my hands on her waist, I shift her body on the upturned log.

"What are you doing?" she snaps. Does she no longer want me to touch her in even the simplest manner? My chest pinches at the thought.

You're so standoffish. I don't think this is true. I'm just quiet. I'm not a talker, but her silence has me questioning my lack of chatter, or at least opening up about a few things.

"I'm washing your hair," I state. She twists and looks up at me over her shoulder.

"What?"

"I know how much it can be a bother." I swallow before I continue. My heart races as I speak. "When my wife was sick, she liked it when I washed her hair. When it all fell out, I cleaned her scalp. We pretended her hair was still there."

Her eyes instantly fill with tears, but I don't want her sympathy. She licks her lips and turns her back to me.

"She was a lucky woman to have such care and attention." I hold my breath, questioning the honesty of her words, but she twists back to face me with a weak smile, letting me know she means every word.

"It's going to be cold at first." Positioning one knee near her, I tip her back over my propped thigh. Then I release her hair from the band, allowing the thick tresses to tumble toward the ground. It's long, so I'll need to watch that it doesn't dip into the dirt. I pour a portion of the water jug over her hair, and she closes her eyes.

"Cold?" I question.

"It's okay," she mutters. *She's* more than okay. Other than when we started, she hasn't complained once about our arrangement. Outside bathroom. Eating from a pan. Even sleeping in a tent. I've had fun with her. Ax throwing, laughing, even a foiled attempt at flipping a burger over an open flame. Letty is a metaphor for life, and I want to live her. Yet disappointment seems inevitable.

"Clara…" I pause, and Letty's eyes snap open. "That was my wife's name. We were high school sweethearts. I was this big oaf football player, and she was a quiet book girl. I always wanted to go into the military, and she only wanted to be a mother. We weren't talkers. Weren't eloquent. We fumbled a lot." I chuckle, recalling our first kiss, our first time in bed, and all the near misses. We grew practiced but not passionate. "It wasn't fair to lose her so young."

Letty nods and water drips onto her forehead. I swipe at it, taking my time to caress the side of her face as I stare down at her. Breaking the connection of our eyes, I reach for the shampoo next to me and squirt some on her hair. Apricots. It suits her. I massage the growing suds around her temple and lift her head for the underside. She hums like she did when we had sex, and I smile to myself. This is a noise I'm not certain I can live without hearing.

"She was thirty-nine when she passed."

"How old are you?"

"I'll be fifty next spring."

Her eyes pop open. "You don't look fifty."

The corner of my mouth tugs upward. "I've got gray hair."

Her eyes narrow, and she checks out my beard. "A few, but you also don't seem that old."

"Thank you." I snort. "And how old are you?"

"I just turned forty."

I gaze down at her. She can't be. "You look so young."

A smile brightens her face although her eyes have closed. "You're a charmer, Mr. Harrington."

Her teasing tone further curls my lip.

"No one ever says that about me." *You're so standoffish*, returns to my thoughts. *How many people have you tried to charm?* I ask myself.

Her eyes open again as I massage her scalp. "Charmer?" she questions.

"Yes."

"Huh," she huffs. "I find you very charming." Her lids lower lazily, but her lips twist like she doesn't approve of this finding.

"And how is that?"

"You're thoughtful and kind. And you obviously took care of your wife. You're a lucky man to have loved someone so deeply. And washing hair is a romantic gesture." My fingers pause on her sudsy locks. She isn't wrong. I loved my wife. Clara loved me. We worked, but it's been ten years. My mother's voice trickles through my head.

It could happen again.

I peer down at Letty. Her blue eyes are cut off from me, but her pink lips pout. She has the perfect slope to her nose and apple-defined cheeks. I want to lower and kiss her, and then I remember again I haven't kissed her. I've touched her and fucked her, but we haven't kissed.

I'm such an idiot.

"Going to rinse now," I warn. "Tell me if it's too warm." I lean forward and drag the bucket of water from the fire. Hoping I didn't let it sit too long, I dip a finger in the liquid to test the temperature. Not hot. Not frigid. I grip the edge of the bucket and pour the water over her suds-filled hair.

"That feels nice," she purrs like she did last night. My dick knocks at my zipper, unfurled to almost full mast. I continue to rinse her hair, doing the best I can to remove all the soap residue. This wasn't a spa-like treatment, but I'm hoping it might help make her more comfortable.

I get one more night, then we talk. There won't be much to say after another night, though I'll admit I'm happy to have another chance with her. *Will one more night be enough?* my heart murmurs, but I dismiss my answer.

When I think I have her hair clear of shampoo, I press at her shoulder blade, helping her sit upright again.

"Better?"

"Much. Thank you. That was sweet of you." She begins to comb her fingers through her hair, separating the wet clumps and spreading the long length.

"Have a comb?"

L.B. Dunbar

Her brows pinch in question, but she answers, "In my bag."

"Be right back." I can't handle rummaging through her underthings again, especially now that I know what they look like on her body. When I was searching for her tablet earlier, I brushed against her collection of thongs and was instantly hard—again. The thin lacy material is so unlike anything Clara wore. Skimpy. Sexy. Spontaneous. Seeing Letty in this barely-there fabric does something to me and not just my dick. It hints at adventure in the bedroom. I curse myself for comparing Clara and Letty. They are obviously unique women, yet the opposition between them is what draws me to Letty. I want the adventure. I want different.

I return to Letty's side and tug another stump up behind her, seating myself on it. My thighs straddle beside hers, and I'm careful not to touch her with my legs although I want nothing more than to pull her back to my chest. Instead, I place the comb in her hair and gently stroke downward, righting the tangles as I go.

"My God, you're hired. Come to Chicago and you can do my hair before the wedding."

I chuckle. "Right, the wedding. Where's it at?" I don't mean to bring up a sore subject, and I'm not good at small talk, but I am curious. I'll do anything to start her chattering at me again.

"The Drake, of course. Overlooking Lake Michigan." I flip open a mental notepad and pencil down the information.

"Sounds fancy."

"Only the best for my sister," she mocks.

"You'll be the most beautiful woman there, I'm sure."

She turns to glance at me over her shoulder. "See, charming." Then her brows pinch, and she looks toward the dying embers in the fire pit. "I don't want to be more beautiful than Dayna, though. I want to go unnoticed on that day and forget the reminders it could have been me. I want it over. Time to move on."

Time to move on. The words ring through my head like a gong. For years, I've pondered what moving on means. I restored my home. I dived into work. I supported my brother with his pub. But none of it has been enough.

80

I finish combing through her hair and scoot closer to her, finally giving in to the tremor in my thighs that want to rest against hers. I risk an arm around her middle and press my forehead to the damp nape of her neck.

"I'm sorry if there was a misunderstanding about last night."

Her breath hitches.

"If I was too rough. If I said something or didn't say something I should have. I apologize." *I'm not good at this*, I want to tell her. *I don't know what I'm doing, feeling, wanting*, I want to say.

"You weren't rough," she replies, her voice dropping. "I liked it."

She's quiet again, and I lift my face to press a kiss to her wet hair, lingering there as I speak. "I don't know how to be with…people." *With you*. How do I be with you?

"With women?" she suggests, curiosity lacing her question.

"With anyone, I guess."

"Tell me," she whispers, and my one-arm hold on her tightens, leaning my chest against her back.

"I was in the military forever. When I came home on a medical discharge, I didn't know where I belonged. Clara had a routine, and I didn't know where I fit. My dad offered me the brewery, but I didn't know anything about running a business. It was like a crash course in economics and marketing. It's my family. It's my name. But it hasn't been enough." *I'm lonely*, I want to tell her. *I've been lonely for a long, long time*, I think, but I don't admit this to her. I just hold her tighter, allowing my face to rest in her wet locks. With a whisper, I say, "My life is so quiet."

"And I talk too much." She chuckles.

"I don't think anything you do would be too much," I mutter. *You're perfect*. When she doesn't respond, I joke, "Your chirping is growing on me." *And so is your hum*. Then she chuckles. *Your laughter, too*, I add to my growing list of noises. Her body, her nearness, her scent. All of her. I don't want to let her go.

12

Night sounds

[Letty]

We spend the afternoon on a short hike, and thankfully, Giant goes at my pace because my blisters have blisters. He surprises me by sharing more details about himself and his family.

His brother Charlie is the mayor brother.

Billy is the pub-owning brother.

James is the motorcycle brother.

"He's the black sheep of the family. He used to be in search and rescue. He claims he has reasons for staying away from us, and I know those reasons, but they aren't good enough to me." Giant scoffs. "Now he's mixed up in all kinds of things, and I don't like knowing he's up here."

Giant reaches for my hand and draws it to his lips to place a brief kiss on my knuckles. To my surprise, he doesn't release my hand, but holds my fingers as we continue to climb through the labyrinth of trees.

"Mati is my sister. Her husband died a year ago August, and she's recently reunited with her best guy friend from high school. It's about time he professes his love for her." Giant chuckles. "Our mother was obsessed with Roald Dahl, and we are each named after a character from one of his books. I come from the BFG. *Big Friendly Giant.*"

I chuckle. It suits him. "That's sweet."

"It's embarrassing," he admits, and I'm about to disagree when he stops us on a large boulder, like a natural ridge. My breath hitches at the view. The valley is breathtaking as the greenery shifts to reds, golds, and oranges. Fall is in full bloom. It almost doesn't look real, it's so picture-perfect.

"Wow," I mumble, scanning the sponge brush-painted landscape. My phone camera would not do justice to this natural image.

"Yeah, wow," Giant says, and I turn to find him observing me. A grin grows on my face. Just his eyes on me have me giddy and all seems to be forgiven from this morning.

His brow pinches. "I haven't kissed you."

I lick my lips and bite the corner. "I've noticed." I pause a second, reaching up for his jaw. "I've never been kissed by a bearded man," I add, scraping my fingertips against the thickly covered edge of his face.

"Think I should fix that?" he teases.

"I think you should." Giant lowers for me, cupping my cheeks in his large hands before taking my lips with a tender kiss. Even though it starts too slow and sweet, like all things between us, it heats within seconds, and our tongues collide. Giant draws me to him, and I melt against his large body, feeling the evidence that his desire matches mine. I want this man again, but I'm content to have him kiss me like he is, like I'm the air he needs to breathe and the color in his wind.

That night, Giant asks if I mind connecting the sleeping bags to make a double one. He slips in next to me in only his boxer briefs and a T-shirt. I start with my pajama pants and a sweatshirt, but he runs hot, so within minutes, I'm overheating, and I sit up to remove my pants. Giant tucks me into him when I'm only half-dressed.

"I'm not good at this stuff," he tells me, and I turn my head to look up at him. My hand rests on his chest while my ear listens to the beat of his strong heart.

"What stuff?" I question. When we returned to camp, he made dinner, stopping to occasionally kiss me before returning to the task at hand. He's pretty good at a few things.

"Holding someone."

My brows pinch. What about his wife? He spoke of her with such adoration and sorrow earlier, my heart broke for him. I turn to kiss his covered pec.

"You're doing just fine," I tell him, wondering how many women he's been with since her. Has he treated them all with the same distance as he's treated me? Did he eventually pull them close with unending kisses? I snuggle into him with the thought.

Clara was a lucky woman.

The idea of her doesn't make me jealous, but the devotion of Giant's love does. I've never felt such dedication, such passion. If love exists, and I believe it does, it must be for other people, not me. However, my sister's wedding comes to mind, and I reconsider when I think of the farce it's going to be.

"Where are your thoughts?" Giant asks, and I shift to glance back at him.

"All over, I guess."

"When you're quiet, I get nervous."

"I thought you didn't like my chirping."

"As I said earlier, it's growing on me." He chuckles, and the rumble against my ear warms my insides. He's on his back, and I'm pressed into his side, so I slip a leg over his. I'm not expecting any more sexual encounters with him. Thinking of his wife makes me raw and sad, despite all our kisses through the remainder of the day. I don't want to compare myself to her, and I don't want to feel like I'm filling a hole for him, but I do want to be close to him. It's nice to be held. Hug therapy—it's a real thing where a person holds someone for an hour. I might enjoy the experience. Then I chuckle. I couldn't hug a stranger, yet that's exactly what I'm doing. However, Giant Harrington feels anything *but* a stranger to me. Something about him sings to my soul. Maybe it's the intensity of the sex last night. Maybe it's the loneliness I heard in his voice when he spoke of his wife.

He strokes up my spine and brushes back my hair from my shoulder. My leg hitches higher on his thigh.

"Dammit, woman," he hisses, and I pull back my head.

"What? What did I do?"

"Just being you. I'm rock solid again." He scrubs a hand down his face and lifts to kiss my forehead. My knee inches upward, nudging the sac contained in his boxer briefs. The firm length of him can't be mistaken. He's huge, hard, and straining.

"Should we do something about this?" I gently nudge upward again with my knee, and he groans.

"I promised myself I'd be good tonight. No more taking advantage of you."

I perch up on my elbow and peer down at him. Cupping his bearded jaw, I turn his face so he looks at me. "Is that what you think? You think you took advantage of me?"

"I didn't exactly ask permission the other night, and then last night…" His voice drifts.

"You did ask, with your hesitation, and then your consideration of me last night. I already told you I enjoyed being with you like that." My voice lowers as I speak the next words. "Please, don't take this experience away from me, okay?"

"What experience?" he questions, his voice rough.

"All of it. The camping, hiking, ax throwing, and the sex."

"Dammit," he grumbles, clamping his hand under my thigh, and then flipping me onto my back. One of his broad legs slips between mine as he holds himself up on an elbow. His thickness digs into my pelvic bone, and then he shifts his body, slipping the other leg between my thighs and positioning himself at my core. He brushes my hair back, peering down at me.

"You're the prettiest thing I've ever seen." His voice deepens as it lowers, and my face heats like a schoolgirl. I can't remember the last time someone called me *pretty*. His mouth meets mine. Hesitant. Sweet. Prickly from his beard. Then his tongue comes forward, and I open. The fire ignites as the kiss flames. The pressure down below builds as his heavy shaft rests against my achy center. His tongue swirls with mine, and my hips shift, finding friction against him, but it's not enough. He kisses and kisses, and my leg hitches over his hip, opening myself to him. He curls a hand under my thigh and lifts it higher, pressing harder at my covered core.

"Never been kissed by a bearded man," he reminds me, groaning against my mouth as he rubs his firm length over my damp thong. "Can this bearded man give you a few other new experiences?" He rubs his hairy chin over my cheek and down my neck, then sucks at my skin to soothe the bristle brush sting. He lowers into the sleeping bag, skimming both my breasts over my sweatshirt until his face is level with my midsection. Then he presses the soft material upward.

"Take this off," he commands. "And open this bag a bit." I lift to remove my sweatshirt and then unzip halfway down each side of the heavy bag. He flips the thick material backward and scrapes his scratchy face up my stomach before rubbing over one breast with his chin. It tickles and teases and then his mouth opens for a swollen globe. His large mouth covers an equally large breast, and I've never felt so consumed. His tongue twirls over the nipple before he pulls back to suck the tip, already peaked and tight. His tongue traces around the stiff nub, flicking over the firm swell before returning to suck the fullness. He releases my breast with a pop before moving to the other one, dragging the prickly hair of his chin over my skin to mark me once again.

Releasing me, he moves down my body. His scruffy jaw scribbles on my skin, writing words I'll want to remember. *He wants me. He's going to devour me. He's going to ruin me.* My sex clenches with anticipation, and my knees open wider, allowing his broad shoulders to slip between my thighs. The stubbled jaw tickles as he rubs his chin over my sensitive skin before his tongue follows. Hesitant like his first kiss, he takes his time, torturing me with a lazy lick and a teasing twirl. Then his tongue flattens, and he laps up my seam. My hips buck, and my head lifts.

"Giant," I hum, slipping my fingers into his hair. He continues to flirt with me until finally his tongue settles in and splits me open. His enthusiasm begins—licking, lapping, lusting. My eyes roll back as I tug at his short locks, singing praises to a higher being until I can't take it any longer. My orgasm rushes me like the thunderstorm from last evening, rolling out of nowhere to roar between my thighs. I cry out as my head lifts again, and I hear him eagerly savoring me. I'm so turned on another ripple immediately follows the first.

"Giant. Oh God, Giant, another one is coming." I exhale. *This never happens.* "I'm coming again." Shocked and overwhelmed at the sensation, I lose control of my body as a second quake strikes as intensely as the first. Stars dance before my eyes in the dimly lit tent, and I fall back to the pillow. My legs shake, and my center drips. I'm spent, and eventually, Giant releases me to suck at my inner thigh. His scruffy beard will leave more marks, and I want them all over me.

Returning north, he presses kisses into my flushed skin as he moves up my body. When he reaches my mouth, he asks, "May I kiss you?" My brows pinch at the question.

"Please," I beg, willing to taste myself on his lips. With equal excitement, his mouth captures mine, and we kiss for several minutes before I pull away.

"My turn," I say, pressing at his shoulders to encourage him to roll to his back.

"Cricket," he warns. "You don't need to do this." Again, I'm uncertain of his cautious tone, but I reassure him.

"I want this." I tug his T-shirt, and he sits up to remove it. Working my way down his broad middle with kisses of my own, I want to do this. I twirl my fingers through the hair on his chest and stroke over his deep treasure trail. This is one of the sexiest parts of a man, and on Giant, it's a trove of lush dark hair leading to gold. I curl my fingers into the waistband of his boxer briefs and pull them down his hips. He lifts, and once I have them to his knees, he wiggles his legs to kick them off.

He's big. Huge. Ginormous. It's ridiculous to think he won't fit as he's already been in me, but my mouth is different. Still, I want to taste him. I want to please him. I want to give to him what he's given me.

"If it's too much—"

I cut him off with a lick of the smooth head, wiping the worried tone from him. Circling round the mushroom edge with my tongue, I hum before I draw him in. Knowing I can't possibly take him all in, I cup his balls and gently squeeze while I suck most of him. His hands cover my hair, stroking back the falling tresses. He bucks once and then apologizes, but I don't want him to be reserved.

I suck harder, pulling him back as far as I can.

"That feels so fucking incredible," he groans as his hips set a slow rhythm, tapping his tip at the back of my throat. My cheeks hollow and increase their suction. Within seconds, he sits up and yanks me off him.

I'm on my back before I can shriek, "I wasn't finished." My mouth drips with the flavor of him. He should bottle this blend at his brewery. I'd drink a full keg.

"This is how I want to finish." He holds himself at my entrance, the wet tip easily slipping through my eager folds. "I'm sorry about no condoms. I had a vasectomy, though, and I haven't been with anyone in so long."

I press up to kiss him, hating this awkward conversation.

"I haven't been with anyone in over a year. And before that, it was with the same man for too long."

Giant groans as he enters me with more care than last night. He's slow and deliberate, and I hum as he fills me. He reaches somewhere I've never been touched before, way down deep inside, and I'm fuller than I've ever felt. The sense of oneness makes me shaky and unnerves me a bit. But when he pulls back, my body chases his, and he chuckles over me.

"I like how you follow me as if you don't want me to leave your body."

"I don't." I exhale, and he rushes forward, forcing me to catch my breath. My eyes roll back as the oneness sensation ripples through my body again.

"You seem greedy," he teases while his tone makes it sound dirty. *Toes in the dirt*, he mentioned, and I want to be all kinds of dirty with this man.

"So greedy." My voice hitches as I clutch at his tight backside, squeezing each firm globe to keep him inside me.

"Jesus, Cricket." He rocks back and then thrusts forward. Repeat. Repeat. Repeat. *Chirp, chirp, chirp* is the friction song our bodies sing as we rub against each other. His large hand grips the back of my thigh while the other covers one backside cheek. He tugs me upward, lifting me a little to shift the angle of his thrusts. I can't describe what's happening to my body. The rhythm. The connection. The emotion.

"Giant," I warn. "It's happening…"

"Another one?" He sounds surprised himself. "Fuck yeah, Letty. Finish."

He rests on one elbow with his hand under my backside. The hand on my thigh lowers between us, and his thumb flicks the swollen, sensitive hood, triggering me to tip over once again. I come alive around him, humming his name, adding it to the night sounds around us.

"Cricket," he groans. "God, you're squeezing me so hard. I can't last." He pulls out, and we both watch as he pulses streams of pleasure on my lower belly. Once finished, he collapses over me too briefly before shifting to pull away, but I wrap my legs around his hips and reach for his biceps, unwilling to release him so soon.

"Not yet," I beg, not wanting the sensation to end. He's larger than me, and heavy, but I want his weight to blanket me. Fearing he'll shut me out again, I won't let him escape. *Not yet.*

13

Twinkle toes and gun-shy

[Giant]

I've been more turned on in the last seventy-two hours than I've been in years, and the morning is no different. I wake with a solid wood, and when Letty nudges her backside against me, I can't resist her.

"Can we do it like this?" I question. The angle will be different once again. Our position last night, the way we moved, the deepness of my thrusts, we were anything but regimented in our rhythm. Letty and I sync. Deep down, I don't want the missionary position, but I want her any way she'll let me.

Letty wiggles her ass against me, and I slip my hand up her hip. She didn't return to her skimpy undies last night, and the discovery makes my dick twitch. I quickly remove my boxer briefs and press my length against her backside.

"You're warm," she teases, rubbing against the length. I'm going to be a whole lot hotter once I enter her. I'm a big man, but she took me deep last night, and I felt something I'd never felt before. Greedy, I called her, but it's total lust on my end. I want her like I've never wanted anyone, and that includes Clara.

I position myself between her thighs as we lie on our sides. "Hitch your leg over my hip." Letty spreads, doing as I ask, and I like how responsive she is to me. She hasn't stopped anything I've asked of her yet.

Don't take this experience from me. My heart leaped when she said this.

My finger dips into her, discovering she's already wet, so I prep her with a few gentle pumps and then I brace myself at her entrance. I'm out of control with this woman, and I slip inside with one long thrust. She yelps a little and jackknifes forward, bending at the waist and drawing me deep from this angle.

"Okay, Cricket?" I worry I've hurt her. Clara was sensitive.

"So full," she murmurs and slips her leg off my hip. The collapse of her thighs tightens her hold on me, and I slip in and out, pistoning like a revved-up engine. I wrap her hair around my fist and tug. Her back arches, and she hums that sound I'm coming to love. My pace increases. The tension builds. I'm not going to last.

"Letty, sweetheart. Get there. It's too much." She slips her hand between her thighs, and her fingers brush my dick slipping in and out of her. My eyes roll back, and I release her hair, gripping her hip instead. *My God, she's glorious.* I want to hold out for her, but I don't know if I can.

When she hisses my name, I know she's close. I'm sweating, straining to keep the orgasm back. When she growls and arches her back again, the tension releases. A shower of my seed pumps into her, coating her insides while she clenches around me. I should have pulled out like I did last night, but I couldn't help myself this morning. I want to fill her. I want to howl at the moon even though it's daylight. My fingers curl over her hip as I still, allowing the release a final spill. When I settle, I tug her back to my chest and press my lips to her shoulder.

"Good morning," I mutter. When she chuckles, the movement of her body jiggles me inside her.

"It is a good morning." She rubs her hand up and down my forearm over her stomach. I want to hold her like this for the rest of my life. Feel her warmth around me and her chuckle vibrating up my spine. I like this woman. But too soon, I'll have to take her back.

Not yet, she said, but soon enough.

My thoughts drift to Clara. I don't want to compare the women, but Clara hated giving head, and truth be told, she struggled at it. When Letty took me deep last night, I thought I'd blow right then. Not to mention, after I licked Letty, she let me kiss her. Clara would refuse, not wishing to taste herself on my lips. *Don't take this experience from me*, she said, and I agree with the sentiment. I don't want to forget one minute. Everything we've done is nothing I've ever done before even though I was a married man.

We rest for a few minutes before I slip out of her. I need to clean up and get her something as well. Camping hasn't been the most convenient

L.B. Dunbar

time for my newfound sexual adventure, but then again, I didn't plan to sleep with the enemy. For a moment, I remember the land and then dismiss the thought. I want to enjoy Letty as much as I can before we talk business again.

"Let me get you something." I slip from the sleeping bag and rummage for a spent tee. She takes it from me and wipes herself. "Hey, I noticed your feet yesterday."

She twists to look at me over her shoulder and then looks down at her covered toes.

"Why didn't you tell me about the blisters?" I ask.

Her head falls back, and she stares off to the side of the tent. "Because I didn't want you to say I told you so." She huffs. She's tough, and I like that about her. I like her. Too much.

"Let me bandage them."

She shifts to her back and chuckles. "You do *not* want to touch my feet."

To prove her wrong, I slip my hands inside the sleeping bag, reaching for her toes. She kicks out at me, but I catch her ankle. Her other foot attempts an attack, but I clutch it as well.

"This could be a very compromising position." I could spread her again and mount her like last night, which reminds me I haven't left the tent to clean myself from round one. She giggles and throws her head back, attempting to wiggle her ankles free.

"Oh my gosh. Do not look at my feet."

I look. She has perfectly painted toenails and nasty looking blisters. "You anti-feet or something?"

"Yes," she huffs, settling her squirming legs.

I chuckle. "So if I were to lift these to my mouth, and say, suck your toes, that would gross you out?"

Her eyes close, and her legs wiggle against my hold. "Yes. Yuck."

"What if I licked the underside?" I laugh a little more, lifting her foot and pointing my tongue at the intended spot.

She makes a puking noise.

"But I want to taste every part of you." She stops squirming and gagging, and her lids pop open. She stares up at me. The petulant child act appears to settle her.

"I'd like that." Her sultry tone makes something rush up my chest. I want her again, but I'm almost fifty and can't quite get there that quick. My thumbs rub at her ankles.

"Maybe once these are healed." The implication is there. Healing takes time, and this hints at seeing her in the future. Her legs relax. "I'll get the bandages but let me clean up first."

I step outside, naked as a jaybird, and use the water in the bucket near the smothered campfire to rinse myself off. The cold shock douses thoughts of seeing her again. Taking a deep breath, I suppress the scream rising in my chest. *It isn't fair.* She wants my land. That's why she's here.

I turn back for the tent and find her sitting up. She wears one of my T-shirts and she's holding the collar up to her nose.

"I'm sorry. I just…" Her voice drifts, and I hold up a hand.

"It's okay. I like seeing you in it." *When I shouldn't.* When I shouldn't think of her wearing my clothes, or coming to my home, or fucking her again. Seeing her in my shirt settles my restless thoughts a bit, and I kneel for my briefs. After tugging them on, I work on bandaging her toes and heels.

"I was hoping to go canoeing with you, but it's a hike. I don't know if those can handle it." I'm referencing her blisters.

"I'm sure I'll be okay. I made it through yesterday, and I'd love to go canoeing." My eyes drift up to hers to find her watching me. "I can't remember the last time I went."

"It's a three-mile hike up to the drop."

She sits up straighter. "I can do it." Her determination shouldn't startle me, but her tone does. She sounds very business-like, and I decide she must use that enthusiasm in her job. The one where she steals land from people. Does she volunteer to tear people from their homes? Does she suggest she go in for the kill to take property out from under people? I curse myself for the sudden shift in thoughts. I just had sex with her. I like her, but what does she think of me? Am I only a business venture? A prospect? Does she do this often?

It's been a year since I've been with anyone. She sounded sincere, and I hate my doubts. I should ask her what we're doing here—what's between us—but I don't because it isn't my style. Confrontation. Communication. Discussion. Not my thing.

You didn't do half the things you've done with Letty with your own wife, my head hammers. Try it. *Try talking to her,* whispers through my thick skull, but the problem with a thick skull is, it's too thick sometimes.

"How about a protein bar breakfast with coffee so we can hit the trail?" I offer instead, ignoring all my doubts, questions, and fears in need of a distraction for the day. It's exactly what the land is worth to me. Distraction from reality, and the reality is, Letty's made it to her three-night minimum, but I wonder if she'll reconsider. I wonder if I can convince her to go home empty-handed but still holding me.

+ + +

We trek the miles upstream to where I keep my canoe. I explain how I come up here often and return the canoe to this launching area in order to ride it back to camp. I vary my destinations, but it worked out to have the canoe in place this weekend.

"When I was a kid, my granddad brought us up here. I told you about his brewing days, but after things were legalized and we established a brewery near town, he kept the land." My chest pinches at the memory of Pap bringing me up the mountain and us traveling back down by the stream. "He built the cabin at the base, but I restored it after he died."

To everyone's surprise, I inherited the land. It should have naturally passed to my dad, but Pap left it directly to me. The will stated he knew I loved the property as much as he did, and one day, I'd need it to remind me who I was and where I belonged. I'd gone off to fight for my country just as he had. And I'd returned a little lost, like him as well. He told me the mountain and the woods would ground me, and it has. I never want to see brown desert sand again.

"Were you close?" Letty asks me as we flip the canoe and push it into the water.

"Very." It's all I can say as my throat clogs. I miss the old man every day. He died while I was still overseas, and I couldn't get home for his funeral.

"He sounds special. I've never been close to someone like that, except maybe my younger brother." It's all she offers, not expanding on him or their relationship.

I help her into the bow and then push off the stern, jumping in at the last minute. Letty squeaks when the canoe jostles.

"I won't tip us. I promise. This water is freezing."

We travel in silence for a bit. The only sound is the lapping of water as I paddle from one side to the other of the vessel. Letty offers to help, but she hinders us at first even though I'm in no rush.

"It's so peaceful," she says, stealing my thoughts with her hushed voice as if she'll disturb the silence. Nature whispers around us with the rustle of trees and the low ripple of the river. We quietly continue until she says, "Tell me a story about your granddad."

I'm surprised by the request but immediately know what story to tell her. I begin with the first time he took me fishing. A river runs behind the properties on the Lane. Technically, the dock was on our neighbor's land—the Chances. I chuckle with the memories of my first catch, which seemed huge but wasn't. Then I tell her about coming up here and learning to hunt.

"I'm not a fan of guns," she reminds me.

"Right. The freezer fairy."

She chuckles. "Tell me more."

I'm surprised at myself as I chatter on the remainder of our trip. I haven't spoken of these memories in a long time, and it feels good to tell someone about Pap, even if a part of me is sad at his passing.

"Those are great stories." She pauses. "I always wanted to be a writer. Tell stories."

I stare at her. She shifted to her side as she listened to me, but she angles her face forward, reminding me of a sea nymph on the front of a boat.

L.B. Dunbar

"Why didn't you become a writer?"

She shrugs, looking off at the distance before us.

"I guess I changed my mind," she says, but her tone tells me that isn't the truth.

"You can always change it again." I nudge the issue because I don't believe her, and for the first time, I wonder if real estate possession is really her passion. *Could she change her mind about wanting my land?*

"Maybe one day," she states, dismissing the suggestion. We near the curve for our camp, and Letty leans backward to glide her hand in the cool water.

"Careful," I warn, but her body tips precariously, and her arm flaps to balance her equilibrium. "Letty," I snap again in warning. Her toe hooks into the edge of the canoe, but it isn't enough. When I reach for her, I rock the vessel, and she dips farther, arching her back. Not even a second passes before her toe slips from the small lip, and Letty's awkward position pulls her backward. I stand, which one should never do in a canoe, and Letty falls overboard.

The water is shallow here, but I worry she hit her head on the bottom. She pops up rather quickly, though, swiping at her face before she lets out a scream.

"It's fucking freezing."

A deep, uncontrolled belly laugh bursts from me. She's a wet T-shirt dream with her soaked hair plastered over her cheeks and her drenched flannel hugging her body. Her already-hip-hugging jeans are saturated as she stands in the water and grips the side of the canoe, trying to wobble it and force me to join her. For a big man, I have the balance of a cat, so I move with her efforts. Her irritation grows, and that only adds to her fierceness. She's adorable.

I use the paddle pitched to the bottom of the stream to hold the vessel in place. "It'd be faster for you to walk to shore." I nod to the land only a few feet away, struggling to suppress my chuckles as she turns to note the proximity. Letty pushes off the canoe and struggles in her sodden clothing to close the distance to the soft dirt of the shoreline. She stomps up the embankment as I steer the craft and eventually beach it. I tiptoe up the cavernous metal and jump out just as we hear rapid fire.

Three sharp shots.

And Letty's on the ground.

"Cricket!" I cross the dirt in two long strides and dive for her. She lies on her belly with her hands over the back of her head. I gently roll her to her side, quickly skimming her body with my hands and eyes. Her chest rises and falls, and she's gone pure white. "Are you hurt?"

"Did you hear that?" Her voice is a whisper, her lips blue and trembling.

"I did," I say, looking up and off toward the trees. Those weren't hunting shots. That was gunfire but not a rifle. *Dammit, James.* I glance back down at her. "Are you okay?"

I'm still not convinced she wasn't shot with the way she dropped. Her front is caked in mud, the dirt sticking from the wetness of her clothing. She slowly sits up with my help, and I brush back her hair, finding grit and fine pebbles mixed with it.

"What happened?" I stare at her. The noise. It triggered something.

Her lips tremble as ghosted eyes stare up at me. "My brother. He was shot in the streets. A drive-by shooting. I saw it happen." There are no tears or sadness, only hardness and fear. "He was only twelve." I pull her to me and hold her listless body against my chest. My hand covers the back of her head. I know all about her pain. The loss. I'd seen too many, too young lose their lives in battle.

"We're getting out of here," I tell her, pressing her back by her shoulders. "It isn't safe." Then I tug her back to me once again, cradling her against my chest. Briskly, I lift her like a bride and stalk to our site.

What are you up to, James?

14

Shot through the heart

[Letty]

Owen.

All I can see in my mind's eye is my brother. His smiling face with a bounce in his step and his hair flopping over his forehead. Him walking toward me. The call of his name and the twist of his head. He went down with three shots, right on the sidewalk before the middle school. At first, it didn't make sense. Not my brother. Not on my watch. But he'd been mixed up with the wrong kids for far too long, longer than we knew. My brother. Dead at twelve.

Should I sell drugs? Would it help us with money? He was so innocent, hopeful and earnest, when he asked. A middle school student with his whole life before him and he was worried about our family finances.

Giant carries me up the slope and the few yards to our campsite. Once there, I demand he set me down. We quickly gather our things. I'm shaking, but my body works without thought.

"I'll come back for all this," Giant says, but I turn on him.

"No. No, we'll get it all now and go together." I'm determined he won't leave me, and I don't want to let him out of my sight. We collapse the tent, and Giant lowers the coolers. I don't know how he got all the equipment here on his own, but we pile and fasten items to the larger cooler, building a makeshift cart. Giant carries the smaller one along with both our packs. It seems counterproductive to me to move toward the ranger station.

Until Giant admits he has a truck parked there.

I'm too out of sorts from all that's happening to register I didn't see a truck the night of the storm nor the morning after. It all becomes clear when we break through the trees near the back of the station. Giant signals for me to remain quiet as if we're on a mission of espionage. He sets all the stuff in the bed of the truck and then helps me into the driver's side of the cab, forcing me to scoot over as he enters. Once he starts the engine, he peels around the old station, the tires throwing up gravel and dirt as he circles to the front of the small structure.

"Fucking James." Giant doesn't look back, and neither do I, as I'm too stunned. It feels like we're fleeing a crime. Fugitives on the run.

We bounce down a worn path, crushed between a wall of trees. Giant wants to speed, but the rough terrain prevents it.

The time passes in silence.

"Say something," he commands, his voice full of an emotion I don't recognize. I don't even know if I can speak my full name.

"I don't know what to say."

"Anything. Just talk." *Your silence makes me nervous.* He swipes a hand over his longer beard, and I realize how damp I am. Everything processes in slow motion. My clothes are soaked. Dirt coats the front of me. My hair is a mess. Giant has a truck.

"Should we have searched for James?"

Giant swipes a palm over his hair and then slams the palm on the steering wheel. He shakes his head, lips clamped in refusal to discuss his brother.

"Ask me anything else."

"How long has your truck been up here?" It seems like a silly thing to ask. He obviously parked up here and unloaded to prepare for us. Then he came down the mountain to get me.

He quickly peers over at me and then away without an answer. *What's happening?*

"Explain to me what happened here?" I bite my lips, chewing at the tender skin as thoughts ramble through my head. Did he plan all this? Did he hope to seduce me? What am I missing?

"James fired a gun, and I got us out of there."

"Not James," I snap, my irritation growing although I'm not certain what I'm irritated about.

Processing: Giant drove up here. He set up camp. He knew I'd show. *Did he set me up?*

"Was this a game to you?" The thought surprises me, but I need to ask.

"What do you mean?"

"You brought me up here, but did you lead me on? I thought we were without amenities or transportation, and it was here all along. What were you doing?" Withholding running water and electricity feels like the least of my issues, though. He sighs and swipes at his hair again, but he isn't offering an answer. In fact, he sheepishly avoids looking back at me, and his jaw clenches, reminding me of our second meeting when he proposed the camping trip.

"You tricked me into going." But did he? I'm the one who went to his cabin. I'm the one who went up this mountain without coercion. What was I thinking? The land. *I wanted the land, but was that really the only reason?* my heart whispers.

"I did no such thing," he snaps, side-eyeing me. "You came willingly."

Oh, I came all right. Six, seven times in three nights.

Three nights. That's how long I think you'll last before the land breaks you.

He was so wrong. Three nights and he broke me because my foolish heart started to believe it was more, it was something else.

His cabin comes into view in the distance. His cabin. The place he inherited from his pap. On the land he isn't going to sell. My gut realizes it although my heart doesn't want to accept it. What was all this about then? Why did we play this game?

"Three nights," I whisper. "You lied to me." The words feel thick and heavy, and I'm shocked by the underlying truth. My body feels dirty, and it's not from the grit mixed in my hair or the mud splattered on my shirt. "Why would you lie to me?"

Again, he doesn't speak. He doesn't defend himself. Instead, he slows the truck, pulling up to the cabin and shifting into park.

"Answer me," I bark, and he flinches. His eyes close, and his knuckles turn white on the steering wheel.

"I'm not giving you the land." This is no longer an acceptable answer or even my question.

"Meaning?"

"I had no intention to sell. Ever."

Ever. The word echoes through my hollow heart.

I didn't plan to marry you, Letty. Ever. Hudson's admission pales compared to Giant's. I feel my dreams crumble and filter through the wind like paper torn to shreds and tossed into the air. Giant's rejection feels like something more, something deeper. It feels so much worse than Hudson's. But why? I hardly know this man. Admittedly, our current situation proves I knew less than I thought.

"Then what was this all about?" *Three nights.* Sleeping with him, enjoying him, falling for him. I glare at Giant, cursing him in my head as the stranger he is, and aching for him as something more in my heart.

His eerie silence is my answer.

"I see." I slowly nod even though I don't see. I don't understand anything. "Foregone conclusion, wasn't I? You challenged me, and I accepted. And for what? For sex?"

What did he want from this arrangement?

"It wasn't just sex," Giant mumbles, but I dismiss the statement as any emotion is absent.

"Did you do it to make me feel...stupid? City girl and mountain man, or something like that?" But that's not what I felt. Used. Betrayed. Hurt. So very hurt. But not stupid.

I nod as if he spoke, as if he said something, *anything* to contradict me and give me hope I wasn't a joke. "Did you think if I slept with you, I'd forget the land?" Then another question dawns. "Or do you think I slept with you to get the land? To make the deal?"

He turns on me, his eyes narrow and dark. "Didn't you? You with your eager eyes and your pert smile, hoping to butter me up and take this from me. Telling me everything has a price. Well, this doesn't." He waves a hand toward the windshield and then slams it against his chest. I don't understand the motion and absentmindedly look at the cabin I'll never enter.

Cozy. Homey. Inviting.

I'll never have a home like this.

I'll never have a man like him, who loved a woman so much he washed her hair.

101

L.B. Dunbar

"You wanted what's mine, and I wasn't going to give it to you. It wasn't even a thought until…" His voice drifts, but I've heard enough.

"How could you think such a thing of me?" My lips instantly quiver. An ax thrown at my sternum would be less painful than what he's suggesting. I would never do such a thing. *Ever.* The word reverberates in my head. Sleep with the enemy. I've already done that with Hudson. Sleep with a client to score a commission. Not on my watch.

Then I hear Uncle Frank's voice. *Anything.* I continue to shake with disbelief. Not like this. I would never strike a deal like this. This wasn't a deal. Things changed. Something happened, at least for me. This was so much more, and for what? Why did I go with him? Why did I sleep with him? These questions have no answer, and it's all a reminder that Giant and I are strangers. I lean forward and rummage through my bag for my car keys.

"I see," I repeat. Licking my lips, I reach for the handle to release me from the truck. "Well, enjoy your land, Mr. Harrington." I realize when a real estate deal has failed, but once again, I've failed to recognize a hopeless relationship.

It wasn't a relationship. It was only sex.

I don't offer a conciliatory handshake as I pop open the door. I've already wasted my heart on Giant and my body, which aches for his, even now, especially now.

Say something to change my mind.

"Officially off duty, sir," I spit, reminiscent of stating I reported for camp when I accepted the challenge. The challenge of this land. The challenge of this man. I salute him with one hand while my other grabs my backpack at my feet. With strength I don't feel, I carry the suddenly too heavy pack a few feet to my car and toss it over my front seat once I've opened the door. I collapse into my rental and reverse, narrowly missing the back corner of his truck.

With liquid blurring my eyes, I peel down the two-tire lane with a sad tune in my heart.

*Country road, take me home, to the place, I belong…*Chicago.

15

Intent to purchase or not

[Giant]

Eight days. Eleven hours. Twenty-seven minutes. That's how long it's been since she drove off, and I didn't say a word to defend myself or apologize for my accusation.

The pain in her eyes undid me. The tears she fought. The courage it took her to get out of my truck.

I wanted to pull her to me the minute I said what I said.

Didn't you?

Didn't you sleep with me in order to obtain my property? Didn't you mess with my heart to get to my land? Didn't you want to stay? Didn't you feel something for me? Didn't you see I'm falling for you?

Three short *nights.*

I slam back the beer, hardly tasting the crisp October blend. My brother Charlie asked me to meet him at the pub for lunch. Being in public is the last place I want to be, but going back up the mountain isn't a possibility for me. She ruined it. My haven has been invaded by memories of a woman with blistered toes, a sweet laugh, and a delicious body.

Charlie is the mayor of Blue Ridge and the baby brother of our family. He took up politics after some of the corruption from our previous mayor came to light. He's been good for the community, working to keep the locals happy and the tourism thriving. The economy has been restored under his reign, especially with the help of one particular business.

Blue Ridge Microbrewery and Pub is my other brother's business. Billy didn't want to work in the factory, but when he dropped out of college, he didn't have a choice. Eventually, he broke free and built a place for people to enjoy our family's brew—and party—which he knows best. Celebrate has been Billy's motto since his divorce from his high school sweetheart, or potentially the cause of it. He's been in business for about fifteen years and along with him, Giant Brewing Company has grown under me.

I thought I'd be military forever, but with the gunshot wound and a medical discharge, here I am.

Alone again.

It sounds like a song Mati's new beau might have sung back when he was a rock star. Matilda's our little sister, the real baby of the family, and the princess as the token daughter after four sons.

"Want another?" she asks me as she works the lunch shift before coaching volleyball in the evenings for the local high school. Her lion-red hair doesn't match any of us boys, as we're all shades of gray at this point. I'm still the lightest although I'm the oldest.

"Keep 'em coming."

Mati pats my shoulder and walks away. Charlie approaches, weaving here and there to greet people as he makes his way to the round table in the back corner. He's like a local hero. James is the real hero in our family, but he disowned us. For the past week, I've tried to figure out what he was doing up at the ranger station and if he was the one shooting his gun. His bike was gone when Letty and I arrived for my truck, but that doesn't mean anything. He's mixed up in some bad stuff, hanging with the Rebel's Edge MC outside of town, and I'm hoping to ask Charlie if he knows anything while we have lunch.

"Good to see ya," he says, slipping in next to me. The table seats four, but he pulls up a chair next to mine.

"Hey," I grumpily reply.

He waves at Mati, who holds up her finger, and Charlie nods. She'll be bringing over a beer for him as well.

"How are you doing?" Charlie asks, and I hate the suggestion in his voice, questioning me on a deeper level. Everyone worries about me. My mental state after returning home. My mental being after losing Clara. My mentality taking on the family business. Now, I have my mother worrying about my sex life. She tried to set me up with Alyce Wright again.

"I suck," I say, surprising myself as I don't give my standard answer of *I'm fine*. I'm not fine. I miss Letty something fierce, and I don't know what to do about it.

How could you think such a thing of me?

"Really?" Charlie's voice hitches. "Does it have anything to do with a request to purchase Pap's land?"

"What?" My head snaps in Charlie's direction, and my eyes narrow. How does he know about this?

"A request to purchase *uninhabitable*"—Charlie air quotes around the word—"land came through the zoning office. Of course, Betty knows the property belonged to Pap, so she brought it to my attention." Betty Jean Murphy was an old family friend of our parents.

Charlie pulls a copy of a legal document out of a leather portfolio he carried into the pub with him. My eyes leap to Mullen Realty Company of Chicago and the name Frank Mullen.

"Goddammit," I hiss under my breath.

"Do you happen to know an Olivet Pierson from this real estate agency?"

"What?" I snap, glaring at my youngest brother.

Charlie examines my face for a minute and then nods. "Huh. That's what I thought."

"What do you mean?"

He rubs a hand over the leather binder. "Last Thursday, I got the strangest phone call." He pauses a second. "A woman with a Yankee accent is on the line, and she starts telling me this story. How she might lose her job, but she wanted to tell me how her company wanted to acquire Pap's land. As I'm listening to her, I look up the company, and they're no small business in Chicago. They buy and sell real estate for all kinds of companies, and they represent a hotel conglomerate who uses their service to secure property for resorts and such." Charlie pauses. "You following me so far?" His brow hitches, teasing me.

"Get on with it," I bark, my eyes aimed at the document, but the words blur.

L.B. Dunbar

"So, this chattering woman tells me how she found some loophole. How the property cannot ever be procured for commercial use. Not only as it's private property, but *because* it's private property."

I could have told her that, I think. *But you didn't,* my heart reminds me. You let her believe she was going to get the land after a three-night camping trip.

I have no intention to sell the land. Ever. The look of horror on her face, as if I'd just stabbed her, slayed me. Did she want the land that badly? Did she really think it was that easy? Fool the mountain man, lure him into lust, and take what's his? I pause at the thought. I don't actually believe that's how things happened between us. In fact, everything happened so fast I'm not certain what the intention from either of us was.

My heart skips a beat. *You knew what you were doing,* it patters. You saw a spark in her, and you wanted the spontaneity of a flame.

"Land held in a land trust means it can only be inherited, not sold. It doesn't qualify for purchase. Nor can it be divided for commercial use. In the case of Pap's, if no family was living to claim the land, it reverts back to the state."

I know all this, and I'm a little surprised Letty didn't. Did she not do her research first?

"Now, you might wonder how this woman knew all this or why she shared it."

Is Charlie a mind reader all of a sudden?

"Turns out, her company set forth this petition, trying to acquire the property to the left of Pap's, but as you might recall, it's unobtainable due to zoning and dimensions and…" Charlie pauses to wave a hand, knowing I'll drown out the legal jargon. "Anyway, they hoped to squeeze you out in the deal, but she wanted to assure me she was working on something as she disagreed with their sneaky antics."

"Cut to the chase, Charlie." My heart hammers in my chest.

"She says upon her visit to the area…Did you know she visited the area, Giant?" He pauses again for effect with an eyebrow hitched, reminding me of our mother. "She found the property *uninhabitable*. Something about no running water, no electricity." Charlie's voice slows. "Do you know anything about this?"

I don't answer my brother. Instead, I lift my glass and down the rest of my beer.

"Then she yammers on about how she learned the mayor of the town was the brother of the property owner, and she wanted to inform *me* of these loopholes." Charlie chuckles like it's the most ridiculous thing he's heard. He's a lawyer. He's my sibling. He knows all this information. "Seems her research skills failed her if she didn't know this information before making a trip down here. Then again, maybe she's their bulldozer. Send her in to handle the locals and hope they don't know anything about their land rights." Charlie snorts, but I'm failing to find the humor in anything he says.

"So?" I grunt. They never would have gotten my property anyway. Charlie already knows this. I know this. What game is she playing now?

"She wanted to personally let me know that the company repeals the petition. She was making certain of it. They were no longer interested in the property. And here's the weird part. She was adamant I know and equally persuasive in suggesting I inform you. Isn't that the damnedest thing?" Charlie's voice lowers, and I feel his eyes zeroing in on me, but my eyes remain on the document before me on the table.

I huff. Based on Letty's grand exit, I assume she'll never look back. The property isn't the only thing she's no longer interested in.

"Then"—Charlie chuckles—"she goes on to tell me we should consider an ax-throwing facility or perhaps a court at the pub."

"What the fuck?"

"I know, right? I mean, that sounds ridiculous. Who throws axes for fun?"

Exactly, I think, exhaling heavily as my heart is ready to burst through my chest.

"However, she mentioned how she learned to fling an ax from an ax master when she was in the area." Charlie's voice rises, thoroughly enjoying this little tale he's sharing. "Then she ends by telling me how sorry she is that her company won't be building in the area because she just loved her time here. The land was so beautiful, she said." Charlie mocks her Yankee accent. He flips a few pages of the document before me.

"The funny thing is, she sounded relieved the project wouldn't happen, despite all her chatter about how great our community seemed. We have the nicest people here, she said. She loved the stars at night. Even the rain was wonderful." Charlies snorts again. "She had the most amazing adventure in the woods, experiencing nature, and really came to appreciate it. No, *love it* were her exact words." Charlie lets out a breath. "And man, does she have words. She's a talker."

Cricket, my heart sings. Always chirping.

I turn to my brother, waiting on more...holding my breath with hope for something else. "And?"

"Here's what I don't understand. Why was she telling *me* all of this?"

I have no idea, I thought.

"Did you ask her?" I ask, my voice sharper than necessary.

"No, I thanked her for the information. Told her how I hadn't visited Chicago in a long time but remember enjoying my stay there. Then I told her I hoped she'd be able to visit here again soon, seeing as she enjoyed *it* so much."

"Did she say she would?" My voice rises as I sit up straighter. Hope is a dangerous emotion.

"Should she?" my brother inquires, lifting a brow as he suddenly plays coy.

"Charlie, don't act like you know something when you don't. There's nothing to tell."

Charlie shakes his head, disagreeing with me. "Here's what's to tell. A woman checked into Conrad Lodge and then checked out, saying she was going camping in the area. She let it slip she was headed to the Harrington cabin. For three days, your place was empty, and you didn't answer your phone. James is called in for questioning about an incident up on the ridge, and he mentions your name as an alibi. Says he saw you with a woman up there."

Jesus, will the whole town know?

"What did James do? And how do you know this other stuff?"

"Cora told Mati who told me. Gotta keep tabs on my siblings." Charlie winks. "As for James, he claims it was target practice. God only knows why he loves that ranger station." He waves a hand, dismissing our brother while knowing all the reasons that particular station means something to our brother.

"You know it's typically my job as the eldest to know what everyone is doing."

"Yes, but then who looks out for you?" Charlie laughs.

I sigh as I look away from Charlie. No one. No more Clara. No more girls. No more Letty.

"I don't need looking after," I snark.

"But it'd be nice if someone did, right? If someone worried about you. Or had sex with you. Or loved you."

"Jesus, have you been talking to Mama?"

Charlie chuckles. "Fuck, no. I just know how you feel." He probably does. Us Harringtons haven't had much luck in love, and he's had one of the worst deals as his wife divorced him right when his small-town career took off. She left behind their adorable daughter, Lucy, as well.

Charlie points to information on the final page of the document. "There's a phone number for the real estate agency in Chicago." He taps the page where a Post-it tab rests below the information. "And she gave me her cell phone number. She said I was free to pass it on to the property owner in case he had questions, wanted details, or just wanted to talk."

"Did she really say that?" *Then we can talk.* We never had the discussion we needed to have after her third night. The conversation I hoped to have where I explained that I couldn't sell the land, and I hoped she'd understand the reasons behind my decision, and then I'd ask her if we could somehow explore what we had, what we discovered between us in our adventure on the ridge.

"No." Charlie chuckles. "But maybe you should call her?" There's a hesitation in his suggestion.

"I don't have any questions," I gruff, more irritated than I should be. Am I angry with her or myself for not explaining everything? "She already admitted she's no longer interested in the purchase."

"And what about you? Are you no longer interested?" His brow tweaks upward.

"I don't know what you're talking about," I lie.

Charlie pats my shoulder. "Sure, you don't." With that said, he stands, leaving the copy of the document and the yellow tab glaring up at me.

Sometimes being a Harrington can be a pain in the ass.

16
Wedding presents

[Letty]

"And he washed your hair?" It's said like a question, but it's more of a statement, and Marcus has turned it into his greeting the last week. It's not *hello* or *how was your day*? It's *He washed your hair*, as if I need the reminder of the romantic gesture from a man who ripped my heart out.

"Sit," I tell Marcus as he pulls out a stool at the high-top table. We're both dressed in business attire, and over the last eight plus days, I've found the clothing itchy and restrictive. I'm exceptionally fond of my yoga pants and sweatshirts on the weekends, but these past days, I've longed for jeans and a flannel in an unhealthy way.

Marcus looks every bit the professional he is with his sandy brown hair perfectly gelled into a mini coif by his forehead. The sides are shaved, which is a modern style with a razor-sharp part. His brown eyes hide behind dark rimmed glasses. He smiles tightly at me.

"Be brave. Be strong."

The night will be difficult, but I find I'm more sour over a man some thousands of miles away than the man kissing my sister on the cheek near the door. Mullen Realty decided to host a party to celebrate the nuptials of Dayna and Hudson at the end of the week, as if we weren't already celebrating Dayna's good fortune all year leading up to her special day. It's turned into wedding week, like Shark Week on television, and being eaten by one might be more pleasurable than the experience of this wedding. *Kill me.*

My uncle Frank beams at Dayna, so proud of the connection her marriage to Hudson Rockford will provide to his realty company. I, on the other hand, have turned into the biggest disappointment again. My contact with one Charles Harrington, mayor of Blue Ridge, Georgia, didn't go unnoticed.

"What do you mean you didn't procure the property?"

"It's not for sale nor can it be sold. Land entailment." I've used the terminology to disguise my failure or, rather, my change of heart. I no longer want us to pursue Giant's land—the land his precious Pap gave to him. It wasn't just because he broke my heart, either; I truly didn't feel right trying to obtain something so precious, so non-materialist from someone so genuinely content with something so simple.

Uncle Frank strangely knew the detail of the land but decided not to include it in the prospect report he gave me. He believed some simpleton in a small town would only see dollar signs and hand over his property for greener pastures. Or in George Harrington's case, green papers with Benjamin Franklin on them. It appears Uncle Frank didn't investigate the Harringtons either. How wrong he was about Mr. Harrington, his attachment to the land, and his lack of desire for money.

"You look lovely. Want a drink?" Marcus says, distracting me from my thoughts. He doesn't mean what he says. He's seen me all day in this outfit—a pencil skirt, a tight blouse, and a stiff suit jacket. I look a little worn from the day I've had, but not as frightening as I looked when I arrived at a hotel outside of Atlanta before flying back to Chicago. I don't know how the woman agreed to give me a room. Maybe it was the tear-stained face and stiff, dirty clothes. I took an extra night to cry myself to sleep in a big, comfy bed with extra pillows after a long hot bath. It was heavenly…minus the crying part.

"I'll have a margarita on the rocks with salt."

"Oh, fiesta time?" Marcus wiggles his ass on the wooden stool.

"Get me drunk time," I say with a laugh although it isn't true. I want to keep my wits this week so I don't say something I shouldn't. I'm over Hudson and my sister, but a little liquid courage might not stop me from spilling the truth. He cheated on me with her. Hudson didn't want the bad press, so he asked that we part, stating irreconcilable differences, as if we were getting a divorce. As if he wasn't seen with my sister at some fundraiser a week later. I didn't want to admit his indiscretion, equally embarrassed that he'd slept with my sister, of all people.

"Gonna make it through this week?" Marcus asks although he knows I will. I'll put on my brave face and big girl panties because I don't want to seem like the bitter, sniveling little sister.

"When's the ax throwing?" I tease.

"And then he washed your hair."

I laugh bitterly at the reference. Yes, he washed my hair, and made love to me, and then he snapped me like a twig.

It wasn't just sex, he said. What else could it have been? His silence had unnerved me, but I had my answer. *Just sex*, is all it was.

Mindlessly, I stroke back my hair, pushing it behind my ear.

"I can't talk about him. Not this week." I've already told Marcus everything. Well, minus a few graphic details. Don't want to get his knickers in a twist. He listened and sighed and held my hand. *He sounds like a good man*, Marcus said.

For the most part, Giant Harrington is a good man. He just didn't understand I would never consider sleeping with someone to score a deal. Something happened to me on that mountain…with him. It was no longer about the land after that first night, and it wasn't just the assistive hand during my self-soothing moment. I'd never done anything like what I'd done with Giant, and it made my feelings all the more real. *To me.*

"So ax throwing," Marcus states, perking up. "Gonna chop some wood." Marcus makes karate-chopping motions over his lap. He's so inappropriate.

"Marcus." I chuckle. "I can't handle your sharp wit. Get it, *handle*? Sharp?"

"Oh, oh, good one. You're quite the cutup." He winks at me, lifting his chocolate martini to his lips.

"That was a good one," I admit with a giggle. "How did you *hatchet*?"

He laughs, and then claps once, holding his clasped hands before his chest. "It was an ax-cident."

I laugh in earnest. "How about he axed her to marry him after I tossed him over." I nod in the direction of my sister and former fiancé, trying to be clever, which isn't my strong suit.

Marcus gives a triple *clap-clap-clap*. "He axed for it."

Tears roll down my face as I guffaw even harder. "I wasn't cut out for him." But somehow, this isn't a joke, and the tears shift from humor to hurt as my thoughts wander. I'm no longer referencing Hudson.

"Oh, honey." Being my best friend, he practically reads my thoughts and hands me two paper napkins. "He's an ax-hole if he doesn't realize how wonderful you are."

I giggle with sadness because I don't consider Giant an asshole. Not even close.

"I did this to myself," I mutter.

"After the way you said he did you, honey, I think you're mistaken. He wanted you as much as you wanted him," Marcus tries to reassure me.

The land. He believed I wanted it more than him, and for a few hours, I did, but then I got to know *him*. The man. And nothing made sense anymore. Can you fall in love with a stranger in three nights? I don't have to *ax* my heart because it's all chopped up.

+ + +

The ceremony is held on a Friday evening because Dayna wanted a night wedding. Also, Friday night weddings are cheaper, but considering the money between Hudson and Dayna, the expense was not spared. Not to mention, my uncle has chipped in to make this a real business affair. Dayna also wanted October for her wedding, but the dresses we wear scream July. Despite the mild weather of Chicago, the breeze briskly blows as the day dips to nightfall, and we shiver in our ludicrous attire while taking pictures down by Lake Michigan. A trolley drives us up and down Lake Shore Drive before returning us to the hotel for the wedding dinner.

Marcus is my plus one even though he was already an invited guest. I didn't have a date and didn't feel the need to find one weeks before the wedding. I only want to sip wine, give my toast, and get the hell out of here. Yes, I need to give a speech congratulating my sister on marrying my ex-lover. It's going to be short and sweet.

May you deserve one another.

The end.

The ballroom is dripping in yellow, and I feel as if I've entered a cream puff. *I hate custard.* I saunter up to the bar. Skipping the celebratory champagne, I decide wine will be my comfort.

"You doing okay?" Marcus asks me for the millionth time. I'm on the verge of making him into a cream puff if he asks me one more time.

"I'm fine," I grumble, reaching for the glass the bartender hands me and guzzling heartily the crisp liquid. It isn't as sharp and tangy as the beer I drank on a mountain ridge under the stars, but it will have to do. It's a weak substitute, I realize and sigh. Marcus notices.

"Remind me why you can't call him?" I made that absurdly stupid phone call to Giant's brother, the mayor brother, and included all kinds of details in my long-winded explanation. Then I left my phone number—could I have been more desperately obvious that I wanted him to call me? I decided it had to be up to Giant to reach out to me. If he wanted to talk, he had to come to me. Which he didn't do.

"Because I'd already said too much, and he accused me of sleeping with him...for business...no less." I exhale, whispering the last part before taking another sip of wine and realizing I've finished the glass. Well, that was quick. "Marcus, you know how I am. I talk too much, but it's normally nonsense. For once, I want someone to listen to me. Really listen."

Marcus's eyes widen as he glances over my shoulder.

"And what is it you would want a certain someone to hear?" His voice shifts as he holds his lips in a strange grimace.

"I want someone to listen to my heart. To what I had to say. Hear how I feel." Jesus, this wedding is making me sappy and sentimental.

"And what does your heart feel?"

"Dammit, Marcus, you know this. I felt something for this man, who was a complete stranger, yet the strangest part was the immediate attraction I had to him. Like he knew me, or saw something in me, or...I don't even know what I'm saying. It's the wine talking."

"Then I'm listening to a damn good bottle of Moscato." The gruff voice behind me startles me, and my eyes widen as I stare at Marcus. The sound certainly didn't come from his lips although it holds all the teasing Marcus would make. My head slowly shakes, but Marcus nods with a matching pace. He knows what I don't. I lift a hand to my upper chest, my heart hammering under my skin, and the pinched smile on Marcus's face curls into a wide grin.

Slowly, I turn to face the rugged tone and meet a tux-covered chest. My eyes climb the tall stature, taking in the black bow tie at his throat and the dark spark to his eyes.

I'm hallucinating, I tell myself.

Before me stands a giant of masculinity, polished with a trimmed beard and combed hair. A sharp gleam graces those bark-colored eyes. His broad shoulders are covered by a fitted black suit like he's a member of the wedding party. My eyes roam the remainder of his large physique, drinking in the tux on him like it's the bubbly wine in my glass. Gone is lumbersexual, replaced by dashy and debonair.

My God, he's tasty.

"What are you wearing?" he asks, his voice gruff, reminiscent of our first meeting.

"*He* washed your hair?" Marcus gasps in a hushed tone from behind me.

"Giant," I breathe out his name with shock and desperation and longing.

"Cricket," he addresses me, and Marcus chokes at my back.

"He has a pet name for you," Marcus practically squeals. "You didn't mention a pet name."

"Marcus," I groan, keeping my eyes fixed on Giant, who isn't grinning, but his lips twist. He wants to smile. He's moving his mouth like he's fighting it, and all I can think about is how I want that mouth on mine.

"This is Marcus?" Giant asks, offering a hand to my friend, but I don't miss how he skims my arm to reach around me.

"George Harrington," he says. "But people call me Giant."

"Mmm...I bet you are," Marcus purrs. He doesn't play his gay card often or to the hilt, but this is over the top, even for him, and Giant quickly retracts his hand. Marcus steps around me and looks back and forth between Giant and myself. "The pleasure to meet you is all mine," he states, and then he continues circling, taking a step behind Giant but still facing me. He lifts his fingers toward his hardly-there hair and makes massaging motions as he mouths his new standard statement. I giggle as I wave him away.

"What are you doing here?" I ask of Giant, still breathless and stunned. He's actually standing before me. *In a tux!*

"Heard there was a wedding happening, and the prettiest woman here needed a date."

I step toward him, fighting the urge to wrap my arms around him and climb his body like the mammoth tree he is. He leans forward to kiss my cheek while he rubs my bare shoulder. It's a little reserved. Where was the wild man from the ranger station? Or the adventurous one the first night in our tent? Or the one who kissed me senseless on our last night together?

You hurt him, I remind myself. *He hurt you*, my brain replies.

But he's standing here before me.

In Chicago. "Let's get out of here," I whisper, and he chuckles, slipping his warm hand down my arm to my fingers. I grip them hard.

"It appears I might be late to the party. Don't you have some obligations tonight?"

"You aren't late." I exhale. It's only been twelve days, twenty hours, and roughly three minutes but not late. "I need to give a toast, but the second I'm done, you're mine," I groan, the wild in me clearly reaching out for him.

17

The man in the mirror

[Giant]

You're mine. I shouldn't like the sound of that as much as I do, but I do. I so do. Her dress is hideous, but she's so beautiful with her chestnut hair piled at the nape of her neck and soft curls framing her face. She's wearing makeup, which I hadn't seen her wear while camping, so she looks different. Still pretty but polished. I want to smear her lips with mine. For a moment there, I thought she'd jump into my arms, but something stopped her. My heart dropped.

I've waited twelve days to see her. I can hold out another hour to have her alone.

"The wedding was on a Friday?" I expected to arrive in time for a rehearsal dinner, surprising her and giving us time to talk. Instead, I walked into the Drake without a room or a plan to find the placard in the lobby announcing the wedding in the ballroom.

"My sister wanted to be unconventional." Letty lifts a glass of wine for her lips. "Just like how she obtained her new husband."

She's already told me she isn't bitter about him and her. It's more the principle of their meeting, and I understand. Cheating is unacceptable. Disloyalty, lies, half-hidden truths. I don't care for any of the sort even though I'm guilty of a few on a minor level.

"When did you get here?" she asks, lowering her glass and looking up at me. So many questions in those eyes, and I want to answer everything.

"About an hour ago. Took a bit to get here from O'Hare." I don't travel much. My nephew Jaxson is in charge of sales and distribution, and he's the one who visits places. I've already been halfway around the world and back, so I'm happy in my mountainous backyard now.

The bartender hands me a local beer, and I sip, letting my tongue roll to distinguish the ingredients. It's not bad. My brother Billy is more a brewmaster than I am, though. He's a closet chemist, and my father learned too late of Billy's benefit to the company. Fortunate for me, I extort my kid brother's skill.

"Did you get a room?" She hesitates as she asks.

"Changed in the bathroom and asked the front desk to hold my bag," I clarify.

"I have a room." Her eyes sheepishly leap to mine. "I didn't want the hassle of driving home, plus I have the send-off breakfast tomorrow morning, which is suddenly optional, and then that's it." Her definitive tone tells me she'll finally be finished with obligations and can let this fiasco go. *Time to move on.*

"Optional?" I raise a brow.

"I might be busy in the morning."

This woman. Her teasing brings a grin to my lips, and I take another sip of my beer. The night isn't passing fast enough.

She doesn't mingle, but as people approach her, she introduces me. Family and more family. Business acquaintances.

Finally, she gives her toast and leads me from the ballroom.

"We didn't dance," I mock although I'm not a good dancer. She laughs as she drags me toward the elevator, holding my fingers like I held hers on our hike. God, I missed her laughter.

When the elevator closes, I waste no time before I rush up to her and flatten her against the back wall. Her heels raise her closer to my height, but I still dip my head.

"I want to be naked with you." I don't know where the words come from, but they're every bit the truth. I want to be bare and raw and honest with her. I said things I shouldn't have said, and I need to apologize. With my hands. With my tongue. With my dick.

"I want to be naked with you," she whispers, her voice shy, but her hips buck forward, and my hand lowers for one. My mouth waters, but I don't kiss her. Once I start, I won't stop because I didn't kiss her enough when I had her on the mountains.

She leads the way to her room and holds the scan card over the magnetic lock. The sharp click releasing the catch is like a pistol shot, and I'm ready to race. When she steps inside, she stops and spins to face me. The door closes with a soft thud, locking us.

L.B. Dunbar

"This is more my camping speed," she teases, swiping out her hand. "Bathroom." She gestures behind me. "Comfy bed." She chuckles. "A fridge."

I laugh with her, but I can't take my eyes off her dress. It isn't her. It's pretty enough, but it's not my Cricket.

"What are you wearing?" I ask a second time.

Letty tugs at the loose material over her breasts and lets the fabric fall back.

"It's a dress. I think. Buttercup yellow," she clarifies.

"It looks like margarine on a biscuit. And the 80s called, they want their prom dress back."

Letty laughs, a bubbly chuckle, and I'm reminded of pebbles in rain puddles. My spine shivers with the sound. I like it too much.

"Take it off," I demand, torn between wanting to talk and needing to skip the formal stuff. She turns her back to me and points at the zipper along her spine. Slowly, I unzip, and the dull yellow material spreads. The dress slips to the floor, pooling at her feet, and she turns back to me. Her hands come to her hips, and I swallow.

"You're the prettiest thing..." I falter, roaming slowly over the nude-colored strapless bra and matching thong in lace. "Fuck that. You're the most beautiful woman I've laid eyes on." Her head tips, and her smile grows, but I can't take my eyes off the bra where her nipples nearly pop over the edge and the G-string of material covering her lower region. And her heels. Fucking strappy and high. She's a fantasy of epic proportions.

I tug the tie from my neck and shrug off the jacket, throwing them at the bed. As I slowly unbutton the cuffs of my shirt and then a few at the neck, I keep my eyes on her.

"So, this is your idea of roughing it, huh?" Once I've loosened enough of my shirt, I tug it and my undershirt over my head from the back of my neck. I kick off my fancy shoes.

She purrs at me, watching me strip. Her eyes are hungry looking, and I'm starving for her. I hold out a hand for her.

"Let's check out the bathroom first."

Her head tilts, but she follows me as I walk backward to the large bathroom. Once we enter, I spin her for the sink, and my hands roam. Up her spine and around her sides, cupping her breasts. I watch in the extra-large mirror.

"God, I've missed you," I murmur, kissing up her neck.

"Me too." Her arm reaches back, wrapping around my neck and holding me to her. My eager palms squeeze at the material over her breasts, forcing the nipples to protrude above the silky fabric. I tweak them collectively, tugging until she yelps. Her hips buck back, and her ass hits my front. I'm rock hard and have been since the moment I saw her.

Correction: every time I've thought of her for the past two weeks, I've been stiff, but seeing her makes me three times more solid.

Two fingers dip into the thin string between her backside cheeks. I stroke downward, and my knuckles brush against her firm ass. Curling my hand under her, I discover her core wet and wanting. My eyes meet hers in the mirror, and I watch her face as I slip into her.

Her mouth opens. Her lids flutter. She releases my neck and reaches back to grip my hip.

"So beautiful," I say, turning into her neck and kissing her again. I work my fingers in and out, not removing the thong but sliding it to the side.

"With this bra exposing your nipples, and the scrap covering your pussy, plus the heels, you're a fantasy. One I'd watch on repeat. I want to fuck you like this, Cricket."

Her breath hitches as she brings her hands around her back to blindly work at my belt. Without releasing my fingers from her center, I push her hand away and single-handedly struggle with the catch, loosening it but not removing it. Then I unzip my pants.

"Push at the sides," I say, talking to her reflection in the mirror, and Letty presses my pants below my hips. I don't want to be naked. Not yet. It's sexy as fuck looking in the glass with me half-dressed and her in this outfit. It's wild, and I want her.

"Giant," she hums in warning. She's close, and I am too. She hasn't even touched me, and I'm ready to lose it. With my fingers in her, I grip myself and position my head at her entrance. I remove my coated digits and press her shoulder blades to lean forward over the counter. Her legs spread, and I bend enough to align myself with her. Slowly, I disappear into her, watching her swallow me. Then I look up to see her eyes on me through the mirror. My hands wrap over her covered breasts and tug the material downward. Exposing each of them, I cup them as I draw my dick back and then thrust forward. Letty grunts.

As I pull back, she chases me, and I smile in the reflection. "Greedy?"

"You have no idea," she mutters.

"Oh, I have an idea," I say, slamming into her. Repeating the motion several times, I clutch at her breasts and delve into her. She meets me thrust for thrust, bent over the counter. "I've missed you every second we've been apart."

"You have?" she gasps as I tap inside her.

"So much."

She smiles back at me. "I like your smile," she says, watching me as I set a pace of driving into her.

"I like you," I say.

"Watch," she whispers as her hand snakes down her belly and lowers into the lace barely covering her curls. Sweet Jesus, I don't know if I can look, but I can't tear my eyes away. She's touching herself, and I know it without fully seeing it. My eyes stay focused on the movement of her hand. Her lids close as her hips buck.

"Finish," I snap, knowing I can't hold out much longer. My spine tingles. My balls tighten.

"Giant," she squeaks, and then my name dissolves as she stills, clutching me within her depths. Her head lolls forward, and I slam into her, holding her to me by her breasts as I have the orgasm of all orgasms.

Stars dance before my eyes, and I lower my head to her shoulder.

"Dammit. I didn't kiss you."

She chuckles with me still inside her. "Well, we'll just have to try again."

18
Baby steps

[Letty]

He slips out of me, and I spin to face him. He finalizes the removal of his pants and socks, and I kick off my own shoes. I step out of my thong and unhitch my bra. Hooking a finger at him, I make him follow me into the double-size shower where he kisses me senseless until our mouths move to other places.

Wrung out, I wrap in a towel while he slips into the comfy white robe provided, and we head to the bed.

"This is a bed," I tease, pulling back the top cover. "With linens and pillows. And oh, look, a mattress." I press on the firmness to emphasize my point. Giant wraps his hands around my waist and tosses me on it, then follows after me. Half his body covers mine, and I love the weight of him over me. I've missed him so much.

He brushes back my wet hair and looks down into my face.

"Was it really that bad? The camping?"

"I survived," I joke before reaching up to cup his scruff-covered jaw. "Actually, I really enjoyed myself. Surprisingly, I miss the place." I might not be able to live in a tent eating food from a skillet the rest of my life, but I do miss being with him and enjoying the experience with him.

"I heard you're no longer interested in the property."

"Giant." I sigh. "I lost interest the first night you made me a hot dog."

"Who knew that's all a girl needed to change her mind? I thought it might have been when I washed your hair."

"That too." I laugh, thinking of Marcus. "And when you taught me to throw an ax."

He leans forward and kisses me, soft and delicate.

L.B. Dunbar

"How did the ax throwing go?" he smirks. "Heard a master ax thrower taught you?" He winks at me, and my skin heats as I recall the things I said to his brother.

"I didn't win, but I hit the mark enough times to scare Hudson. I told him I'd learned to chop wood as well." I mimic the motion of chopping by knocking the sides of my hands together. Giant shifts to his side, perching up on an elbow and looking down at me.

"As long as he knows his wood is off-limits."

My lip crooks. "Not interested in anyone's wood but yours. And I'm not talking about the trees on your property."

Giant chuckles and draws a line along my collarbone with the tip of a thick finger. His expression darkens, and I know what's coming. We need to talk.

"We never talked about your brother."

Owen isn't who I expect us to discuss first, and my lips twist as I bite the corner. "Do we need to talk about him now?"

"I think we have a few things to discuss that shouldn't wait any longer." Giant isn't wrong, but we're jumping into the deep stuff by tackling Owen first. I swallow the lump that always forms in my throat before I talk about him. I nod and explain again the circumstances of my younger brother and his gang affiliation.

"Owen was only four when our father died, and he hated Uncle Frank. Being six years younger than me, I was like a second mother to him. He was a little lost with our mother working, and Dayna acting as second parent but never doing a good job." Some parent she turned out to be. "Gangs are prevalent everywhere in and around Chicago, but it's not all colored bandanas and acid wash jeans hanging off a kid's ass. Kids with means can just as easily get hooked up with the wrong people, and Owen did. We struggled with money for a bit, and he was a worrier. He'd lost his way around middle school and got in with a rougher crowd in seventh grade. He suggested he sell drugs to help us meet ends." I chuckle with the memory of Owen telling our mom he wanted to help out. *Be the man of the family.* "He wanted Mom out from under Uncle Frank's controlling nature. Mom couldn't handle budding-teenage Owen." I recall how babyish his face was while his body was growing

124

into the makings of a young man. He was smarter than he gave himself credit. Smarter than our mother recognized. He just needed guidance, and I tried to be there for him, but it wasn't enough. I was only eighteen. "I was his older sister, but I couldn't protect him." Liquid fills my eyes, and I blink back the pain as the memories fill my head. Giant reaches out with a thumb and swipes at the tear before it falls.

"I mentioned he was shot on the sidewalk outside his school. I was there to pick him up and give him a ride home. I didn't see them coming." Loud cars with trashy music are common around a school. It could have been any car with any group of kids, but this car was looking for Owen. I leave out the details of screams and blood and holding my brother in my arms.

"When I heard James's gun, I freaked out. It's also triggered by thunder." My eyes close, embarrassed by admitting such a weakness. Giant cups my cheek, forcing my eyes to open.

"I totally understand. I've seen my share of surprise attacks, and the horrific results in the military." His voice drops. "But on a sidewalk in a city with a kid, it seems so unthinkable."

I brush aside the robe and point at the wound near his left shoulder. "Is that how this happened?"

He huffs with his own set of memories.

"We were on a mission, and one of our men was injured. I was shot lifting him into a helicopter. The soldier friend needed to be helivaced out, and suddenly, so did I."

I lean forward to kiss the wound.

"You have a new appreciation for life once you almost lose it," he states. However, I remember what he told me—how he didn't know where he fit when he came home. How his wife had a routine. How he joined the brewery business. *What's been in his life for him?*

The mountain. A gift from a beloved grandfather.

"I'm sorry about the land." Should I tell him why I wanted it? Will he understand? It's a lot to take in from someone he just met.

He stares into my eyes, twirling a piece of my hair between his thumb and forefinger "*I'm* sorry for what I said."

My head shifts on the mattress, and I roll my body to my side. My hand rests on his chest, feeling his heart rhythmically pulsing under his warm skin. "Did you really believe I slept with you for your land?"

"What I said was a knee-jerk reaction. Why else would you be interested in sleeping with me?" His throat rolls as he swallows, and I open my mouth to speak, but a few fingers of his cover my lips. "You seemed too good to be true and wanting *me* didn't seem like enough of a reason to give yourself to me."

"Giant," I softly whine, reaching up to cover the trimmed scruff on his jaw with my hand. "I'll give myself to you a hundred times if you'll take me. Of course, I want you."

"You're very different from what I've had in the past."

I cringe at the thought. It sounds kind of bad when he says it like that.

"No, no, this is all good. My…" He pauses as his eyes shift to my shoulder. "My sex life hasn't been as wild as it's been with you. It's been rather tame, in fact, and I'm enjoying the difference."

I tip my head up to take his mouth, and we kiss briefly. I'm not certain how to take what he's said. Is he comparing me to his wife? To other women? Either way, I guess I'm glad I'm not the same as everyone else. He pulls back, looking over at me again.

"I don't think I'm explaining myself very well," he says, and I perch up on an elbow while he falls to his back, looking up at the ceiling. "I'm not good at communicating my feelings." There's mockery in his tone, and I imagine he's been told this a time or two. He does have a standoffish demeanor, which I accused him of, but I want him to open up to me.

"Try," I whisper.

"This seems like an awkward time to discuss it, but Clara was sensitive. We were two kids bumbling through the dark at first. Over time, I wanted a little more, but Clara couldn't handle it. Certain positions. Certain locations. We really only had one position, and she would accept sex in only one place—the bedroom. It wasn't awful, but it wasn't spectacular." He rolls his head to look at me and sheepishly smiles. "It was more functional. We weren't adventurous."

I fight the smile forming on my lips, not wanting to give away how pleased I am with what he's said. *Oh, so that kind of different.* My hand scrubs over his firm pecs, exposed from the open robe. My fingers play with the hair on his chest while he seems lost to the memory. He exhales.

"Anyway, I heard what you did, or rather, I got your message. What made you think to contact Charlie and not me?"

"Honestly, I didn't have your number."

"Don't you do any research before you go after a property? Why didn't you call the brewery?"

"Would you have spoken to me if I called?" I pause, sheepishly chuckling. "I don't really know what I was thinking with that ridiculous call to your brother." I lower my face to the coverlet, hiding from the heat of Giant's eyes. "I hoped Charlie could pass on the legal jargon, and you'd understand it wasn't the land. It's you that I want," I mumble the muffled words into the duvet.

"I want you, too." He shifts to his side, and I turn my head to face him. His lip crooks, and he kisses my shoulder. "I think I'll always want you."

The words startle me and shoot right to my heart like an arrow on a mission. I don't know how to respond. *I think I'll always want him, too.* I brush away thoughts of the distance between us and the impossibility of being with him for always.

"What made you decide to come to the wedding?" It's quite the grand gesture to show up unannounced.

He chuckles. "I heard you needed your hair done."

I laugh with him. "I'm kind of a mess right now."

His fingers comb into my hair, brushing it back from my face so he can clearly peer into my eyes. "This is my favorite look on you."

Gah. This man. "Charmer," I tease.

"Hmm, let me see how else I can charm you." He leans forward for my jaw. When he nips at the juncture between my shoulder and neck, I'm totally charmed.

+ + +

We make love in the bed, and neither of us misses the fact that it's different once again. We've been rather wild and reckless but this, this is slow and purposeful. Soft hands caressing skin, and fingers lingering to outline bodies. Long kisses and deliberate movements. I come undone in a way I never thought I could while we take our time with each other. A new deal is sealed, at least for me.

I'm in love with this man.

Hook, line, and sinker.

The next morning, we agree I need to make an appearance at the send-off breakfast.

"One cup of coffee, and then we flee." Giant laughs, but I'm serious. I don't want to share him with my family, not yet, and I only have him until Sunday afternoon.

My sister Dayna and I look nothing alike. While I'm dark featured, she's light, and she greets me with all the falseness of a nosy Nelly, which is what she is when it comes to Giant.

"And who is this tall drink of water?" she flirts, and I want to smack her hand when she goes for Giant's chest. Fortunately, he intercepts it and makes an awkward show of forcing her to shake his hand instead. "Well, my, what a grasp you have."

Giant slips an arm around my waist and tugs me to his side. "I've been told it's all the better to hold an ax." He jiggles me against him, and my sister flushes, not understanding the private joke. She'll never know the strength of his hands, though. Not on my watch.

"Come. Meet Hudson."

Giant's face wrinkles in disgust, and I interject. "We're only having a cup of coffee, and then I'm going to show Giant the city." He claims he's been here once or twice, but he'll see it through new eyes with me as his guide. Navy Pier is our first stop.

While I'm hoping to escape Hudson, I can't escape my mother or Uncle Frank.

"Cassandra Pierson, meet George Harrington." Giant doesn't correct his name when he meets my mother and the Southern charm pours off him.

"A pleasure to meet you, ma'am." Mom is easily impressed. My mother is a smaller woman with bleach-blond hair to cover all the grays, cut in a sharp bob coming to her chin. She wears a surprised smile while she shakes Giant's large hand.

"George Harrington," Uncle Frank interjects. "Your name sounds familiar." He pauses a moment. Frank is your typical Italian-looking mafia man minus the mafia. He's loud and brutally *frank*. "You're quite the big guy, aren't you?" Frank makes a muscle with his arm and aims it toward Giant as if he should be impressed. Then Frank realizes something. "You're that property we lost." Frank's eyes shift to me and back to Giant.

"Actually, I wasn't lost. Letty found me," Giant murmurs, tugging me into his side once again.

"Damn shame. Olivet, here, cost us a big deal," Frank continues, ignoring Giant's attempts to be sweet and lessen the awkwardness. My eyes close a second, but Giant gives me another squeeze. *Please don't blurt out the dollar amount*, I whisper in my head as Frank is famous for oversharing.

"Some things are more important than making a deal, sir," Giant corrects.

"Like what?" Frank scoffs, and Giant's mouth opens again to speak, but my mother steps in.

"Now Frank. It wasn't her fault. You know she only had one thing on her mind." My mother turns to me, and I hold my breath. *Oh God, she wouldn't.* "The baby."

Giant stiffens at my side, and it's my turn to clutch at him. My fingers fist in the back of his shirt.

"Right, another foolish idea of yours," Uncle Frank agrees. He shakes his head and looks up at Giant. "What do you think of this baby business? Adoption." He scoffs as though it's a dirty word.

"I think Letty can do whatever she pleases, sir," Giant says, surprising all of us. Mom's brows rise while Frank crosses his arms.

"Indeed," he says, like the British man he's not. He doesn't agree one bit with Giant's assessment. In fact, he disagrees wholeheartedly as does my mother.

L.B. Dunbar

"It was a pleasure to meet both of you. If you don't mind, I need some coffee. I don't function well without it," Giant mutters, his voice struggling to remain level instead of rough. He's saving all of us from an awkward confrontation. My mother laughs, agreeing that coffee is a necessity in life, and points us in the direction of the carafes on the buffet. I follow Giant who has released his hold on me.

"Please let me explain," I mutter through tight teeth as I come up next to him while he pours a cup. He offers it to me.

"Oh, I intend to hear every bit of this story," he hisses, and the rugged edge to his tone returns.

+ + +

After taking an Uber to Navy Pier, we begin a leisurely saunter along the old Naval pier. Restaurants line one side until the carousel while the right side is open to the lake—reminiscent of an ancient shipping dock. As we stroll, I feel as if I'm doing the walk of shame, minus the sex and last night's clothing, but I have nothing to be ashamed of. I jump right in.

"It all started with Hudson. We weren't really going anywhere, and I think in my heart of hearts, I knew we would never marry. I wasn't in a rush until, suddenly, I was. I wanted a baby when I hadn't really entertained the idea beforehand. Because a baby solves everything," I mock myself. "Hudson didn't want children. When he finally told me he never had any intention of us marrying, something snapped."

I swallow back the pain. Not at losing Hudson but at the cruelty of what he did. He made me false promises. I brush a hand through my hair even as it continues to blow forward in the wind. Giant walks with his hands in his jacket pockets. It's a brisk day for October. There's more gloom than sunshine, and the cloud cover presses down on me like this history.

"I'm forty, and I didn't see the prospect of getting married to anyone else. The loss of Hudson was more than losing a man. A worthless man, I might add. I lost a dream, or so I thought. Marcus and his partner had begun trying to adopt, and it sparked the idea I could do it on my own. I needed this for me."

130

I keep my eyes forward, not risking a glance at Giant, fearing his judgment like all the rest of my family.

This is insanity. You can't raise a child alone, my mother said even though she'd done the very thing herself. Then again, my uncle stepped in to help her out. Where was the family loyalty when it came to this decision for me?

"In vitro with sperm implants seemed too complicated and a risk at my age. I'm not too old to have a child, but I didn't want to wait for things to take. It could have taken months or years, which I don't have. There are so many children who need a parent now, and adoption seemed more immediate…" My voice drifts as I recall all the babies I've seen in and out of the Bundle, a private adoption agency on the Northshore. "I just wanted someone…for me."

I blink away the tears. My sister is on her second marriage. She has three growing sons she hardly deserves. *Did I mention the irony that Hudson hates children?* It didn't seem fair some days, but I don't want to be jealous. I don't want what she has. A superficial first marriage. A business arranged second one. Empty relationships with her sons.

"Why didn't you tell me?" His rugged voice is full of sympathy instead of anger, and it's almost worse. I don't want pity. I want someone to be excited for me.

I shrug. "It isn't something I could easily bring up. Hey, while you teach me to throw an ax, I wanted to tell you I'm adopting a baby."

He snorts, and I look over at him. He squints into the distance before us. "So when do you get the baby?"

"I don't, actually." I swallow the lump in my throat. I'd been passed up again right before I went to Georgia. Maybe it's another reason I did what I did. The spontaneity of a trip. The uninhibited sex with a stranger. The total release of all the hurt feelings inside me. He turns to peer down at me.

"What happened?"

"I didn't make the cut. It isn't that they aren't willing to give me a baby as a single mom, but if a married couple comes forward or ones with more financial stability, they take precedence."

He's thoughtful a moment, his brows pinching. "Why's that?"

I shrug again. "Money talks. Everyone has their price." I choke on the words. Giant stops, and I take another step or two forward before I spin to face him.

"Is this the reason you wanted the land?"

My shoulders fall, and I look away. "I needed the commission. Adoptions costs money. If I had a little more, I'd look financially secure. The sale of your land would have garnered a sizable kickback for me, as well as secured a position as partner within my uncle's company. It's all about providing a stable home." I shake my head. "It doesn't really matter anymore," I say, masking the truth. I'm heartbroken once again, but I tell myself it isn't my time yet. I smile weakly, looking up at him. "There'll be another baby, another day."

I turn to continue walking, but Giant stops me with a hand on my upper arm. "Wait a second. This is important. You should have told me." Irritation roughens his voice, and he looks genuinely pissed.

Here comes the breakup.

"Why, Giant?" I stare at him. Are you sorry you came to Chicago now? Do you want to take back all the amazing sex we had? Do you want to renege the sensation we both felt as we made love last night? "It isn't a great conversation starter." I'm teasing, sort of, but the truth is, it isn't something I easily share. This adoption business—as my family carelessly calls it—is really important to me.

You can't do it as a single woman.

You shouldn't do it as woman without more means.

Who would want to be a single mom?

I would. Willingly. And I'm tired of defending myself. It's no one's business but mine. That's the point. A baby. For me.

"Letty, you should have told me about the money." His voice remains rugged.

"And what could you do about it? Sell me your land?" I pause, exhaling in frustration. "I don't want it." It's not about the land, per se, but the money, and I don't want either from him.

With a puzzled expression on his face, he states, "We could figure something else out."

I laugh without humor. "No." For some reason, I see the wheels turning in Giant's eyes, which makes me both uncomfortable and ridiculously hopeful, but I don't want to rely on someone else. That's the point of this adoption. A baby. For me. Someone who needs me. For once, someone who needs *me*.

"Why not?" he snaps, his voice returning to mountain-man Giant.

"Because I'll figure it out on my own." *I always do.*

He steps forward and cups my shoulders. "But you don't have to." He stares down at me, but I don't know what he's saying. It would be too much to hope he's saying all kinds of things I shouldn't assume.

"You're sweet." I give him a genuine smile, even if it's only half my lips. He is sweet, and I bet Giant Harrington is the type of man to take care of things, to fulfill obligations, and stick where he doesn't want to be stuck because he thinks he's doing the right thing.

"I'm serious." His voice deepens, irritation remaining.

"So am I."

He nods, but disagreement fills his eyes. He doesn't let me go. His eyes grow serious and sharp, peering down at me while his hands slip to my shoulder blades. "I'm here for you. You can talk to me. I'll do whatever you need, but I need the truth."

He's right. There have been a few too many secrets between us, but could I have laid all this on him after only three nights of amazing sex? I wouldn't have thought so, but I should know better. Everything with Giant has been different.

My lips purse as I fight a smile, risking a little more of myself. "The truth is, I like you, and I didn't want to scare you away. A baby screams commitment, and that's not what I'm after. But thank you. If you're willing to be my friend and stick around for some moral support, I'd love to have you be here… well, not here *here*, of course, because you live in Georgia…but here for me." The reality hits me. He doesn't live nearby, and he won't be close enough to help me, but I don't want to lose him. There's so much more I've left unsaid. So much I couldn't dare to ask of him.

"Okay," he says softly, his voice the lowest I've ever heard. He tugs me to him, holding the back of my head as I take a deep breath with my cheek against his chest. He kisses the top of my head before sliding me to his side, keeping his arm around me, and walking us forward. I'd like to think the steps are metaphorical. We'll go forward together—as friends—long-distance friends, with benefits, lots of benefits, but a niggling feeling tells me I might lose him for good once he leaves this time.

19
Just friends. My ass.

[Giant]

Friend? I don't want to be her fucking friend. I don't know how to define us—*her*—but friend is not my intention. I want her as my lover, as a partner, as a...I can't even consider something more. I shouldn't think it. But my heart jumps around like a monkey trapped in a cage, rattling the iron bars in hopes of release.

It could happen again, Giant, my mother said a few days before I left for Chicago as if her sixth sense, Mom-powers already knew something was out there. Someone.

Friend is not what I want.

We continue down the pier, the wind blasting around us as I prompt her to tell me more despite her initial protests. She explains how adoption works.

"It's very scary. A biological parent could come back and demand his or her parental rights. I don't want any issues. I just want a baby outright."

I hold her tighter to me, but I don't feel close enough. My gut twists with the reality of her financial situation. She assures me she's well enough off and dismisses the commission once again, but I want to help. I just don't know how without offering her thousands of dollars, which I know she won't take from me.

We leave Navy Pier and travel to see The Bean where we take tons of selfies. I don't typically take a lot of pictures on my phone, but we smile and kiss and act silly. Finally, I have her phone number, and I save an image of just her to the contact. A photo of us becomes my new background.

From Millennium Park, we travel to Willis Tower, formerly Sears Tower, and wait in a long line to go to the observation floor with the Sky Deck, a room hanging off the tower with a see-through floor. Letty goes inside the three-sided glass box, trembling from the height, and peers out at the steel jungle of buildings. It's nothing compared to being on a mountain ridge overlooking a natural landscape.

"I could never live here," I blurt, realizing too late it's a bit insensitive.

"Why not?" she asks, her voice small as her eyes remain on the skyscrapers and rows of houses below. Chicago is very grid like.

"Too many buildings, too close together. I need space."

Letty stands before me, my arms around her, trapping her against the glass with her back to my front. She nods as though she agrees with me, but she doesn't say a word. Does she like living here? Would she like us to be closer? Would she continue to see me? Would she consider moving?

The last question surprises me, but I instantly realize I'd love to have her in the mountains with me.

"The mountain," she whispers.

"It's also the brewery. I'm in charge." I don't work for my dad. I'm the boss. I'm a forty-nine percent owner doing one hundred percent of the work.

Letty's head softly rests on the glass, and she rolls it back and forth. "I know that." Her voice is too quiet for someone who has talked almost the entire day.

My stomach grumbles, and Letty shifts to glance at me over her shoulder. A soft chuckle slowly restores her disposition. "What was that?"

"I'm hungry." It's true. We grabbed a Chicago-style hot dog, one steamed by a street vendor with no ketchup allowed, and ate as we walked to the Tower, but I need something more substantial. "Would you be upset if I wanted a couch and a television set?"

"I think I can provide that," she teases. "Ready to head home?" A smile forms on her seductive lips, and I give her a too-short kiss. A moment later, I register what she said.

Her home. *Here.* A long way from mine.

"I can't wait to see it," I assure her.

+ + +

I shouldn't be surprised, but her place is another closed-in space. A condo on the fifth floor in a building surrounded by concrete. It's funny how I can sleep in a tent, but this wouldn't work for me. It's cozy, but I'd be claustrophobic here.

We stopped back at the hotel to retrieve our bags and then took another Uber to her place. She hasn't driven me anywhere, and it's a foreign concept. I love to drive my truck.

"So food?" she says, clapping her hands. "I don't have a campfire handy, but I'm wicked good at using this." She holds up her phone and jiggles it. "Delivery?"

I stare at her.

"What are you hungry for? We can order in anything you'd like."

We decide on something we don't readily have in Blue Ridge—Chinese food. When she starts reading off the names with moos and choos and I don't even know what, I just tell her lots of meat and vegetables are good enough for me.

"How do you feel about football?"

I chuckle. Is this a woman after my heart? "College or pro?"

"It's Saturday, so it has to be college tonight."

I toss myself on her couch and kick my feet up on her coffee table. "Game on."

She curls up next to me while we mindlessly watch Georgia play Alabama. It's comfortable like this and reminds me of similar moments with Clara when we were young. Of course, I spent months away from her, and once I permanently returned, we didn't cuddle anymore. I had my chair. She had her corner of the couch. For a moment, I'm saddened by the memory.

Letty is so different from Clara. Her laughter. Her smile. The things she lets me do to her. The things she does to me, like absentmindedly stroking down my chest with the game on the TV. I can hardly concentrate as another part of me is turned on.

The food arrives, and my arousal needs to be put on hold. Letty drinks wine while she offers me more locally brewed beer.

"This is nice," I finally say as we lounge on her couch with full bellies. We're both drowsy from a day of cool, fresh air and alcohol. She leans up and presses her lips to my neck. "That feels nice, too."

I chuckle until her tongue licks at the skin just under my beard, and then her mouth sucks on the section. She lies on her side, her back to the couch cushions while I lie on my back. Her leg hitches over my lap as she continues her sipping kisses. I cup the back of her thigh and close my eyes, mellowing under her attention. A sigh escapes, letting her know one more time how nice she feels. I like her mouth on me. I like how she looks at me. I even like how much she can chatter.

She continues to kiss me, moving her body over my legs and sucking at my skin. Her fingers begin unbuttoning my shirt. Last night, we made love—slow and soft—and I enjoyed every second of it, but I want her a little wild again. The tender moments are almost too much. Too close. Too intense. I don't think we should go there with the distance between us. I came here to give her an apology. I think I'm going to leave here without my heart.

She tugs at my shirt, loosening it from my pants. I quickly sit up and remove both my flannel and my T-shirt with one tug. Then she presses me back to the sofa, returning to cover me with the tip of her tongue and openmouthed kisses.

"Whatcha doing, Cricket?" She doesn't answer me, but hums against the dusting of hair at my waistline. She works at unbuckling my belt and unzipping my zipper. Within seconds, she has my briefs and pants off, and she stares down at me from where she stands next to the couch. The only light in the room is the glow of the television, and she mutes the sound. Then she tugs her sweater over her head. Jeans lower next. Slowly, she removes her bra, watching me as I watch her. I'm enjoying the strip tease act as she wiggles her hips to remove her undies.

Finally, she straddles me, flipping her hair over one shoulder.

"Cricket?" I question as she remains silent. I have no doubt about what she's doing, but there's an intensity to her gaze. The way she's soaking in my body with her eyes. I twitch between her thighs. My hand palms up her side, reaching for a breast and squeezing her nipple. My other hand remains behind my head, casual and calm, which isn't what I feel. My heart races. My dick strains. Just looking at her makes me hard, and then she settles on my length, coating me with the wetness soaking her.

"You drunk, sweetheart?" I chuckle under her as she rides my length, not yet inside her, but slicking over me all the same.

"Just feels good," she hums, her eyes closing, and I kind of like that she's getting off by being on me.

"Whatcha need, honey?"

"I want to ride you."

Jesus. "Yes, please."

She lifts a little to set my tip at her entrance. Her hands brace on my chest. "Ready?" she exhales, and before I can answer, she slams down on me.

I grunt and buck upward. She groans in response. We fall together, and then I lift my hips. She yelps, sitting upright. Her hands go behind her head, and she raises her hair. She presses up on her knees and then drops down on me again. My eyes roll back until I see her hands slipping down to tease her own breasts. She's putting on a little show for me, and I grip her hips, forcing her up and down, listening to the slick sound of her swallowing me while she teases her nipples. Her fingers eventually lower, and I watch as she touches herself while I disappear inside her. Her movements are wild. She's riding me as requested. Hips roll. Tits bounce. Her hair falls over her shoulders. I love how she's taking what she wants. She's giving me everything I need.

I love her.

The thought hits me hard, and I thrust upward, determined to fill her with all of me. She hums louder, and I want to bottle that sound and take it with me to listen to on repeat. Then she settles, slowing her ride as she clenches around me. Her lids lower as she rocks over me, her orgasm lingering. My fingertips press into her skin.

"I'm comin', sweetheart," I warn before I jet off deep within her. I'd love to give her the baby she wants. The baby she so lovingly deserves. But I can't.

If only we'd met earlier in life...

L.B. Dunbar

The ridiculous thought escapes me as she falls over my chest, spent and breathing heavily into my neck. I wrap my arms around her, holding her to me while she holds me inside her.

I don't want to let her go. Not yet.

+ + +

Sunday, we head to brunch. It's what she does with friends, she says, only today she wants me to herself. We window-shop as we walk back to her place. The temperature has dropped.

"Hang around for a bit, it will change again." She laughs about the Midwest weather, but there's something deeper in her comment.

Could I stay here?

I can't. I have too many responsibilities back in Georgia.

Could she leave?

She can't. She's waiting on a baby.

I don't like the odds of hopeless, so I smile through clenched teeth as we make our way through the morning with my departure weighing heavily between us.

When we return to her place, time becomes awkward. It's almost as if we know I need to leave too soon.

"I can't thank you enough for coming to the wedding." It was only the reception and not long enough, but I lean forward and press my forehead to hers as we stand in her living room. "It was the best of surprises."

"Why do I feel like this is goodbye?"

"Isn't it?" she softly asks, and her voice cracks. I pull back to find a tear slipping down her cheek.

"Cricket, what's this?" I tenderly swipe at the tear, holding her face in my hands.

"I'm never going to see you again, am I?" Another tear falls.

"Do you want to see me again?" I weakly smile with hope.

"Yes." Her enthusiastic nod brings a quiet chuckle from me.

"Then let's work this out, okay? In two weeks, the pub hosts an Oktoberfest. Can you come back to Georgia?"

"I think so. Let me check my calendar." She pauses, another tear slipping from her eye. "I'll make it work."

"There's my Cricket. She never gives up." I lean in for her mouth, and we kiss through her salty tears before I have to tear myself away and head back to Georgia.

20

Home visits

[Letty]

Giant wants to pick me up in Atlanta, and I can't contain myself when I see him. I leap for him when he greets me at the airport. I pepper his face with kisses, locking my legs around his waist although I'm certain I'm too heavy for him. He's laughing until his mouth catches mine, and then he holds me in place, kissing me hard before pulling free.

"That's better than any homecoming, and I'm already home." Giant doesn't talk much about his military experiences, but over the past two weeks, we've talked every night on the phone and sent sexy texts throughout the day.

"I've missed you," I blurt, not shy of my feelings at the moment. I'm so happy to see him, and his expression matches mine. He grabs my bag and my hand, and then we head to his truck. It's a beautiful day as we climb the mountain, and he tells me more about Oktoberfest.

"The event is Billy's grand idea to draw people into the pub and celebrate our beer. It's worked. He's been surprisingly successful." I have all the Harringtons straight in my head, but I'm nervous to meet them. It's obvious from our nightly conversations that his siblings are close minus James, and even there, Giant misses the brother below him in birth order. Their parents—Elaina and George—are still important to them, too. I want to make a good impression, a lasting one, even if I don't know how long Giant and I will last.

We plan to stay at his home. He has some obligations to Oktoberfest the following morning, but he promises me they won't take long. His house is on the edge of town, and it's closer than the cabin. I'll miss the mountain, but I'm excited to see where he lives. I'm also anxious. This will be the home he shared with his deceased wife, so I worry there will be hundreds of reminders of her.

I'm gently surprised when there isn't. The living room is masculine with a bright red plaid couch and two brown leather chairs, one well-worn from a big body. A large stone fireplace is the focal point, whitewashed with a built-in bookshelf on one side. The dining area is behind the couch with the kitchen next to it. It's one great room. The space is neat and minimal, and all male minus any sign of his deceased wife.

"Did you…do you have pictures of her?"

He stops where he's walking, sets down my bag, and turns to face me. "I used to keep pictures of her everywhere until one day I just couldn't look any longer. So I boxed them all up. I keep one in my room, but I put it away." His eyes drift to the floor, sheepish of his decision.

"I don't want you to feel like you have to hide her. You were married, happily, and she died. It's okay." I wish to reassure him, but I don't know how. I don't have experience with a man who has already been married, who has already loved another. He isn't comfortable discussing her with me, but I know he'll tell me anything I ask about her.

I just feel like I'm betraying her and hurting you when we talk about her.

I can respect his feelings.

"I feel better with the picture down," he says. I step up to him and cup his face.

"I'm honored to be here." He glances up and over my shoulder.

"It's much different than it was. I changed everything after a year. Furniture, paint colors, even tweaked the layout." The house looks like a sprawling ranch from the outside with false dormers, but there's a second floor below us, hidden in the cliff. A porch the length of the back of the house is half screened in and half open, and my eyes are drawn to it.

"Want a complete tour?"

"I do." I nod with a grin, and Giant leads me through all the rooms. On the lower level, a pool table centers a room with another fireplace. A hot tub in a screened-in porch is off this man cave. We climb the stairs again, and I notice a glass-paned door leading to a second floor.

"What's up there?" I ask.

"Nothing of consequence," he answers. It's a vague answer, but I let it slide as he leads me to his room. When we step inside, he tackles me to the bed. "Too soon to have sex with you?"

I chuckle beneath him. "Nope."

+ + +

The strange thing about sex in his bedroom is it didn't feel right. I mean, it felt amazing, but something was off, and I just chalked it up to the distance and reacclimating ourselves to one another. I'd never had a long-distance relationship, and we're still so new to each another. I'm excited to be here and learn more about his life, but we weren't the same people we've been in his bedroom.

After sex, he makes me dinner. This time, it's on a grill on his deck instead of a campfire.

"I bought the house to keep Clara in one place." He smiles weakly. "She didn't want to continue traveling everywhere with me, and some places weren't meant for her. I was career military but didn't make it a full twenty like I planned." He's quiet for a moment. I don't want him to be shy about talking about her, but the hesitation he had during sex is present again. He pours me more wine and opens a second beer for himself while our steaks cook. He continues to tell me minimal details of his military time but emphasizes the distance. "I went for long spans without seeing Clara. It was difficult at times."

I don't know what he's telling me, but I listen all the same.

When he serves dinner, we switch topics to the adoption process. I haven't heard anything more.

"And there's a time constraint, you said? You'd have to petition to remove the baby from the state for any reason." Once I have a child, the finalization process could take a year. I wouldn't be able to leave Illinois without permission from my adoption liaison. Again, I'm not sure where he's going with his line of questions.

Finally, we shift to an easier subject—Oktoberfest and his family.

"You'll meet the whole crew tomorrow." He shakes his head. "I hope they don't scare you away."

"I'm not easily frightened," I say.

"Oh, I've noticed. Although they might be worse than bears."

The night is cool, but a fire pit near the table keeps us warm. Candles scattered around the deck give off a romantic atmosphere. The backdrop of the mountains is reminiscent of our time on a higher ridge. Soft music plays through an outdoor speaker, and Giant reaches for my hand, gently tugging at my fingers. "Dance with me."

When we stand, he pulls me into him, and we sway like teenagers pressed together.

"I'm not a good dancer," he mutters. It's more of a moving embrace, and I'm warm and comfortable in his arms.

"You're just fine," I say. "Quite charming actually."

He huffs before speaking. "I should have danced with you under the stars." The assumption of where is clear, and I tip my head back and gaze upward. There are plenty of stars to be seen here.

"This is pretty perfect," I tell him, dropping my eyes back to him.

"Yes, you are."

I smile. "See? Charming."

"I don't know about that. I think it's more *your* doing. I don't know how to be around you, yet I just be."

My brows pinch. "You don't have to be anyone special or someone different, honey. I love who you are."

He stops moving and shifts to lean against the railing, putting his backside to it while he pulls me between his open legs. His hands loop around my lower back, and my palms rest on his chest.

"Is it strange being here?" Somehow, I know he doesn't mean Georgia.

"Is it strange having me here?"

"Yes and no. I'm happy you're here. More than happy. My home is my home, but I can't shake this feeling…"

"Have you had many women here before?"

"Never."

I'm shocked and honored to be the first, but it also explains his hesitation. "You don't have to replace her." His heart was full of her once. I know I can't compare.

145

Giant sighs. "That's just the thing. You have. It's hard to explain. I...I need you. You're good for me."

My insides warm further. "You're good for me, too." I tip up to kiss him, and our mouths slowly move, drawing out each other's lips— sucking, sipping, savoring. We stand under the aura of stars, within the candlelight and near the fire pit, and breathe in each other with only our mouths. It's the most romantic moment of my life.

+ + +

We don't make love that night, and I don't complain. We kiss and kiss and kiss some more, and then we climb into his bed like an old married couple. Only he tugs me close to him, breathing in my hair and smelling my neck as if taking his time to get used to me in this bed with him.

He wakes early to help his brother, promising me he'll return soon, but by ten o'clock, I'm restless. He hasn't returned my call, and he doesn't have a second car. A quick GPS check confirms I'm eight miles from town. Feeling brave and overzealous, I decide I can walk to Blue Ridge. I haven't really spent time in the small town, other than my one-stop shopping at Duncan's for camping clothes.

By the time I reach a diner in the city's center, I'm drenched in sweat and irritated with myself. I collapse into a booth.

"Hi honey, need some coffee?" A very pregnant woman with a Southern drawl, blond hair, and the bluest of eyes asks of me.

"That'd be great."

"You passing through?" she asks, eyeing my sweat-stained shirt and workout leggings.

"Not exactly. I'm staying with a friend and took it upon myself to be ambitious. I walked into town from his place, but it was harder than I thought. The dips and climbs of the road made it seem a lot longer than eight miles."

She lightly chuckles as she fills my cup. "Where you staying at?"

"George Harrington's."

Coffee dribbles over the edge of my cup, and she quickly pulls a rag from her old-fashioned diner uniform and swipes at the spill.

"Giant?" She gasps.

"Yes," I say confidently, but my smile falters as she stares down at me.

"I can't believe…I mean…that's wonderful." Her voice rises an octave. Another woman passes behind the enthusiastic waitress, and Blondie stops her. "Dolores, this here woman is staying with Giant." Blondie turns back to me, and I read her name tag. Hollilyn. "What's your name, honey?"

I should stop myself from offering too much information, but I can't seem to help it. "Olivet Pierson. Letty." I lift a hand to shake hers. Hollilyn shakes mine, and the other woman with piercing eyes stares at me.

"Welcome to Blue Ridge, Letty," the brunette with sad blue eyes says. "I'm Dolores Chance." Dolores of Dolores's Diner. I surmise she is the owner.

"You have a nice place here," I say, taking in the worn-paneling and roughened tile. It's quaint, if tired looking.

"Where you from?" Dolores asks.

"Chicago."

Her brow rises. "And you know Giant…?" Her voice drifts, suggesting I provide an answer.

"It's complicated," I say, waving a hand to dismiss the subject.

"Those Harringtons are." She chuckles lightly and pats my forearm. "You let Hollilyn know what you need. Enjoy your stay."

I order a breakfast of eggs and bacon and check my phone again. No response from Giant. I've also noticed my service goes in and out.

I randomly scroll through social media and my emails until Hollilyn returns with my food. A few minutes later, a man enters the diner and greets Hollilyn. While I eat, I have the strangest sense of them watching me. Finally, I look up and Hollilyn approaches.

"I didn't want to disturb you, but this is Jaxson Rathstone. He's Giant's nephew and works with him at the brewery."

Jaxson tensely smiles and extends a hand. It's clear he doesn't want to be introduced to me as he tersely greets me. "Nice to meet you."

"She says she's staying with your uncle," Hollilyn offers.

"Hollilyn," he hisses. He's a good-looking man, and I'm guessing late twenties for his age. His eyes are all Harrington. Dark and intense.

"What? I just thought you'd like to meet her." Hollilyn turns to me, and Jaxson mouths, "I'm sorry," from behind her. I smile and shake my head.

"Have you seen your uncle this morning?" I pick up my phone as way of excuse. "Having trouble with reception."

"He's still at the warehouse. I'm heading over there after I grab a coffee. *To go.*" He reaches for Hollilyn's elbow, and she steps away from the table, catching the hint to fetch his drink. As she walks away, he tips his head toward her. "Sorry about that."

"No worries." I pause. "I'd drive to the warehouse, but I don't have a car." I don't know why I offer this information, but Hollilyn must have sonic ears because from her place near the coffeepot, she hollers, "Jaxson can give you a ride."

I look up, taking pity on the mid-twenties man. With his dark brown hair and matching eyes, I can see a slight resemblance to his uncle and wonder what Giant looked like as a younger man. "I bet your mother warned you about stranger danger. You don't need to give me a ride. I'll just find an Uber." The words tumble out before I know if Blue Ridge even offers the service.

"You'll be hard pressed to find that here." He chuckles. "And my mother also warned me about one-night stands and look where it got me." He winks as he nods in the direction of Hollilyn.

I'd be taken aback by the insult if Hollilyn hadn't approached, swatted Jaxson on the arm, and then said, "You love me."

He chuckles without directly answering her, but his eyes light up, and I imagine he does love her.

"I can give you a ride. You look innocent enough." He winks again, and I decide charming must be a trait of Harrington men.

21
Oktoberfest

[Giant]

"Letty?" My tone rings surprised as I see her standing in my office door, a bit disheveled, with my nephew next to her. Charlie turns in his seat. We've been discussing a few things—legal stuff—and I note the time on my phone. I'm two hours later than I planned to be. I also have a few missed messages from her. She's been waiting for me.

Shit.

Thankfully, she doesn't look pissed.

"Imagine my surprise at finding this pretty lady at the diner," my nephew says, all flirtatious for someone about to have a baby with a girl he won't admit he loves. "And she says she's staying with you."

"How did you get to the diner?"

"I walked." She leans against the doorjamb, crossing her arms, which only emphasizes the outline of her body. Thick breasts. Hourglass hips. Her hair sits in a messy bun at the base of her neck. She looks edible, and I'm upset again that I didn't take the opportunity last night. My head got in the way of my heart, and I became overwhelmed with her in my place. Letty is so vibrant and energetic, and I like having her here. We should have had sex all night, but my bedroom shut me down, and I wonder if it's the picture of Clara *in* my dresser.

Or was it guilt that I'd finally moved on?

Charlie had been giving me a pep talk before Letty arrived.

"How you doing with Letty here?"

"Wonderful." I sighed.

"And it's not strange in the house?"

"It's very strange but in a good way." I smiled, thinking of our romantic dinner on my porch. I pulled out all the stops, surprising myself at how much I wanted everything perfect for her.

"Mati said she had trouble with it." Charlie means our younger sister whose new love was an old friend. My sister lost her husband in a

149

car accident over a year ago. Needless to say, she moved on much sooner than I did.

"You know Mama's going to have a field day with this."

Yes, my mother who called only a few days ago to arrange another dinner between myself and Alyce Wright. I'm worried I'm feeding Letty to the bears, but I also think my mother's going to love her.

"And your relationship is open, right?" My brother's marriage was full of deceit, so I'm certain he means honesty, not a relationship where we see other people. At least, I hope we aren't seeing other people. I'm not seeing anyone else, and I don't want Letty to either. Like I told her, we'll work this distance thing out.

I spent several months each year apart from my wife throughout our twenty years of marriage, sometimes up to eighteen months back during the Iraq War.

And how well did that really work? my heart whispers.

It made us distant and lonely even in the presence of each other. We loved one another, but we didn't know one another after my years of service and separation.

"Letty," Charlie says, standing from his seat and offering a hand to her. "I'm Charlie."

"The mayor brother," she confirms, and her cheeks flush. She must be thinking about her phone call to his office.

"Sure." He chuckles.

"There are so many of you. I keep it straight by associating your profession with your name."

"Oh goodness, what's his profession?" Charlie teases, glancing over at me.

"Resident sex god."

I choke on air.

Charlie stammers.

Jaxson bursts out laughing.

"Giant, she's a definite keeper," Jaxson says once he settles his laughter, sounding like James, the biker brother.

"Well, uhm…on that note. I'll leave you to it," Charlie says, turning red around the collar. "I mean, I'll leave you to do it." His eyes widen. "I mean—"

"I think we get it," I say, standing.

"I didn't mean to clear the room," Letty says, a sly grin on her face.

"Oh, we were only hiding out from Billy. Pub owner brother," Charlie clarifies. "He's a pain in the ass today."

"I can't wait to meet him," Letty teases as I reach her, and she steps under my offered arm.

"Don't be too eager," I say, leaning to kiss her forehead.

"Aww, you two are just the cutest," Jaxson drawls, sounding more like his mother, my sister.

"Mama's gonna have a field day," Charlie repeats, pushing my nephew out the door and pulling the door closed behind him.

"I really didn't mean to interrupt," Letty says, looking up at me. I reach around her and lock the door.

"And I really didn't mean to be gone so long. I'm sorry." We only have so much time together, and I should be hanging out with her, not my brother. I can be with him on the days she isn't here.

"So sex god, huh?"

"That was too much, wasn't it?"

"Maybe we should test it out." I lean forward and kiss her, urgent and earnest. Why didn't I make love to her last night? In my office, I'm as turned on as she always makes me, and within seconds, I'm moving her toward my desk.

"You said you never kissed a bearded man before," I tease, keeping my mouth against hers. "How about desk sex?"

"Here?" she chokes, excitement mingling with her surprise. I love surprising her, and I love how she surprises me by letting me do what I want with her body. *You love her*, my heart screams, but I ignore it. It's too much, too fast. I can't.

I hitch Letty up onto the edge of my desk.

"You walked to town? I'm a terrible host."

"I was getting antsy. Too much energy waiting for you."

"And how ready are you for me?" I slip my hand between her thighs and palm her over her yoga pants, but it isn't enough. She tilts up her hips, and I tug down her pants, underwear too. Sliding a finger into her wet center, I find my answer. *So ready for me.* I rush to undo my belt and lower my pants. "God, you make me do crazy things." I exhale as I drag myself against her wet folds, readying myself to enter her. She tips back on her elbows, her legs spread wide.

"You make me crazy, too," she hums, a pleasant sound mixing with her words. I slip into her, and she falls to her back. Her legs hitch up and wrap around my hips, and I lean forward, bracing my hands on either side of her. I thrust up and pull back, setting a rhythm to keep us attached.

"I'm kind of a mess," she softly says, her hair falling loose of the messy bun as her hands reach above her for the opposite edge of my desk. Papers slip to the floor.

"You're fucking gorgeous," I say, straining as my pace increases. I slip my thumb between us, watching as I play with her clit while I disappear inside her. "I love to watch this. Watch us."

I look up to find her eyes bright and intense on me. She licks her lips as if she wants to speak but fights it.

I love you, my heart hammers. *Tell me you love me, too.*

I shake the thought, falling deeper into her body. Letty closes her eyes, her head tipping to the side as she bites her lip.

"Finish, Letty," I growl, wanting her orgasm on my desk where I'll remember her and this moment each time I sit here. Her back arches as she stills. Clenching me brings the result I desire. I let go inside her, feeling free of the hesitation I felt in my home.

Maybe we should just stay in my office.

Maybe I should just get my head together.

+ + +

That evening, we have dinner inside the Blue Ridge Microbrewery and Pub although the festivities are primarily outside. Billy is insanely busy, along with my sister, Mati, working the tent. Charlie's making his mayoral rounds. Even James and a few of his cronies are present on the outer periphery. But the most important people for Letty to meet are my parents.

George Harrington Jr. is a good judge of character. Elaina Harrington is just judgmental.

"Giant." My mother breathes out my name as though she hasn't seen me in years. It's the same sound of relief she had each time I returned home unharmed. Even when I was harmed, her relief came with the fact I lived.

"And who is this pretty young thing?" my father teases, reaching out to kiss Letty's cheek. Letty offers it and blushes.

"I'm Olivet Pierson. But you can call me Letty."

"And you can call me George." His warm smile eases the tension I didn't know she was holding in. Her shoulders relax. Was she nervous to meet my parents? I guess I'm anxious as well because I exhale when my mother beams a smile at me.

"She's lovely," she mouths as if Letty isn't present and can't hear her. They join us for dinner and unknowingly grill Letty, but she takes all their questions in stride. Good thing she likes to chat and doesn't seem to mind the rapid-fire inquiries coming from my mother.

"Elaina, honey, I think you've asked enough. My only question is which beer do you like best?" my father jokes, cutting off my mother when she gets to question thirty-seven in what is clearly an unwritten list of *are you good enough for my son?* I think I'll make my own decision, thank you very much, Mama.

"Time for the tent," I suggest, and we head out to the overcrowded canopy set up between the pub and the bookstore named BookEnds on the opposite street. The covering takes up the first block of Third Avenue.

"Let me introduce you to a few people," I shout over the volume of beer drinkers slowly getting hammered on Giant Beer. I walk Letty through the crowd, introducing her to Cora Conrad, Mati's best friend, and Alyce Wright, who smiles without hurt feelings when she sees I've got a girl on my arm. I point at James, who nods at Letty, and then we make our way to the temporary bar.

"Billy," I call out. "This is Letty."

L.B. Dunbar

My brother has streaks of silver in his hair while the scruff on his jaw remains jet black, and we tease him that he must color it. His eyes sparkle when he sees Letty, and he wipes his hands on a rag before coming to the end of the bar and pulling her into a hug. He holds on a second longer than my liking, and I force my hand between them.

"She feels nice," he teases, and I want to punch him even though he's only looking to get a rise out of me. He's my brother, and I know he'd never, ever go after my girl, but I don't like the thought that some other man might want her too. When I push him back by the shoulder, he chuckles with a gleam in his eyes.

"I see how it is," he says with a clap of his hands and then rubs them together. Letty laughs, and Billy smiles deeper.

"What's your flavor, honey? I'll let you taste anything you like." The innuendo in my brother's voice raises the hairs on the back of my neck.

"William Forrest Harrington," I warn.

Letty looks back and forth between us a second. "I don't understand that one."

Billy's expression slowly falls, and he tilts his head. "What do you mean, love?"

"Roald Dahl," Letty explains, and Billy's eyes shoot up to me.

"You told her the family secret?" He's aghast. "She really must be special."

I glare at my brother, not liking the direction of his comment.

"Roald Dahl?" a feminine voice says at my side, and I turn to see Roxanne McAllister, owner of the bookstore and my brother's nemesis. One brow rises in question as she glares at Billy. No one understands the deal between these two. They act like they hate each other. Roxanne glances over at Letty. "Billy is the name of a character in a short story called 'The Minpins' by Roald Dahl. It's a cautionary tale about not going into the woods." Roxanne glances back at Billy with malice in her eyes. "Seems appropriate."

Letty covers her lips with two fingers, biting back a chuckle. "Oh my," she says under her breath, and I tug her to me.

"What would you know about playing in the woods?" Billy mocks.

"More than you'd know about reading a book," Roxanne snaps.

Letty's mouth falls open, and I watch as the two spar.

"Oh, good one." Billy covers his chest over his heart with both hands. "Ouch, I'm hurt that I don't read."

"It's better than being anywhere near your wood," Roxanne retorts. Her eyes narrow on Billy.

"Go away," he stammers, shooing her with the back of his hand.

"With pleasure." Then she turns to Letty. "If you need a good book, come visit me."

"And if she needs good wood, she can come to me," Billy adds, puffing up his chest as he bellows his comeback. Only I'm not liking what he said one bit.

"Fuck that," I say, glaring at my brother.

"I didn't mean…" Billy turns red, which isn't easily accomplished on him, and Roxanne chuckles as she turns and walks away.

"That woman…" he groans, turning back for the bar.

"Well, they certainly sound familiar." Letty chuckles, and I peer down at her.

"What do you mean?"

She responds by pointing back and forth between us.

22

Hot tubs are hot.

[Letty]

Tipsy and tired at first, I have renewed energy when we return to Giant's home. I'm not going to be able to fall asleep so easily tonight.

"Mind if I try out that hot tub downstairs?" I ask, my words a bit slow but not too slurred.

"Mind if I join you?"

I'm happy he asked. We've had a good night. Lots of laughs and him holding me under his arm. He's been kissing my temple and making a real show of me as his to this town. People have given us a knowing smile all night, and I feel like they know more than me, but by the time I was three beers in, I no longer cared. I still don't. I just want to continue enjoying him.

We decide to strip naked for the hot tub, and I sink into the bubbly warmth. With the crisp fall air coming through the screens, the juxtaposition of heat from the water is soothing. Giant and I sit opposite each other, shyly smiling while our toes brush underneath the water. Eventually, he grips my ankle and pulls my foot to his mouth. He bites the pad, which causes my knee to jerk, but I'm not as repulsed as when he suggested kissing my feet while we were camping.

"You should put one of these up on the mountain. Maybe at your cabin."

"There is one."

I don't recall seeing it, but I didn't get a good look at his place. In fact, I haven't even seen the inside.

"That place is special to you." He's already explained the inheritance from his pap.

"The house was so dilapidated when Pap gifted it to me. I think he knew I'd need the project when I got home. I'd need the solitude of the woods and the work with my hands. Idle minds are not good for those with dark memories."

My eyes fall to the wound on his shoulder, and my chest aches. I can't imagine him not in the world. Not in my life either. I want to keep him.

"You'll have to show me sometime."

"You really miss it?" he teases, but there's something more in the question.

"It was more than I expected. Peaceful. Serene."

"That's what the brochure would say."

I push water at him. "That's what I'd say. I found a little of myself that I didn't know was missing."

His lips crook in the corner. "Really?"

"I've been a little lost since Hudson. Not that I miss him. Lying, cheating bastard. Then I missed another opportunity with a baby." I chuckle, but my voice saddens. "I just thought I was moving in one direction, and then I wasn't. It's the story of my life. I thought I'd graduate college and go one way and ended up where I'm at."

"And that is…?"

"I sell real estate when I wanted to write books."

His brows pinch, waiting me out. "I was an English major eons ago. What else would I want to do besides teach, which I didn't want to do. I wanted to read and write. Period." I chuckle at myself and my twentysomething dreams.

"And you can't do it now?"

I stare at him, his big brown eyes questioning me with sincerity. "I-I never thought about it. I mean, I work all the time and travel."

"Do you like that?"

"No," I offer a little too harshly and a little too quick. "It's a job."

"Could you do it anywhere? Sell real estate?"

"I wouldn't want to." The words rush out again, and his eyes widen. *Why is he looking at me like that?* "I mean, I wouldn't want to sell real estate somewhere else because I don't really want to sell it at all." I can't believe I'm admitting this to him. I don't think I've even admitted it to myself. I'm miserable at my job, but saying it out loud makes me feel guilty. It's a decent job, and I need the money for a baby.

"If you could do anything, anywhere, what would you do?"

157

L.B. Dunbar

"Write books," I say a little more confidently. "I'd write a book."

"About romance?" he teases, wiggling his brow.

"Well, I certainly have good material lately," I flirt.

"Sex god." He pats his large chest.

"Among other things." I giggle. It's so much more than sex. I feel connected to him in a way I can't explain. Maybe it's because of the mountain and our experience up on the ridge. I proved to myself I could camp, and he opened me up to an adventure I didn't know I needed.

After covering his face with bubbles, he pulls himself from the tub. "I'm too warm."

He's hot, actually. So hot. His broad chest. The patch of hair. The trail leading lower. His dick, which isn't extended but still large. His arms. His hands. I love this man.

Even if it seems too soon, I love him.

His eyes dip, and his grin turns mischievous. "Let's go upstairs."

+ + +

I'm wrapped in a towel covering the middle of me while Giant has one wrapped around his waist. I lead the way and note the time over the clock on his stove.

It's after two in the morning.

As we cross the living room, heading for his bedroom, Giant cups my elbow and tugs me to a stop. I turn to him, and he leads me between the furniture to the well-worn brown leather chair.

"Sit," he commands, his voice deep and rough, and a tingle runs up my spine. I sit with the towel still around me, but he untucks it as he lowers to his knees before me. "Sit back."

The leather is cool after the heat of the hot tub as I lean back, and he pulls the towel out from under me. He scoops under my knees and drags me to the edge of the cushion. Then he lowers his head and laps across my seam. I flinch at the sudden touch—cool on warm again. He smiles into the crease. Then he sucks on my clit, and I fall under the spell of his tongue. Charmed.

The flat pad separates me, dipping between the folds as his mouth deepens the seductive kiss on my lower lips. His head bobs, and he moans against sensitive skin. My feet lift for his shoulders, and my fingers delve into his hair.

"Cricket"—he sighs—"you make me so wild. I want to do all kinds of things to you."

"I want you to do everything to me." I can't think of one thing I'd deny this man.

He continues to work me with his mouth until I'm on edge.

"Finish." One word and I want to do as he says. "Scream, Cricket. Fill this house."

He nips me, and I let loose. My knees fold against his head, and my fingers tug at his hair. I call out his name, filling the room as he asked. I'm hardly done when he tugs me from the chair.

"Flip." Again, I do as he says, my knees hitting the soft material of my damp towel on the floor as he presses my upper body to the cushion of the chair. My nipples peak to attention as they meet the cool leather. His hand twists into the messy bun I made to keep my hair up while in the hot tub, and he fists it, giving it a tug as he slams into me. I cry out. "Again."

He pulls back and thrusts forward, the angle deep. Every time I think he can't reach anywhere new in me, he does. He rocks his hips, forcing me upward before slipping into my channel. Then he repeats the motion.

"So wild," he mutters behind me. "I can't stop myself. I want you so much." His voice strains as he takes me harder, faster, deeper. I'm close once again, and then he pulls out.

"No," I whine, but he lifts me under my armpits, and we shift positions once again. He sits in the chair and guides me by my hips to climb over him. I easily slip down his stiff length, filling myself once again.

"This," he says. "I want to see you fall apart over me. In my chair. Every time I sit here, I'm going to picture you over me, under me. In my mouth. On my dick."

His words spur me on, and I lift and lower, holding his shoulders as I gyrate over him. I stroke at him in a way my clit rubs on the bone near his dick. The sensation is divine, and he presses at my hips, forcing me back and forth.

"Take me," he groans as I ride him, finding my pleasure until he's hissing.

"I can't...Too much...Feels so good." He stills, and the pulsing within sets me off. I come, digging my nails into his shoulders as he holds my hips, pinning me to him. Moonlight streams into the room, hitting a section of his face as his neck strains.

Sex god. Mountain man. Lumbersexual. He defines each word.

Suddenly, I'm tugged down to him, and he wraps his arms around my back, holding my shoulder blades so my bare breasts cup his face.

"I love this," he says, kissing between them. "I love everything about you." He looks up at me with such adoration and fear and hesitation and surprise. I lean down and kiss him soft and tender, telling him I feel all the same emotions.

When we finally fall onto his bed with him on his back and me on my stomach next to him, I reach for his jaw and scratch the scruff.

"I love you," I whisper before exhaustion sweeps me under.

23
Waffles with little ears

[Letty]

"Papa." The word jolts me upright in Giant's bed, and I turn for him as he's already leaping out from under the covers. We fell into bed naked and exhausted, and I twist to find bright daylight streaming through his windows.

The patter of little feet resonates down the hall, coming toward this room, and Giant stands, reaching for his pants on the chair and tugging them on. He looks around the room for something and then takes three steps to his highboy dresser. Briskly opening the drawer, he pulls too hard, and it jams. He slips a hand into the slim opening, tugs out a T-shirt, and roughly pulls it over his head. Another call comes closer.

"Papa."

My heart drops to my stomach, which roils and coils, and not just from the excessive amount of beer I drank last night.

Giant steps for his bedroom door, not even acknowledging me, and wraps a hand around the handle.

"Papa?" I question, bile climbing up my throat. *As in Dad?* Giant's hand pauses on the doorknob, but his back remains to me.

"Grandpa," he clarifies, without looking back. His forehead hits the wood barrier to the hall for a mere second before he opens the door only a crack. "I'll get rid of them. Just. Stay. Here." His words are almost angry as if gruff Giant has returned. He slips through the opening he made and shuts the door behind him.

The second the door closes, I rush for his bathroom, emptying the contents of my stomach. *Stay.* What kind of command is that? Am I dog?

When I stand from the toilet and look in the mirror, my face is ashen. My lips dull. My eyes too bright.

Papa. Grandpa.

He has fucking children. He has grandchildren.

161

L.B. Dunbar

I lunge for the toilet again, but nothing other than liquid comes out. On shaking legs, I stand, splash water on my face, and then brush my teeth.

Stay here. I'll get rid of them.

Oh, no. Not this again. I will not be invisible.

I'm forty and about to do the ultimate walk of shame—meet the children after fucking their father senseless. I fix my hair into a tight bun and slowly cross his bedroom for my bag. I pull on clean clothes. Jeans and a long-sleeve shirt are the best items I have left. I wore a dress last night to the Oktoberfest, but it smells like beer and…it's down by the hot tub where I left it.

I pinch my cheeks for color and pull on my proverbial big girl panties.

"Well, here goes everything," I whisper as I tug open the door a little too harshly and step into the hall. The noise of little girl voices and an older female fills the great room. A second strong feminine voice joins the first.

As I step to the edge of the room, I stop when two sets of eyes meet mine.

"Dad?" the one questions while the other just stares at me.

Giant turns with a girl roughly three years old in his arms. Another little one sits on a stool at the kitchen island.

"Hello," I say, my voice cracking.

He has children. He has grandchildren.

Giant looks from me to the girls and back. The little one in his arms wiggles to be released to a second stool. I feel as if I'm walking through deep water as I cross the living room, approaching the gaping mouth, wide-eyed women who appear to be in their mid-to-late twenties.

I extend a shaking hand, hoping they can't see how much I tremble. "I'm Olivet Pierson. Letty." I choke on my own name. Not a Livvy or a Vette or an Olive. Just Letty. Invisible.

One young woman circles the island, extending her hand for mine. Her hair is a light amber color, but her eyes match her father. "Ellie. Ellie McCabe. These are my daughters, Kali." She points at a light brunette with eyes matching most Harrington offspring. "And Essie." The second

162

Silver Brewer

brunette has brilliant green eyes and mischief in her little smile. She lowers her face away from my prying gaze. "And this is my sister, Sarah." Ellie points at the other woman.

Awkward silence falls around us as Giant still doesn't speak. He isn't looking at me, and I refuse to look over at him.

"We're here for breakfast," Ellie explains.

"Well, then," I say to the little girls. "What are we having?"

"Waffles," they cheer in unison. "With ears," the younger one—Essie—adds. I look up at her mother in question.

"Mickey Mouse ones. My dad..." Her eyes shift to Giant. "He makes them when we come for breakfast."

My heart is ripped into tiny little shreds, and while I should pack my bags and storm out of this house, never to look back, my pride wouldn't allow that scene. Instead, I'll suffer through this breakfast, humiliated and awkward, and make my presence known while feeling empty in my chest.

"Waffles with ears sound delicious," I say, stepping toward the kitchen as if I know where anything is.

24

Relationships of fathers

[Giant]

The hurt in her eyes pains me more than the bullet wound near my shoulder. She won't look at me but keeps the tight smile on her face as she addresses my daughter.

Ellie, named after my mother, is twenty-eight years old and a beautiful mother in her own right to little Kali, five, and Essie, three.

"We live in Atlanta," Ellie explains, speaking on behalf of herself and her sister.

Sarah, so like her mother, is quiet, shy, and stunned. She hasn't closed her mouth yet while Ellie nervously chatters, filling the awkward silence while she rattles in my cabinets.

"Daddy makes breakfast the last Sunday of each month. That's our deal." Ellie isn't being defensive. She's stating a fact. Breakfast. The word distracts me, and I step around the island.

"I got it," I mutter, pulling out the Mickey Mouse waffle iron I thought would be a fun treat for the girls, and entice them to want to come to my house.

"I teach ninth grade English," Ellie states, and my chest rips open again. Letty told me only last night how she studied English and wished to write a book.

I love you.

There's no denying what she said to me before she fell asleep.

Yet she hates me today, and I don't blame her.

It isn't that I forgot about my monthly breakfast date. It's just...I forgot it was this weekend. And I forgot to mention I had children although I didn't really forget them.

"What are you reading with your class?" Letty asks, prompting Ellie to keep talking.

"Close your mouth," I mutter to Sarah as I pass her for the refrigerator. She clamps it shut and shakes her head.

"I'm Sarah," she says as if Ellie didn't already handle introductions five minutes ago. Letty smiles at her and reaches out a hand. She doesn't offer to shake so much as wraps both hers around Sarah's and squeezes.

"It's nice to meet you, Sarah." The affection warms my insides as Sarah struggles with social situations. Her shyness keeps her from acting confident. "And what do you do?"

"I'm studying to be a veterinarian, but for now, I work at an animal clinic."

"What's your favorite animal?" Letty prompts, encouraging Sarah to speak. My breathing comes quicker. She's being so nice to my girls. My girls who were shell-shocked by someone other than their mother coming out of my bedroom. My girls who have told me to date, but I told them it would never happen.

I break eggs and add flour, but I can't even calculate the measurements in my head. I'm making a mess. A mess of everything.

Letty comes around the counter and gently pushes at my hip. "Why don't you let me?"

"I thought delivery was your specialty." I'm trying to tease her, but my voice remains stilted as I speak.

"I think I can handle a few waffles. With ears," she adds, addressing my granddaughters. Kali looks up, hopeful of success. She's so like her mother. Essie, on the other hand, is a little deviant like her father. The absentee dad. I was like him. Always working. Never home. Missing everything important to my girls. I didn't want that for the next generation, yet Ellie picked a man like me. Mick is in the military.

"So how did you meet Daddy?" Ellie asks, interrupting my thoughts of her husband.

"I wanted to buy his land."

"Pap's land?" Sarah asks, horrified at the thought. She enjoys it almost as much as I do, loving the wildlife in the woods.

"Yes. But then I had a change of heart."

Kill me. She's driving the knife deeper because it's *my* heart that changed, and she'll never love me after this.

"And when was this?" Ellie asks, digging for more details.

165

"A month ago." Letty stops whipping the batter. *Has it really only been a month?* I feel like I've known Letty a lifetime. I want to know her for a lifetime. I glance from Letty to Ellie, begging my daughter for a moment.

"Let's go wash our hands," Ellie announces, and the two littles jump from the stool. "Sarah, come help us." Sarah stares at her sister a moment until Ellie, not so inconspicuously, nods to follow her. Kali skips. Essie follows. Letty turns her head toward the French door leading to the second floor.

"Nothing of consequence? Their rooms are up there, aren't they?"

"I can explain everything," I mutter.

Her eyes close, and I'm certain she's heard those words before without good results.

"I should leave," she hisses under her breath.

"I don't want you to." With everyone out of the room, I tug Letty to my chest, where she lands against me like a brick wall, stiff and tense. *Noooo*, my heart screams. The feeling reminds me of Clara, and I want to smash the bowl of batter and throw the waffle iron across the room, which would be so unlike me. Clara wasn't cold, but she didn't melt into me like Letty does. She didn't respond to my touch like Letty. She didn't give me…

"I need a minute," Letty mutters, disrupting my thoughts and pulling away from me. She heads for the back deck, and my stomach flips with unease. I can't relive what I had with Clara. I loved her, and I don't fault her for anything we had in our relationship, but Letty has been so much more to me, so liberating, and I can't handle her shutting down. In bare feet, the wood slats of my kitchen floor feel cold, chilling me in the briskness of the morning. I stare out the window after Letty, and my hand slams on the counter.

Dammit. Dammit. Dammit.

"Dad?" Ellie stands before me, and I quickly look up.

"Yeah, honey?" Eyes which match mine stare at me, apprehensive and curious.

"She's pretty."

I lick my lips. "I know." She's the prettiest woman I've ever seen. Clara had a simple beauty, a grace about her quiet nature, but Letty is stunning. *Don't compare*, I criticize.

"She seems nice."

"She is." I exhale, crossing my arms over my chest as I lean back against the opposite counter. Letty's kind, and when I consider her adoption reasons, she has a good heart. She's a good person.

"And you like her. I mean, she spent the night so…"

"I do. Like her. I…feel a lot of things for her." I'm not certain I should be having this conversation with my twenty-eight-year-old daughter. My girls and I aren't emotionally close. I'd been gone too long, too often, and when I finally came home, hurt and broken, I didn't know how to interact with them. Then their mother died, leaving me with two teenage daughters and no clue how to be a parent. Thank goodness for my mother and Mati. I did the best I could, but we lived separate lives. It's one reason I lost them both to Atlanta.

"It's okay to love her, Dad."

I stare at my girl. *When did she become such an adult?*

"I really fucked up here, Ellie Belly."

She chuckles at the long-gone nickname. "Well, unfuck it."

I should admonish her for her language, but instead, I just laugh. She steps up to me, and I open my arms, pulling her into my chest and kiss the top of her head.

"Dad," Sarah softly speaks, and I glance over Ellie's head to see her sister hesitantly looking back at me. I release one arm, holding it open for her. As Sarah walks into the embrace, I can't remember the last time I held them each close, held them collectively like this. I shudder to think when it might have been. *Ten years ago.*

"I like her," Sarah says, giving her stamp of approval.

"I like her, too," I repeat to my younger daughter. "In fact, I think I love her."

Sarah pulls back from the hug with tears in her eyes as she glances up at me. "It's about time," she whispers.

Time to move on.

+ + +

"Are you going to be our Mimi?" Kali asks, and I drop my fork. Letty nervously chuckles from her seat at the dining table.

"No, sweetheart."

My stomach drops next. *Why not?* Why can't she be their grandmother? Would she not consider marrying me? Both thoughts bring me up short. A bigger thought is why am I thinking such a thing.

"Oh," Sarah says, glancing from Letty to me. "Oh, I misunderstood."

Letty finally looks at me, concern in her eyes, before gazing back at my youngest daughter.

"I thought—" Sarah stammers.

"Okay, time for dishes, waffle ears," Ellie announces, cutting off her sister. The girls stand from the table, and the little ones follow. Letty picks up a plate, but Ellie reaches for it. "We wash if he cooks."

"Sounds like a good plan. I need to pack anyway." Her voice sounds as distant as she feels from me.

Ellie stares at Letty. "What do you mean?"

"Well, I live in Chicago."

"Chicago?" Sarah squeaks. "That's like a thousand miles away."

"Exactly," Letty states with a chuckle. "If you'll excuse me a few minutes." She disappears down the hall to my room, and my eyes flip from my girls to the hallway.

"Chicago?" Sarah questions again.

"Dad, go unfuck this," Ellie growls.

"What's unfuck mean?" Kali asks, and Ellie groans.

"Something your father needs to do often, but don't mention it to him." I should chuckle, but instead, I follow my daughter's advice and head for my room like a petulant child about to have my favorite toy removed from me for life.

25
Invisibility cloak malfunction

[Letty]

I start out folding and end up rolling my clothes into a ball before shoving them into my bag. The bedroom door opens and closes behind me, but I don't turn to him.

Suddenly, I'm bitter and resentful when it isn't his fault. He has everything I want. He fell in love. Got married. Had children. Works a dream job. Has a mountain retreat. His life is…perfect.

"Cricket."

The nickname makes me bristle, and I close my eyes, blindly forcing my clothing into my open bag. Two hands land on my shoulders, and I stiffen.

"Please. *Please*, don't be like this."

"You made me invisible again. You made them invisible." I spin to face him.

"What do you mean?" His face is stricken, and anguish fills his eyes. He really has no idea. "Hudson used to do this. Treat me like I wasn't present. People would be surprised to learn he had a girlfriend or to discover we lived together." I pause, drawing in a deep breath. "How could you do this? You lied to me."

"I…" He closes his lips as quickly as opening them. "I omitted."

"Same difference!" I snap. Hudson omitted telling people he had a girlfriend. He didn't acknowledge my opinion or decisions. He forgot to tell me he never planned to marry me. I turn away from Giant again, but he stops my restless packing by wrapping his arms around my chest, pinning mine to my sides. His front to my back, I don't want to melt into him, but I want to melt. I close my eyes once again, encouraging myself to stay strong and hoping my tears won't fall. I'm too angry to cry.

"I didn't want to share you with them."

169

"Don't you mean *them* with *me*?" I mutter to the window before me, noting the mountainous view. My heart breaks a little when I recall our time up on the ridge.

"No. That's not what I mean." He spins me in his arms and holds my shoulders again. "I didn't want to share you with anyone. Not yet. You're mine. Not mine as in possession, but as in just for me, and selfishly, I wanted to keep you all to myself."

"That's bullshit. I met your family this weekend."

"My siblings. My parents. But my girls…it's different."

There are so many things I want to sling at him, but I bite my lip. His girls should be the most important people I meet, but maybe that's why I haven't met them. Maybe he didn't want me to ever meet them. An introduction would be another crossover between me and his past.

"I didn't know how they would react, and then I didn't want their reaction because I knew it didn't matter. I wouldn't give you up, no matter what they said. Then they surprise me and like you, which shouldn't have been a surprise because you're amazing. It's just been strange for me..."

"Because this is where you lived with Clara, and now I'm here."

"Yes. No," he says, his brows lifting. "I don't know." His tongue-tied chatter could almost be endearing, charming even, but I'm no longer looking to be charmed by him.

"I don't intend to replace her."

"That's not it. That's not it at all." He tugs me as he walks backward until he slumps down to sit on his bed. His hands come around my lower back, trapping me between his open thighs. "I-I loved my wife, Letty, but she was nothing like you. I don't want to compare the two of you because you are both unique women, but Clara and I, we fell into a routine. We fell into silence, and then she got sick. I…I don't know what I'm saying. I'm not explaining this right. All I know is you come along, and you're just life to me, Letty. Noise and energy and just everything I didn't know I was missing. It isn't that I don't want you here. It's that I don't want you to leave. Ever."

My hands come to his shoulders, hating how much I want to hold him. How much I love the feel of him under my palms, and how much I want to believe him.

"What are you saying?"

"I'm saying I think I'm in love with you, and I don't want you to go home."

"Giant," I begin, looking up and around this room. "You can't even make love to me in this room. Her picture is jammed in your dresser. She's all around you."

"No, no, Cricket," he says, lowering his head into my stomach.

"I can't stay here," I whisper. "I need to go home."

He's already had all I've been longing for, and the last thing he'll want to do is do it all over again. And I don't want to settle for jumping in midship. I want to fall deeply in love, get married and have children. I'm selfish, I guess.

I push back at his head and cup his jaw to tip his face up. Leaning down to kiss his lips, I intend to keep it tender, but the moment our lips touch, his mouth opens, devouring mine with tongue and teeth. We gnash and spar and nip until I need to pull back before I give in. Before I let him take me on this bed where he can't make love to me.

"I...I think you're pretty amazing, Giant Harrington. The best."

I step out of his embrace, allowing our fingers to be the last connection before releasing him. Then I return to packing, keeping my back to him. I won't let him see the tears because crocodile tears have no place in this bedroom any more than I do.

+ + +

"Letty, may I see you in my office?" Uncle Frank's tone warns me, and a cold ripple runs down my spine. It's been ten days since I saw Giant. Ten days since his first email and I worry Frank has broken through the intra-net and scoped out the letter.

Cricket,
I spent long periods of time without talking to people. Times when

171

I wasn't allowed to communicate. I can be silent and quiet and still, but you make me restless, and I want to talk. You aren't speaking to me, and I'm unnerved by it. I miss your voice. Your chatter. Your laugh. I miss the beat of your heart and the warmth of your body next to mine.

I'm not an expert with words, so I'm going to ramble here. Bear with me a bit.

When I was eighteen, all I wanted was to join the military. I wanted out of my town, away from my dad and his business. Pap understood. I was quiet and large and not good at much. Clara was similar. Shy, bookish, and interested in me. I was shocked. Pap was not. He told me she was a good woman, but I needed bigger things.

The CliffsNotes version is this. I enlisted. Clara went to college. We eloped. I went to basic training and was deployed. Home on leave, she got pregnant. Motherhood was what she wanted more than anything. Another tour. Another baby. I'd moved up the ranks. Pap warned me I was going too far and gone too much. I didn't know how to explain myself. I didn't know what I wanted. I wasn't certain I could come home. Then he died. I got shot months later and didn't have any choice. I was surly and upset, suffering from PTSD and guilt. Clara stood by me. Then she got sick. I stood by her.

I don't want to romanticize us, Clara and me, but I don't want to defame what we had either. On the other hand, you're special to me, different, and I felt guilty. For wanting your wild nature and craving it. Guilty for knowing the sensation of being with you—inside you—and having it be some of the best moments of my life. I miss your touch. I miss your kiss. I miss the way you look at me as if you see me and understand what I need. You're the opposite of me, yet we mesh.

Silver Brewer

You're always on my mind and in my heart, Letty. I want us to work, and I know we can.

I'm sorry I didn't tell you the truth about them. I'm sorry I didn't tell them about you.
I'm just sorry.

Please come back to me.
All my love,
Giant

I'd read it so many times I have it memorized, yet I still haven't responded. A new email came every day after the first. He told me more about his girls, about their lives, and then he told me about the brewery. I cried each time I received one.

"Uncle Frank." I address the only father figure I'd known since childhood. My mother's brother has been a pillar of support, but it doesn't mean I'm close to him. Dayna is his angel. I'm his disappointment.

He motions for me to sit in one of the two chairs across from him. His large modern desk of glass on a metal frame is cold like his demeanor toward me.

"You've been different these last few days," he begins, folding his hands over something on his desk. "More focused. More driven." I've thrown myself into the job I finally admitted I hate as a means of distraction. Determined to get any commission and convince the foster system I can be a parent has become my new goal. Seeing Giant with his children opened my eyes to one thing—I don't want to miss out on the things I want most in life, even if I do them in a slightly backward manner.

"We'd like to send you to Tennessee to look at a property. Securing it will make up for the loss in Blue Ridge."

Nothing in the world can make up for the loss I feel from that town. I miss Giant like crazy, but I'm too stubborn to give in and respond to him. He lied to me. He kept his children from me. He kept me from them.

173

"What are the specs?" I halfheartedly listen as my uncle drones on, knowing I'll review the material later before attending the meeting. My thoughts drift to Giant and almost hitting him with my car. His sweaty, broad back. His muscular, sculpted chest. The hair leading lower.

"Olivet," my uncle snaps. "Are you listening?"

"When do I leave?"

"Tomorrow." It's a Thursday.

"I'm good to go." I stand and reach for the folder I assume holds the necessary information. It's a small area in the Smoky Mountains, not dissimilar to Blue Ridge. It's also only an hour or so from it.

Country roads...take me to the place I belong.

26
Emails and phone tales

[Giant]

Eleven fucking days.

This woman is torturing me, yet I know she's reading my emails. Knowing her, she can't possibly ignore them even if she's ignoring me.

We had the longest ride of my life when I drove her to Atlanta later that fateful Sunday. Silence heavier than a ton of snow from the mountain filled my truck. I didn't know what to say, and I admired her conviction not to speak. Not a word.

Eventually, nearing the airport, I pulled over and parked.

"Say something," I begged.

"I don't know what to say." She hugged her purse to her chest the entire hour ride as if it was a life preserver holding her afloat. *"Lying is the one thing I can't handle, Giant."*

That ex of hers was a fucking idiot to cheat, which is a lie, and I've done something similar. Only my heart is hers.

"I want to see you again."

"I don't know," she replied, her voice falling lower. Her lip trembled, and she bit the corner. I reached for her chin, forcing her to look over at me.

"You're so far away," I whispered. She kept her distance, and I didn't like it. For a woman who followed my lead or made me go with the flow, her stiff demeanor rattled me. *"I don't want you to leave."*

It wasn't fair of me to ask her to stay. Even after all I learned.

Charlie helped me investigate adoptions in Georgia. I wanted to ask Letty if she'd consider moving here and adopting here, so we could be closer and see each other more often. It was a selfish thought. Asking her to give up her home and job was a lot, and then...my girls. I didn't mean to hide them. I meant what I said. I didn't want to share her. Once Letty met them, my girls would want more of her, like me, but I didn't want to give her up to them. Not yet.

175

L.B. Dunbar

Letty stared at me across the bench seat of my truck. "What more are you hiding?" she asked.

"Nothing. I swear. There's nothing else to know." It's the truth. I'm a simple man. I made a mistake here, but there's no other agenda.

"I don't know anything about you."

She's wrong. So wrong. She has opened me up just as she claims I've done to her.

"That's not true. You know I'm good at throwing an ax. I can make eggs over a campfire. I like to wash your hair. I love your laugh." I'd give anything for her laughter instead of the tears filling her eyes.

"Giant." She exhaled. "I can't do this."

"Why not?"

"Because you already had everything," she blurted.

"What do you mean?"

"Marriage and children. Love and happily ever after."

"She died. How was that happily ever after?" I hate myself for snapping at her or even considering that Clara and I hadn't been happy. We were. We were content.

A tear trickled down her face, and I popped the latch on her seat belt, tugging her to me.

"Cricket. Please," I groaned, holding her to my chest and stroking my hand down her hair. I inhaled her scent, hoping to memorize it. Apricots. It made my mouth water. She is spring rain to my snow showers.

Thankfully, her arms wrapped around my neck, and she hugged me back. I thought we were good, and then I dropped her off at the airport.

My heart crashed as she walked away, and I wondered if Clara felt this loss each time I left home. This fear that she'd never see me again. That I'd never return.

That's how I felt when Letty entered the terminal and then didn't answer my emails.

"Whatcha drinking?" The teasing sound of my brother snaps me from the memory. I'm sitting in Blue Ridge Microbrewery and Pub on a Thursday evening.

I'd sent Letty an email every day since she left me, telling her everything I haven't said and more. I kept it light, reminding me of the communication I once had while in the military. The action sparks my determination to make it work with Letty. I've had a long-distance relationship before—across an ocean—so I can do this again across a few states. It's only a short plane ride between us.

"Whiskey," I say, rolling the glass between my fingers on the bar. I'm more of a beer man, but tonight calls for the hard stuff. Eleven days. No conversation. I'm the only one talking in those emails.

I look up to find Billy watching me. "What's going on?"

I'm not an open book with my siblings. I don't delve into emotions, digging into my feelings, but I need to tell someone.

"Letty left me."

Billy's forehead furrows. "You broke up?"

"Something happened." I pause. "I didn't tell her about my girls, and they practically caught us in bed."

Billy chuckles while I fail to find the humor in the situation. Reading my countenance, he coughs into his fist and tries to look sympathetic. The forced expression is lost on him. He's too good natured.

"And…

"She was upset I hadn't told her I had children."

"Does she know about Clara?"

"She does."

"And she wasn't upset about her?"

"I told her all the facts about Clara. I omitted the part about children."

Billy whistles. "Why?"

"I didn't want to share her." It's the sappiest, most honest thing I've ever told anyone.

"What does that mean?" Billy chuckles.

"I knew the girls might love her, get attached, and I just didn't want to share." I pause, swiping a hand down my beard. "She wants things, and I didn't know if I could go down that path again." *Marriage and children. Love and happily ever after.* Then again, it's all I've thought of

177

L.B. Dunbar

since she left. I can see myself married to her. I see my daughters accepting her. I see us together. "But I don't want to lose her."

"Seems like the answer is obvious," Billy retorts, reaching for the whiskey behind the bar and refilling my glass.

"What's that?"

"Give her what she wants. Then you'll get what you want. It's win-win."

"Who's winning what?" my sister asks as she comes to stand next to me. It's rare to see her at the bar on a weekday evening. Her girls' volleyball team is headed to the state finals.

"Giant wants Letty. Letty wants Giant. It's win-win."

"She doesn't want me."

"What did you do?" Mati asks. How is it always the man's fault, yet I know I'm to blame in this round with Letty.

"I omitted."

"Is that like lying but calling it another name?" Mati's eyes meet mine, and her brow arches.

"I didn't lie." I meekly smile. "I withheld the truth." It wasn't like I *denied* my daughters existed. I just didn't mention them. The justification sounds bad, even in my head.

"And the difference is...?"

I shake my head as my youngest sibling speaks like our mother. Mati pulls up a stool next to me.

"Although I guess I shouldn't talk," she states, lowering her voice. Billy pulls out another shot glass and fills it with more whiskey.

"What do you mean?" Billy asks.

"I've got to tell Denton something, but let's keep to Giant. This is important. You love the woman, right?"

"How do you know that?" I question, and Mati rolls her eyes.

"Giant, when you take a woman up to Pap's or bring her to your home, and you've never done those things before, it's got to be more than a shag."

"Shag?" Billy smirks, disgust on his face. "Is this England? He's bonking her."

178

Mati rolls her eyes again. "He's not bonking her. He's in love with her."

What the hell is bonking?

"You just want everyone to be in love because you are. *Mati and Denton sitting in a tree*," Billy sings.

My brows pinch. "What are you, five?" I huff.

"Forty-six and loving every minute of it." He winks as if I should understand. I don't. I haven't had the cavalier one-night stands my brother's had for the past sixteen years. I've been much more selective, and it feels as if I haven't enjoyed myself until I'm almost fifty.

"Anyway," Mati draws out. Her hand comes to my wrist. "I know it's difficult. You want to move on, but you don't know if you should. You want to feel something again, but what you feel is guilt for wanting that something. *I know*," she stresses, and my sister does know. Her husband. My wife. Both taken too young. "But you have to let go, Giant." Her voice softens. "It's been ten years. She's never coming back, and you already know that. You aren't betraying her. You aren't harming her memory. The memories will always be there, but it's time to make new ones. With your life. The one you're still living."

She's right. And I know she's right.

"It's just…I think I love her, and it all seems so fast."

"Well, nothing can be slower than twenty-seven years." Mati chuckles as that's how long it took her to reconnect with Denton. I don't want that much time to pass. I want twenty-seven years *with* Letty.

"Look, slow, fast—"

"In, out," Billy interjects, thrusting his hips at the bar. Mati slaps the wooden top.

"Can you try to remember I'm your sister for five seconds? Anyway…" she starts again. "I don't think there needs to be a time limit on love or grief. Grief ends when you're done. And love begins when you're ready."

You're so ready for me, Letty. The words drift into my head, reminding me of her on my desk. She is always ready for me, but it's been more than sex. So much more.

"I think I need to get back to Chicago and do some groveling," I say, picking up my phone from where it lies on the bar.

"You've been to Chicago?" Billy asks.

"Try to keep up," Mati teases.

"I need to go," I say, slipping from the stool. My phone buzzes in my hand, notifying me of an email. Hastily, I open it while I stand at the bar because the notification is from her, in response to my last email.

You're so far away.

+ + +

"Cricket." I breath her name into the phone when she answers on the second ring.

"Giant." She sounds equally as breathless.

"Are you okay?" Her email worries me, and I tap my fingers on my steering wheel as I sit in my truck in a parking spot on Main Street.

"I'm...I'm in Tennessee. I know it isn't exactly next door, but it's closer than Chicago, and I wondered if you'd be interested in—"

"Yes."

She giggles, and I smile, a spark of hope flickering before me. "Well, that was easy, but you didn't let me finish."

"I'm easy." I laugh.

"You're very difficult, Mr. Harrington," she teases. "Easy is not a word I'd use to describe you."

"What word would you use?" Say charming. Say anything. Just let me hear your voice. It's so good to hear her voice.

"Does *hard* work?"

"Hard?" I choke out. "I can be hard for you." I don't know where the flirting comes from. I should be apologizing, groveling...Dammit, I should have sent her flowers. I swipe a hand over the thick hairs on my jaw, but she continues to chuckle.

"Well, maybe we could talk before we get to the hard part."

I laugh uneasily. "Talking is the hard part."

"I know." She sighs. "But I've missed your voice."

"Me too. I mean, I've missed yours." *And your smile, your laughter, your arms around me.* "So you're in Tennessee."

"Yeah, I have a meeting tomorrow to look at a property. My uncle's giving me a second chance to make up for losing out on yours." She isn't upset, and I can hear the smile in her voice. "I thought maybe Saturday, or whenever you're free, if you're free...I mean—"

"Just tell me where you are," I snap, harsher than I intend but desperate to get an answer. I press the ignition starter, then reach for the navigation system in my truck.

"I'm in Appleton, just outside Knoxville. Have you ever heard of it?"

"Yes, I have. There's a vineyard near there, right?" I know exactly where she is, and I type in the name of the lodge when she tells me where she's staying. Then I reverse onto Main Street.

"A vineyard, yes." The line goes silent for a moment, but I don't want to let her go.

"So...uhm...how have you been?" I'm not good at small talk. When I called home while I was overseas, Clara did most of the talking, filling me in on the girls, my family, and any other gossip until my time was up.

"Lonely," she admits, and my heart breaks. I know the feeling.

"I'm sorry. I mean, I'm sorry for what happened with the girls. Well, not the girls because they adore you just as I do, but I mean, I'm sorry for not telling you."

"When did you become the chatterbox?" She giggles, and then silence falls another moment. "I know you're sorry. I am too. I might have overreacted a bit, but it was a shock, Giant. I mean you mentioned Clara and motherhood, but you hadn't even hinted at children, and then there they were, staring at me. Literally the elephant in the room."

"I wouldn't say an elephant," I good-naturedly mock. "More like a stunned bear."

"I was stunned but so were they. Are they okay? Their reactions suggest finding a woman in their father's house doesn't happen often." Is she fishing for something? I'm not going to hold anything else inside.

"I already told you, there's never been another woman in my house. Ever. Not my bed, my hot tub, or that damn leather chair I can't sit in without thinking of you."

She softly huffs into the phone. "Then why didn't you tell me?"

Haven't I explained this? I didn't want to share her. "Letty, have you ever wanted something for yourself? Something you didn't know you wanted until it was before you, and then, even though you want to shout to the world, *look what I found,* you're also afraid others will want it too?" I take a deep breath. "I've been longing for something different, some kind of spontaneity that I couldn't name, couldn't imagine, and then, there you were. *You.* You're what I've been longing for." It's all true. My life has been predictable. Routine. I've been waiting for something more, and I finally have it in her.

"I understand what you mean." Her voice drops lower. "It's how I feel about you, too. It scares me."

I'm terrified by what I feel because it seems like too much, too fast. Yet, just as Mati said, how can I put a time limit on such things? I've been waiting a long while for this feeling, so I don't want to easily give it up. Letty remains quiet for another minute. Seems I've taken up her trait of needing to fill the quiet space, so I start talking about my girls.

"They liked you. Ellie called me the next day and asked when I'd see you again, then when would they see you again, and would they get the chance to spend more time with you." It was exactly how I knew they'd react. Curious. Eager. Hopeful. My daughters wanted the best for me, even if we weren't terribly close. We had a routine, so I didn't lose them completely: once a month Sunday breakfast at my house, their choice of days in the month to visit my parents' house, and then every other Wednesday for dinner in Atlanta. Phone calls were once a week because…I didn't have much to say.

"They were sweet once the initial shell-shock dulled a little. Your granddaughters are lovely." There's a sadness in her tone when all I want to do is keep things light, but I know we'll have to dig a little deeper.

"I'm sorry again about the Mimi comment. I don't know where that came from. Mick has parents in South Carolina, and they see them from time to time."

182

"I didn't mind," she replies, and another flash of hope ignites in me. "I just think I'd like to become a mother before being considered a grandmother." She laughs awkwardly. "It seems like the natural progression of things."

"How is that going?"

She explains the progress of her adoption request and how the foster system is hopeful of finding someone for her. She really wants a newborn but will accept any child under five. She wants it to be a boy. "My reasons relate to Owen. I want to make up for where I once lacked." It's a tall order, and no child will be a replacement for the brother she lost. It also wasn't her fault he died. "I think one thing that upset me about your girls is you having them. I'm jealous, Giant. You already raised children, and you're on to grandchildren. I haven't even started yet."

"It isn't a competition," I say. "Or a race."

"I know that," she says, resolve in her voice. "I just…sometimes, I feel like I'm losing time, and I'm frustrated by the process of things." The defeatist tone doesn't suit her, and I want to wrap her in my arms and tell her she can do anything, *have anything*. Sometimes, what we want takes time. Like me finding her.

"You've already had it all." She's quieter as she adds, "The last thing you'd want to do is to start over."

"Don't tell me what I wouldn't want." The words are curt, and I shift on the driver's seat, tightening my hands on the wheel as I mutter a quick apology. I don't want to fight with her because starting over feels more and more like something I do want. Like a second chance.

"Fine. I shouldn't make assumptions, but I don't know what you want, Giant, and it's a lot to discuss. We haven't known each other very long, and we've already had so many misunderstandings between us."

You, I want you. No misunderstanding there.

"Nothing's between us," I emphasize. My voice deepens, demanding, "No more holding back."

Silence lingers for only a second.

"Would you want to do it all again?" she cautiously questions, but before I can answer, she nervously chatters. "Maybe that's something we

L.B. Dunbar

can talk about on Saturday when you're here. I'd feel better if we talked face to face."

I agree, only we won't have to wait until Saturday before we're face to face.

"So how is the beer-making business?" she interjects. I'm not letting this conversation slide, but I need to say some things when I can see her reaction, as she said, so I blow out a breath as I envision my office—and my desk—another place I can't look at without thinking of her. I tell her about the upcoming holidays, which are a busy time for us, and how wholesale has really increased over the two years with Jaxson as head of sales and distribution. I'm proud of my nephew and offering him the job was the least I could do after all his mother did for my girls. Plus, keeping the business in the family is important to me.

She yawns, and I pause. "Am I keeping you up?"

"I'm so sorry. I don't know where that came from, but I've been awake since four this morning. Frank makes us take the cheapest flights, and the early-bird six a.m. was the least expensive."

"No worries. You get some rest. I'll be there soon."

She chuckles, and then the sound halts. "Wait? What? You mean Saturday, right? You'll see me on Saturday?" Is that hope in her tone?

"Actually, I'll be there in an hour."

"An hour?" she shrieks. We've already been talking for one, and it's only another hour to the lodge. "You don't have to come here tonight. I have meetings and—"

"I'm already on my way, and I'm not turning around. If you want to wait to see me, I'll just book a room when I get there."

"You don't need to get a separate room." Her voice lowers.

"Are you sure? I can always—"

"We already shared a tent as strangers. I think we can handle a hotel room with two beds." I'm a little crushed at the notion of separate beds, but I chuckle nonetheless at the mention of the tent.

"It was a little wild that first night, wasn't it?" Who *almost* finger-fucks a woman he only met two days prior? One who got under my skin from the moment I saw her.

"It was." She exhales, and I hear her shy smile through the phone. "I think of it often."

Me, too. "Oh yeah, what do you think about?"

"Your hand guiding mine." Her voice drops a little lower. "And you leading me to touch myself."

My dick leaps to life, and I shift to adjust. "Cricket," I groan.

"Then I imagine you touching me instead of my fingers. You were so close." Her breath hitches. Here's my spontaneous, unpredictable, always ready for me girl.

"Are you…are you touching yourself now?" The heel of my hand rubs down the zipper of my pants. I can't take care of myself while I drive, and I don't want to. It's been eleven days of torture without her. I want my hands on her and hers on me.

"Not yet." She sighs. "But I want to."

"Don't," I snap, which thankfully draws another giggle from her.

"Why not?"

"I'll be there in thirty minutes."

"You just told me an hour," she teases.

"I'm breaking every speed limit." I'm already going dangerously fast on these backroads, and I'm hoping I don't miss the switchbacks I need to take as not everything is properly marked in these parts.

She chuckles. "Okay, I'll hold out, but I'm wet, Giant. So wet."

Fuck. "Cricket, two beds or not, we aren't sleeping separately. We can talk all you'd like, all night long if you want, but you will not touch yourself without me present."

Her laughter fills my chest, and my heart pumps with excitement. "There aren't two beds here, honey. Only one, with me in it, waiting for you."

"Damn, girl, I'm going as fast as I can."

"That's what I'm hoping you'll say once you're here."

I groan through the phone. "Soon."

And then we both laugh. It's so good to laugh with her.

L.B. Dunbar

27
Lodgings and loving

[Giant]

I'm nervous, and I swipe my hands on my pants for the tenth time as I walk to her room. I sent her a text when I arrived, and as I cross the lobby, I rethink what I've done. I should have gone home and showered. I don't even have a change of clothes or a toothbrush.

I comb my fingers through my hair as a door down the hall opens, and she steps out. Still dressed in a tight skirt that hugs her hips and a blouse cut deep to reveal a hint of cleavage, she takes my breath away. She's barefoot, though, and her hair is piled on her head. I want to run the rest of the distance, but I inhale and rub my hands on my pants again.

"Hey," she says as I near her. She smiles slow and sheepish.

"Hey." She's holding open the door, but I reach over her for the heavy plank, and she steps into her room. I follow, and the click of the shutting door sparks something in each of us. I don't know who moves first, but within seconds, we're on each other. Lips on lips and hands in hair. Her hips buck forward, and I scoop her up.

"My skirt," she mutters, not able to wrap her legs around my hips.

"Needs to go," I demand with my lips still against hers. She fumbles with the zipper at the back while I tug her blouse up and over her head. I stare down at her in a nude bra and black panties. Like the greedy man I am, both hands reach for a breast and squeeze. Her head falls back as her fingers pull my shirt from my pants. I release her only long enough to tug my shirt over my head and stand bare chest to her covered breasts. She unhooks her bra, and I tackle my pants, kicking off my shoes and stepping out of my jeans.

I'm rock hard and straining in my boxer briefs. With exaggerated breathing, we stare at one another.

"Should we talk?" I swallow the question, knowing I want nothing more than to be inside her, but if we need to clear the air, I can wait. *A few more minutes.*

186

"I don't want to talk," she whispers, and I'm in her space immediately.

"Thank fuck." My mouth crashes to hers as my hands trace the outline of her body down to those black panties. I press them down her hip, and she wiggles so they fall to the floor. I walk her backward until she connects with the wall.

"You can't lift me."

If she's daring me, she'll lose because I shove my boxers down to my feet and then lift her as I stand upright. She squeaks, but I swallow the noise as her legs spread and she wraps them around my body. I'm frantic as my dick twitches between us, desperate to enter her.

She's right. I can't do this and give her what she needs.

I spin us for the bed, and then we fall onto the mattress. She lets out a laugh as she bounces and then quiets as I guide myself to her entrance.

"Giant," she whispers, her eyes meeting mine and growing serious. "I've missed you so much."

My mouth covers hers again, telling her in that kiss how much I've missed her. Her legs spread farther, and our bodies find their way. I enter her while our mouths remain attached, but as I climb inside her, we separate our lips, both moaning in relief.

Welcome home, I think.

"You feel so good," I say, dropping kisses along her neck while I draw back and then rush forward.

"So good," she mutters, keeping pace with me, just as eager as always to keep me inside her. We dance the oldest dance known to humans, and then I spin, dragging her on top of me. She sits upright, and her hair tumbles from her bun. Her breasts jiggle with each roll of her hips. Her fingers scrape at my chest.

"I love you," I blurt, and she stops moving.

Her eyes widen. "What?"

"I love you. I don't want anything else between us, so that's the last secret I have. I'm in love with you."

"I…"

I buck up, forcing my dick as deep as I can to prevent her from speaking. She grunts at the sharp intrusion. I'm hoping to distract her from telling me she doesn't feel the same.

It's too soon. That was too fast. We didn't talk yet.

"Dammit, Giant. Hold up a second."

I stop bucking under her while she sits with my dick buried inside her. "Hold up? Did you just say *hold up* in a Southern drawl?" More stalling.

"George Giant Harrington, you just let me talk before you move another muscle."

I stare at the determination in her eyes with fear in my chest.

"I love you, too, honey. I love you, too." Her voice softens as her shoulders relax. We peer into each other's eyes in what should be an awkward and difficult moment, and it is. I feel vulnerable and raw, as if she can see into my heart, into my soul, and then she moves, the tempo slower than moments ago. She rolls and nods, her hips swaying while her head lolls. Her eyes close, and I follow her lead, soaking up what we've said while drowning in the connection.

She shifts after a few minutes, sliding up and then slamming back down. I sit up, and her legs flip from straddling my lap to wrapping around my backside. I bounce her up and down, dragging her over me with guided force and relishing the friction.

"Giant." Her voice hitches as her clit rubs lower against me.

"Touch yourself if it helps. Let me watch." Her hand slips between us.

Damn, she's so hot. "Finish," I hiss, as I'm too close to the edge with her doing what she's doing while I disappear inside her.

"I'm coming," she hums, and I still, pulsing inside her as she clenches over me. It's incredible to orgasm simultaneously. I feel one with her in a way I've never felt before. Her arms wrap around my neck as every drop drains out of me. She doesn't let me go, even when we've stopped, and I hold her pressed to my beating heart.

I'm never letting her go again.

+ + +

When I wake, I see Letty exiting the bathroom in only her skirt and a black bra. *Damn.*

"Where you going?" I ask, rolling my head to see it's seven in the morning.

"I've got to go soon." Her voice is low as she comes to my side of the bed. I sit up and reach for her waist, tugging her to me to pressing a kiss between her breasts. She giggles before she pushes me back. "Honey, don't be teasing me. I just showered, and I don't have time. I need to be at Caldwell Woods by eight thirty."

I fall back dejected and slip the sheet down to my hips. "I've got a wood you can inspect." I'm teasing her, but her eyes grow dark and hungry. She hums, and then she reaches down for my dick that's standing at attention. Her fingers wrap around me, and she tugs.

"Now, who's teasing who?" I groan, my eyes closing as the pressure around me increases. When my eyes open, she's bending at the waist, pulling her hair over one shoulder and opening her lips. "Cricket." I've hardly finished her name before she draws me into her warm mouth, swallowing me to the back of her throat.

"Sweetheart," I groan again, stroking over her hair as she twirls her tongue around me. My hand skims down her back, over her curvy ass, and lowers for the hem of her skirt. I slip my fingers up the backside of her leg, lifting the material with the climb as her mouth sucks in earnest, drawing me deep. My fingers find her...

"You're soaked, Letty." I love how ready she is for me, and I slip a finger under her thin panty, delving deep while she grunts against my dick. The vibration ripples up the vein, and I choke. She's so fucking sexy with my finger up her skirt and her mouth on my dick. This woman? *Incredible.*

It doesn't take long before I'm warning her I'm close, and she rocks on my finger. I add another, and her knees buckle. Her teeth scrape up my shaft, and I explode. My eyes close under the sensation, but my fingers still work her until she releases her lips, groaning my name. She comes, holding my dick in her wet palm while drenching my fingers.

"Woman, a man could grow used to this."

She chuckles. "You're such a charmer."

I slip my fingers from her and sit up to take her mouth in a brief kiss.

"I really have to go," she whispers after a minute. I nod, acknowledging once again to myself I never want her to leave me.

She returns to the bathroom to freshen up, and I use my T-shirt on the floor for the time being. When she comes out of the bathroom, her eyes soften despite the gleam of naughtiness after what we did.

"I wish I could stay for coffee, but I'll be back in a few hours."

"I'll be here," I tell her, hoping she reads more into the words. I swallow back all the emotion and let the words escape. "I love you."

She crosses the room and cups my face. "I love you, too." Another too quick kiss and then she's walking away. The door clicks shut, and I fall back on the bed, replaying last night. Our frantic lovemaking. Our declarations. Our talk after both.

"I want us to work," I told her as we lay on our sides, facing each other.

"How would that be?"

"I don't want to bring up the past, but I've done this before with a greater distance. We'll have to commit to it. Phone calls. Text messages. Emails." I reached for her face, hinting at the unanswered messages I sent her.

"I got them all, and I read them every day. Sometimes more than once a day." Her eyes lowered to my chest.

"Why didn't you answer me?"

"I didn't know what to say, at first. Then I thought I might have overreacted a little. Then I decided we wouldn't work. I mean, where does a long-distance relationship lead?"

"Where do you want it to go?" There was something she wasn't saying.

When she didn't answer, I asked something else to take off the pressure.

"How about we just try it for a bit?" I suggested. "Let it run its course." As if it would run out—which it won't, for me. I'd never have enough of this woman.

190

"Okay," she whispered, hesitant and uncertain. I kissed her forehead.

"Speaking of commitment, I'd like to make sure we're on the same page. I'm a one-woman man, and I'd like to ask the same of you."

"You want me to only see one woman?" she teased, and I chuckled, but I held out for her answer.

"You don't even have to ask. It's only been you since the moment I saw you slinging an ax."

"Ax throwing?" I laughed.

"No, chopping wood, when I almost hit you. You're all I could focus on."

"Sex god," I teased.

"Lumbersexual god."

"I'll show you limber," I said, reaching out for her and tugging her over my chest.

"Lumber," she corrected, giggling over me. "Lumber, like wood."

"I can show you that, too." And we headed off to round two for the night.

My body feels a little used and abused. Sex twice in a night and then a blow job in the morning—I'm one lucky man. Plus, she loves me.

I smile to myself.

She says she loves me.

I stretch and twist to sit up in bed when my phone beeps. Her name pops up on the screen.

"Hey baby," I say after she whines my name into the phone. "What's the matter?"

"The rental car won't start. The desk clerk says he thinks the battery's dead. I called the rental service, but I don't have time to wait for a jump start."

"I'll be down in a second."

L.B. Dunbar

28

Something new from the old

Giant to the rescue. It's cold outside, and I'm inside the lobby, pacing while I wait for him to exit the elevator.

"Don't fret," he says when he sees me, and his warm smile puts me at ease although I'm freaking out. I don't have time for a car breakdown, not after I took the time to satisfy this delicious man. I couldn't resist. He was all long and hard, stretched on his back with his shaft upright and ready. I wanted to climb him, but then I'd be even later than I already am. "I have cables in the truck."

It takes me a moment to realize he means jumper cables, and he leads me out to the parking lot. I'm parked facing a row of bushes with a car on either side of mine.

"How would you feel about me just driving you?" Giant asks, and I glance up at him.

"I can't ask you to do that. You already drove here in the middle of the night. Then we stayed awake most of the night." My face heats, recalling the little sleep we had and the reasons.

"Letty, let's be straight about this. I'd cross an ocean for you, if I needed to. This"—he points at his truck—"is nothing." With a hand on my back, he leads me to the passenger side and helps me in. When he enters the driver's side, he adds, "As long as you don't mind that I'm still wearing yesterday's clothes."

"We can go back to the front desk and get you a toothbrush," I suggest although I really don't have time to go up to the room.

"No worries. I already used yours."

My mouth falls open, and I stare at him as he starts the engine.

"What? You already had something else of mine in your mouth, Cricket. Sharing your toothbrush is the least of things to consider."

I laugh with relief as he pulls out of the lot, and we begin the drive to Caldwell Woods.

I love how easygoing he is today. We talked, and I'm relieved we came to some agreements.

"How about we try for every two weeks?" he asked. It seemed too long to wait, but it wasn't too much to ask. He'd never move to Chicago, and he was clear on that when he came to the wedding, but he seems okay with visiting. I wonder what it means for the long-term, but as he said, let's just see where things lead. I couldn't answer him when he asked, where did I want us to go? How do you tell a man you've known for a month that you want love and marriage, and children and happily ever after with him? Especially when you've just said I love you to one another.

Did it happen too fast? The fullness in my heart says it didn't.

"I want to invite you to Thanksgiving."

I was shocked at the invitation—and honored. He's told me about his closeness with his family, which is the opposite of my relationship with mine.

"Are you sure?"

"My mother adored you when she met you. She'd love to have you. Besides, it will stop her from setting me up on more blind dates or dinner arrangements."

My head turned to look up at him. "Does she do that often?"

"She did." I waited for more. "But since I told her how much I like you, she stopped."

"Like me? Aww…are we going steady?"

"Yes," he teased. "Steady. Very steady." Then his mouth crashed into mine, and I forgot all about his mother setting him up with other women. Committed, he told me. I was all his.

"So what do I need to know?" he asks, interrupting my thoughts. "Let me be your sidekick, your Marcus. What do I need to know to get him to sell?"

I snort at the reference to Marcus. Giant and he could not be more opposite, yet I love them both for different reasons.

"Well, the property is actually located on a small lake. There once was a resort there. A whole town opposite it at one point. A few buildings remain but not the physical town itself. All the homes are gone."

Giant side-eyes me. "Wait. Caldwell Woods? Wasn't that the location of an old electrohydraulics plant or something?"

"It was." The town was built up around the waterworks business and consequentially destroyed when the company moved to a larger city. Most of the land was either still owned by the original plant or returned to the state of Tennessee to go wild. "The piece of property we plan to look at is managed by a recluse."

Giant shifts to look at me before turning his eyes back to the road. "That doesn't sound safe." He pauses. "I don't like that you were going to go there alone."

"It's fine," I say with a dismissive wave, but I must admit meeting a man I didn't know in the heart of the woods near an abandoned village doesn't sound all that smart. Then I glance over at Giant. Well, it might have worked out a little bit once before, but Blue Ridge isn't desolate. "Don't want me shacking up with a stranger in a tent to obtain the land, huh?"

Giant scoffs. "Don't want you shacking up, period. No tent unless it involves me. And yes, I'm a little concerned about your lack of stranger danger."

I laugh. "What about me? I could have been the ax murderer."

"Considering I've seen you throw an ax, that's highly doubtful."

"Hey," I whine, but then I reconsider. "Why did you take me up that mountain without knowing me?"

"Honestly, I didn't think you'd show."

"But you prepared everything."

He twists his lips and side-eyes me. "I was hopeful."

My smile grows. "And why was that?"

"Because from the moment I met you, Cricket, I could tell you were something special. Spontaneous need, remember?" He quickly glances at me. He told me last night how he wanted something different, something he didn't know he needed, and apparently, that's me. I'm all warm inside with the thought. "And I don't regret one minute of that decision to take you camping, even if I did it under false pretenses."

He was never going to let me purchase the land.

"I don't regret a minute of it either."

He reaches for my hand and brings it to his lips, kissing my knuckles and then holding it against his thigh.

"I love you," he whispers, shy and quiet.

"I love you, too," I say. *More than you know.*

+ + +

Mr. Samuel Calder is an old man, full of stories and memories of the land—what it once was and what he hopes it can be again. A resort sat on the property once upon a time. Ironically, we can't get to the site without taking a boat to the secluded location *across* the river—he corrects me, it's not a lake—and Giant eyes me again, hinting at my lack of stranger danger. There's no boat to transport us, but the remains of a landing on both sides of the river hint at what once was.

"I promised my Annie I'd restore it for her. I wanted her to come back to me." Mr. Calder's elderly expression speaks of lost love, and my heart breaks a little. With his advanced age, it might be too late to regain whomever the woman was to him.

However, I'm hopeful of the interest from the hotel company, considering there was once one there. Mr. Calder describes how the resort looked. It's difficult to envision its past majestic until Mr. Calder shows us some faded pictures of a lodge, golf course, pond, and patio. With the verbal image Mr. Calder paints in addition to the worn photographs, my imagination sees a resort something the likes of *Dirty Dancing*. We spend an hour listening to Mr. Calder recount memories of the old place as we traipse along the opposite shore of the river. I don't know what I was thinking because I'm not well prepared in my heeled boots and tight skirt. It reminds me of when I met Giant. I was equally unprepared for meeting the large man graciously walking next to me, discussing the land with my perspective client. Mr. Calder's weathered skin and liquid blue eyes hold so much passion for this place and its memories.

"Been in my family for generations." His voice drifts, and I'm not certain if he's talking about the property or the company.

"Company moved upstream, but the resort went on for years after." His eyes remain sad as he looks across the water. "Then it disappeared as well." He already explained how the company razed the nearby community. His fingers shake as he reaches for his forehead and rubs. "But I'm going to bring it back. Bring her back."

I look from Sam to Giant, whose brow pinches with concern. This man must be in his eighties. I fear his Annie might be dead.

"Where did Annie go?" I whisper, curious about the deep love he evidently felt for this woman.

"California." His voice carries over the water like a greater distance divided them.

"I'm sorry," I say, not certain why I apologize.

"Never let anything divide you." Sam pauses. "Not family, money, business, or a river." He chuckles to himself for a moment and then turns back for his car. I glance at Giant again. The two men have hit it off. He looks as confused as I feel over Sam's references.

We each shake hands with Mr. Calder like old gentlemen did in a time gone by. An unspoken agreement sits between us although I'm not certain I've acquired the land. Sam mentions the name of his lawyer, who also happens to be his grandson.

"He's about your age, so when you're ready to ditch the giant, I'll set you up." He winks at me. He's been a flirt all morning.

"You remind me so much of Annie." Whoever she was, she held his heart for a lifetime, and mine pinches at the thought of such a memory. Our hearts retain true love, despite its end. Is this how Giant feels about his wife?

It's sweet and sad, and I want to hug Mr. Calder to assure him she probably remembered him with longing, too.

"We didn't have these fancy, newfangled cell phones. We communicated through pickle jars." He chuckles softly to himself, reminiscing about the fodder of young summer love, and once again, his expression shifts to memories far away. *Dirty Dancing* returns to my thoughts, and I imagine a young Sam sneaking off to parties and kissing his lady friend down by the water. "Can't remember where I placed the last one." He looks around the late fall landscape, suddenly confused. "Don't know if she ever got my message."

After a moment, he reminds me once again to contact his grandson. "He handles all the money. Told me I wasn't good with numbers." I'm sensing his family took away his right to make decisions, but I don't question why he's the one meeting us instead of his grandson.

I'm quiet as we drive back to Appleton, my mind racing with Mr. Calder's hints of once upon a time, and his loss of happily ever after. It's the makings of a romance novel.

Giant and I stop at a Walmart to buy him a change of clothes, and I snoop around. I rarely go to one of these superstores, so I'm fascinated. I find odd things I don't really need, like a daily planner, a notebook with a typewriter on the cover, some fancy markers, and a pretty pillow.

"How will you get that in your suitcase?" Giant teases. I shrug.

"Maybe you can keep it for me." Two weeks and I'll be seeing him again.

+ + +

"Was someone with you?" It's the first thing my uncle says to me as I enter the office on Monday.

"Excuse me?" I don't know why he's asking although I know who he's referencing.

"Mr. Calder's attorney contacted me. He told me you met with his grandfather." I stare at my uncle. What is he getting at? Samuel Calder, property manager. "You were supposed to meet with him. Drake Calder."

No. *No.* "The paperwork clearly said Samuel Calder." I'm adamant I didn't misread the email confirming our meeting time and location.

"Samuel *Drake* Calder," my uncle emphasizes. "The grandson. At his office in Knoxville."

"Knoxville?" I would never make a mistake like this. Caldwell Woods was the location. I knew where I was going. *Not to mention, I wasn't far from Giant.* I brush away the thought. If my uncle discovers I

197

entertained seeing Giant as a secondary mission the moment he mentioned Tennessee, he'll accuse me of being flighty.

"The documentation reads to meet Mr. Samuel *Drake* Calder at his office. Instead, you met his grandfather at the property location."

"How did his grandfather know to be at the property then?"

"That's a very good question." Uncle Frank glares at me, but the question I've asked is the same one I want answered.

"Mr. Calder was very excited about a resort on the property." I recall the time Giant and I spent with the man. He wanted it restored to its original glory. *For my Annie*. He was so sweet.

"The old man wants one built there, but he isn't selling."

"Yes, he is. We shook on it." He gave me his word I could have the property. I realize as I'm speaking how ridiculous I sound.

"First of all, nothing's ever permanent unless it's in black pen on a dotted line, Olivet. Secondly, Mr. Calder's attorney, the old man's grandson, was quite adamant the property will not be sold. *Now*."

"Then why did you send me there?" Is this a test? I don't understand.

"Because the grandson was willing to sell the land until you spoke to his grandfather."

"I don't understand." I don't.

"It appears the old man won't part with the land for some silly reason." Silly? Annie? *It's romantic!* "The grandson has the power of attorney for the property and was going to sell despite the old man's objection."

"Well, that sounds awful, trying to sell a man's land out from under him."

"Mr. Calder isn't of sound mind." Frank levels a stare at me as if that should explain everything.

"He seemed lucid to me." I think back on our conversation. His humor. His flirting. His recall of the resort and a woman who never left his heart. "He was very excited about a resort on the property."

"Because he thought you were a builder. You and your friend. He thought you were there to rebuild the former resort, not purchase the land for *another* resort company. He was very confused." My uncle stares at me as if I confused the man and I'm to blame for twisting things. This doesn't make sense. The papers stated the location, the owner, the meeting time.

As if reading my mind, my uncle twirls a pile of papers on his desk and pushes them toward me. It clearly states the property for purchase. The owner's name as Samuel Dean Calder. Meeting time at eight thirty in Knoxville.

Wait. *Hold up.* That's not what…

"I don't understand," I repeat. How could I have been in the wrong place, miles from where I should have been at the right time? How was the older man there? "He was waiting for me."

Uncle Frank shakes his head. He doesn't believe me.

"It seems your friend made quite an impression, and Samuel senior went back to his grandson to tell him of the good news. Imagine Drake's confusion as he'd been wondering where his eight thirty appointment had been, and he discovers you'd been at the property with his senile grandfather."

Again, I wonder how Samuel Calder, the elder, was present at the property, and my heart sinks at the slow realization that I've majorly fucked this up. An intelligent, organized businesswoman and I've made a huge mess of this second chance given to me by my uncle.

Where was your head? I can hear Frank asking without him asking. Giant. My head was wrapped around Giant as were my legs and my heart.

"There must be a mistake. I'll just call—"

"You'll make no calls," Uncle Frank warns. "In fact, you're staying put. I don't know what's up with you, but for the past two weeks, your head has been in the clouds. Just when I thought you were finally buckling down and getting serious about being a partner. This is the second attempt at a large land purchase you fucked up. Is this all that baby business? Are you hoping to get *pregnant* instead?"

My mouth gaps open to defend myself, but he continues. My uncle has never spoken to me like this before. He spits out the word pregnant like it's acid in his mouth. Is he insinuating I'm sleeping around?

L.B. Dunbar

"We're keeping you local, Olivet, where we can monitor your sales and assist you. I can't afford to lose more deals because of you."

My chest hurts, stabbed by his words. I didn't do anything on purpose, and he's making it sound as if I have.

"But he was there…" My voice drifts as I see my uncle wants no explanation, no excuses.

"Dayna's going to speak with the grandson and try to smooth things over."

"Dayna?" I shriek. Not only will she be the ultimate betrayal, especially if she does secure the property, but honestly, I think she'll muck it up even more. It's the second time in a month we've tried to obtain land with questionable means, and I'm relieved we haven't gotten what we set out for. We don't appreciate the history of these people or the land they love.

"Plant your feet back on the Earth," my uncle demands, implying my head is in the clouds, but he doesn't realize how much I want to do just that. Dig my toes in the dirt. Dip my hands in a river. And enjoy.

I stand to dismiss myself and walk out of his office.

+ + +

"He what?" Giant asks, and I ache for him. It's been twenty-four hours, and I miss him already. I don't know how I'll last for the next two weeks. I want him to hold me. I want him to distract me. I want him here.

"He accused me of not being dedicated to becoming a partner." I pause, letting the words swirl around me as they have from the moment my uncle spoke them. Was he really wrong, though? Do I want to be partner if these are our practices? *Yes, think of the baby, the one I don't have.* Giant's prolonged silence rouses me.

"Hello," I call out, wondering if I'd lost the connection.

"Can I ask you something?" His tone is serious and quiet. I hear the hesitation, and my blood races through my veins.

"Sure." I'm not confident in my answer, but I won't deny him anything.

"Do you really want to be partner, Cricket? I mean, you told me you took the job because you didn't find anything else." He pauses again, and I recall telling him these things. How I fell into a rut and stayed. "You could always do something else."

"If only," I snort, but wasn't I just thinking these same thoughts?

"Why not?" He's silent for a moment as if he's waiting for an answer. *I'm* waiting for an answer.

Why not?

"Because I'm forty, and this is the only work I've ever known."

"You can learn something new." He pauses. He thought he'd always be military and now runs the brewery. "Are you happy there? You don't sound happy there."

"No, but that's not the point. I need this job." This job is security for me. It's what I need to prove I'll be a sound provider for a baby. The agency assures me my employment status is imperative to receiving a child.

"What about writing?" I've been thinking a lot about Mr. Calder and his story. The hints of his love affair linger in my head. The way he spoke of his girl. The memories so vivid. The pickle jar love note.

"It's not that easy." I sigh in exasperation. However, curiosity haunts me about the old resort, Sam's romance, and the mystery of the past town, but I can't just drop my job and write a book, hoping it will make me the kind of money I need.

"I could provide for you." The comment brings an awkward silence. I swallow the lump in my throat. It's a generous offer, and I know he means it wholeheartedly, but I couldn't accept.

"That's sweet of you, but it's not about me." I wait a moment for the rest of the statement to sink in.

Are you trying to get pregnant? My uncle's words still sting.

"Right. A baby." He doesn't ask about the progress of my application, and I'm wondering if he's one more person on board the Letty-shouldn't-do-this train. I'm too emotionally exhausted to argue with him and ask him what his tone means. Giant sighs.

"Will he fire you? Because of me?" I've told Giant about the misunderstanding and who Sam Calder thought we were. The genuine concern in his voice makes my heart ache for him again.

"He won't fire me because I'm family." Uncle Frank would never let his sister down by letting me go even though he'd love nothing more. He doesn't have his own children, so his only hope of continuing the legacy of Mullen Realty is through his nieces, or at least Dayna especially since she has Hudson. I wouldn't trust either of them, but that's just me. The future of the company seems secure, at least from one niece.

"I can't wait until you're back here and see how a family should treat you." The comment stings because it implies my family doesn't treat me well, which they don't. Still, it hurts to accept the reality.

"It's another reason I want a baby. I'll treat him differently. Very differently. He'll be my family."

"A baby boy. You know, I thought all women dreamed of little girls."

"Maybe someday," I say, but I don't believe I'll adopt more than one child.

"Harrington brothers seem to only have girls. I have two, my girl has two. Charlie has one. But my mother had four boys, and Mati had twin sons. It's like an unknown curse. There isn't anyone to carry on our name." He says it with such pride and concern, I'm a little sad. I suppose a son of a son is important to a family legacy.

"What can you do about it? I guess that leaves James." I laugh at my joke, but Giant falls very quiet. "What did I say?"

"Nothing, sweetheart." The drop to his tone tells me not to ask, so I move on.

"So, two weeks? That's a lot of nights with my vibrator."

Giant chokes. "Your what?"

"Bunny ears," I tease.

"I...I want to see." His voice drops again, and I squirm a little with excitement. This man has certainly been an adventure. One I'd take again and again.

29
Baby blues

[Giant]

Thanksgiving isn't for three more days, but people act like today starts their holiday. I'm sullen and somber for some reason, but when Letty's name pops up on my phone, I feel a little lighter.

"I'm getting a baby."

It takes me a second to register what she's said before I've even said hello.

"A baby?" I choke before I realize what she means. "I mean, a baby. Tell me everything." It's so wrong that I'm a little deflated with the announcement. I'm happy for her. I am. This is what she wanted, but I don't see myself going the baby route again. I've already been there, and while I'd like to say I've done that, I didn't. I wasn't home when Ellie was born. When Sarah was due, I was scheduled to deploy. She came early just so I wouldn't miss the experience, but I still wasn't around for diapers and late nights and breastfeeding. Not that Letty can do that last one.

"You don't sound happy," she says, her excitement waning a bit.

"No, no, I am. Bad day. Tell me all about him."

"He's beautiful. They sent me a picture. He's three months old, and the mother abandoned him. Brought him to the hospital and left him in the emergency room. After running a battery of tests on him, he needed some immediate medical attention. She was a young woman who didn't take care of herself and couldn't take care of him."

"What?" *Who abandons their child?*

"Yep. My adoption liaison called me right away. She said I'm the perfect candidate."

"Medical issues? That don't sound too good, Cricket." There could be potential for all kinds of heartbreak if the child has a disease or an addiction. Who knows where this mother came from or what she did?

And what happens if she returns? But Letty's already told me she has faith in the system.

"Whatever he needs, as long as he's mine. And the good news is, I only need to wait out the abandonment for six months instead of a year for the adoption to stick." It all sounds worrisome to me, but Letty's enthusiasm is contagious. "I'm so excited." She squeals into the phone, and I wish I was there to celebrate with her. I want to be excited for her, but my heart selfishly sinks a little more because I know what's coming after my next question.

"When do you pick him up?"

"Tomorrow." Her voice cracks again with her eagerness.

"What about Thanksgiving?"

"I'm so sorry, Giant. I can't travel under the adoption rules. I can't go anywhere for six months." Reality slowly sets in, and her voice falters as she repeats, "Six months." The words echo through the phone like an empty cave.

I swallow back the fear in my throat. "We can do this," I encourage.

"Will you still want me in six months?"

We haven't really talked about this possibility—the *what-if*—of her getting a baby. I'm not opposed to long-distance dating. Nothing against her being a single mother. But a new baby and the distance? The future with a baby? Even I'm starting to doubt the situation.

"Six months is nothing, Cricket." I've done longer stints without Clara, but when I think of how that really worked out for us, I'm not certain I'd promote a long-distance relationship. Sure, it was okay for us, but if I had to do it all again, I'd want a little more continuity. Daily physical contact being number one on my list. With Letty, I thought I might have a second chance, but again, I'm suddenly skeptical. I don't tell her my thoughts, including the ones where I was hoping to convince her to move here. She could adopt here. She could work here. Blue Ridge might not be the real estate metropolis she has in Chicago, but a change of scenery might be what she needs.

"Please be happy for me."

"I am, sweetheart. I really am. This is exciting. You're going to be a great mother."

"I am," she says with her feisty determination to get the job done, but tackling a baby isn't quite like obtaining real estate. "I hate to dash, but I've got to go. I have so much to do. Clear the office in my condo. Buy a crib. Purchase clothes. Get some diapers." She laughs. "I never thought I'd hear those words cross my lips. I'm excited to change a diaper." She's giddy as she rambles, and I can picture the grin on her face. I want to kiss those smiling lips, but I can't. Not yet.

"You get settled, and then I'll come to you," I tell her.

She quiets a little. "You know, I don't expect…I wouldn't ask you to come here all the time, but I just can't—"

"I'm not worried about making this equal travel or wherever your pretty little head is taking this. We'll work it out. I promise."

"I just don't want to take advantage of you. If it ever becomes too much or you can't see yourself handling the baby, just…please…be honest and let me know your feelings. I'll understand. I will."

What's she saying?

"I'm not going anywhere, and neither are you. Go get your baby and your crib and your diapers. You'll be rethinking those diaper changes at two in the morning when you haven't had any sleep." I scoff, hoping to lighten the mood. "And call me tonight."

"I love you," she says breathlessly through the phone, and for the length of those three words, I actually believe we'll be all right.

"I love you, too, Cricket."

+ + +

"What's up with you?" Billy guffaws, pounding me on the back while we hang out on Thanksgiving Day at my parents'. Elaina Harrington is in full force when her family gathers, and nothing is forgotten. Food. Beer. Desserts. I'm stuffed from overeating and a little heartsick without Letty present. The focal point of this holiday is the newest addition to our family, Christopher Jaxson Rathstone, Mati's grandson. CJ's adorable, and Mati gloats about another boy when all us brothers only have girls. Baby talk seems to be surrounding me lately, and I'm suffocating.

"Nothing," I snap, lifting another beer to my lips.

"Uh-huh. Trophy Room. Now." Billy brushes past me and walks down the back hall from the living room to a room off the garage. It's a silly name for a room, but the enormous shelving unit once held all our sports' trophies and contest ribbons, along with our high school senior pictures. Board games and gaming systems were stored in the cabinets below the shelves, and a large screen television sits in the center opening. Eventually, wedding pictures replaced the trophies, along with framed images of all the grandbabies. This room was our man cave as teenagers, conveniently located off the garage so we could sneak out, stash beer, or bring a girl into the house undetected.

"Talk," Billy demands, and I want to tell him to mind his own fucking business. He's been just as ornery today.

"Letty got a baby."

Billy's eyes widen so big I think they'll pop out of their sockets. "She was pregnant?"

"No, idiot." I swipe a hand over my beard. "She adopted a baby. And you're catching flies." His mouth remains open, gaping in disbelief.

"Did you know about this?" he asks, his lips slowly closing.

"Of course." I sigh.

"And you aren't happy?"

I lower to the old leather couch that has seen better days and its fair share of naked Harrington ass on it. "I'm happy for her. Thrilled. This is what she wants."

"But...?" He rolls a finger, encouraging me to tell him more.

"I just...I hoped we'd have some time together. Long distance is hard enough. Actually, I was hoping to convince her to move here, but now with the baby thing, she can't leave Illinois for at least six months. Maybe longer."

"It's not a *thing*," Billy retorts, and I'm about to tell him he knows what I mean, but he doesn't. Billy and his ex-wife, Rachel, never had children. I briefly explain the adoption process and restrictions. "I don't think I see the big deal. Put a ring on her and get her down here in six months."

I chuckle and scrub a hand over my jaw, stroking my thick scruff. "Doesn't it seem a little fast? It's hardly been three months."

"Is there a time limit on these things?" Billy finally lowers to a chair opposite me, reminding me of what my sister said a few weeks ago. Billy and I both married our high school sweethearts for different reasons. Billy had stars in his eyes over Rachel. They were that image of a perfect couple: Homecoming king and queen, most likely to live here forever. He wanted to have sex with her, and she held out until their wedding night.

"I don't know," I whisper.

"Look, I'm not the man to offer advice about love." He scoffs. "But I'd have to say if the timing is right now, there's nothing wrong with acting on it." This is Billy's philosophy on life. Since his wife left, he's been living in the moment, screwing just about everything crossing his path for the past sixteen years. He's out of control, but he's my brother, and I love him.

"I just don't know."

"What don't you know? I already told you that if you make her happy, you'll be happy. If she wants the baby, accept the baby." His voice lowers as he speaks, and he turns a little ashen.

"You okay?"

"Yeah, I gotta thing...but we aren't talking about me."

"Did you get someone pregnant?" I sit up a little straighter.

"Not exactly," he says lowering his head and squeezing his hands together. Then his elbows hit his thighs, and he covers his face with his hands.

"What did you do?" I hiss.

"I... I'm a father."

"To who?"

"She's sixteen."

"You got a sixteen-year-old pregnant? What the fuck?" I feel a little sick to my stomach.

"That's how it happened." He chuckles. "And I mean the child is sixteen, not the mother, dumbass."

"William Forrest," I reprimand. "This isn't a joke."

"Do I look like I'm laughing?" He lowers his hands from his face.

He doesn't, actually. He looks sick to his stomach. "How? When? What? Who?"

"It's a long story, so let's finish yours first," he says. On that note, Charlie enters the room. He smiles big and bright at me.

"Man, the memories in here." He chuckles. "What are you two doing back here?"

"Hiding out," Billy mutters.

"Billy's a dad," I reply.

"What the fuck, Giant?" Billy snorts, looking up to glare at me.

"What the hell?" Charlie asks, staring down at our brother.

"It's a long story, okay, and we're in here for Giant, not me. He's the one questioning if he wants to be a dad again."

"I am not."

"Who did you get pregnant?" Charlie asks, turning on me.

"No one. Letty adopted a baby."

And damn Charlie, he smiles. "Well, alright." Charlie knows the details as I've already spoken to him about the legality of adopting in Georgia, should I convince Letty to move here.

"She can't leave Illinois for six months." I stare at my brother, but he doesn't acknowledge the concern in my voice.

"And you won't see her until then?" His brows pinch in question.

"No," I begin. "I plan to still see her."

"Then what's the problem?" Charlie asks. He's the family member who understands a long-distance relationship as his ex-wife lived in New York while he was here. It didn't end well for them.

"See?" Billy mocks as though he's an authority on advice. "Win-win."

"No win-win. I want Letty here, and she can't be." I sit up straighter as my voice roughens.

"For six months," Charlie clarifies. "That's nothing. The bigger question is, do you want a woman with a baby? A newborn, Giant. Your girls are in their late twenties. You have grandchildren already. Are you willing to start over again?"

Am I? I mean, I want Letty, sure, and I'll take all that comes with her, but a baby?

"Why is this suddenly so hard for me?" I whisper.

"Guilt," Charlie mutters. He's not wrong. Guilt pecks at me because of my girls. I wasn't there for them as babies, hardly as toddlers, and emotionally distant while they were teens. I've done it all wrong with them. "But it will pass, Giant."

"I don't know what any of this means. Do I ask her to move in? Should we get married? Do I adopt the baby?"

"Don't you think that's a little fast?" Billy snaps.

"You're the one who just told me there wasn't a timeline and to put a ring on her."

"I mean, don't you think you should talk to her before assuming she'll do any of those things. Like marry you, for one."

He's right, and my shoulders slump. Maybe she doesn't want to get married. Maybe she just wants a baby. She's told me over and over she isn't looking for any commitment from me. My girls tell me plenty of women do this nowadays. Single mom power without the hassle of a husband. Still, Letty seems like she'd like a partner. She's told me love and marriage, children and happily ever after.

Charlie laughs. "Giant, you should see your face. I've never seen you so love-sick and forlorn all in one expression. You're normally so brooding. *I'm Giant. Don't talk to me.*" Charlie throws his voice to sound deep and rough as he mocks me.

"Now, he's all *I'm in love with Letty,*" Billy teases with a feminine twist.

The door to the Trophy Room opens, and our father leans in, holding the doorknob. "You boys might want to come out here before your mother finds you." He winks, as this is something he'd say when he caught us drinking in this room or a girl under one of us. James was the main culprit in his day, and I suddenly feel the loss of him.

"Coming," Charlie says, always the kiss-up, always the good kid. He's a politician, so it's in his nature.

"Seems *coming* is the problem," Billy mutters as he stands from his seat.

"Only for you," I say, standing as well and wrapping a hand around the nape of his neck, tenderly shoving him forward. We all walk out of the room with laughter on our lips but questions in our hearts.

The crowning moment to the holiday is when my nephew proposes to his girlfriend, who just had their son. He gives a toast, acknowledging our dad for his beer-crafting skills and then...

"And to Hollilyn, the mother of my child. Who could have predicted this is how it would end?"

Who could predict, I think—a woman demands I sell her my land and then follows me up a mountain to go camping?

Jaxson nods to his son in Hollilyn's arms, and she pinkens. Their son is the result of a one-night stand that turned into many nights thereafter.

Would it be so bad to have another baby? Would Letty want to share him with me?

"But if I could have known the path would lead me here, I would do it all over again. I only wish I'd met you sooner, so I hope I'm not too late to ask."

If we could only know where life would lead.

If only I'd met her sooner... I dismiss the thought. I loved Clara, but I want Letty in a way beyond what I felt with my wife.

Jaxson lowers to his knee before the overstuffed chair where Hollilyn sits, and she breaks into tears. Mati gasps as we all see what's coming next.

"Will you be my wife and share the rest of my nights with me?"

Hollilyn struggles to stand from her seat, and Mati's man, Denton, pops up to take the baby from her arms. With another hand, he helps her stand while Hollilyn nods and nods.

"Don't do it," Billy whispers, and I knock him in the back of the head from where I stand behind him. He's seated on the couch next to my sister.

"Yes, yes, yes," Hollilyn says, staring down at the ring Jax holds up to her. Jaxson murmurs something to her, and she pulls back to give him a kiss, which deepens rather quickly.

"That's how they got in trouble in the first place," Billy says, and Charlie laughs next to me.

"Jaxson," Mati snaps, clapping her hands once as if that will break them apart. She sounds every bit like our mother.

"As if you don't kiss him like that," Billy mutters to Mati implying Denton, and Charlie snorts.

I know someone I'd like to kiss like that, and I hope I'm not too late.

30

Gratitude

[Letty]

When I try to explain to my sister that being a mother overnight feels strange, she tells me it's because I didn't have the nearly ten months of incubation of the baby in my stomach. I hate her a little more.

The nurses said I should talk to the baby, but babies don't verbally respond, so I spend all day speaking to myself.

Then there's this whole switch to calling myself mom. Mommy has been even harder.

"Mommy loves you." I stare at my beautiful boy rocking in the baby swing, relieved he finally stopped crying. I lie on the couch on my side, watching him tick-tock back and forth. I'm so tired, but I feel wired. I wonder if he knows I'm not his biological mother. Does he wonder where his birth mother is? Does he know she left him? I worry she'll show up one day to reclaim him. The agency warns against sudden attachment, yet Dayna says it's important to form an immediate bond. What does she know about children, though? Her boys are as distant from her as if they weren't her kids.

The agency cleared the baby of all initial medical concerns. They thought he might have a heart murmur and ran a bunch of tests. Heart surgery would have been imminent, but the diagnosis passed. Now, I just need to look for typical milestones of development. I'm already an anxious mess. It's been a rough couple of days, and I've been tackling most of it on my own. I skipped the family tradition of gathering for Thanksgiving. I can't remember when I last ate a meal. My eyes are drifting shut when there's a knock on my door. I will myself not to answer it. *No one's home*, I want to say, but instead, I get up, hopeful it might be a family member deciding to visit me.

I peek through the peephole and then whip open the door.

"Giant," I hush-whisper, staring at him in disbelief. I must be dreaming. I've gone delusional. I'm hallucinating.

"Cricket?" The moment he says my name in question, I leap for him. *Oh my God*, he feels so good as my arms loop around his neck, and I tug him tighter to me. I melt into his embrace, inhaling his neck, addicted to his scent. Then I remember I can't recall when I last showered.

"Oh my gosh, Giant. What are you doing here?" I pull back from him, my voice rising, and then the baby cries. My shoulders fall. *Well, that was only a hot minute.* Giant chuckles and steps inside, closing the door behind him. I continue to stare. He should be home with his family. "It's Thanksgiving."

"Actually, that was yesterday," he teases, and I look toward my windows. It's been dark and gloomy for the past two days, and with the lack of sleep, I guess the days have run together. I swipe a hand over my hair—finding it greasy—as Giant watches me. I'm a mess. "You're the prettiest thing I've ever set eyes on."

I should cry.

I want to cry.

I'm too tired to cry.

He steps up to me, hugging me again quickly before pulling back and walking over to the baby swing. He stops a step before it and stares down at my son. *How weird is that to say?*

"He's—"

"He's biracial," I interject, and Giant turns to me, brows pinched in question at the sharpness of my voice. I'm sensitive because of the high-pitched surprise in the voices of my mother and Dayna, their judgment apparent.

"I was going to say he's a king of kings," he states. His brows remain pinched, but a grin spreads on his face.

"I'm sorry." I fold down to the couch. I'll need to get used to reactions without sounding defensive, but the disapproval from my mother and sister has eaten at me for days. I don't see skin color. In fact, I didn't make any specifications on my adoption request. I wanted a healthy baby boy. I wanted a child, any child who had an economic disadvantage so I could give him all the love he deserved, which is why I registered with the foster system.

213

"My family hasn't been very accepting." His skin is a rich tawny color with eyes a deep onyx. His hair is as dark as fresh-tilled soil after rain. He's beautiful, and I already love him. "His birth mother is Latino; his father African American." The liaison knew this information from birth records in the hospital where Finn was deserted. I shrug. I don't care about any of that. "His name is Finnikin. Finn for short."

Giant squats before Finn who has stopped fussing even though our voices woke him and the swing stopped moving. "Can I pick him up?" He looks at me over his shoulder, and my heart weeps.

"Of course." The new mom in me wants to tell him how to pick up a baby—support the head, hold the back—but then I remember he has children and grandbabies. He knows how to handle a baby, and at three months, Finn already has more strength than I expected. Giant scoops Finn out of the seat and stands, spinning to face me. The baby looks so small in his large hands, and then Giant cradles him in the crook of his elbow. I'm speechless as my ovaries explode. *I didn't need them anyway*, I tell myself as the man I love holds my baby to his chest. Finn seems mesmerized by Giant's warmth or heartbeat or something.

"He's quiet," I say, breathing a sigh of relief and frustration.

"Sometimes they need a fresh set of arms," he says, the expert father. "Clara used to get so mad when the girls cried all the time, and then a family member would come over, and they'd be angels." Giant's head lifts, and he looks at me. I can't decide if he's worried at the mention of her or concerned at the state of me. I brush back loose hair near my face.

"I haven't showered." *Lately*.

"When's the last time you slept?"

"I'm not sure."

"Go shower. I've got him for a few minutes."

My eyes narrow. "You spent days with me in a tent without running water," I snap, implying we didn't exactly bathe while camping.

"Yeah, but then you smelled like me, not baby spit-up." He winks, and I want to snap again, but instead, my shoulders fall. I'm failing at this mother thing. "Come here." He tips his head, so I stand and walk over to him where he spreads out his other arm and pulls me to him. He kisses my forehead. "I love you."

"I'm so glad you're here," I whisper, and a tear escapes. Once the dam breaks, I know there will be no going back, so I suck in a breath to contain them, but another traitorous one releases.

"Hey," Giant says softly. "Shower." It's like he knows I need the solitude despite the tears, so I step out from under his arm.

A half hour later, I feel like a new woman. I *am* a new woman, and my heart accelerates when I see Giant pacing my living room, rocking a baby, with *SportsCenter* on the television. He looks up at me with a grin, and I muster a smile although I silently curse Finn for sleeping. *Little traitor.*

"Why don't you dial up some dinner?" Giant teases, gazing back at Finn, and my heart swells at the image. Finn looks so natural in Giant's arms, or is it Giant looks calm and collected with Finn tucked into him? Either way, it's a reminder I want Giant in my life, in Finn's life, but I don't see how that will happen.

Thinking of Giant's request, I'm ready to retort *this is why I didn't marry*. I'm not someone's little woman, raising children and making meals. I'm an independent female. Then I see him nod to my phone on the coffee table, and I chuckle to myself. Oh, right. The little woman knows how to dial a phone for delivery, and I realize a second later, I might not mind a home-cooked meal with a man in my house.

+ + +

After the warm shower and a hot meal, I'm drained of energy, but my anxiety gets the best of me as I prepare for a long night. I've read about this—*colic*—and I'm convinced Finn has it. It's like a timer goes off in his little system at nine o'clock and for two hours, I'll be pacing this living room trying everything to make him stop wailing.

"You didn't tell me why you're here?" I ask, sitting next to Giant on the couch. Finn rests in the car seat at Giant's feet. "I mean, I'm thrilled you are, but this is a surprise." I hate to ask because I'm so grateful. I can't do a heavy conversation with him, but I'm definitely

215

L.B. Dunbar

stumped by the impromptu visit. His Thanksgiving plans involved being home with his family, and it's only the day after the holiday.

"My nephew asked his girlfriend to marry him."

"Jaxson, right?" The one who drove me to the brewery and was dating the very pregnant woman at the diner. I knew they'd had their baby. "A proposal prompted you...?" There's still a question in my voice.

"I'd just finished a discussion with my brothers." He keeps his eyes on his plate. He finished each bite of his moo shu pork while I couldn't finish my shrimp fried rice. "We were talking about you and me, and I was questioning where we were going, with Finn suddenly in your life, and then we walked into the living room, and Jaxson popped the question right there in front of everyone." He pauses, rubbing his hands on his thighs.

"And this inspired you to hop on a plane to come see me?" I'm flattered but concerned. "What are you wondering in regard to Finn?" Is the idea of a baby too much for him? I know he's already raised children. Maybe he's not interested in going through it again. Maybe the reality of my situation is catching up to him. Maybe he's breaking up with me, which seems silly considering he bought a last-minute plane ticket on a holiday weekend to fly thousands of miles, but still...

"It's kind of a heavy topic with all you have going on." He sheepishly glances at me and then away.

"Just spit it out, Giant. Are we breaking up because of Finn?" My heart sinks to my stomach, and my shrimp fried rice wants to come back up. He shifts to face me.

"Absolutely not." His expression is serious.

"What are you saying then?" I'm so confused, and I can't process. I gaze down at Finn, who is making a squinty face.

"I'm saying, I know it can be rough to be alone with a new baby. You don't have much family support, and I can't be here all the time. I'm worried about you."

"Well, don—"

He holds up a hand to stop me. "I can't predict the future, Letty. I don't know where we'll go next, but I don't want to lose you. As for

216

Finn…I'm just concerned. I've already been this route of long distance and babies. I don't want you to be hurt."

My mouth falls open, and I glare. "Well, then don't hurt me," I snap.

Giant stares back at me, and my skin prickles. I don't know why I'm so on edge. *You're exhausted.*

"I still don't understand what you're saying. Just spit it out, Giant." My tone remains irritated although I shouldn't be barking at him.

"I want you to move to Georgia in six months."

Well, that's not what I thought he'd say.

"Why?" The singular word is said a little too harshly and a little too direct as if the thought wasn't ever a thought. I instantly want to reel it back in, especially when his face falls, and he looks down at Finn who's fully winding up for his nightly bawl. Suddenly, I want to join the baby with a good cry. I'm messing everything up.

"I guess…I thought…I don't know." Giant stands without finishing his thought and picks up our plates from my coffee table. My eyes follow his retreating back. I want to run after him. I want to tell him I didn't mean it how it sounded. I just want to understand. Moving to Georgia? That's a big step. I don't know what I'd do for a living, or where I'd live, and any of these concerns are moot until I pass through the six-month timeframe of abandonment and post-adoption.

"Giant, I—" As soon as I speak, Finn breaks into a wail, and Giant disappears down the hall for my kitchen.

I glance over at Finn and sigh. This is so much harder than I thought it would be.

What do you want? I scream in my head, not certain whom I'm directing my thoughts at.

Men are so confusing, no matter what age.

31

Finnikin of the Rock

[Giant]

As I wash the plates and listen to Finn cry down the hall, I wonder what I'm doing here, and then I want to punch myself for bringing up the subject of moving. She's overwhelmed, and a discussion about our relationship status and our future is not on her radar like it is mine.

I want a plan.

She wants peace and quiet.

I let her deal with her son while I clean up her kitchen. I wash the baby bottles and take stock of her grocery needs. Then I go into Finn's room and find a small pile of laundry. Taking it to the washing machine, I begin a load and notice another sitting in the dryer. I fold the tiny clothes, marveling at their small size.

He'll grow into a man, someday. *He better appreciate his mama.*

I think of how she defended Finn from my first impression. I don't care about his skin color, but she didn't mention she was doing a trans-culture adoption—not that it matters. It doesn't. I just didn't know.

I want to kiss her senseless for her big heart. She's doing a good thing here, and I need to be on board if I want to keep her. Which I do. In fact, I want to keep both of them. From the second I saw him, I felt possessive of him. I want him to be the best of men, and he's going to need a man to teach him how. Not that Letty won't be a wonderful mother in her own right, but there are still things a man needs to teach a son. *A son.* Does she want a father figure for her boy? Would Letty ever take a husband? Would she let me be Finn's father?

The night wears on, and Letty grows frustrated, but she won't let me help, and I feel helpless watching her. Eventually, she tells me to go to bed, and begrudgingly, I do as sitting on her couch watching her pace seems to upset her more. After another hour of crying, though, I get up and demand she give Finn to me. He settles within minutes, and I set him in his bassinet in her room.

"I hate you," she whispers, swiping at her eyes as I crawl in behind her. She doesn't mean it, and I know it.

"Why?" I press a kiss to her shoulder.

"You did that so easily. I'm terrible at this."

"He's just frustrated and more so as you grow frustrated. He can't calm down when you can't, and you're tired." I'm trying to be sensitive because I know if I say the wrong words, she'll snap.

She's quiet for a moment, and I think she's falling asleep, but then she speaks. "I'm sorry about earlier. I didn't mean what I said, but you did sort of surprise me."

"I shouldn't have brought it up," I begin, but she shifts to look at me over her shoulder.

"I can't come visit you, and it isn't fair to have you only visit me. I don't know how this will work for us, but I'm so grateful you're here now." I lean forward and briefly kiss her.

"I've gone nearly eight months without seeing my family in person, and that's not going to happen to us. I can handle six months."

"Still—" She interrupts, but I interrupt her right back.

"I want to be here for you. I promised myself if it ever happened again, I'd be available for the whole thing. I'm sorry it won't be that way. I can't leave the brewery behind, but I'll be here as often as I can.

"I'd never ask you to do this," she tells me. "As far as moving—"

"Cricket, can you forget I mentioned it? Let that brain rest a little bit. Get some sleep, okay, and we can talk about all this another day."

"I love you," she mutters, her voice falling quieter as I stroke up and down her back. Those words are all I need from her as a sign of commitment, a sign we'll figure it out.

"I love you, too."

+ + +

"I miss you," she whispers through the phone after telling me Finn fell asleep on her shoulder.

It's mid-January. Eight weeks down. We haven't spoken again about her moving to Georgia or what the end of six months will entail.

I'm gun-shy to mention it, so I bide my time and fly to her every few weeks. This is an off weekend, so I'm home and we're doing our nightly phone call.

"I miss you, too. I miss Finn." He's so much more than I thought he'd be. I didn't think I'd want to start over again at almost fifty, and I'm actually a little surprised at the encouragement from both Billy and Charlie to take on fatherhood again. I haven't mentioned the baby to my parents yet, using the excuse Letty's too busy with work to travel to Georgia.

She still worries the mother will show up and want to stake her claim on Finn. I send up a silent prayer each day that doesn't happen. Letty's a good mother despite her fears or maybe because of them. She wants a good future for the little guy, and so do I.

I never considered boy versus girl. It isn't an either/or; I just wanted healthy children, but I'm feeling this connection with Finn I can't explain. Maybe it's because I wasn't there for my girls as infants. Maybe it's because I have practice at being a dad. Whatever it is, I love the kid as though he's mine. I want him to be mine. Letty makes no hints about marriage or moving in or sharing Finn, though, and I won't ask for fear it will result in another disagreement. We seem to be on shaky ground despite the constant communication and the occasional visits. Our lovemaking has become less enthusiastic than our first meetings because she's exhausted. I feel her slipping from me, but I'm not ready to release her.

"How's the writing coming?" The last time I was there, she was scribbling notes in a notepad. When I asked her what she was doing, she said just jotting down ideas. I snuck a peek while she fixed a bottle for Finn.

"Are you writing a book?" I asked.

"Just playing around."

"Tell me," I demanded. I wanted to know what she was thinking, especially since she hinted this was something she wanted when she was younger.

"I just can't get Sam Calder and his Annie out of my head. Or the town. It's like an unsolved mystery. The place. Their love. Did she come

for the pickle jar? Did she get his message, whatever it was? It's a great story." She shrugged nonchalantly, but I don't want her to blow it off.

"You should write this. Make it your own or call him and get more details." She smiled half-heartedly and handed me the bottle. I liked feeding Finn. I liked holding him close, and when she fell next to me on the couch, leaning her head on my shoulder, I liked how it felt to be connected. Each of us touching as though we're a family.

"I thought up a few more ideas, but it's hard to concentrate with a lack of sleep. I'm learning to type while holding Finn."

I hate her struggles. I hate how alone she sounds. I want to be there for her. I want her here with me.

"I can't wait to read it."

"It's going to be embarrassing."

"Why?"

"Because you might recognize some scenes, Mr. Lumbersexual."

I chuckle, lying back on my bed. If I close my eyes, I can feel her next to me, pressing against me.

"You know I'm always limber for you."

"I miss sex," she whispers, and my dick twitches.

"Mmm…me too." My hand slips into my pants to straighten my growing length.

"I hate how I'm not in the mood." *And I release myself from my pants.* "Mommy-itis, I guess. Feeling a little not so pretty and desirable."

"You're desirable, darlin'. Very desirable."

I hear her shuffle through the phone. "Hang on," she whispers, and I assume she's setting Finn down in his crib. Then I hear a door close.

"How desirable am I?" she teases, and a smile curls my lips.

"Want me to talk you through it?"

"Yes, please. Guide me." This has become our code for leading her to touch herself like I did the first night we were together in the tent.

"Take off your shirt." I hear the phone shift and know she does as I command. "And stroke over your nipples." I slip my hand back into my pants, tugging at myself. "Show me."

I hear her gasp through the phone. "Giant?"

"Let's get on FaceTime. Lower the phone." We've been playing with the visual more and more. She shows me Finn and his progression, and it's amazing when Finn recognizes me and my voice through the video. She hangs up, and I send the FaceTime connection. When the visual pops up, it's her finger swirling around her breast.

"Fuck, that's hot," I groan, squeezing myself.

"Show me how hot," she hums, and I lower the phone, giving her a view as well. It's naughty and dirty, and I can't help myself. I'd never dream of doing something like this, showing off my dick while I get off, but I hear her purring through the line, and I want to give her anything she wants. "Watching you touch yourself makes me so wet."

She holds nothing back, angling her phone to show me her fingers dipping lower, and it's better than porn. This is live action, and while I want to be with her, this is the next best thing. Her sounds. The sight of her fingers disappearing into her pants.

"Take them off," I choke, stroking over myself as the tightness grows. She shimmies her yoga pants to her hips and then her fingers disappear between her thighs. She hums, and my eyes close a beat, imagining my fingers entering her. Imagining her sitting on my dick. Imagining her mouth on me.

"Cricket," I groan. *So close.* Her breath hitches.

"I'm close," she whimpers, her fingers moving as the phone jiggles.

"Fuck," I hiss as hot streams pour out of me, coating my hand. She's watching me from her vantage point, and she swears as well as her fingers still, and she rocks her hips. Damn, she's hot. "I miss you so much," I cry out, wanting to touch her, feel her, surround her.

"Me too," she whispers, coming down from the high. "It's never enough."

Never enough. I don't want to be alone. I don't want her to be alone.

"Soon, right?" It's the first hint I give. We only have a few more months, and then we'll talk. Then we'll figure it out. We just need to wait a little longer.

+ + +

Letty applied for Family Medical Leave Absence, asking for the full three months despite the fact she didn't give birth to her son. Her uncle was an ass about it, but human resources warned him he had to honor her rights. HR happens to be her mother. Score one point—finally—in the mom category.

Due to a snowstorm in Chicago, I miss a weekend at the end of January and can't reschedule until the middle of February. Around Valentine's Day, she's sick with a cold, and Finn seems to be teething. She's miserable when I'm there, and I feel helpless. We don't make love, and while it's not the be all and end all, I miss our physical connection.

As we near the end of February, her three-month mark quickly approaches.

I'm just not ready to leave him. That's silly, right? Women go back to work all the time after having babies, and I didn't even have him, technically. I just...I don't want to leave him with someone other than me, she tells me one night. I don't have any answers for her.

Come to Georgia. Marry me. Stay home to raise him. These are my thoughts.

"You look miserable," my father says to me as he walks into my office. I sigh and scrub a hand down my face. I've just gotten off the phone with Letty. "What's going on?"

My parents know that Letty and I have a long-distance relationship. I've let them believe it's because of work issues, which is partly true.

"Dad, I have something to tell you." Like a child of thirteen when I broke his fishing pole, the one Pap gave him as a kid, I feel sick. Thankfully, my father's calm reserve back then dismissed the situation as an accident. I might have left out how James and I were playing lightsabers with it, but still. This is so much bigger than a fishing pole accident.

"Letty has a baby."

"Is it yours?" I can't tell if my father is hopeful or concerned, but I quickly explain how Letty was in the adoption process before I met her. I also explain how I'm struggling to find my place in her life with the distance and the new little man.

223

L.B. Dunbar

We're dating, but are we more? I want us to be more, but I don't want to pressure her. She's under so much stress already, and after her reaction to my suggestion she move to Georgia, I don't have the heart or stomach to bring it up again. I don't mention this part to my father.

"When your mother had each of you, I struggled as well. She was so busy caring for each of you, it's a wonder there was another one." He chuckles, and I don't want to consider my parents having sex, but within seven years, they had five children. "Motherhood was her dream, and her pride is wrapped up in each of you kids. Where did I fit in then?"

I hold my breath, afraid for some reason.

"I was her rock. She's a strong woman, but even a mountain risks erosion, and when your mother felt herself crumple, she relied on me. I provided for you financially, but I like to think I had my own place in developing who you are. A boy needs a father to show him how to be a man." He takes a breath and smiles to himself, and I grin as I had the same thought regarding Finn. "And a man needs to lead by example, by loving and cherishing his wife." He narrows his eyes at me. There's no doubt my parents have loved each other well over the years. They never spend a night apart despite him taking late nights at BRMP or working long hours at the brewery. "*Your* place is in her heart. In her bed. Are you the rock? The soft landing? The comforting shoulder? Wherever or whatever she needs from you, that's where you fit in."

"I want to be all those things, but I want her here with me."

"You want the boy?"

"Is that really a question?"

"It is. Do you want the boy to be yours? He's still a baby, right? And he needs a daddy." He waves dismissively at me. "Oh, I know Letty can probably handle him as a single mother, but kids still need a father figure. Who will that be to him?"

I want it to be me. I don't want to even think of Letty with another man, or another guy becoming a dad to Finn.

"Are you ready to love him?"

"I was in love with him the moment I met him, just as I was with her." The feisty woman leaning over her car, trying to talk me down.

Name your price, Mr. Harrington. I could never have predicted it would be my heart.

Then I consider Finn. His sweet smile when he looks at me. How he tips his head on FaceTime like he recognizes my voice. Letty grows frustrated when he settles for me so easily when I hold him, but I secretly love it. It's as if he likes me back, and he knows I'll never let anything hurt him. He's safe with me. With us. I love my girls, but a boy... there are so many other emotions.

My father is thoughtful for a minute before he speaks. "We have no Harrington boys, Giant. All my boys had girls. My girl had boys." We stare at one another, thinking of James but not mentioning what happened to him. "Mati's sons are just as much Harringtons, but they don't carry the name."

I'm not certain where my dad is going with this.

"Dad, he's...uhm...he's not white. Not that it matters to me or should to you, but I feel like I should mention it." I also feel like an ass because I'm mentioning it.

"If you want her, you accept what's hers."

"I understand that."

"Blood is blood, son, and we all share it. The entire human race shares it. Family, that bond is what we make of it." He taps his chest, understanding we Harringtons are tight, and that's how he always wanted it to be. He stands without another word.

"Thanks, Dad," I call after him, still confused how to act or what to say. He pauses at the doorway to my office.

"Can you name him George? If you decide to adopt him." I sit up a little straighter. Adopt him? I'd thought it briefly before, but with my dad's suggestion... If I marry Letty, I can adopt Finn. Even if I don't marry her, if she doesn't want marriage because she's all I-am-woman-hear-me-roar, and we only live together, I could still adopt him. It would be a little extra security for him.

"He's already named Finnikin. Finn. She named him after some character in a book." *Finnikin of the Rock*, she told me. He was a strong character who went after the princess and did all he could to bring her safely home where she belonged.

225

L.B. Dunbar

Bring her home where she belongs.

"Finnikin Harrington," my father says, and my heart races as he speaks the name. "That's a damn fine name, too."

32
Mothers know best.

[Letty]

"I have a proposal for you."

My throat catches air as Giant's voice rings through the phone. I hadn't even said hello before he spoke. This isn't how I envisioned being asked but—

"I'd like to take three months off and come stay with you. Like my own FMLA. I can watch Finn while you go back to work. This gets him to nine months old." His voice sounds almost giddy with the suggestion, and giddy is never a word I'd use to describe Giant. "I want to adopt Finn with you."

"What?" My voice comes out strangled in both shock and question. I look up at Marcus, who came to visit me when I got some distressing news. I hold up a finger and cross the living room for the hallway. The line remains silent a moment. I don't know what to say. Giant adopting Finn was something I hadn't considered. Well, I had considered it but only in my fantasies of family. But he isn't even asking to marry me. He's asking to adopt Finn. And on today, of all days. "Giant, I—"

"I love you. You love me. This can work. I'll come up there and stay with him and begin the process. Whatever needs to be done."

Giant doesn't legitimately live here, so I don't see how the courts would accept him.

"Then what?" I wonder, my voice dropping as my head hits the wall behind me. I can't have this conversation. Not today. *You should tell him*, my mind whispers.

"I don't know," he says, his voice hesitant, the distance between us spanning more than a hundred miles. I've felt us drifting apart over the past few months. We talk every day, and I relish the time, but something has shifted between us.

"Giant, I don't think that's a good idea."

"Why not?" his gruff question echoes through the phone.

L.B. Dunbar

"I appreciate the offer, but I don't think adopting Finn is a solution. Or even a plan. I didn't foresee sharing him. Selfishly, I saw a baby for only myself." It's true, but it's not. I never envisioned being alone. I wanted love and marriage, a baby plus a husband. A family of my own. It all came together so differently in my dreams. I want Giant but not out of duress. Suggesting he adopt Finn feels like a scramble, grasping at loose ends to hold onto something falling apart.

"I don't think this will work." My voice drops even lower as I close my eyes.

"What won't work?"

I don't reply, a lump forming in my throat.

"Don't do this," he quietly pleads, sensing where I'm going with my comment. I swallow the lump clogging my airway as I prepare to do what I think is best under the circumstances. I walk back into the living room and sit across from Marcus. Wiggling my fingers, I reach out for his hand. I need support. I need to be strong.

Be brave. Be strong.

"I found a nanny. She's young, but she'll come to the condo, and my work is flexible enough that I can do most of it from home. Frank isn't allowing me to travel, so this is covered."

Marcus's eyes open wide. He mouths, "*What are you doing?*" while I shake my head at him. I close my eyes, squeezing his hand.

"I love you," Giant mutters, his voice rough and low, so low I can hardly hear him. I swallow again, the lump now the size of a boulder and choking me. My heart feels just as heavy.

"I love you both," he says, and my breath hitches. Finn. *He loves Finn?*

"You're the best thing to ever happen to me." My voice cracks. "Along with Finn." Finn comes first for me. He'll always need to be first.

"So that's it?" he whispers. "We can't even discuss this."

"I don't see any other way." Ask me to marry you. Ask me again to come live with you. Tell me everything will be okay. Don't make it only about Finn, my son.

A shuddering breath releases with my thoughts. I'm doing what I think is best as Finn's mother. *Don't form sudden attachments.* I am

228

attached, and I don't want to lose him, though it's a strong possibility. Giant's grown attached to him as well, and a tear rolls down my cheek with the thought.

I refuse to look at Marcus even though he's tugging my hand, begging me through the physical contact not to do what I'm doing.

"Goodbye, Giant," I whisper.

"Bye, Cricket," fills the line, and then he's gone.

+ + +

"Tell me I did the right thing," I say, still holding Marcus's hand across my coffee table.

"Do you want me to tell you the truth?" he asks, jiggling Finn on his right thigh. Finn is almost six months old, and he's grown so much in the three months I've had him. Holding his head up, pressed against Marcus's belly, the miniature human being with his dark, trusting eyes is a marvel.

Did I do the right thing for you?

"Lie to me," I mouth, tears clouding my eyes as I stare at my son.

"You did the right thing." The lie hurts as much as the decision. For the past three months, Giant has come to see me every two or three weeks, and having him in my home has been amazing. He's a great pseudo-dad, and my imagination ran away with me each weekend he was here, envisioning us as a family. But the more I imagined us together, the more unfair it seemed. We were on a one-way street, and we weren't driving in the same direction. This—*us together*—only reinforced what I want deep down inside. I want love, marriage, and a baby in the baby carriage, along with happily ever after. I want it all with Giant while Giant has already had these things.

I don't want a weekend-only father for Finn. I lied to him. It wasn't that I didn't want to share Finn with another person. My little man could use a male mentor in his life, but I couldn't let it be someone coming and going. I want stability for Finn. Stability I didn't have as a child after my dad died and Uncle Frank played father figure when it suited him. Owen needed someone consistently, too, and so will Finn.

After Giant's one-time suggestion to move to Georgia, we never discussed the future again. I had all kinds of questions but didn't ask them. Should I move away from Chicago? Did I want to keep selling real estate?

I've thought a lot about myself since I've had time off from work. What do I want for me now that I have Finn? Is real estate really my calling? Is motherhood the only thing that will define me? What about the next forty years of my life?

And when I am free of the adoption restrictions, what will I do about Giant and our long-distance relationship? Continue to travel once a month to see him with a small child? It doesn't seem fair to anyone. We can't keep playing part-time, weekend lovers…with a baby in the middle.

I want to adopt Finn. What was he thinking?

I didn't ask. I don't want to ask him to do something I know he can't—live here. He'd hate it. He already told me as much, and as the owner and director of his company, he shouldn't leave the brewery. And if I lose Finn, as today is hinting, there won't be any Finn to adopt, which clears Giant of feeling any obligation or whatever he's feeling to make this happen. I won't tie Giant down. He's the type of man to stick, but I don't want him to be stuck. As much as he doesn't admit it, he's already been in that position. I don't want to make concessions in my life as I've done with real estate and settling for a Hudson, and I can't ask Giant to do the same. He wants an adventure with me, but what kind of adventure can I offer him—single mother compared to an empty nester? Another child when his are grown? He has grandchildren, for heaven's sake. I had to make a choice, and for now, I choose me and Finn because I can't lose Finn.

Which reminds me of this morning's phone call from the adoption liaison. The birth mother has been found. The mediator assures me they can get the biological mother to sign off on Finn, but I'm on edge. She's abandoned him, yet she has all the rights to him. It isn't fair. It isn't just. I could use Giant's support, but I don't want to involve him. I understand this makes me wishy-washy when I need to be firm. Stable. Reliable. Here for Finn.

"Can I tell you the truth now?" Marcus asks, interrupting my rambling thoughts. I haven't been able to stay focused on any one thing over the past few months. "You look miserable."

The tears fall in earnest at his comment, and I release his fingers to cover my face with my hands.

"I am," I say into my palms, and Marcus shifts to sit next to me.

"Honey, I don't understand. You love him. He loves you. Why didn't you tell him?"

"I just…I don't know what I want." Another lie. "I don't think I'm being fair to him by having him come here every other weekend, and right now, I need to prove stability. I need to show the system I'm the more stable choice."

My personal life is under scrutiny, and the adoption liaison suggested I remove any thing not solid in my life. Giant is solid, but he's not mine to keep, and the process doesn't want to see a part-time lover, part-time father figure coming and going from Finn's life.

"I thought Giant came willingly."

"He did."

"He washed your hair." His voice softens, but I snap.

"Stop reminding me how he is one of the most romantic men I've ever met." I can't tell Marcus how one weekend when Giant was visiting, we struggled to get in my bathtub together, and he did it again. Then he curled me over the edge of the tub and took me from behind. The images in my head make me miss him already.

Marcus rolls his lips inward, staring back at me with wide eyes.

"I'm sorry," I mutter, lowering my head again as the tears continue to fall.

"Listen to me. That man did not travel hundreds of miles every few weeks because he didn't want to be with you. He had no reason to come here, Letty, other than you and this baby, which isn't even his, and he just offered to adopt him."

Marcus isn't wrong, but I need to do what I think is best. I can't have the liaison think I'm a flight risk or flighty with a long-distance relationship. I need to show I'm stable, concrete, and willing to stick for Finn.

231

What will I do if the system takes Finn from me?

Marcus held my hand to keep me steady in my resolve to end things with Giant. I know me. I was cracking under the tone of Giant's voice, but I had to do the right thing.

"He wants you," Marcus states. "He wants Finn. I don't see the problem. He just offered to play daddy while you return to Mc-Hell-in." Mc-Hell-in is our nickname for Mullen RE although Marcus doesn't really dislike his job as my assistant.

"*Play* Daddy," I remind him. "Not be a daddy."

"Don't *play* semantics with me," Marcus warns, lifting an eyebrow. "He just offered to come stay for three months."

"Three months, not forever."

Marcus glares at me.

"And what if they take Finn from me?" I whisper. Marcus's eyes soften. He knows the fear is real as he and his partner still haven't been matched with a baby.

"Don't think such negative things. Be brave. Be strong. Think positive thoughts."

"If only it were that easy," I say, swiping at the tears which continue to streak my cheeks. "I don't want Giant to sacrifice for me, for Finn. I don't want him to put his life on hold, especially under these new conditions. I can't have a...a lover...living here. And say I do keep Finn, what happens after the next three months pass?"

"He washes your hair?" Marcus teases in question, but when I scowl at him, his expression turns stern. "Why do you have to question everything? That's what love does, Ms. Pierson. Gives. Holds. Sacrifices." He doesn't need to remind me Hudson did none of these things. Four years with one man, and nothing. Four months with another, and everything. Love is a strange beast.

"*When* you've completed your six months," he emphasizes with full confidence that I won't lose Finn. "You get out of here," he suggests, making it sound like a prison break. Like it's just that easy to spring free. Quit the job. Sell my place. Move several states away.

"What do I do? Drop everything and go to Georgia. He hasn't asked me to do that again, and I don't know how to bring it up. I don't want to suggest I move there if he doesn't want that anymore. I don't want to push him into something when he's already done the marriage thing. He's offering to come here to be nice because that's the kind of man he is. He isn't suggesting something long-term." I sigh. "Besides, I have bigger concerns to consider right now." I stare down at Finn on Marcus's lap.

"Letty, just stop it. You don't think he can love again? He's told you he loves you. You don't think he wants this baby? He just suggested he'd adopt him. Maybe it wasn't on his radar a few months ago when you hiked a mountain and slept with him in a tent. I doubt *you* were on his meter stick until you suddenly were."

"Marcus," I warn him and his euphemisms.

"Something happened right. You connected. No man travels hundreds of miles to see a girl if he doesn't want her permanently. Nor does he wash her hair."

"Marcus!" I growl.

"I'm just saying. Letty, so what if he hasn't asked? It's the modern age. Look at Peter and me. Ask Giant or, better yet, be your demanding self and tell him: I'm moving to Georgia. Ask *him* to marry you!"

Marcus and his partner had this unconventional question. When you're gay, who does the proposing? Marcus decided to ask Peter to marry him. Peter's the one who proposed a child through adoption.

"That's ludicrous," I admonish.

"And so is throwing away the love of your life. And don't tell me Hudson was him because I'll never believe you. I've seen you with Giant."

Marcus met us once for brunch, and another time, we had dinner with him and Peter. He's seen Giant and I together. We laugh. We stare. We touch.

I exhale in frustration. "I didn't do the right thing, did I?"

"Want the truth this time?"

I shake my head, but I'll listen.

"I don't think so, honey." His squinting eyes tell me I should have been honest with Giant. Told him the stress I was under. The news I received.

233

L.B. Dunbar

"I know," I mutter. "But it's not like I can call him back and say, hey, I'm a nut-head lately, forgive me. Or better yet, race down to him and grovel at his feet." I can't leave Illinois, and I want to curse the adoption process even though I understand its reasoning. I want to raise my fist and scream. *I am a good woman. I deserve this abandoned child. Why can't you trust me?* But I don't want anything to get in my way of keeping Finn forever.

Nothing's permanent, Olivet, until it's in black ink on dotted lines. It might be Uncle Frank's only decent advice.

"If you call him, I think he'll understand you're a little off balance lately. And yes, typically an apology works best, and when groveling, so do blow jobs, but we don't need to discuss that."

My head can't wrap around the fact I won't be giving Giant one of those to make up for what I've done. I won't be kissing him or touching him or anything ever again.

"You didn't even tell him about Mr. Calder?" Marcus reminds me, and I sit up, brushing at my cheeks.

Marcus gives me a disapproving look once again. It took a few months of persistently pestering one Drake Calder, grandson and attorney to Sam, to forgive me and then get what I wanted—an interview with the old man. I'd been hurt after what my uncle thought I'd done, but I couldn't shake the feeling there was a reason I met Mr. Calder, the elder, in the wrong place at the right time instead of his grandson. Maybe it was the romantic in me, but I couldn't let it go.

"Why didn't you at least tell Giant about that?"

Never let anything divide you. Not family, business, money, or a river.

Oh Mr. Calder, how right you were, yet what about miles and miles of distance? His girl moved to California, and he never got her back. Why didn't she come back? I bet she was afraid. I bet the resort in her memories didn't match the reality of her heart, and she couldn't turn back. Her summer of love was all a fantasy. A great adventure. One she'd never forget.

My shoulders fall, and I reach for Finn on Marcus's lap, needing the comfort of holding my child. Once he's in my arms, I remind myself

234

I need to think about more than me. I need to continue with my initial plan despite the stabbing pain in my chest. I need to do what's best to keep Finn.

"I think I need to let the poor man be." My resolve returns just a little bit. The best thing for Giant is to set him free.

33

Brotherly love

[Giant]

Three more months have passed, and being the last week of May, her six months are up any day.

"You look like shit." A gruff male voice mocks me while my throat burns with another swallow of whiskey. I should be over at Blue Ridge Microbrewery and Pub, celebrating the Summer Fling Sample Thing Billy thought up as another draw to the bar. Samples and such will be provided to introduce our summer brews, but I couldn't handle the festivities.

"Surprised to see you here." A heavy hand pats my shoulder, holds a moment, and then a man sits on the barstool next to me. I turn to face James. This is his hangout. Ridged Edge is a bar on the outskirts of town, appropriately named, as well as owned and operated by Rebel's Edge, the local biker club. James is second in command. He joined them at a low point in his life. They aren't hard-core one-percenters, but they've had their share of unsavory dealings. It's one reason I didn't feel safe with Letty up on the mountain with him nearby.

You're the best thing to ever happen to me, along with Finn. Then don't walk away, I wanted to shout during that phone call months ago, but I heard it in her voice. We were over.

"It's a free country because of men like me," I slur, rousing myself from thoughts of Letty. I went off to fight for America. James decided to do service Stateside. Search and rescue was his calling, and he became a ranger in the Smoky Mountain area, saving people on terrain more familiar to him than the dry, arid desert was to me.

"Thank you for your service," he mocks, rapping on the bar and then holding up two fingers. This place isn't their secluded club. It's open to the public who might want a little taste of danger and maybe a one-night stand. I'm contemplating both, but then Letty pops into my thoughts once again, and I know it isn't true. I'd never have a one-night stand again.

"What brings you here?" My younger brother's rugged tone matches my own.

I hold up my low glass and jiggle it for him. The amber liquid inside sloshes from side to side like my stomach. I'm trying to ignore the ache in my heart.

Selfishly, I saw a baby only for myself.

She was lying. She wanted it all, and I was willing to give it to her. "I'm having a shit day," I mumble. A shit week. A shit month. A shitty few months. So much *shit*.

James snorts next to me. The bartender brings him a few fingers of whiskey in a lowball glass like mine and slides another in front of me. James taps my glass with his before lifting it to his lips. "To women."

I huff and stroke a hand over my beard. *I need a trim.*

"Lost my girl," I mutter, shocked to admit the words out loud to my absentee brother. Being closest in age compared to my other siblings, he was my best friend as a kid. Two years younger made no difference. Then I went away. Life got in the way.

His head swivels, and he stares at the side of my face. I don't need to look over at him to know he understands me—what I feel and what I'm thinking. He's lost many women in his life.

He exhales. "Damn, I liked her." He doesn't mean it in any other way than he was impressed by her when he met her that one time up at the old ranger station on the mountain. She held her own against me even with him as an audience. The time reminds me…

"What were you doing up there? At the station last fall?"

James turns his head forward, staring at the glass bottles along the opposite wall while I face him. His profile is similar to mine yet not the same. He has more gray hair—silver actually—despite being younger than me. A scraggly patch of hairs circles his mouth and lines his jaw, heaviest on his chin. His blue eyes are as sad as I feel, but the edge to his cheeks tells me he's keeping it in. Maybe we aren't so dissimilar after all.

L.B. Dunbar

"Camping." He's lying, and we both know it. As he told me, the station isn't a campground.

"We heard shots." I pause, giving my brother time to explain himself.

"That was target practice." Sarcasm drips from his voice.

"That's what you told Charlie. Want to tell me the truth?"

James's lip tweaks at the corner of his mouth, and he stares back at me, his eyes admitting he knows I know he's lying. "You always were the smartest of all of us."

I chuckle without humor. "You know Charlie is the smartest."

James snorts. "Let's get back to your girl. What happened?" His voice shifts, and I hear the familiar sound of him buried beneath the tough exterior he's built over the last few years. The voice of my brother, the best friend, who could read me and my silence better than most. He doesn't typically chat with us as his real family, resigning himself to the club as his brotherhood, but I'm grateful for a moment he's acting like the brother I once knew and still love.

"It's a long story, but the short of it is, she adopted a baby, and she didn't want me to be part of it."

I want to adopt Finn with you.

Then what?

"Ouch," James mumbles. Talking about a child is the last thing I want to do with my brother, but he continues to question me. "Why'd she adopt?"

"A number of reasons," I say, not wanting to give away all of Letty's secrets. "But I think most of all she just wanted a family after a jilted relationship."

"How do you fit in there?" He scoffs.

"I was the next guy." My attention turns back to my brother, and he stares at me, pain resonating in his eyes. He's the only Harrington with blue eyes.

Was I some kind of transition man for Letty? I don't believe it for a second, but still, I have my doubts. What were we doing all those months besides playing house? I thought we were building something, biding our time until time passed, and we could take the next step.

238

James nods next to me, knowing all about "the next guy" syndrome.

"Women sure do know how to sock a punch," he mutters, giving away his only weakness as he turns his attention to the liquor in his glass. He stares at the whiskey before taking a deep swallow of the burning liquid. "I'm sorry, man."

Silence falls between us another minute. It's one of the best qualities about my relationship with James. We don't need to fill any quiet with useless chatter.

Cricket certainly could chirp, and I almost chuckle with the thought until I remember how sad I am not to hear her voice, her sounds, her hum. My dick weeps at the same time it jolts for attention. My entire being misses her.

"Evie didn't call." The admission startles me as much as him sitting next to me. Evie Pepperly was the love of James's life, and he never mentions her name. Never. But I know about his pact with her. Once a year, she guarantees to call him. It's always around this time. *Fuck*. I don't know who has it worse. Then I peer over at my brother. Him, he definitely has it worse than I do.

"I'm sorry, man," I reply to him as he did to me. He shrugs, but he isn't so nonchalant over this missed call. He won't tell me more, and his demeanor tells me not to ask.

"You know," he begins after another moment. "If she was my girl, I'd fight everything in my way to keep her."

Considering Letty is the main thing standing in my way of obtaining her, I snort.

"I'm serious. A baby wouldn't keep me away from a woman if I loved her. It would redouble my efforts to be with her instead."

Oh man, this is going to get real deep, real fast if we start talking about kids, but then a thought occurs to me. An elderly voice fills my head.

Never let anything divide you.

Sam Calder. That man had loved someone deeply. Enough that he wanted to rebuild a resort in hopes his lost woman would return. What could I build for Letty to bring her back to me?

239

"It isn't the baby that's holding her back," I mutter although I'm not certain that's true. She wanted everything: love, marriage, family.

I sit up straighter on my stool.

Family. Did she misunderstand? Did she not see I wanted it all with her as well?

Don't do this, I said, but did I explain myself to her? It wasn't only adopting Finn; it was about marrying her as well. It was about building a family.

Fucking hell.

I scrub a hand down my face. "Love sucks," I mutter although I don't mean it. The love I've had with Letty has been everything to me. I'm not certain I've explained myself to her, and now, it's too late.

"Don't I know it," James mumbles. Then he taps my empty glass with the edge of his and downs the rest of his whiskey. "You win. You look pathetic, old man." His lips twist as the corner crooks into a half-ass grin, and I'm reminded once again of us when we were younger, always trying to one-up each other. God, how I've missed him.

"Speak for yourself," I snark, reaching out to ruffle his hair as though he were still a kid. His hand catches my wrist before I can touch him, and our eyes lock. The hold he has on me is tight and meaningful, a warning. My sign he's no longer my kid brother. "Sorry," I mutter.

"Me too," he says, releasing my wrist and lowering his hand to his thigh. His fingers spread and then clench together. He closes his eyes for a second. His body trembles.

"Still having nightmares?" I question, pushing him another inch. "You know I understand." It's my olive branch. My hope that he'll turn to me as his big brother, like he once did when we were kids. Turn to me like he should have when things turned sour for him.

"I'm not doing this with you." He immediately stands. His hand hovers in the air, and then he retracts it to his side. "Happy Birthday, big brother."

I'm surprised he remembered. The marker of my birth coincides with a low time in his existence.

"Thanks," I mutter, but he's already walking away. Fifty years old. Why do I feel like this is the story of my life? People always walking away. My wife is dead. My girls live in Atlanta. And the woman I believe to be the new love of my life doesn't want me involved in hers.

I continue to watch James retreat until a woman saunters up to him, wrapping herself around him, and he kisses her temple. The affection looks forced. His emotions are locked back within his jaw.

To brothers, I decide as I lift my empty glass. Then I pick up my phone to call Charlie for a ride. I'm too buzzed to drive.

An email alert catches my attention before I make the call, and I absentmindedly click the notification when I see the sender is Mullen Realty.

The court settled in her favor after the mother signed over her maternal rights. Thought you'd like to know she's finally free and gets to keep the baby.

All the best, Marcus Klurg.

What the fuck? Was Letty in jeopardy of losing Finn? Why hadn't she told me?

I stare at the message.

She would have called me if she wanted me to know. It's clear she doesn't. She got what she wanted with Finn, and he'll have a great life.

I just wish I could be in it—with both of them.

Instead, I delete the email and call my brother Charlie for a ride home, where I'll be going alone. Always alone.

34

Name your price

[Giant]

After my lacking celebratory drink with James, I give in to the longing to isolate myself. I head up the mountain the following weekend. I haven't had the heart to come to the cabin all spring, sensing memories of Letty would be all around me, but she never entered the place. We'd been higher up on Pap's land instead. And I want the solitude.

The heavy thwack of an ax splintering wood does nothing to ease my thoughts or the worrisome questions within my head. Why did Marcus send the email and not Letty? How had Marcus found me? I assume my information is office knowledge after Letty's attempt to solicit me for my land. I want to smile at the memory of her, but instead, I hammer down at the wood with more force. I don't want her to be a memory. I want her in my arms, in my home, in my heart.

I walk up the porch of the cabin to stack an armful of chopped wood by the front door and then return to the yard, preparing to start chopping another pile when an SUV clears the trees and exits the narrow drive.

Now what? I mutter in my head. No one comes up here. You'd have to be really lost to stumble upon this place.

The SUV draws near, and my fingers clench harder at the shaft of the ax in my hand. My chest heaves as I consider throwing it at the windshield to stop whoever is driving recklessly close to me. The vehicle stops short of my wood pile, and the driver door opens. For a second, the offending driver is hidden by the large door. Then, out steps a woman, one I recognize immediately with my eyes, my heart, and another body part that hasn't been used on the regular since some time back in the winter.

Cricket, my heart screams, but I don't speak to her.

"Mr. Harrington?"

Is she serious? I watch as her throat rolls with a swallow, and her hands clench at her sides. Her eyes stay focused on mine. She's wearing tight jeans with flip-flops and a tank top. Her clothes hug her body, outlining a form I've missed with each passing second of the past few months. It's warm for late May. The trees are all in bloom, and the sky is bright, but I can't take my eyes off her.

"George Harrington the second?" she formally inquires, and I drop the ax in order to cross my arms. I turn my head away from her, staring off in the distance. *She's kidding me, right?*

"Giant," she whispers, and I close my eyes. My heart squeezes. I want to run to her, wrap her in my arms, and inhale the scent of her hair. Mouthwatering apricots.

Then I want to shake her for breaking my heart.

"Where's Finn?" I ask, turning back to the SUV and wondering if she left him somewhere back in Chicago at her home.

"He's sleeping." She hitches a thumb in the direction of the vehicle.

He's here. She brought Finn with her. She's free to travel about the country.

"What are you doing here?" I don't want to ask. I want to wait her out and hear her explanation before I sound desperate; however, my voice is rough and the question harsh. Her hands clutch together before her, and her head lowers.

"I don't suppose you'd believe I was in the area. That would seem a little impossible. Then again, I could say I'm looking for property, which I am. I'm looking to make an investment for a buyer, and I heard this is a good area. Pretty trees. Lovely sky. The male scenery isn't too bad, either."

Not this again.

She's rambling to fill the space, and her lips curl up at the corner, pleased with herself. If she's flirting with me, she's going to have to try a lot harder. I'm hurt. We've had no contact since the break-up phone call. The rip-me-to-shreds-and-throw-me-away-in-the-wind phone call. I wrote a hundred emails and deleted them all. I never received one from her. I want her reasons. I want to understand.

You destroyed me, I want to yell at her while she stares at me all adorable in her tight jeans and teasing smile with chirping lips. Lips I want to kiss. I'm a fucking contradiction.

243

L.B. Dunbar

"There's nothing for sale here," I say, keeping my tone curt. My heart races, and my arms tighten around my chest, willing myself to stay still and not approach her.

"Perhaps in town?" My brows pinch. *What does she mean?* "Or something in the general area?"

What? "Land's empty and owned for miles."

"I could build. I know those Duncans have a construction business in the family."

What the…?

"You can't build out here, Letty," I snap, and she flinches at my voice.

"I remember."

My nostrils flare. *What's she playing at then?* Did she really return in hopes of gaining the land? What is she doing here? What does she want? I want to tell her to go home and leave me alone while at the same time, I want to pull her to me and fuck her in the front grass.

"Name your price, Mr. Harrington."

Is she fucking kidding me?

"There's nothing left here." I practically growl at her, my arms lowering to my sides. I mean, what can I say. I'm nothing. There's nothing for her. She took all that was important to me. Her. Finn. My heart.

"Name your price. Everybody has one," she states, holding firm as she takes a few steps toward me. Her fingers open and close, forming fists of control. I didn't realize I'd moved, but suddenly, we stand closer to one another, only a foot or two apart.

"Mr. Har—"

"You. And Finn. That's my price."

She stills while her breath hitches.

Dammit. *Why did I let that slip?* My head lowers to face the ground. I scrub a hand over my trimmed beard. I'm waiting for her to step back, enter her big rental, and drive off. Instead, two feet with pink-painted toenails come into view near the tips of my boots. Slowly, I lift my head.

"Sold," she whispers, and my eyes widen.

What is she saying?

244

"If I camp on the mountain, will you forgive me?"

"Cricket." I sigh. Dammit, why is she so cute? No, beautiful. Fucking beautiful.

"I can hike up the mountain and back," she offers.

I fight a slow grin that wants to curl my lips. My fingers twitch at my side.

"What about ax throwing?"

"Maybe."

"I've been practicing."

"Really?" I'm astonished.

"Yeah, remember there's this bar in Chicago? I went there before the wedding. I scored a—"

"Anyone ever tell you, you talk too much?" I can no longer fight the smile threatening my lips.

"Yes, this grumpy mountain man once did. He made me sleep in a tent on the lumpy ground and eat out of a pan."

Sheepishly, I gaze at her. "I thought he was a lumber something or other. And I don't remember you complaining." Are we really doing this? Are we flirting with each other? There's so much to be said, but my heart leaps in my chest even though I still don't understand what she's doing here.

"Lumber*sexual*," she draws out. "And no, I didn't complain. In fact, I liked it. I loved it." She swallows as her eyes hold mine. "I…I still love you."

My head flicks back while my shoulders fall, and the tension slips out of me. I don't know if I feel sucker punched by her words or if I've lost my breath.

She still loves me.

"What are you doing here?"

"I…I was thinking of moving to Georgia." My brows rise so high the skin on my forehead crinkles. "There's a little house in town for rent, and I'm thinking of—"

"Fuck that," I bark.

L.B. Dunbar

"Excuse me?" Her hands come to her hips, standing off with me, and I see a hint of the woman I first met, the one who sparked my interest to play with her and dare her to go camping with me.

"You are not renting a house in Georgia."

"And why not?" Her eyelids flutter as her face pinks.

"Because if you're going to live anywhere, it's with me." I don't know where the demand comes from, as I should phrase it as more of a suggestion, but I'm finished suggesting ideas to this woman.

"Well, aren't you presumptuous? Or do I seem like a foregone conclusion?" Her smile grows, and her cheeks brighten. Damn, she's the prettiest thing I've ever seen. "You think you can smile pretty at me with that sweaty back and heaving solid chest." She points at my waist. "With your manly hairs dipping into your pants and I'll just do as you say."

I look down at my bare chest, noting how my pants sit a little lower on my hips. My head lifts, and I meet her glowing blue eyes, matching the sky above us.

"Does that work for you?"

"If the price is right." She pauses. "But I have a price, too."

"Because everyone does," I mock. *Aw, shit.* I feel like I'm on a roller coaster ride, holding my breath on the ups and losing my stomach on the downs.

"No. But. Well, my price...is...I want you to love me and adopt Finn. Once you marry me."

We stare at one another.

Did she just say what I think she said?

Is she...?

"Cricket?" My voice strains as she lowers to one knee, digging for something in her pocket.

"Giant Harrington—"

I hold up a hand to stop her. I don't want to stop her, but this isn't how it should be. I'm prepared to do the asking. In fact, I've been prepared for months and have just been waiting out the time.

"Will you do me the honor of marrying me and accepting my son as your own?"

246

One finger covers my lips to hold back the laughter rumbling up my throat.

"What?" She stares up at me from her kneeling position, holding a thick dark ring between her fingers. I reach down for her elbow and tug her upward to stand before me.

"Woman, I've wanted to marry you since I saw you in Chicago in that hideous dress at your sister's wedding."

"Really?" Her eyes widen as her hand lowers, but I catch her wrist, holding the ring-supporting fingers between us. My eyes remain on the thick band.

"Actually, I take that back. It was the night in the ranger station." I tug her to me, her breasts knocking into my chest with the ring still in her fingers. "When I took you from behind during a thunderstorm."

"And that sealed the deal?" She giggles while an admonishing brow tweaks upward in question.

"Knew I'd never be able to live without you from that moment forward," I say, swearing it's true as I dip my forehead to meet hers.

"You had me at ax throwing," she teases, and I wrap an arm around her, pulling her even closer, still keeping her hand with the ring between us. "I'm sorry for what I did. I should have never broken up with you. I've missed you every day and—"

Her chattering stops the second my lips meet hers. Her tongue slips along the seam of mine, and I open, allowing her in, so happy she's home with me. My home. Our home. We savor one another, feeling as if it's been years yet only yesterday. I don't want to ever lose her again.

"Is that a yes?" she asks, pulling back from me and glancing at the ring still braced between her fingers.

"Let's have you hold that for a bit," I say. Her lips fall, and then a squeak comes from the vehicle.

35

When a door opens

[Letty]

"It's Finn," I quietly say, crestfallen he didn't respond to my proposal. Instead, he looked like he wanted to laugh. Laugh me off the mountain perhaps. I'd deserve it. I took a chance, and this is what I get.

You broke up with him. That's what you got.

"I'll get him," Giant offers and steps around me. He hasn't taken the ring from my fingers, and I don't know what to do next, so I slip it back into my pocket, feeling foolish and idealistic. He stops as I haven't moved and watches the ring disappear in my pocket. His mouth opens and then shuts.

I deserve the hesitant treatment. My heart aches, and I blink back the sting in my eyes.

"Why did you rent such a big truck?" he asks, opening the back door and leaning in to unclip Finn from his car seat.

"I didn't rent it. It's mine."

Giant stands upright, holding Finn to his shoulder. "It's yours." His eyes narrow. "Did you drive here? From Chicago?"

"I did."

"That's a long drive alone. With a baby." He jiggles Finn at his shoulder, pressing a kiss to the side of his head. "Who is growing into a big boy?" He smiles at Finn and then turns back to me. "Why?"

"I wanted to get to you as soon as I could, and Finn needs so much stuff. It was too complicated to fly. And I just..." I wasn't really thinking. As soon as I knew I could leave the state, I packed our bags and all Finn's necessities. I put my place up for sale. Marcus is my realtor. I had to get to Giant. In person. I couldn't call him or send a text. I needed to see his face if he rejected me.

In hindsight, I might have been hasty in more than one decision.

"Cricket, that wasn't very safe," he admonishes.

"Ten hours plus stops. He was such a good boy." I reach up and rub down Finn's back as he stares up at Giant. "Remember Giant, Finn?" I ask him as if he can answer me, but he turns his head, recognizing his name. Then he looks up at Giant and tugs his beard. Giant moves his little hand and sucks at his fingers. He's so sweet to him.

I want to adopt Finn with you.

I guess he's changed his mind. I feel sick. I drove all this way, nerves eating at me, and now...I'm just tired.

"What time did you leave?"

"Around three a.m." It's close to six in the evening now. He eyes me for a minute, still playing catch with Finn's fingers as they reach for his beard. Giant's mouth sucks them in.

"You hungry?"

Not really. "I could eat." I slip my hands into my back pockets, which forces my breasts forward, and Giant's eyes lower to the cleavage swelling out the top of my tank. It's warmer here than in the Midwest, and I'm sticky from the drive and the heat.

"I'll make us dinner," he says, but there's an awkwardness between us.

"I should probably go to Conrad Lodge and check in." I drove all this way and suddenly feel like I need a minute away from him.

"Didn't you hear what I said? You're moving in with me."

"But I..." *I just asked you to marry me, and you didn't answer.* "I think maybe we should talk about a few things first."

His expression holds firm. He's given me a hint of a grin but nothing like the smiles he used to give me. No laughter, which I miss. I remember wondering what it would be like to hear him laugh. *Would it rock my world?* It did. In more ways than one.

He kissed me, searing and sweet but not enough. More like the marking of territory but not the possession of my heart. He doesn't want me.

Then why is he insisting I move in?

"We can talk over dinner. You got any bags?"

"A whole trunk full of stuff." Finn doesn't travel lightly, and I didn't know how long we'd be staying, if we stayed at all. I'm suddenly too exhausted to consider turning around and driving seven hundred miles back home. I don't feel like Chicago should be our home. With Giant is where we need to be.

You're moving in with me.

Why? He didn't agree to marry me. I'm an idiot.

Giant walks to the back of the SUV and pops the door open. He whistles low as he looks at Finn. "She never did know how to pack."

"Hardy-har. Most of this is his." The pack and play portable crib. A bouncing seat. Diapers. Bottles. Clothing. Teething toys.

Giant hands me Finn and takes the portable crib and a duffle bag in hand. He walks around the open door, and I assume I'm to follow him.

My heart hammers as I finally enter his cabin. The inside is rustic but cozy. The living room spans the length of the front of the house with a giant fireplace as the centerpiece. An overstuffed couch faces the fireplace with a bearskin rug on the floor. On one side of the chimney is a ladder leading up to a loft.

"My girls slept there. It was the original sleeping quarters. The rafters are low, and there's a mattress on the floor." Giant nods to the door next to the ladder. "My room is back there. I'll set Finn's crib up in there. It will be easier than hiking up and down that ladder. The kitchen's on the other side," he says, tipping his head to an archway opening to the right of the chimney.

"That's not real, is it?" I ask of the rug.

"What do you think?"

"Wayfair dot com, I hope. Otherwise, Sarah might be upset," I suggest, referencing a popular online homeware retailer and his animal-loving daughter. Giant chuckles, not answering me. He takes Finn's stuff in his room, and I follow. The bed is made up with a camp blanket in red and black plaid. It's a four-poster bed, and I can't imagine his big body fitting on it. Then I imagine other things—like my wrists tied to the headboard or me bent over the footboard—and I want to cry at the ache in my core. He's never going to enter me again. He wants to be roommates. I want a husband.

"You okay?" he asks, and I weakly smile.

"Yeah. I'm good." *I'm horrible.* This isn't the greeting I'd hoped for, but I was too romantic in my thoughts. I'd propose. He'd say yes. Then he'd say he loved me, forgave me, and couldn't live without me.

Knew I'd never be able to live without you from that day forward.

He heads out to my SUV for another load and drops most of it just inside the cabin. "We can sort this later. I'll start dinner."

He's so...standoffish again.

"Can I help?" I ask although I don't know how or what I'd do. I'm losing the fight with tears as my eyes burn and my nose prickles.

"I got it. You look tired. Need a shower or a nap?"

I need both, but I'm afraid to leave his presence, and what about Finn? *Oh, my poor boy.* What have I done to us?

Giant walks up to me. "Why don't you surrender him to me? Take a shower. Lie down. I'll have dinner ready in an hour." My brows pinch in question while his lips twist, and he nods to his bedroom. "Go."

+ + +

The tears of emotional exhaustion fall as I shower in the small bathroom off his room. Like everything else in the cabin, it's cozy and comforting, and the sensation of fluffy towels and Giant's soap overwhelms me. I inhale as I wash and hold the towel to my puffy eyes when I finish. I slip into fresh jeans and a T-shirt and then climb onto the bed. The scent of him fills my nostrils as I roll into the pillow. My eyes close for a minute, and then I feel a dip behind me. I stiffen, feeling caught doing something I shouldn't have.

His hand comes to my hips and skims up my side, hovering below my breasts, nudging at it but not cupping it.

"You're really here, right? I'm not imagining you." His nose dips into my wet hair, and he inhales. I shiver at the touch. His hand skates back down to my hip, tugging me back against him. His hard length rubs against my ass, and I arch my back. Instantly, I'm wet and ready and wanting him.

"Giant," I hum.

251

"Later tonight, I'm going to take you so hard, Letty. I'm going to make you wish you never broke my heart."

"Oh God," I whimper, wanting the punishment and fearing the revenge.

"I broke my own when I did it." I exhale, rubbing my backside against his firmness. "I'm so sorry, Giant. So very sorry."

"We'll see," he says, kissing my shoulder and then lowering for my neck. He nips me hard, and I cry out, spinning to face him. His lips crash mine again, tongue forcing its way into my mouth. I whimper and moan and whine for more. I want him to take me. I want to give me to him.

He pulls back too quickly, too harsh. "Dinner's ready." And I want to cry out, *let me be your feast. Let me nibble on you instead*, but I keep all my thoughts packed away like my bags by his front door.

He rolls off the bed and holds out a hand for me. I follow, standing to face him, and then he tugs me into him again. A hand dips into my hair while another covers my ass. He pulls me into his chest, finding my lips again and kissing me hard. I don't struggle. I don't fight. I swallow each punishing kiss.

"God, I've missed you," he says, pulling back and closing his eyes as if he's just admitted too much. His forehead lowers to mine and rolls against it. Then he breaks away, releasing me, and I wobble, feeling breathless and wrung out although he hasn't touched me. Not really. I'm on the edge of an orgasm, desperately aching and hot. *Damn him.*

Answer my question or kick me out. Just don't torture me like this, I want to scream.

Instead, he turns for the door, and I have no choice but to follow his lead.

36
Punishment and proposal

[Giant]

We're quiet as we eat the chicken I prepared. Letty gives Finn tiny shredded pieces and then feeds him mashed peaches from a jar.

"He's grown so fast," she says, breaking into our silence. "It's a wonder to watch him change."

He can sit upright now, and he holds tight with his fingers, testing out his legs. He looks ready to stand, run across the floor, and take over the world. A king of kings, I called him, and he's appropriately named for the fictional character in the book Letty likes.

"What ever happened to the book you were writing?" I don't know why I think of that other than considering Finn's name is from a story.

"Funny you should ask." She pauses and reaches for her water glass. "Remember Mr. Calder? Did I mention I've been in contact with him?"

No. I haven't heard anything from you in months.

"I asked him if I could write his story." My head pops up, and I meet her eyes. "I couldn't let it go. The mystery of the town, the history of the resort. His story with Annie. I wanted to know more. I interviewed him a while back and then told him I'd be in the area. I asked him if I could meet with him."

I sit back in my chair and cross my arms. "Pretty sure of yourself," I scoff.

"I'm suddenly not sure of anything," she says, keeping her head lowered as she pushes her food with a fork. My brows pinch. *What isn't she certain of?*

"So how does that work with him?"

"I'm going to interview him a second time. Have him proofread what I've written so far. His grandson is a pain in the ass. Drake had the land on the market, which is why I went there, but when Sam found out the truth, he was very upset. It's sad."

My eyes question hers. "What are your thoughts?"

"I'd love to rebuild the resort for him, but I don't have that kind of capital."

"But you know how to find buyers or investors. Could you help him out?"

"I don't know." She sets down the fork and looks up at me. "Think that's a possibility for him?"

"I think Old Sam might like the idea."

She beams, and I swear my home doesn't need electricity when she looks at me like that. She lights up the whole place. "I could trade him. His story for my help."

"Sounds like a plan." I lean forward again and pick up my fork.

"Of course, that's near Appleton, two hours away."

The silence stretches between us.

"What happened to your nanny?"

"Oh…" She turns red, playing with her food again. "That didn't work out." She closes her eyes, keeping them closed as she licks her lips. "Actually, I didn't have a nanny lined up."

My fork clatters to the plate. *Did she lie to me?*

"Then I did hire one, and…I didn't like it. I didn't like her being in my house and dealing with Finn. I want to raise Finn, not share him with someone else."

And we're back to this.

"I remember."

"No," she says, reaching across the table for my wrist. "Not like that. It's that I don't want to share him with a stranger. I want to be home for him. I want to give him a family."

"I think you need to back up a bit. What about your job?"

Her hand slips from my wrist, and I watch it retreat.

"I quit my job. I put the condo on the market." She shrugs. "I guess I just leaped, and if it doesn't work out, I'll figure out something after I finish Mr. Calder's story. I have enough savings to last me a year."

I stare at her. *Just like that.* She left it all behind. For me? For us?

"Letty, let's be straight here. What were you hoping?"

She looks away and brushes at her cheek. If she cries, I'm a goner, but she turns back to me, dry-eyed.

"I was hoping you'd say yes to me...to Finn and me...but I don't want to pressure you. I know I made a mistake. A big one. I didn't think I was being fair to you, so I set you free. Only my heart wouldn't let you go. I was hoping...but...I can see I'm too late."

She stands, lifting her plate. Stepping forward, she goes to walk past me to the sink, but I catch her forearm.

"Who said you were too late?"

Finn drops his cup off his booster seat, and we both look in his direction. He smiles over at me, and Letty pulls free of my grasp. She sets the dishes by the sink and then returns for Finn's cup.

"Cricket," I demand. She didn't answer me.

"I think we should talk later."

Yes, talk, but I have other plans as well.

+ + +

Letty gives Finn a bath, and then he wobbles around my cabin, holding her fingers, stretching his legs, and cooing as he goes. When he starts rubbing at his eyes, Letty gives him a bottle, and he falls asleep against her. It's a vision I want to see every night. She disappears into my room to set him in the portable crib and then returns to the front room.

"I only have beer," I say to her, rising from the couch and heading for the fridge. "It's a summer blend. I have one that's made with lemonade, our Summer Shanty, and one that's more berry, Berry Brew."

"A Summer Shanty would be fine."

I return quickly, finding her sitting on the couch, her knees tucked under her as she faces me.

"Thanks," she says, taking the beer from my hand. I fall onto the cushions next to her. We remain silent for too long, and I feel forced to fill the quiet. She's the one who chirps, but she's surprisingly not speaking.

"So," I huff out.

"So," she whispers.

I exhale. There's so much I want to say, ask, do, and I'm afraid if I don't, I'm going to lose her forever.

"I got a very cryptic email from Marcus a few days back."

"Marcus?" she shrieks, and I watch her swallow hard.

"He said something about you being free, and the courts ruled in your favor. I assume since you're here, the adoption passed."

"Well, there was a bit of a hiccup, but it's all settled now."

I stare at her, telling her with my glare she needs to speak.

"The birth mother was located, and I panicked. That day you called offering to adopt Finn…I had gotten the news earlier in the day that I might lose him. It was the only thing on my mind."

I sit up straighter, focusing on her as she looks down at her beer, chipping at the label with her nail.

"The biological mother reneged her rights. My liaison said it would have been a difficult fight if she wanted custody as they found her in a drug house on the southside of town. There was no way she could have taken care of a child, but there was still a risk…"

I stare at her. "Why didn't you say something? I could have helped you. I could have been there for you." What was she thinking?

"I don't know how," she says, lifting her eyes to me and blinking at unshed tears. I don't know how I would have helped her either, but I could have been there for her, been moral support or physical comfort.

"It hurt, Letty. Hurt damn bad when you let me go."

"I'm sor—" I hold up a hand to stop her from speaking. I need to get it all out, and then she can chatter away at me.

"I want to say I understand why you did it, why you pushed me away, but I don't. I promised you I was all in and committed to making it work."

"And I didn't think it was fair to you. I didn't want you to feel trapped. I didn't want to be trapped—not by you, but the process—and I didn't want to drag you in. I didn't want you asking to share Finn because it seemed like the only way. And on that day, I didn't even know if I'd have Finn to share with anyone."

"Because you don't want to share him."

"That isn't what I meant."

"Then tell me what you did mean."

She sighs, and I'm expecting little white lies, but she's surprisingly honest. "I want it all, and it didn't seem right to ask it of you. It didn't seem fair to ask you to take on Finn when you've already raised your children."

"You didn't ask me, though. I offered, and you took the choice from me."

"What was I supposed to say? *Gee, Giant*, that sounds awesome. I want you to adopt my son, but you hadn't mentioned marrying me. I mean, I want to marry you because I love you, and I'm pretty sure my son loves you, and I think you'd be a great father and a good husband. But it seems like too much…" Her voice drifts. She looks over at the chimney.

"Yes. Yes, you were supposed to say those things if you wanted them. But you told me marriage wasn't in your plan, that sharing Finn wasn't in your plan, Letty."

"I've always wanted it. I told you, love and marriage, and a baby and happily ever after, but I didn't want to ask…I wanted it to happen."

She swipes a hand through her long, chestnut hair, and I want to wrap it around my fist. I want to tug on it until she gives in to me, until she sees she robbed us of months together.

"I want all those things too, Letty, with you and Finn." Her head turns back to me. "But I'm angry right now. I want to forgive you and punish you. I want to hate you and love you."

"Want me to beg? Want me to play *Naked and Afraid* on the mountain? Want me to kneel before you?" she snaps, and my irritation grows.

"Yes."

She takes a long pull of her beer and uncrosses her legs to stand from the couch. She walks to the fireplace, places the beer bottle on the mantle, and then turns to face me. The light has dimmed in the room as the sun has dipped. I don't have a fire burning as it's just warm enough, and my heart heats anyway with adrenaline and frustration. She pulls off her T-shirt, standing before me in a pink bra. Then she shucks off her jeans, exposing a matching panty. She wasn't wearing shoes or socks.

She lowers to the bear skin rug on both knees and places her hands on her thighs. Holding my gaze, she looks vulnerable and scared, and my heart races both guilty and thrilled at her position.

"I asked you to marry me today, and you refused."

"I did no—"

"It's my turn to talk. I'm sorry for what I did to us. I'm sorry for saying there wasn't another way or not believing you loved me or loved Finn enough. I didn't want you to feel pressured into something you've already experienced. I was scared of losing Finn, so I pushed you away."

"But my experiences haven't been with you, and I want them to be," I say, sitting forward and setting my beer on the floor at my feet. She holds up a hand.

"My turn." She rubs her hands down her bare thighs, and my mouth waters. "I'm sorry, Giant. That's all I can say. I'm sorry." Her voice cracks, and I can't take anymore. The sorrow in her eyes. The vulnerable position. I lunge for her, catching her before she falls back.

"Where's the ring?"

"What?"

"The ring you offered me earlier."

"In my jeans."

"Get it." She crawls to her pants, and my gaze follows her. I lick my lips, watching her ass in the air. She pulls the ring from her pants. "Set it on the fireplace edge."

Her brows pinch, but she turns on her knees and does as I ask. After placing the circular band on the concrete ledge, I crawl up behind her, and she stills when my hand rubs down her spine.

"Giant?" she questions.

"Stay just like this." She nods without looking back at me, and I rise to quickly undress. When I kneel again, behind her, I unhook her bra, allowing the material to fall down her arms, then cup both breasts. I tug her back to me, up on my lap, against my thighs. I nip her neck like I did earlier. Hard. And her back arches as she hisses my name. She presses her breasts into my eager hands while the back of her head lands on my shoulder.

"Don't ever take my choice from me again," I whisper into her ear as my nose traces up her neck. "Never take yourself from me again."

"Okay," she yelps as I bite her again.

"Shhh. We don't want to wake Finn until I'm finished."

"He's almost ten months and sleeps for several hours."

"Hours?" I tease. "Won't be enough time. I need days. Months. Years."

I squeeze both her breasts, tugging them forward to pull her nipples to tight peaks. I twist the firm nubs, and she whimpers, bucking back at me, my bare dick hitting the seam of her covered ass.

"Lean forward. Hands on the edge." She does as I say, placing her hands flat on the stone ledge. She's on her knees, and I slip mine under hers, so she straddles me. With one fierce rip, I tear the material of her cotton undies down the middle, tugging them to the sides to free her two globes of perfection. I cup them each, lifting her a little to bring my hard length against her center.

"So wet," I hiss as my tip brushes her core. I flinch at the connection. We're hot, wanting, ready. She kneels upward, positioning me at her entrance and then slams down, drawing me into her. We both let out a loud groan, and I cover her mouth with my hand while pressing my head into her shoulder. She stills to hold me in her depths. I've never felt this before. Not like this. Only with her.

"I love you, Letty." I speak low and deliberate at her ear. "Don't ever take that from me again."

"I love you, too, Giant. So, so much, and I'm so sorry. I was scared you wouldn't want what I want."

"The only thing I want in my life is you." My hands come to her hips, and I lift her forward and then tug her back down on me. Her hands balance her, and I repeat the motion until we form a rhythm. She bounces over me, up and down, up and down, and I watch as I disappear into her. My hand snakes around her hip, finding her clit and flicking at it. "This will be fast and hard, Letty, but next round, I'm taking my time. This is the punishment. Round two, I'll forgive you."

"Punish me," she whispers, and I take control, rubbing her clit and guiding her with one hand on her hip. We're sweating and sliding, skin

L.B. Dunbar

slapping and suction sounds, and then she hums, and I slam her down on me, holding her still as she clenches around me, milking me hard, as I release months of pent-up frustration and desire.

"I love you," I repeat into her shoulder, my mouth open and sucking at her salty skin. While I'm still inside her, I reach for my T-shirt behind me and slip it under her. It's going to be a mess when I pull out. She giggles as I release her, but I hold her hip as I reach for my jeans next. I dig in the pocket and then place something next to her ring for me on the stones.

"Giant," she whispers.

"I had it back on Valentine's Day. Cliché, I know, and then you were so sick. I wanted it to be a good memory for you and me, but nothing is going to top you getting on one knee in my yard and asking me to marry you. So maybe we can promise that from this day forward, we'll do things together."

I reach around her while she still kneels naked before me, and I pick up the ring I placed next to hers.

"I didn't say yes earlier because I wanted us to say yes together, Letty. It's always been yes for me."

"Giant. I…I'm so…Are you asking me to marry you?"

"Isn't that what I just said?"

She chuckles, and I realize it isn't exactly what I said. "Yes," she says. "Yes, it's what you said, and what I say. Yes. To us. To all of us." She spins without taking the ring and cups my face, giving my lips a tender kiss of acceptance. When she pulls back, she reaches for her ring for me and holds it up.

"Together."

"Love and marriage. A baby and happily ever after, Cricket."

We slip the rings on each other, and I like the look of hers on me. A black titanium band sized large enough to fit my big finger. Hers is a sparkling solitaire diamond on a silver band.

"It fits," she says as I squeeze my hand and then flatten my palm.

"You fit me best," I say, surprised at the comfort and the feel of the ring. I look up at her and bring her lips to mine with a hand on her jaw.

260

As I kiss her, relief washes over me. She's going to be mine. No more leaving. No more distance. All mine, all the time.

I pull back but continue to hold her face.

"Letty Pierson, I would love to be your husband and a father to Finn."

"Thank you," she mouths. "I would love for you to share this adventure called parenthood with me and be my partner in all things."

My mouth crashes hers again. She has nothing to thank me for. It's going to be my honor to love and cherish her for all the days of our life.

37

Fatherhood

[Letty]

Finn wakes while we kiss at the fireplace, and I chuckle when we break apart. Happiness fills me to my core, but I also feel a little silly being caught naked. Not that Finn's old enough to see us.

"Here." Giant hands me my T-shirt, and then he reaches over for his boxers. He destroyed my underwear, and I marvel at his strength and the sexiness of it. *Lumbersexual.* He redefines the term.

"You get him. I'm gonna grab a few things."

Giant follows me into his room where I search for clean underwear and then pick up Finn and nestle him against my shoulder. He settles in, not really needing a nighttime bottle. Giant rustles around behind me, and then he follows me back into the main room. The light is completely gone from the day, and the evening temperature has settled in. Giant starts a small fire and spreads a blanket over the bear skin rug.

He tosses two pillows on the blanket.

"Lie down with him." I do as Giant asks, setting Finn next to me as I curl on my side. Finn remains asleep, and Giant perches on the other side of him. Up on an elbow, he looks down at Finn and then over at me.

"I love you both," he says, and my heart leaps. He reaches for my left hand, pulling the diamond to his lips and kissing over it. "So to be clear, we're getting married. You're moving in with me, and...I'm adopting Finn."

"Yes," I say, keeping my eyes on him. His smile grows, and he leans over Finn to kiss me too quickly.

"Everything I've been wanting is right here."

"What about your girls?" I whisper, not wanting to break our bubble, but they are his family.

"That would be awkward." His brows rise, implying they wouldn't really fit in the space around us.

"Giant," I hiss, knowing he's teasing me.

"Okay. Let me try to explain this. I love my girls, but I can't go back. I can't redo what I didn't have. We have a relationship now, and it's good. It works, but we jumped in when they were adults. I want another chance." He looks down at Finn. "I want to be better."

"Honey, I'm sure the girls think you're the best."

"And I think they are. But Finn's going to be a best, too."

"He is," I whisper, gazing down at my boy. *Our boy.* "Finnikin Harrington."

"You'll give him my name?" Giant's brow rises.

"I'll be taking yours, too."

His smile grows once again, warmer than the firelight. "I love you."

"Love you, too."

Giant lies down, his arm coming over both Finn and me, and we stay there for a long time, just staring at one another.

+ + +

When it seems Finn has settled, Giant pulls the portable crib into the front room, just outside the door to his bedroom.

"What are you doing?" I ask groggily.

"I can't make love to you with him in the room."

"Oh," I say, sitting up, my back creaking from being on the floor for a bit. I scoop up Finn, hoping not to disturb him, but he's in that heavy, dead-weight sleep. I place him in the pack and play with a kiss and then follow Giant into his room. We leave the door open to listen for Finn but quietly slip into the sheets.

"Forgiveness fucking," I say as Giant climbs in over me, naked as can be. My legs spread, taking his wide hips between my thighs.

"Love, Letty. Only making love." His fingers slide down the center of me, between my breasts and over my stomach until they dip into my underwear and find my clit. I purr as he takes more time and care to tease me, circle me, drawing out the anticipation before slipping two fingers into me.

"So deep," I whisper, feeling lazy and loved as he slowly plays me. Giant struggles to remove my underwear, then hitches my leg over his hip. His tip meets my entrance, and he easily slides into me, deliberate, purposeful, and filling. I lift both legs over his lower back, and he cups my backside as he rolls his hips. We move like a dance, taking time but building quickly to another rushing orgasm.

"It's been so long," he says into my neck.

"Too long," I say.

"We're going to do this every night, Letty."

"Promises, promises," I tease until he moves in a way a new spot is discovered. I squeak, and his head pops up.

"That's my promise, Cricket. Spontaneous."

"Again," I whisper, and he flinches upward a second time. My eyes roll back as my arms wrap around his neck. "I'll never get enough of you."

"That's the plan."

We don't stay slow for too long before we are both rabid and needy, releasing once again together. He's just so much and everything I've ever wanted.

When he pulls out of me, I shudder at the loss, but he's quick to return, cleaning me up and then crawling in next to me and tugging me to his chest.

"It's always going to be like this," he tells me as if he's asking or warning or wanting.

"It will always be like this."

He kisses my shoulder, and then we sleep.

+ + +

In the morning, I wake alone with the door to the bedroom closed. I find a fresh T-shirt in Giant's drawer, pull it on, and then head out to the main room. A soft masculine voice drifts from the kitchen.

"So what do you think, little man? Is it okay to marry your mom? And how about me becoming your dad? You good with that?"

I hear Finn making incoherent noises in response.

"I'll teach you how to fish and hunt, and brew beer, and of course, when you're older, catch a girl. You'll learn all the traits of being a Harrington from me as your dad."

"Dada." I freeze. Giant must have too because not a sound comes from the kitchen. I step forward and see Giant staring at Finn. His dark orbs leap up to mine, wide-eyed and surprised.

"Did he just…?"

"That was his first word," I say, my voice low. *Little traitor*.

"I never…I wasn't home…" Giant sets the jar of baby food on the table and pinches at his eyes.

"Giant." I step forward for him, wrapping my arms around his head as he falls against my belly. "Honey?" I comb over his hair, but he shakes his head into my stomach.

"Dada," Finn says again, and we both look over at him.

"Thank you," Giant whispers, and then peeks up at me. "Thank you for this. For him. For you."

Epilogue
Wedding Bliss

[Giant]

"What would a wedding be without ax throwing?" I hear Letty explain to Billy, and I chuckle. "I'm telling you, it's all the rage."

It's a beautiful fall day, almost a year from the date I first met Letty. I guess you could say she's obtained my property after all as she has agreed to be my wife. We have no interest in selling, though. In fact, we've made the cabin our residence. It's a little bit of a haul to the brewery from here, but I don't mind. I'm widening the drive, so we don't run into trouble during the winter months. Then again, I can't think of anything I'd like more than to be snowed in with Letty.

We'll be adding onto the cabin although Letty doesn't want to make too many changes. She's adamant I keep the floor plan, so I can remember Pap's original structure, but the addition will be our personal touch to make the cabin our home. Letty needs an office as she did interview Sam Calder again about his Annie and the resort. She published her work in September, and she's had a good run of the story. I don't understand all the particulars, but she's hitting fancy lists and beaming with pride, and that's all that matters to me.

I want my girl to be happy.

She tells me every day she is.

"I don't think I can build a court right in town," Billy replies.

Letty's trying to convince Billy he needs to incorporate this activity into the bar's attraction, Our wedding is tomorrow up on the ridge where we camped, but tonight we celebrate in a casual manner where Letty and I met. I didn't want a bachelor party although Billy was more than willing to hire strippers. Instead, we set up a spot for ax throwing and a picnic dinner for our rehearsal.

Actually, I take back what I said about the strippers. Billy said he knew where he could get one, but he didn't suggest we hire one. My brother has changed a little bit. He's still a flirt, and he's still wild, but he's settling. Seems fatherhood might agree with him or maybe it's the new woman in his life.

I jostle Finn on my hip although he's getting so big. He's just over a year, as Letty adopted him when he was three months old, and my adoption of him will be final soon. It feels like I've known him a lifetime. A lifetime I didn't know I wanted until I met Letty. I had those spontaneous needs, but this was more spontaneous than even I imagined.

"Just throw the ax," Letty encourages Billy. "It's surprising how good it feels."

Billy gives me an eye roll, and I chuckle. He's under Letty's spell just as most of my family is. My dad adores her, winking at me when he catches me staring at her. My mother claims she's relieved she can stop setting me up with available women and tries to take credit for introducing me to Letty.

"You know, if I hadn't directed her to the cabin, you might have never found her."

My mother is wrong, but I let her think she's right. I didn't find Letty. She found me.

Billy thinks my future wife is hot, and he likes to tell her and me how good she looks, but that's as far as he'll ever take it. He's opened up a little bit about what happened to him, and I think he's learned his lesson about women. At least, I hope he has.

"Yeah, William, just take the shaft and give it a toss," Marcus shouts, and I snort as I jiggle Finn once again. He wants down to the ground, but I'm hesitant with all the axes flying around.

"I'll take him. We'll sit safely on the porch," Marcus says to me as he reaches for Finn. "Uncle Marcus will keep Finn away from the big bad ax-men." His teasing, whiny voice makes me laugh once again. Speaking of flying things, Marcus is full of puns and euphemisms, and I'm glad he's here for Letty. He's the only family she invited to our celebration even though he isn't directly family. She was adamant that if her family couldn't accept Finn for who he was, she didn't need them judging her wedding day either, or her. Nothing about our ceremony will be traditional, and I can't wait.

"Ready for a tussle?" Letty teases Billy, wiggling her brows.

"You know I'd give you a toss any day," Billy flirts. It's in his nature, and if he wasn't my kid brother, and I didn't know he was just playing, I'd toss him right to the ground like I did when we were kids and make him scream uncle. Billy isn't really a fighter, more a lover, and he'll be the first to tell a woman such things, but I know my brother would fight for love if it crossed his path.

"Quit hitting on my wife," I snap at Billy with a smile.

"She isn't yet," Billy teases. "I can change all the conditions."

Letty laughs and shakes her head. We've written a list for our wedding vows, ones Billy will read off tomorrow as he obtained an ordained minister's license so he could wed us. Stranger things have happened, it's true. Anyway, Billy calls the list our conditions for marriage instead of our vows, but Letty and I know the truth. This is our promise to each other.

To love one another.

To communicate our needs.

To spend time outdoors.

To never go to bed angry.

To be open to adventure.

To treat each other as equals

"There's still time," Billy addresses her. "I know the way out of his secret lair. I can save you from the big bad wolf." His voice teases, and Letty's eyes leap to mine.

"I kind of love the big bad wolf," she says, keeping her gaze on me. "Especially when he threatens to eat me." She winks at Billy, and the ax my brother is holding slips from his hand. The metal head thuds on the packed dirt at his feet, and he stares at Letty before he bends at the waist and laughs.

"Good one, Letty," Marcus encourages from his spot on the porch, and I'm happy Finn is too young to understand.

"Oh, my God, Giant. She's definitely a keeper," Billy says through his trickling laughter.

He has no idea. I'll definitely be keeping her all for me.

And there's nothing I'm looking more forward to than tomorrow, when Billy, as the minister, will ask us that imperative question—if we'll take each other as husband and wife—and I tell everyone, "I do."

+ + +

BookEnds – bonuses and such

Want to read where the Harringtons began with their sister, Mati? Go back here > Second Chance.

Want to read more #sexysilverfoxes? Start here > After Care.

Want to add *Silver Player* to your future shelf so you don't miss the release date? Go here > Silver Player and keep flipping pages for the first chapter in Billy's tale.

Want to stay up to date on all things #sexysilverfox and L.B. Dunbar? Join here > Love Notes

+ + +

More by L.B. Dunbar

Did you enjoy this story?

Please consider writing a review on major sales channels where ebooks and paperbooks are sold, and perhaps you might like some of my other work:

Sexy Silver Foxes/Former Rock Stars
When sexy silver foxes meet the women of their dreams.
After Care
Midlife Crisis
Restored Dreams
Second Chance
Wine&Dine

The Silver Foxes of Blue Ridge
More sexy silver fox shenanigans from the Harrington brothers.
Silver Brewer
Silver Player
Silver Mayor
Silver Biker

Collision novellas

A spin-off from After Care – the younger set/rock stars

Collide

Rom-com for the over 40 - standalone

The Sex Education of M.E.

The Sensations Collection

Small town, sweet and sexy stories of family and love.

Sound Advice

Taste Test

Fragrance Free

Touch Screen

Sight Words

Spin-off Standalone

The History in Us

The Legendary Rock Star Series

Rock star mayhem in the tradition of King Arthur.

A classic tale with a modern twist of romance and suspense

The Legend of Arturo King

The Story of Lansing Lotte

The Quest of Perkins Vale

The Truth of Tristan Lyons

The Trials of Guinevere DeGrance

Paradise Duet

MMA chaos of biblical proportion between two brothers and the fight for love.

Abel

Cain

The Island Duet

The island knows what you've done.

Redemption Island

Return to the Island

Modern Descendants – writing as elda lore

Modern myths of Greek gods.

L.B. Dunbar

Hades
Solis
Heph

Penny Reid's ™ Smartypants Romance
A spin-off from the Winston Brothers collection
Love in Due Time
Love in Deed – coming Spring 2020
Love in a Pickle – coming Spring 2021

Turn the page for an excerpt of *Silver Player*, Billy Harrington's story.

Nibble of Billy Harrington

Silver Player – coming January 2020

1

Jokes on me

[Billy]

A young girl walks into a bar…

I'd like to say this is the start of a bad joke, but it isn't really.

It's my life.

It all started as I was giving my sister a pep-talk about getting back out there. Dating again. Open yourself up to someone new. I practically wrote the book on this cheerleading speech as it's the philosophy I've lived by for the past sixteen years.

"Hey, boss, there's a girl here to see you," a new busy boy addresses me. Blue Ridge Microbrewery and Pub is my pride and joy, and the staff is a second family. Our waitstaff is pretty consistent, but with summer ending and college kids going back to school, we lose a few, gain a few. Our specialty is a house beer brewed by my family's business – Giant Brewing Company. My family has been brewing beer for decades, although my oldest brother is the official Giant in the title. I didn't want to work directly under our father and when Giant returned from the military and Rachel left me…well, let's just say the pub was my gift— happy thirtieth birthday to myself.

My youngest sibling Mati sits across from me in my office. Her lion-red hair doesn't match the rest of my siblings who have varying shades of gray happening as we grow older. She's one of the consistent workers, as head waitress, human resources sort-of, and event concept coordinator. Basically meaning, Jill of all trades. Mati's husband died over a year ago and she isn't sure if she should follow her heart and do the horizontal shuffle with her once best friend from high school who recently returned to Blue Ridge. It has taken twenty-seven years for them to reunite.

L.B. Dunbar

Me? It took me a dozen years to wise up about sex. More like a dozen years of having sex. Random. Wild. Uninhibited. I'd been a blind fool over my high school sweetheart back in the day but that's a story for another time

"I'll be there in a minute," I tell Hosea.

"Always something," my sister mutters under her breath standing from the seat opposite my desk. I chuckle to myself, not in the least concerned I just admitted to my sister I'd slept with someone I shouldn't have. Someone clearly stalking me. I wasn't in any rush to get out to the bar area, but I didn't want to keep someone waiting, especially if it's a lady.

"What's up?" I address Clyde Bebzine. Clyde looks a little like a hot mess with a wild beard and thick sandy brown hair. He's a few years younger than my forty-six but still close enough we get along well. He tips his head in the direction of a young black-haired beauty sitting on a bar stool—and I mean young—like not legal to sit at the bar but it's okay because it's the middle of the afternoon. Her light brown eyes pierce me to my core and there's something familiar about those eyes. She'd be a looker minus the emo shit she has going on. Pasty-skin. Kohl eyeliner. Nearly black lips. Midnight colored fingernails. I immediately dismiss the sensation of recognition. Every woman looks familiar to me.

They got breasts. They got lips. They got fingertips.

Only I don't do the young ones and regardless of a body looking like a twenty-something woman she still has the face of a teen.

"May I help you with something?" I ask standing behind the bar while Clyde wipes some glasses dry near me. We're prepping for the nightly rush of those appreciating local craft beer and community camaraderie. I opened the bar with the intention of improving our little down area, hoping to attract tourists and locals alike to boost our mountain ridge economy. Blue Ridge Microbrewery and Pub is my baby.

"I'm looking for Billy Harrington," she states, like she's about to deliver a message. Her voice rings rough as if she's a member of *The Godfather* or something equally mysterious despite being youthful and female. Her eyes scan my body as if she likes what she sees but she's also sizing me up. I'm over six foot with silver in my hair but dark scruff

274

on my jaw. My brothers tease me, thinking I dye the facial hair for visual contrast. They'll never know the truth…besides…the ladies are attracted to the dichotomy so what do I care. *Keep the ladies coming*, and there's a double meaning in that declaration. Only I don't dip lower than thirty years old lately. Those twenty-somethings want the spanking and the baby girl nickname and the daddy issues. *No thank you.*

"What can I do for you?" My voice teases and I hear Clyde chuckle next to me.

"You him?" She pauses. "You look different than I thought."

I'm a little surprised she might have thoughts about me one way or another. Her expression clearly tells me she'd eat me up and spit me out, so I don't think when I say:

"Not interested in fulfilling some daddy fantasy, honey."

I reach for a rag and begin swiping at the wood bar top although it already shines with cleanliness. Her Tennessee-whiskey eyes on me are making me nervous all of a sudden and the way they narrow, the sense of familiarity washes over me once again.

"You're sick. I'm your daughter and you would be the furthest thing from my fantasy."

My hand pauses on the bar. The hint of country music fades to the background. The sound of some afternoon sports competition on the television drones to silence. The voices around me trip and mutter to a stop.

What did she say?

"Excuse me?" I chuckle along with choking and then clear my throat as if the action will open my ears and clear my hearing.

"The only daddy issues I have is the issue of you being my dad."

"I…" What. The. Fuuuuuuu*ck*. My brain wants to say impossible. My dick knocks against my zipper saying, *maybe.*

No.

No, this can't be.

I always wrap that shit up. No leaks. No tweaks. No just a dip and I'll pull out. Full coverage. Every damn time.

"I…" I can't seem to find words, so she spears me with a few more.

L.B. Dunbar

"Yeah, I can't either," she states as if she read my thoughts, somehow mysteriously knowing what I think. "And an absentee one on top of it. You win father of the year, Billy Harrington. *Not*."

With that, she raps her knocks on the bar, hops off the stool, and sashays her black-jeaned ass out of my bar.

No joke.

(L)ittle (B)lessings of Gratitude

As always, a special thank you to the readers who have enjoyed reading about characters a little older and a little wiser, but sometimes equally ridiculous as the younger set.

A huge thank you to my team (that's fun to say): Melissa Shank, Shannon Passmore and Jenny Sims. For keeping the story steady, the cover beautiful, and the words grammatically correct. An extra thank you to Heather M. this round with early reads and suggestions. And Karen, as always for a final set of eyes.

Thank you to Tammi, Sylvia, and Krista for keeping up with Loving L.B. and being such good people in my life.

To all the readers in Loving L.B. who make me laugh, make suggestions, and share hot images of those older dudes. Much love.

To all the bloggers and loyal reviewers from those blogs, thank you for your years of dedication, or if you are new to me, thank you for taking a chance on the ole girl.

To author groups who keep me in the know, constantly learning, and often reflective, especially Alessandra Torre Inkers and my fellow Smartypants Romance sister-authors. Indie-publishing is equally dauntind and exciting, and I'm grateful to be among such amazing people.

To the community of Blue Ridge, Georgia. I didn't know you were real when I made up what I thought was a fictional town. I've been to visit. It's lovely there. Thank you for allowing me to make you my fictional home.

And finally, to my family: Mr. Dunbar, my ultimate silver fox, and our litter who have all grown too quickly – MD, MK, JR and A.

+ + +

About the Author

www.lbdunbar.com

L.B. Dunbar loves the sweeter things in life: cookies, Coca-Cola, and romance. Her reading journey began with a deep love of fairy tales and alpha males. She loves a deep belly laugh and a strong hug. Occasionally, she has the energy of a Jack Russell terrier. Accused—yes, that's the correct word—of having an overactive imagination, to her benefit, such an imagination works well. Author of over two dozen novels, she's created sexy rom-coms for the over 40; intrigue on an island; MMA chaos; rock star mayhem, and sweet small-town romance. In addition, she earned a title as the "myth and legend lady" for her modernizations of mythology as elda lore. Her other duties in life include mother to four children and wife to the one and only.

+ + +

Keep in touch with L.B. Dunbar

www.lbdunbar.com
Stalk Me: https://www.facebook.com/lbdunbarauthor
Instagram Me: @lbdunbarwrites
Read Me:
https://www.goodreads.com/author/show/8195738.L_B_Dunbar
Bookbub Me: https://www.bookbub.com/profile/l-b-dunbar
Tweet Me: https://twitter.com/lbdunbarwrites
Pin Me: http://www.pinterest.com/lbdunbar/
Get News from Me:
https://app.mailerlite.com/webforms/landing/j7j2s0
AND hang out with me: @Loving L.B. (reader group)
https://www.facebook.com/groups/LovingLB/